THE VICAR OF STEADSHALL

To Carol,
with thanks
for her patience
and
understanding.

By the same author:

Once Upon An Island

Olive's Boys

The Other Side of England:
PART I: THE HOMECOMING

The Other Side of England:
PART II: NO WORK, NO BREAD, NO HOPE

The Other Side of England:
PART III: LAW AND LAWLESSNESS

Troubled Country

Love and Hate in a Small Town

The Vicar of Steadshall

JOSEPH CANNING

I am indebted to many sources for my research,
too numerous to be listed here: one in particular, however,
was *Parish Life with a Troubled Vicar* by Peter Patilla.

ISBN-13: 978-1481971560
ISBN-10: 1481971565

Prologue

WILLIAM WARBURTON was standing by the porch, huddled inside his topcoat against the early morning spatter of rain, when the moustachioed constable and the paunched chairman of the school managers, a wholesale grocer by the name of Henry Bowden, entered the yard.

All along the railings of the back-street, East End school, the eyes of the mothers who had brought their children there that morning were fixed upon him, as were those of the children gathered in small whispering groups. Defiantly, William Warburton straightened to face the two men: nearby, the church clock was striking a quarter-to nine.

'Mr. Warburton,' the portly chairman began, coming to a halt a safe distance from the tall, thin schoolmaster, 'I have already asked you to leave these premises. You should not be here.'

'I have as much right to be here as you,' was the calm reply he received.

'You have no right, sir, you have been dismissed,' the rotund chairman went on. 'You were given your notice to quit three months ago. That time has now expired. As of this morning, you are no longer the master at this school. You must leave these premises immediately or you will be charged with trespassing.' He looked towards the constable for confirmation, but, curiously, received none.

Irritated, the chairman turned back to the schoolmaster. 'Be sensible, Mr. Warburton. There is no way you can remain. The rector will not allow it. By your words and your deeds, you have insulted him and the other members of the management committee. If you do not leave, I must ask the constable here to put you out.'

'I do not consider myself dismissed,' William Warburton answered him quietly, looking from the wholesale grocer to the stony-faced constable and wondering whether he intended doing anything at all since he was hanging back a good two yards behind the chairman: he came to the conclusion that perhaps he might not.

'I have never been given a hearing,' the schoolmaster added, more emboldened. 'No one has ever asked what I have to say on the matter. I am not leaving here till I have seen the rector.'

The greengrocer sighed, exasperated by the other man's intransigence. 'The rector will not see you. Everything about this matter was carefully considered by the school's managers three months ago. It was not necessary for you to be present. The decision we took was unanimous. What would you explain if you had been present? Again, I beg of you: please, Mr. Warburton, leave these premises. Do not make this any worse than it has to be. It is bad enough that I have to do this in front of the children.'

It was at this point that the constable stepped forward, hoping to end the impasse. 'I think it would be advisable if you were to leave, sir, as the gentleman asks,' he said quietly, an air of authority in his tone: yet the discerning ear of the schoolmaster thought he still detected a certain weary reluctance in it, as if he wished he were not having to be a part of what was happening and had better things to do.

'I thank you for your advice, constable,' William Warburton responded politely, 'but I see no reason why I should leave. I have never tendered my resignation and I refuse to do so. Therefore, I consider myself still the master here.'

A note of desperation now crept into the chairman's voice. 'Could you not just put him out on to the road, constable?' he pleaded.

'I should be unwilling to do that, sir,' the constable said, rather surprisingly, addressing the chairman, but keeping his eyes on the schoolmaster, as if expecting he might do something foolish, like strike the shorter man. 'However, if you were to take hold of his collar, sir, and guide him quietly and peaceably out through the gate and down the steps to the pavement, I will stand by you and see that he does not strike you. That is the best I can do in circumstances like these.'

With another deep sigh, now almost of regret, the wholesale grocer went behind the lanky schoolmaster, reached up to take hold of the damp collar of his topcoat just below the nape of the neck and, with a gentle push, steered him unresisting through the throng of gawping children towards the gate some thirty yards off. It was only when he reached the top of the steps that William Warburton attempted to twist himself free, whether in one last attempt to remain at the school he had served for the past three years or just to be the master of his own now inevitable exit none of the watchers knew.

His antagonist, though a foot shorter, was, however, much heavier and more muscular and had anticipated just such a move. Even as the schoolmaster turned, he quickly brought both his hands together in the small of the other man's back and, with one hard thrust, sent him stumbling down the five steps to the road below.

William Warburton just about managed to keep his balance – and with it his dignity – as he stumbled across the pavement on to the road: then straightening, he brushed at his lapels and coat front, as if they had been tainted by the other's touch, pulled his scarf more tightly about his neck and, with a defiant lift of the head, walked off into the February rain, towards where his wife, Martha, was watching and waiting…

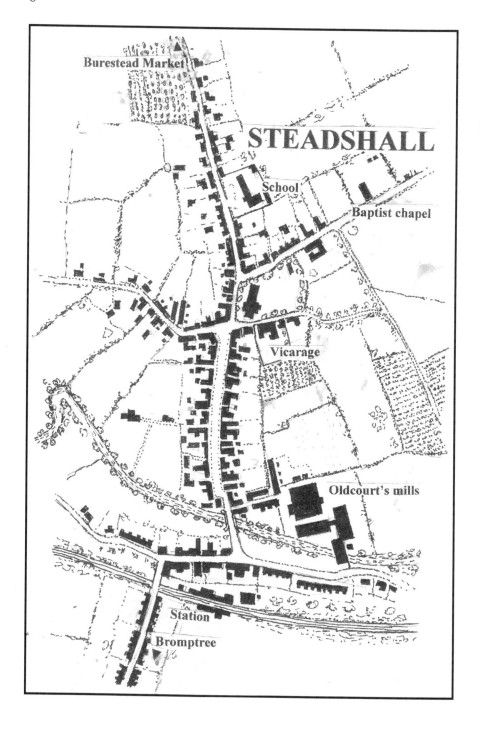

ONE

WHEN, after an eleven-month absence, the Reverend Hugo Scrope returned from his trip around the world to the small market town of Steadshall in the north of the county, it was just unfortunate that he chose to do so on the very day that the Baptists marched in procession from their old meeting place along the Bromptree road west of the town to their new chapel east of it on the road to Wivencaster. For it meant the two hundred and fifty worshippers and Sunday school scholars, walking four abreast, with banners held aloft and a fifteen-strong brass band at their head, had to pass through the centre of the town and climb the long hill of the High Street, which they did just as the carriage containing the Reverend Scrope, his spinster sister Agnes, his fourteen-month-old daughter Elizabeth and a young nursemaid by the name of Sarah Pockett attempted to exit the forecourt of Steadshall station right at the bottom of the self-same hill.

'What is all this?' the Reverend Scrope demanded of his young curate, the Reverend Henry Smallwood, who was driving: it was as if he held him personally responsible for the long column crossing in front of the carriage and blocking their way.

'I am most sorry, your reverence,' the Reverend Smallwood apologised from his seat, reddening with embarrassment. 'It is the Baptists' procession – I had hoped it would be over before you got here. Today is the "grand opening" of their new place of worship.'

'What new place of worship?' the Reverend Scrope demanded, disapproval clearly evident in his tone.

The curate swallowed hard and began his explanation: there was no way he could proceed, anyway. 'While you were away, sir, the Baptists bought the old manor house along the Wivencaster road, demolished it and began building their new chapel six months ago. It was finished last week.'

Such news was very much not what the Reverend Scrope wanted to hear on his return and certainly not within minutes of stepping down from the train. Goodness gracious! When he had left to start his round-the-world trip, the Seventeenth Century Jacobean manor house was still standing, though empty, its owner preferring to live amid the fleshpots of London rather than in the drowsy isolation of Steadshall. Neither had there been an inkling that the Baptists were seeking to build a new chapel: to all intents and purposes, they were 'safely housed' in an old joinery shop a mile out along the Bromptree road. Now, here was his curate telling him that the Baptists, the principal Dissenting 'religion' in the town, the fastest-growing, ahead of even the Primitive Methodists and the Primitive Congregationalists, therefore, his greatest rivals, who seemed to want to have their finger in every pie – here he was telling him that, while he had been away, they had built themselves a new chapel in the grounds of the old manor house, the self-same manor house he had coveted for a long time as a replacement for the draughty vicarage opposite the church!

Every time he had passed it, ever since he had arrived in Steadshall nine years before, he had thought that it would make a grand vicarage someday, a suitable residence for himself, as befitted his status in the town – the new lord of the manor, so to speak, certainly, the town's most prominent personage, ahead of the mayor, who was elected by vote, anyway, whereas he had been called to his eminence by God himself.

Though the old manor had been in a somewhat dilapidated state, it would still have been quite habitable if the necessary repairs had been made to its tiled roof and to one of its walls, which bulged and was cracked from the eaves to the ground. Four years after his arrival in Steadshall, he had even written to the owner in London to ask whether he would be prepared to sell it and the half-acre of land on which it stood. 'Never!' had been the owner's reply. 'And certainly not to you!'

The owner had given no further reason, but he had heard tell that the man was a hedonist, a profligate libertine, the debauched scion of the family who had once lived in the manor house and were long departed from the town. He had never told anyone of his request or the rebuff he had received, but had simply fumed quietly to himself over the years, vowing that, if ever it did come up for auction, it would be his – he had the money to outbid anyone, certainly anyone in Steadshall. Now the Baptists had bought it, demolished it and built a chapel of all things where it had stood.

'Where did they get the money to build a chapel?' the vicar asked, equally as impatiently, as if that too were a blame to be laid at the curate's door.

'We do not know exactly,' the Reverend Smallwood replied, half-turning on his seat to give a slow shake of the head. 'We have tried to find out, but we have been unable to do so. It seemed one minute they did not have the money and the next they did. We can only surmise a well-to-do benefactor has helped them. Who, we do not know. The first we heard of the intended sale was a month after you had gone, sir, when notices were put up for its auction, but then that was cancelled, though we do not know why. The next thing we knew was the Baptists had bought it. There were rumours of some kind of skullduggery, though again we do not know exactly what. I have heard a whisper that the Baptists paid an excessive amount for it, just to get it, and that the bill of sale gave a smaller amount concocted between them and the owner for taxation purposes and that the owner pocketed the difference, but we cannot prove it. They used much of the brick and timber from the demolished house to build the chapel and defray their building costs. If I had been able to write to you while you were away, sir, I should have been able to inform you of all this.'

The Reverend Smallwood had not been able to do so simply because, for the first seven weeks after the Reverend Scrope had left the town, the vicar had been aboard ship, sailing to Australia to visit his other sister, Charlotte, and her husband and their five children, in Melbourne. He had stayed with them for six months so any letter from the curate containing information of interest about what was happening back in his parish – and the building of a new chapel by the Baptists would have been more than just 'of interest' to him – any letter from the curate would have reached him in good time, in a matter of weeks, though what he could have done about it from the other side of the world – had he wanted to do anything – would have to remain a matter of conjecture.

Unfortunately, such was the nature of the Reverend Hugo Scrope that he had singularly failed to leave a forwarding address in Australia with either his curate or the two churchwardens, his own warden, Walter Crowfoot, or the people's warden, Samuel Gough, feeling that the details of his sister's and his brother-in-law's address and business in Australia were of no concern to anyone back in Steadshall. He certainly did not want anyone in the town addressing a letter to *'The Reverend Hugo Scrope, % Wilkins's Ladies' Emporium, Moonee Ponds, Melbourne, Victoria, Australia.'*

Anyway, after his six months there, pestered by flies and mosquitoes from the marshy ponds on a nearby flood plain and creek, he had set sail across the Pacific Ocean for California and had been out of touch for five further months, only reappearing, so to speak, when his ship from New York docked at Liverpool. Even then, he had made no attempt to contact his curate, but had made an immediate detour to the West Country to collect his daughter and his second and much younger sister, Agnes, who had cared for the child during his absence and was now returning with him and the sixteen-year-old nursemaid to live at the vicarage and be the mistress of the house and the child's governess, having once held the same position for several years with a family in Somerset.

Not till he had arrived in London from the West Country the previous evening did he think to send a telegram to his curate announcing that he would be returning on the one-thirty train from the junction at Steymarket, a halt which lay three miles outside the old Roman town of Wivencaster on the main up-line from London.

Knowing of the Baptists' procession – posters had been put up all over the town that week announcing it and the 'grand opening' of the chapel for two o'clock – the Reverend Smallwood's one hope had been that the Baptists would have completed their march through the centre before the vicar arrived, or that, perhaps by the Grace of God – and he had fervently wished He would intervene – somehow the vicar's train might be delayed by anything short of a derailment. Of course, had he had the time, he would have wished to write to the vicar and suggest that he perhaps delay his return till the Sunday, or even strive to arrive on the Friday, ahead of the procession, since he could hardly go to the Baptists and ask them if they would be so good as to postpone their march and opening ceremony to another day just because his vicar was returning to the parish.

In the end, the best he could do was to get the gardener-cum-stableman, Old Thomas, and his helper, the Upson boy, to wheel the vicar's largely unused and cumbersome carriage out of the carriage house, polish it and harness the two ponies, Flora and Frederick, in the shafts: then he had driven to the station to await his arrival and extend a 'welcome home in the name of the people,' see him and his party safely seated in the carriage, ensure that their trunks and boxes would be safely delivered to the vicarage by one of the waiting carriers and prepare to leave...

As they waited for the procession to pass, in the vain hope that it would appease his vicar's obvious growing irritation at the length of it, he informed him of the 'good news' – that four hundred of his own loyal parishioners and scholars from the parochial school were at that very moment waiting at the school at the top of the town to welcome him home themselves and that, further, a tea and an entertainment had been organised as well, though perhaps organised was a little inaccurate and 'arranged' would have been better. There had been nothing 'organised' about the great scramble that morning to get the people to attend, to get the sandwiches cut and buttered and the cakes, jellies and trifles made: in fact, the women were still completing it all, covering the tables with cloths and laying the cups and plates and lining up the chairs even as he left the schoolrooms for the station.

The news of it did not exactly placate the vicar, for the simple reasons that, for one, they were forced to follow the tail of the Baptists' procession all the way up the High Street as there was no room to pass it and, for two, some among the townsfolk waiting on the pavements to watch the procession go by on that bright March Saturday mistook them for a part of it – which the Reverend Scrope in no way was or ever would have been – and, worse, since he was in a carriage at the rear, took him for an important functionary of it, not realising that their vicar had returned after eleven months away...

TWO

MATTERS DETERIORATED further at the top of the town where the High Street widened and ended abruptly in a row of high-fronted shops which faced back down its length: to the left of the line, the Siblingham road branched off obliquely and ran along the top of a high ridge: to the right, the way continued ahead for forty or so yards as the narrower Head Street, till it met the junction with the Wivencaster road coming in from the right, after which it became the Burestead Market road, lined on both sides with houses.

Unfortunately, the destination of both the procession and the vicar's carriage lay along the same short stretch of Head Street, if only together as far as the junction with the Wivencaster road, where they would diverge. The vicar's carriage would continue straight on up the Burestead Market road for a further quarter of a mile to where the parochial school stood, while the Baptists' procession would turn right and march out along the Wivencaster road for a similar distance to the gates of the new chapel, where a platform, festooned with flags and bunting, had been erected in front of its imposing front steps and main doors.

As it happened, the self-same posters which had been pinned up all round the town that week, advertising the procession and 'grand opening,' had also announced that a 'grand bazaar' was also to be held as part of the proceedings in the grounds of the new chapel and all were welcomed to it. A dozen trestle tables had been set up at the side of the building, each sheltered by a striped awning and decorated with bunting and flags and each manned by ladies of the chapel, selling all manner of useful and fancy articles – garden implements and household crockery, umbrellas and walking sticks, ornaments and vases, men's and boys' second-hand boots, working shirts, jackets and trousers, women's hats, shoes, dresses and blanket shawls and children's boots and clogs. On one stall, there were homemade cakes and buns and twists of sherbet and on another even a few books for sale.

In consequence, a crowd of two hundred and fifty or so, with children among them, had lined both pavements along the short run of Head Street to the junction with the Wivencaster road, first, to watch the procession go past and then to follow its tail to the new chapel: and since, to the Baptists, the procession and 'grand opening' of their new place of worship were advertisements for the continuing growth of their brand of faith in the town, it was an opportunity for 'recruitment' not to be missed. At a signal from the bandmaster, the band, hired from Wivencaster for the occasion, halted by the low wall of St. Andrew's churchyard – the Reverend Scrope's own church, which overlooked that very spot – and, oblivious to the presence of the town's vicar and his party at the tail of the procession impatiently wanting to get on, formed itself into a circle in the road, effectively blocking the way up the Burestead Market road. They then proceeded to treat the onlookers to their renditions – their very own renditions – of five popular hymn tunes: and when they had finished, it was the turn of the children's choir, who had been marching immediately behind them, to add their shrill version of *Jesus Wants Me For a Sunbeam,'* which further frustrated the party in the carriage some forty yards back.

While the band played and the children sang, the wearied marchers remained stationary in their serried ranks, turning deaf ears to the curate's exasperated cries from his driver's seat of 'Make way there! Make way!' either because there was no way they could 'Make way!' or because they were drowned out, firstly by the sounds of the trumpets, trombones, French horns, tubas, cornets, pipes and drums, and secondly because at that moment the bells of St. Andrew's began a loud and joyous peel.

At the instigation of the curate, a young boy had been posted at the church gates to look back down the hill for the vicar's carriage, with instructions upon sighting it to run swiftly to the church tower door and shout to those inside, 'He's here! He's here!' which he gleefully did – at which point, the six ringers pulled hard on the bell ropes and a full peel was begun to announce the Reverend Scrope's return, in consequence of which the band played louder still to make themselves heard above the clanging of the bells.

All the party in the carriage could do was to slump back in their seats and call upon the young nursemaid to quieten the crying child, who had been awakened by the cacophony of band and bells, which the poor girl was singularly unable to do and so passed her across to the vicar's sister, who, to everyone's surprise and relief, somehow managed to do it.

Eventually, though the bells tolled on, the choir finished, the band reformed its ranks, the waiting and wearied marchers perked up again and they all set off along the Wivencaster road towards their new chapel, followed by the many who had gathered at the junction, in their excitement all pushing in front of the vicar's carriage and taking no notice of the curate standing in the driving seat again and waving his arms again and calling out again for them to move aside.

It was all very displeasing to the Reverend Scrope, not at all the way he had imagined his homecoming would be. 'For goodness sake, sit down, Smallwood!' he cried sharply. 'You are making a spectacle of yourself. They will be gone eventually. You need not draw attention to us.'

The younger clergyman did as he was ordered, reddening visibly yet again, this time not because of the other's admonishment but because, when he had turned in response to the vicar's harshness, he had caught the eye of his sister and she had smiled sympathetically at him: and no woman had ever smiled at him in that way before that he could recall: it was all very unnerving. Fortunately, it was at that moment that the bells stopped and he was able to turn his attention to the front, flick out the whip and set the carriage in motion again towards the school.

All that morning at the school, while their wives had fussed about inside, doing what women did upon such occasions, several of the male parishioners had worked to erect an eight-foot-high triumphal arch over the gateway, adorning its two pillars with evergreens and hanging between them a large banner with the words 'Welcome Home' painted on it in large black capitals. Not that the Reverend Scrope appreciated any of it: for, when the carriage finally drew up at the gate, he was more concerned with appraising the importance of the line of dignitaries waiting in the yard to greet him, leaving the curate to jump down hurriedly from the driver's seat and help his sister, who was still holding the child, to descend.

The dignitaries waiting in the schoolyard were headed by the mayor, Alderman Wilkins, and his lady, and followed in order by the town's two surgeons, the elderly Dr. Henry Iveson, in his mid-sixties then, and the younger bachelor Dr. James Langham, still in his early thirties, the town's two solicitors, Charles Inglis and Hubert Sparrow, the town clerk Cedric Pringle, the town surveyor Henry Frost, seven of the town's councillors, then the secretary-treasurer of the parochial school's management board, Joshua Linkhorn, who was also Hubert Sparrow's senior clerk, and last, but not least, the Reverend Scrope's own churchwarden, Walter Crowfoot, and the people's warden, Samuel Gough. Except for the mayoress, the other wives waited inside.

Agnes, his sister, whom no one had met before, was introduced to each in turn, while the nursemaid, who at the vicar's insistence had had the child returned to her, stood apart with the curate and consequently was not introduced to anyone. All the while, the Reverend Scrope was conscious of the sound of the band heading for the new chapel drifting across the meadow in between: thankfully, it eventually fell silent, but only because it had reached the gates and a number of dignitaries had made there way up on to the platform in front of the chapel steps.

To those looking on, most were strangers: they had come from other places, from other Dissenting chapels dotted about the Hundred, the county and the region. They were there that day not just to witness the opening of a new Baptist chapel but also to signal a challenge to the Church: that in Steadshall, as in other places, it should no longer take for granted, as it had for so long, that their vicar and his curate were the prime saviours of people's souls: from then on, there would be other players in the game.

In the schoolyard, the handshaking over, the vicar of Steadshall, his sister, the mayor and his lady and the other dignitaries all went inside, followed by the curate and the young nursemaid. Over at the chapel, the triumphant speeches were just beginning…

THREE

INSIDE THE SCHOOL, which was the sole educational establishment in the town, the four hundred parishioners and scholars waiting to greet their vicar gave three hearty cheers at his entrance, some appearing actually pleased – or at least feigning delight – to see him back among them. Others, a closer observation would have revealed, seemed to be unsure whether they should give such an enthusiastic outward display of emotion, for, though they joined in the three cheers called for by Walter Crowfoot, they did so with lowered heads and solemn, even apprehensive, faces.

What the curate could not tell the vicar was that, upon receipt of the telegram, he and the two churchwardens had spent the whole of the previous evening and half of that morning going round the town drumming up support, even cajoling some reluctant parishioners to turn out by reminding them that the Church owned the rental on their cottages: they were not exactly threats, but the matter of 'black marks' and their 'duty' to their vicar and God were mentioned on several occasions.

For the gathering, another small band of male parishioners, like those who had built the arch outside, had spent all morning clearing away the school's desks and benches and decorating its long main room with flags and bunting: they had even built a plank stage at one end on which the vicar and the dignitaries would sit at tables set there, removed from the hoi polloi. The women, meanwhile, had placed vases of daffodils and crocuses along trestle tables arranged in three lines down the length of the room, each covered with white table-cloths and each laden with plates of cakes and buns, bowls of blancmange, jugs of orangeade and lemonade and yet more plates piled high with buttered slices of bread, one line for the adults and the other two with smaller chairs for the children. At each end of the latter tables, lady members of the congregation had been delegated to sit to ensure there would be no misbehaviour among the children while they ate their free teas – no hurling of buns at each other, no spitting in the lemonade or dropping dead flies in the blancmanges to hear the girls scream, as the boys were wont to do on such occasions when overly exuberant.

Fixed to the wall at the back of the stage, where the Reverend Scrope and the other dignitaries were to sit, was a second large banner, made that morning by the older children of the parochial school, with the words 'Welcome Back, Vicar' worked in letters of laurel leaves on a white ground. An observant person would have pondered on the fact that, if the Reverend Scrope noticed it, he gave no sign of doing so to those gathered there, no acknowledgement of gratitude, but went straight up on to the stage, almost as if it were not his way to smile upon people and to praise them, almost, too, as if he expected such things to be done and would have taken note only if they had not been done.

Once the vicar, his sister and the dignitaries were settled at their tables, the curate made a short speech of welcome, which, because of the hubbub all around, mostly coming from the children eager to begin their tea, amounted to little more than what he had said at the station: 'Welcome home, sir, welcome home. We are glad to have you back among us…'

It was followed by three more cheers, led by Walter Crowfoot again, who stepped forward eagerly to orchestrate them and stepped back in some embarrassment when the second round of cheers was not as hearty as it should have been or as he had wanted it to be.

The Reverend Scrope – surveying the faces staring up at him and still not discerning a blank face among them, but seeing only smiles and interest – kept his reply short and to the point, expressing his own thankfulness for the kind and hearty reception he had received and the gratitude he felt at being safely home once more to live and labour among them – his friends, his parishioners. That done, there was a clatter of boots on the bare boards of the schoolroom and the hasty scraping back of chairs as the hundred and fifty or so children present rushed to seat themselves at their tables.

As courtesy demanded, the Reverend Scrope and his sister took tea with the mayor and his wife at one small table on the plank stage, while the other dignitaries and the curate seated themselves at other tables: the nursemaid, Sarah Pockett, had earlier been shown into the smaller infants' classroom, where the pupils' desks and benches were all stacked, so she took her tea alone, still cradling the child Elizabeth in her arms.

FOUR

HE WAS STILL mulling over the schoolmaster's absence when his warden, Walter Crowfoot, stepped to the front of the stage again, just as the tea tables were being cleared, and, clapping his hands for silence, especially among the boisterous children, made an unapologetically obsequious plea, 'begging' the Reverend Scrope 'to give those of us who are unlikely ever to leave England's blessed shores an account of his travels around the world,' which the vicar was pleased to accept.

He did not think the half-hour he took too long a time to regale them with his account of the many things he had seen on his travels, beginning with the perils he had faced on his voyage to Melbourne the sightings en route of great whales and porpoises rounding the Cape and the many sharks he had seen while crossing the vast Indian Ocean. Once 'landed at Melbourne,' he was able to paint a vivid, if somewhat disdainful verbal picture of society in Australia as he had found it, so different from their own, he told them, markedly lacking in culture and the arts, as he knew them, often devoid of the niceties of society, more brash and more hurried in their outlook, less respectful, he thought, to their elders and betters, though he was pleased to see the general respect in which they still held the Mother Country – England. There were other redeeming features, such as the long weeks of pleasant sunshine he had encountered on his arrival in what was Australia's autumn and the many different species of birds and peculiar animals which he had never seen before.

During his several months there, he had not remained all the time in Melbourne with his sister and her family, he told them – carefully omitting any reference to her husband's business or his Moonee Ponds address – but, at his sister's instigation, had travelled north to the port of Sydney, interested to see the actual Botany Bay, to which only forty years before, England had still been sending her convicts: indeed, during his time in Australia, he was quite sure that he had spoken to many of the self-same ladies and gentlemen who had been sent there.

There were other drawbacks to life 'Down Under,' he thought, which anyone among them who might be contemplating a future there would do well to ponder, such as the great distances between the towns, far, far greater than in their own country: in Australia, a town might be as far from the next as a town in Cornwall was from a town in the Highlands of Scotland. And there was, too, he had found when he had gone up into the State of Queensland for two weeks, the sticky late autumn heat with which he had been unable to contend himself, poisonous spiders and poisonous snakes and armies of red ants and, he had been told, of great man-eating saltwater crocodiles which infested the river mouths in the north of the State. In his travels, he had, of course, come across some of the indigenous blacks, the Aborigines, as they were called, but they did not mix with the white man and seemed 'quite docile, almost child-like, in their deference to their European betters.'

In that all-too-short half-hour, he was also able to tell them that he had had to leave Australia before the fierce heat of summer arrived and had crossed the vast Pacific Ocean on a four-masted trading vessel, suffering storms, heaving seas and a hurricane and that the Pacific was not always 'so pacific,' which drew a polite laugh from those who understood the joke and a puzzled silence from those who did not. His ship had called at various volcanic island groups en route, where he was able to observe the native islanders upon each and make notes about their looks, their dress, their homes and their habits, especially the peculiar adornment of the faces of some of them, which he now was able to describe to them in detail. He was pleased to see at all those places that there were a good number of missionaries, who were at least turning the natives away from their heathen tendencies and educating them in the ways of Christianity, even if most of the missionaries were German Lutherans, Swedish Calvinists, French Catholics and American Presbyterians.

When the boat docked in the port of San Francisco in the State of California in the United States of America in the mid-November, he went on, he had spent several more weeks touring the immediate area of that city and the great State itself, being particularly astounded by a forest of huge-trunked redwood trees in the upper State, some so broad that a tunnel had been cut through the trunk of one wide enough for a horse and cart to be driven through. 'The belief is,' he said, 'they are so old that they were growing at the same time as Jesus was walking in Galilee.'

While on America's West Coast, he had travelled to two of California's neighbouring States, both with names peculiar to English ears, Arizona and Utah, especially to see a great gorge, called the Grand Canyon, if they did not know it, a mile deep, many miles wide in places, cut over many thousands of years by a great river flowing through it and so long it would stretch from where they stood all the way to Paris and beyond. They could not possibly comprehend its vastness without seeing it for themselves.

After that, he returned to San Francisco and took passage early in the January on the new 'transcontinental railroad,' as the Americans called their railway line linking the West Coast to the East Coast, and, while the 'railroad journey' had allowed him to see much more of the vastness of that 'great country which is America,' he had not been overly enamoured of its prairie country in the centre, thinking it all too flat and uninteresting, very much of a sameness when covered as it had been by mile after mile of snow. Indeed, he was thankful that he was able to reach New York City in just over a week by train, for in times before the railway such a journey done in the summer by wagon would have taken him five or six months to complete – and in winter sometimes not at all, so he had been told – and had that been the case then he would not have been standing before them, would he?

Some among the gathering smiled wryly to themselves and kept their heads bowed: but, as far as the Reverend Scrope was concerned, they all seemed to be listening to him with rapt attention, save for some of the younger children who had begun to fidget. Fortunately, the lady members of the congregation sitting with them were able to still their scuffling feet and limit their distracting departures to the lavatories at each end of the schoolyard.

Only when he had safely reached 'Liverpool and home,' thankful to escape the bitter New York winter for England's warmer climes and thankful, too, to survive the gale-whipped seas they encountered on the crossing – only then did one small child breathlessly interrupt to ask whether he had seen any Red Indians on his travels. Amid laughter, he was able to say that, yes, he had seen several Red Indians, but they were just sitting huddled inside blankets beside the tracks at the railroad stations at which the train stopped on its journey across the great continent. Their nearness to God-fearing Christians seemed to have subdued their warlike natures and the ones he saw were doing nothing more than selling brightly coloured beads and other trinkets to passing train passengers: they all seemed quite unthreatening, utterly peaceful, in fact, which disappointed the boys of his audience, who appeared to have hoped for something more bloodthirsty from his encounter with them.

At the end of his speech, he was quite pleased by the warm reception he received, though he felt the clapping could have lasted slightly longer than it did and could have been a little more enthusiastic: however, the mayor was gracious enough to compliment him on the eloquence and insightfulness of his address. Even Agnes smiled and gently laid a hand on her brother's sleeve as a complimentary gesture before going off to find the nursemaid, still seated in the smaller infants' classroom and still cradling the child Elizabeth.

The only dispiriting note was that the mayor and his lady and both the surgeons, Dr. Iveson and Dr. Langham, found it necessary to excuse themselves before the entertainment for the evening began, which it did after a somewhat unseemly scramble by the rest of the children for the four lavatories, so much so that Miss Dunsmore had to go out to the boys' end and physically push and pull them into line and clip a few ears in the process, till one queue was formed, with the smallest boys going first. The girls were much more orderly.

The two solicitors, the town surveyor, the town clerk and the councillors, however, all remained and dutifully sat through the songs and recitations, some whimsical and some sad, as well as the musical pieces, smiling as best they could and politely clapping at the end of each offering. First, a choir of Sunday school children sang 'Village Bells,' conducted by Miss Dunsmore, followed by a recitation of 'Tom and His Cruelty' by the spinster Miss Martha Holmes, then a second off-key rendition of 'All Things Bright and Beautiful' by the same children's choir, before Mrs. Mabel Craven sang 'Before All Lands' and 'There's No Place Like Home' in a trembling mezzo soprano voice. That was followed by an overly long instrumental piece on piano, flute and harp which few recognised, performed by three ladies of debatable talent from the congregation, the spinster Iseley sisters, Miss Henrietta and Miss Hermione, and the equally elderly Miss Celia Plunkett. Further renditions of 'Come Soft and Lovely Evening,' sung by Mrs. Hilda Pringle, wife of the town clerk, and 'Cherry Ripe,' sung by Miss Gwendolyn Cropper, aged eleven, brought the entertainment to a close.

The unnoticed but authorised absentee from all of this was the people's warden, Samuel Gough, who had been dispatched surreptitiously to see what he could see of the goings on at the new chapel and to make a report, though he seemed to go rather too willingly for the vicar's liking, with a slight smile on his face, as if he knew what was awaiting the others over the next hour-and-a-half. He returned after the entertainment was over with a report which was destined to displease the vicar even more on his first day home: but then some things could not be helped.

What he had found was that the Baptists were holding a similar tea and entertainment in their new chapel for their two hundred and fifty or so congregation and Sunday school scholars and that the bazaar had done brisk business all afternoon, especially among the many townsfolk, who should more readily have been at the church's celebration, but had followed the band to the new chapel to see what they might buy cheaply off the stalls.

'There must have been two hundred or more of them milling about,' Samuel Gough reported. 'If I'm not mistaken, the Baptists seem to be going out of their way to attract the townsfolk away from us, your reverence. This new chapel is bigger than their old meeting house. They say it will seat upwards of two hundred and fifty and they have installed a pipe organ, specially brought from London, to play during their services. They were playing it while I was watching. I hear they're paying for it with the money they got from the sale of their old meeting house – fifty pounds, so I've been told.'

Again, it was not exactly the news the Reverend Scrope wanted to hear on his return, far from it...

FIVE

THE COMBINATION of the overnight stay in a dreary London railway hotel, hardly able to sleep because of the child's crying in the next room – which the foolish girl of a nursemaid had been unable to quell – followed by that day's tortuous rail travel and having to sit through the three hours of the tea and entertainment, had wearied the Reverend Scrope more than he had expected.

First, there had been the slow train journey that morning up the main line from London to the Steymarket junction and then a wait of a half-hour before a jolting six-mile train ride to the smaller station and junction at Lapperchall along the branch line to Burestead Market and Edmundsbury, followed by a further wait there for a train to coal up and replenish its water before setting out on a second six-mile trundle to Steadshall along a second branch line to the market town of Hilvershall just over the county boundary.

That had been followed by the embarrassment of being caught at the tail of the Baptists' procession, then the tea and the entertainment – all very frustrating, all very tiring, not what he would have wished for himself, his sister and his daughter. The one highlight had been the talk he had been able to give: that had pleased him: as for the rest, it had been somewhat of an imposition which he had borne with as much good grace as one could muster in the circumstances, especially as so many of the town's dignitaries had turned out to greet him: that, too, had pleased him.

It was with more than a sense of relief that, to the accompaniment of 'three more hearty cheers,' this time given at the instigation of the Reverend Smallwood, he climbed wearily into the carriage. Agnes, now cooing over a wide-awake child, and the nursemaid Sarah were already seated, helped into it by the curate, who had again volunteered to drive them back down Head Street to the vicarage and, indeed, was already in the driver's seat, whip in hand, waiting.

Along the Wivencaster road, the band outside the Baptist chapel had struck up again. 'They must be having some more evening's entertainment,' the curate declared, setting the carriage in motion.

'The man has a penchant for stating the obvious,' the vicar thought to himself. To his way of thinking, 'more entertainment' meant that there must still be people milling about outside the chapel and, if people were still milling about there at that hour, they could well be his own parishioners, possible defaulters, turning towards the Baptists and away from his own church. He would ask his two churchwardens to find out their names, if they could, just so as he would know...

As the carriage rattled back down the Burestead Mart road away from the school, he could not help but think that it might have been better if the curate had waited till the Monday and held the tea and entertainment beginning when the parochial school closed. For he would already have returned to the vicarage, the empty vicarage, the house where exactly one year previously *she* – Jane, his young wife – had died in childbirth: the worst part of his return would have been over: he would have already entered the house and made his peace with the ghosts of memory he had left behind when he had set out on his tour: the tea and the entertainment had delayed that.

The suddenness and shock of her death had come back to him like a stab to his heart when he had first sighted the church tower rising majestically through the surrounding trees and above the rooftops of the town as the train approached along the valley – that the mortal remains of the woman who had stood beside him at the altar a mere two years before, to whom he had made love in the great bed, who had sat with him at breakfast, dinner and supper for almost a whole year now lay in her grave amid those same trees.

Curiously, however, coming up the hill from the station, when he had looked towards the old church, it had not been because he was thinking of her or her grave, but to note the further weathering while he had been away of the tower's buttresses and its four pinnacles. They had long needed repair: he knew that, just as he knew that he could not allow God's House to be neglected for much longer: it was tantamount to sacrilege to allow it to remain as it was. It must be made a priority, he had said to himself, something he would need to discuss with the two churchwardens and even the mayor and councillors.

He had intended to have the tower surveyed before he had left for his round-the-world trip, perhaps even with a view to beginning repairs – or at least launching the fund-raising to carry them out, for he knew they would need quite a substantial amount. But her death had thrown him: for the first week afterwards, he had walked around in a daze almost: in the end, there had been nothing for it, he had had to go to see Dr. Iveson and ask his advice on what to do about his continual sleeplessness, the strange chills he felt all over his body and the heavy weight pressing down upon him all the time, almost as if he were carrying an invisible sack of something on his shoulders.

To a degree, time and his travels had eased the pain he had first felt at her loss, just as it had dimmed his memory of her last hours as she lay in the big double bed they had shared for so few months, her forehead soaked in sweat, moaning to herself, at times threshing her limbs as the sickness engulfed her and drained away her life, while the new infant lay sleeping peacefully in a cot beside the bed. He did not know why the Good Lord should have called her to Him so young – at just twenty years of age – but he had tried to understand and to accept that His wisdom was greater than his own.

When she had died two days after the birth, he had accepted it as 'God's will,' just as he had told so many of his parishioners over the years that it was 'God's will' when their loved ones 'passed over': that God should be calling their souls to His presence in heaven was, to him, as unshakeable a belief as '... *in the beginning, God had created heaven and earth... that He had divided the light from the darkness... that He had created every living creature that moveth... made man in His own image and given them dominion over the fish of the sea, over the fowl of the air, over the cattle, over all the earth and over every creeping thing that creepeth upon the earth...*'

He had been fully aware at the time of their marriage that there had been gossip and comment within his own congregation that he, a man of fifty years then, should be taking as his wife a girl of nineteen years, even if her father had seemed quite thankful that anyone should even make the request for his eldest daughter's hand, especially as she was somewhat short-sighted, wore thick spectacles and was plump and poorly educated, except in her Bible learning. But then, after all, she was only the daughter of an impoverished curate from a small village near Norwich, had had no formal education other than a few years with a governess, and, till he had come along, had been nowhere more distant than the main town of that county, having lived always at home with her father and three sisters, her days spent solely assisting him in his duties about his parish.

Aboard ship on his voyage to Australia, there had been occasions, when he had thought especially fondly of her and had wished that she could have been with him, especially during the week it had taken them to round the Cape, battering against a heavy swell, and there had been no one to comfort him or to help him as he lay prostrate in his bunk. The memories of Jane bringing his tea and biscuits to the vicarage study in the early afternoon when he was dozing or writing his sermons, laying out his clothes each morning, tidying his books when he had finished in the study of an evening, arranging his meals, careful to ensure that nothing was ever put on his plate that he did not like – those and a score of other things he had recalled as pleasant memories of her devotion to him, and especially her devotion to his physical needs at bedtime.

However, he also had to admit to himself that there had been other times when her presence would have been an embarrassment, especially when he been in the company of others aboard ship more of his own intellect: for, whatever Jane had been – small, demure, shy, loyal – she had not been endowed with an intellectual capacity even remotely approaching his own, though of course, he would have wished her safely at home in the vicarage rather than lying under a mound in the churchyard and, whenever the thought of where she now was came to him, he always hastily corrected himself.

Only after he had committed her body to the grave had the loneliness of his life engulfed him: the sudden realisation that he was again alone after so short a time of their partnership, that he had no companion with whom he would be able to pass his days and his later years. The fact had depressed him for several weeks after the funeral, worn him down almost: so it was almost as a relief that he had taken up the suggestion of Dr. Iveson, one of his regular churchgoers, a committed Christian and a valued member of the parochial school's management board, that he make the voyage to Australia to visit his other sister, Charlotte, and her family in Melbourne as a distraction from his worries. It was at the doctor's suggestion, too, that he had gone on across the Pacific to America, to make a 'round-the-world trip' of it, rather than return straight away to England, convincing him that the sea air of an even longer voyage and the extra time spent away from the hard work of what was undeniably an arduous parish to minister could only do him good and would more than help him to recover his old indomitable spirit and his zest for work.

Fourteen-month-old Elizabeth, he consoled himself, would always be a reminder of his dead wife, as would the ogee-shaped, polished granite headstone with a scroll and roses emblem above her name and dates which marked her grave. On the morrow, he promised himself, before Holy Communion, he would go to her grave and inform her of his return so that her spirit would know to look down upon him from heaven: the parishioners would expect it of him and he did not want to disappoint them.

'We are here, Agnes,' he said at last as the curate halted the carriage in front of the vicarage, a three-storey, plaster-fronted Georgian building, with dormer windows set in the roof, which lay a short way down a narrow side lane off the top of the High Street and directly across from the low south wall of the churchyard.

As they dismounted, the Reverend Scrope first, his sister and the child next, helped down by the curate, who then extended a helping hand to an apprehensive Sarah Pockett bringing up the rear, a young boy came out of the shadows to help carry inside the small bags they had retained. He was a parishioner's son who, in the absence of Old Thomas and the Upson boy, had been bribed with tuppence by Walter Crowfoot and sent running on ahead for just such a duty: once he had done that, he was also to help the curate unharness the ponies, Flora and Frederick, take them to their stables and give them a good brushing down, while the Reverend Smallwood reversed the cumbersome carriage into the carriage house. During the vicar's absence, he had been given the use of his smaller trap and the two ponies and so was well versed in harnessing, unharnessing and manoeuvring vehicles through the carriage house's low arch.

At least Walter Crowfoot's wife and Samuel Gough's wife had had the good sense to go into the vicarage that morning with two other women of the parish and dust the place, open up the shutters and the windows to let in some fresh air and remove the sheets covering the furniture: and that evening, while he had been at the reception, one of them had gone back to light a fire in the front parlour and in the large bedroom, his bedroom, *their* former bedroom, so there would at least be some warmth in the house, for it had been a chilly day, despite the sunshine.

After he had warmed himself in the front parlour, he went up to the nursery, where Agnes and the nursemaid Sarah were trying to lull the fully awake Elizabeth to sleep: but she was fractious and uncooperative, so he retired to his own bedroom, where he found fresh linen had been laid out and the bed had been turned down ready. The ladies of the parish had indeed been thorough: he must remember to thank them.

He was glad that there was nothing of his dead wife on show: all her things, her dresses, her underskirts, her 'other clothing,' her brushes and combs, her gloves, her shoes, shawls and hats, all had been put away in a trunk before he had left. He had done it himself so that when he walked in after his many months away, he would not be instantly reminded of her and thus her absence.

As he undressed, the happenings of the day came back to him and he mulled over them for a while: the fact that four hundred of his parishioners – albeit a hundred and fifty of them children, who were there solely for the free tea – should have gathered to welcome him showed that he was still well respected among the townsfolk, as he expected himself to be. Also, he must not forget, his worship the mayor and his lady, several councillors, both the town's surgeons and other minor dignitaries had attended his welcome home. Indeed, the mayor himself had told him that, on hearing of his intended return, he had cancelled his and his wife's proposed attendance at the Baptists' ceremony in favour of attending the function in the schoolroom. That above all else had pleased him: to put one over on the Baptists and, by extension, the two other Dissenting denominations in the town, the Primitive Methodists and the Primitive Congregationalists.

Kneeling beside his bed, he thanked God for guiding him home in safety so that he could once again be among the people he knew, his parishioners, in his church, in his parish, to do the bidding of his Lord: then he climbed wearily into the large bed, pulled up the covers to his chin and waited for asleep...

SIX

TIRED AS HE WAS, however, he did not sleep at all well – he did fall asleep, but awoke repeatedly, his mind troubled by something Joshua Linkhorn, the secretary-treasurer of the school management board, had said to him as he was crossing the schoolyard to leave, even drawing him aside so that the two of them might not be overheard.

'I regret having to broach such a matter on the very first day of your return, your reverence,' the secretary-treasurer had tentatively begun, a little too tentatively for the Reverend Scrope's liking, as if he were unsure whether he ought to mention what he was about to say at all, 'but it is perhaps just as well that you have returned when you have. I have been speaking with the other school managers and we feel that a meeting of the management board should be called as a matter of some urgency. There are two serious matters which need to be discussed, sir – very serious matters indeed. The others managers are all in agreement with me that a meeting is required and ought not to be delayed.'

'What matters?' the Reverend Scrope demanded: it all sounded most disturbing.

The secretary reached inside his coat, drew out a folded sheet of paper and handed it to him: it was a printed sheet, embossed with a Government symbol at the top, a 'final notice' from the Department of Education in London, in fact, ordering that accommodation must be found in the parochial school by September for eighty-five infants of the town and the adjoining hamlet of Bourne Brook, a mile-and-a-half to the south of Steadshall, who would all be of an age to start school then: if not, a School Board would be imposed upon them.

'Mr. Crowfoot found it tacked to the door of the church last week, sir,' the secretary said with a weary sigh. 'It was put there by the town clerk, Mr. Pringle. We cannot keep it a secret because one was attached to the door of each of the three chapels as well, including the new Baptist chapel. It is common knowledge about the town.'

The Reverend Scrope read the notice again and pulled a face. It was not exactly a great surprise to him: two months before he had set off on his round-the-world trip, Walter Crowfoot had warned him that a small group of 'busybodies,' as he had dubbed them, most of whom were Dissenters, had written to the Department of Education in London requesting a School Board be imposed on the town. The vicar had thought little of it at the time: in his view, the request came from people who simply wished to air their importance on matters which did not concern them and which were competently dealt with by others – namely himself and the parochial school's management board, on which no Dissenter sat. He would not have them on the board on any account: the parochial school was a Church of England school and would remain a Church of England school and the school's managers would all be members of his church or, like himself and the curate, ex-officio members. There would be no Dissenters elected to it.

After all, the Church had been providing an education for the children of the poor in the town at its own expense for the past thirty-eight years, ever since 1848, and only as their numbers had grown with the advent of the Elementary Education Act of 1870, which had decreed that all children between the ages of five and ten had to attend school, had they sought a grant from the Government to assist them.

Nothing had come of the Dissenters' request and he had sailed off to Australia thinking the matter done with. No, it was not a surprise, but it was still disturbing.

'Yes, it would be better if we were to discuss this at a full meeting of the managers,' the Reverend Scrope agreed. 'We will meet tomorrow afternoon at the vicarage. Please ensure Doctor Iveson and the others are informed. And the other matter, Mr. Linkhorn?'

The solicitor's clerk allowed a group of people to pass out of earshot. 'Her Majesty's inspector of schools made his annual visit recently,' he said quietly, 'and the managers have obtained a copy of his report. I have to say that what he has written is a matter of concern to us all – great concern.'

The Reverend Scrope turned sharply to him. 'For what reason, Mr. Linkhorn?'

'I think, your reverence, I should bring the inspector's report round to the vicarage so that you might see for yourself,' the secretary replied, 'if that is all right with you, sir?'

With the people gathering by the gate to wave him and his party off, it was no time to enter into a discussion on the imposition of a School Board from London or the merits or otherwise of a schools inspector's annual report: so, for the sake of his sister, Agnes, who wanted to get to the vicarage to put the child to bed, and the young nursemaid, who was yawning behind her hand and looking very tired, two o'clock at the vicarage on the Sunday afternoon was agreed.

Whether it was the conspiratorial way the secretary of the school managers had spoken which disturbed his sleep that night or the unfamiliarity of his own bed after so long a time away, he did not know. It was certainly something. Of course, it could have been the appearance in a dream of his long dead wife, who walked into the bedroom as though she were still alive, said something to him which was unintelligible and went out again. For some reason, in his dream, he found himself following her as she moved through the various downstairs rooms – front parlour, dining room, his study, the kitchen and scullery – arranging some flowers in a vase here, plumping some cushions there, checking the time on a mantel clock, before languidly picking up a book and going out through the French windows of his study into the garden. He felt a sudden need to engage her in conversation, to hear her voice again, to make contact with her now that she was 'no longer dead' – now that she was 'alive again' – to ask her how she was, to say how sorry he was that she had died when she had and hope that she did not blame him for it. Sadly, death in childbirth happened to many women: it was not his fault: it was not men's fault: it was just natural: he had not wanted it to happen to her and he was sorry it had: what else could he say?

Peculiarly, so long did he seem to spend with her in the garden watching her pruning the flowers and the bushes, then sitting on the garden bench in the sunshine to read her book that, when he awoke with a start, he thought it must be the middle of the night. But, when he looked at the clock on the wall opposite, he found it was not yet midnight and he had been asleep for just over two hours since retiring at nine o'clock. Along the landing and up in the nursery, he could hear his sister's voice and that of the nursemaid Sarah trying to soothe Elizabeth, who, having finally fallen asleep, had woken again and, finding herself in a strange place, had become frightened and was crying again. Thereafter, he slept poorly: the same thought kept recurring in his mind, he could not blot it out: that the Baptists had built their chapel while he was away as a deliberate challenge to him personally: and when the second dream came, it was of him standing in a pulpit preaching to an empty church. Not a soul was there, neither Walter Crowfoot nor Samuel Gough, nor even the old sexton, Amos Rowley: all were gone, Agnes among them, to the new Baptists' chapel.

He did sleep eventually and was awakened by his sister entering the bedroom with a kettle of hot water, which she poured into the basin on the washstand, before pulling back the curtains. A shaft of pale sunlight came streaming through, illuminating the gently circling cloud of dust disturbed by his sister which was floating between the bed and the window. Breakfast would be in half-an-hour, she said, and he would need to hurry if he were going to attend Holy Communion, as it was almost nine o'clock.

The thought briefly occurred to him that Agnes, then thirty-two, eighteen years younger than himself, just five-feet-two-inches tall, with wire-rimmed spectacles and her dark hair tied back in a bun, ought really to have been married long before: there was no hope for her now, of course, so she might as well live with him: it would be cheaper to have her as a housekeeper and a governess-cum-motherly aunt for the child than to pay someone else. She was quite capable, good at arranging things and she cooked well enough, though in time he would have to hire someone else to prepare their meals so that she might devote more time to Elizabeth as she grew and became more active, for the nursemaid Sarah, having had no real experience of children, was really little more than a minder and a companion to the child: just somebody who was always there for her.

His mind would have continued musing along those lines, prescribing for his own comfort, his own security, ordering his life now that he was back in Steadshall, ready to start again after his absence, had not a clatter of plates downstairs interrupted his reverie. Jumping out of bed, he said a hurried prayer of thanks to God, both for his return and for his survival through the night, washed himself in the basin, quickly shaved the bare parts of his face, trimmed his side-whiskers and his moustache with the small scissors he carried in his valise, dressed quickly in his dark suit, with a clean shirt, remembering to put on once more the clergyman's collar which he had not worn in months, and then went down to breakfast.

In the dining room, Agnes had prepared a meal of porridge with treacle, fried eggs and bacon, fried bread and a pot of tea from the groceries which he assumed the ladies of the parish had laid in the previous day, the same ladies who had taken off the dust covers and cleaned the place. There was just himself and his sister at the long table: the nursemaid Sarah was eating in the large kitchen, at the same time feeding a mush of milk, breadcrumbs and porridge oats to a fractious Elizabeth.

It was still only a quarter to ten when he pulled the vicarage door shut and crossed the narrow lane to his private entrance to the churchyard: though the two wardens were already inside the church, no members of the congregation had yet begun to arrive, so he was able to cross between the headstones to his wife's grave unseen. He was glad to see that the sexton had kept the plot tidy and had planted flowers and cut the grass around it with a scythe: it would not have done to allow the grave of the vicar's wife to be overgrown by grass and docks and thistles.

Her grave was positively the last to be dug in the old churchyard, for it had become so full over the previous two decades as the town had expanded that no further burials could be carried out there, save for those who wished to be lowered into the same grave as a long-gone wife, mother or husband. The new dead now were laid in neat rows amid the grassy paths in the new 'public cemetery' along the Wivencaster road, a former cow meadow a short way beyond the Baptists' chapel, purchased by the town's Burial Board and given two ornate high gates for its entrance to 'replicate the Pearly Gates of heaven.'

The drawback, as far as the Reverend Scrope was concerned, was that a 'public cemetery,' by its very definition, meant that it was for the disposal of persons of *all* denominations, Church of England, Primitive Methodist, Primitive Congregationalist and Baptist: even two Quakers from the Society of Friends' meeting house in nearby Hamwyte had been laid there, but thankfully, in the view of the Reverend Scrope and a great number of his flock, including the vicar's warden and the people's warden, as yet no Roman Catholics. Nor as yet had they established a church to the 'anti-Christ' Pope in the town, which was just as well since the vicar of Steadshall had no time for the 'incense swingers... the Pope blowers... the bread mumblers... the bead rattlers,' as Walter Crowfoot was wont to call them, and even less time for the Dissenters, since they seemed determined to challenge his ascendancy and their pastors were not even trained clergymen.

The main Baptist lay preacher, Thomas Chiddup, was 'a carpenter' by trade, the Primitive Methodist preacher, Hezekiah Coker, was nothing but 'a tenant farmer' with a smallholding out along the Bromptree road and the Primitive Congregationalists' usual preacher,

Gabriel Grout, was a 'blacksmith': not one of them had ever seen the inside of an ecclesiastical college and probably not the outside of one either. The Reverend Scrope found it all very disconcerting at times, very disconcerting indeed...

SEVEN

SIMPLY BY BEING back in England, back in his parish, among his own parishioners again after eleven months away, the Reverend Scrope had hoped, even expected, that he would feel revitalised, re-energised, ready to tackle the myriad problems which pastoral work in a parish could throw up, meeting it with renewed vigour, with a greater spirit. Somehow that thankfulness, that earnestness, that desire had evaporated in the few short hours he had been back. When he had awakened that morning, he felt drained of energy, as if it had leaked from him while he slept: somehow, the happiness he had felt getting off the train and being back among his people had been tarnished, his willingness dissipated, first by the triumphant procession of the Baptists, then by the news from Joshua Linkhorn and, finally, by his own sad return to the 'empty' house.

His hope was that the service of Holy Communion that morning would reinvigorate him, though it did not please him that Agnes informed him at breakfast that she deemed it necessary to remain at the vicarage to see to the child as Sarah Pockett was having difficulty in soothing her. On his first Sunday morning back, he would have expected her to have joined him in holy worship: people would expect her to be there and she would not be: it was all too much and he entered in a subdued mood.

Not unexpectedly, the church was full, with every pew taken, even the row of draughty seats near the bell tower door, which was often left empty: the Reverend Scrope would have been dissatisfied if it had been otherwise. Save for leading the congregation in the Lord's Prayer at the beginning, he was content to allow the Reverend Smallwood to take the service as he had prepared himself to do, letting him lead the worshippers through the responses, accepting his choice of hymns without calling for any changes and listening without interruption to his sermon, which the curate had already given earlier at his own church, St. Mary's at Bourne Brook.

For, when the vicar had gone away, it had meant a suspension of the rights of presentation to enable the Diocese to reorganise the two parishes and changes had had to be made in order for the Reverend Smallwood to be able to look after both. It had been a long and hard eleven months for him. For a start, Bourne Brook St. Mary's main service on Sundays had had to be brought forward to half-past nine so that it would finish at ten-thirty: the curate would then jump into the vicar's pony and trap, which he had borrowed for the purpose, and drive quickly to St. Andrew's, where at eleven as usual he would be following the procession down the aisle ready to begin the main service there – and to give them the same sermon.

Instead, on his first morning back, the Reverend Scrope sat in the chancel and observed, which was how he came to conclude that there was a certain sense of guilt showing on many of the faces – a guilt of absences, if he were not mistaken – which told him that, from the number of smiled greetings he received as people entered, quite a number of the congregation were there simply to have him *notice* that they were there, which to his mind suggested that perhaps they had not been so dutiful while he had been away.

When the service concluded, he went outside to join the curate in shaking hands with the more respectable of his departing parishioners, a chore which he had always disliked and which he would have preferred to have avoided had it been possible to do so. As soon as the churchyard had emptied, he allowed the curate to go back to his lodgings along the Siblingham road for his midday meal, as, in the absence of Joseph Padwick and his wife, he had a Sunday school to take at two o'clock with Miss Dunsmore. It was not kind-heartedness on the Reverend Scrope's part: the real reason was that he wanted to speak to his warden and the people's warden alone: there were questions to be asked of what 'other things' had been happening in the parish while he had been away, things about which he ought to know.

His first question as he sat in the vestry some minutes later and opened the pages of the parish register was as disarming as it was polite: 'So how have things been in the parish, Mr. Crowfoot? Well, I hope?'

At that particular time, Walter Crowfoot would have preferred to have been asked almost any question other than that one: but it had been put to him and he would answer his vicar as truthfully as he could and hang the consequences!

'To be truthful, your reverence, I cannot say things in the parish are as well as they should be,' the warden replied. 'I regret to have to tell you we have had certain problems, sir.'

'Oh, and what problems are those, Mr. Crowfoot?' The whole time he had been away, the Reverend Scrope's one great fear had been that matters in the parish would be allowed to slide, to drift, to decline, if his steady hand were not on the tiller. That he had come back just in time to 'stop the rot' became evident as he perused the most recent entries in the parish register: what he had feared had indeed occurred. No sooner had he set out on his travels, it appeared, than several regular members of his congregation had seized the opportunity to defect to one or other of the Non-conformist chapels.

'We lost fifteen regular churchgoers all told early in the May,' Walter Crowfoot told him apologetically, hoping that the blame for the desertion of his vicar's flock would not be heaped upon his shoulders when people clearly did things of their own free will. 'They just left without saying a word. I had no warning it was going to happen – none at all, your reverence – nor did Mr. Smallwood. Come one Sunday, they just didn't show up in church. Most seem to have gone over to the Baptists. One family have started going to the Primitive Methodists' chapel in Rosemary Lane and two more families have been going to the Primitive Congregationalists in Kings Road since last September, but it is the Baptists who seem to be attracting most of them, though what for, I don't know. They seem to spend more of their time meddling in the affairs of the town than looking after their souls. The number of Dissenters in the town seems to be growing quite rapidly, sir, but it is the Baptists who seem to be growing the most. They could grow even more now they've opened their new chapel.'

The Reverend Scrope made his displeasure known by the sharpness of his tone. 'Yes, I realise that, Mr. Crowfoot,' he snapped. 'What I would like to know is: was anything done to bring these defaulters back to the Church?'

The inference in the question was clear. 'There has been no slackness or neglect of duty on our part, I assure you, Vicar,' Walter Crowfoot protested, nervously twisting his hat. Had anyone else but the vicar put that question to him, they would have received a short and very sharp answer, but before his vicar his response was muted to a sigh and a spreading of the hands to show his helplessness. 'Mr. Smallwood and I called on several of them and tried to persuade them to return to us, but they were all adamant – they preferred chapel to church. They said they did not want to come back and preferred something simpler, like the things the Baptists and the Methodists were doing.'

'Is that the only reason they gave?'

The two wardens looked at each other, faces reddening: knowing the truthful answer to the question, neither was willing to state it, each hoping that, if it had to be given at all, the other would be the one to speak. For the honest answer was: 'They don't want to come back because of you, Vicar, and they won't come back till you have gone from this parish. The greater number of the people of this parish – nay, this town and several of the villages around it – do not like you, or love you or pray for you and do not like going to church because of you. They fear you and some despise you...' And so on.

Fortunately, as he asked the question, something else caught the Reverend Scrope's attention, so his head was down and he was turning the page as Walter Crowfoot gave an answer which was only partly truthful. 'We didn't ask, your reverence,' he said, which was a lie. 'They just said there was more singing in the Dissenters' chapels and they liked to sing,' which was the truth. 'We wondered whether it had something to do with the hymns we were choosing. We tried a few of their hymn numbers at the morning service, but it didn't seem to do any good. Nobody came back. If I remember rightly, two more families left after that.'

The Reverend Scrope looked up briefly, then bowed his head to the register again: he seemed to have accepted their reply – *seemed to have accepted it* – for the only noise he made was to sniff, to clear his throat and to murmur something to himself which they did not catch: another matter recorded in the register had caught his eye – and that, too, disconcerted him.

'I note there seem to have been fewer baptisms,' he said, raising his head once again, this time solely to regard his warden, Walter Crowfoot.

'That was mostly due to the scarlatina outbreak we had in the June,' Walter Crowfoot explained, his cheeks reddening under the vicar's chastening. 'Then there was an outbreak of diphtheria at the beginning of August and a bout of the sweating sickness later in the same month which affected mostly the old folk. We had twenty-five deaths in total in the parish during the three outbreaks, ten of them being old folk, as expected, and the other fifteen all young ones, six of 'em new-born babes, more's the pity. The good Lord saw fit to take the six youngest before they had been brought to church, so Mr. Smallwood anointed them where they lay and, though we told him he was wrong, he would not make a charge for doing it – not even a reduced charge – though we told him he should, but he wouldn't. He said the babes had a right to go to heaven even if the families couldn't afford to pay for their funerals. Also, of course, it means the number of burials don't show up as actual burials in their own right, so to speak, because some of the dead babies were put in the same coffins as some of the older folk that had also succumbed at the same time. As you know, it's done hereabouts to save their parents the expense of paying for their own coffin and grave, but also so's the little ones are not buried alone and have someone with them on "their journey up to heaven." Three others were buried together in the same coffin to keep each other company and, as you can see there, your reverence – ' He stepped forward and pointed to an entry in the register. ' – the Guardians paid Mr. Smallwood's fee to conduct that burial and also for the coffin and the shrouds for the three little ones as none of the parents was able to provide it themselves and there weren't no older folk being buried that week, as I recall.'

Almost wearily, the Reverend Scrope turned his attention to the number of weddings over the months he had been away: that, too, was down, from twenty-seven in the previous twelve months to only nineteen in the past year. 'Why are they down?' he demanded. 'Are people giving up getting married in the sight of God?'

Walter Crowfoot could only spread his hands again and shrug his shoulders. 'We have impressed upon the young ones that they ought to get married in church, but some of them don't seem to care whether they are married or not, your reverence. They are quite content to live in sin and say it is cheaper and they don't need a piece of paper to bind them to each other – they do that in bed.'

'Is that so,' cried the Reverend Scrope with a snort, clapping the register shut. 'Well, we shall see about that, Mr. Crowfoot. I shall want a list of names of all couples who are living in sin. It is a matter of expediency. If they do not marry in a church, they will not bring their children to be baptised in church and our numbers will deteriorate even further and, with it, the Living of this parish.'

His next question was very much an outcome of Walter Crowfoot's previous revelation. 'And how many bastards have been born in the parish while I have been away? Do you know?'

'Ten in all, your reverence,' Samuel Gough answered, eager to be able to say something which would put him in a good light and not allow his fellow warden to hog all the news, 'though three of them died during the scarlatina outbreak. It was as if God had sent an avenging angel to smite their mothers for their wickedness.'

'Amen to that,' said the Reverend Scrope.

'Amen,' said the two wardens together.

The consequence of all this, of course, was that revenues from all means – baptisms, marriages, burials, prayers for the dead, the 'churching' of women who had given birth, general collections, charitable donations and the like – were down quite sharply from the previous year – another matter of disconcertion for the vicar. His time away was proving to have been costly, for the parish, the Diocese and the Church in general...

EIGHT

WHATEVER HE DID, the Reverend Scrope was determined to save his parish from what he considered to be 'the nightmare' of a School Board being imposed upon the town: to him, they were an 'abomination' to be avoided at all costs. Thus, the first part of the meeting of the school management board, which began two hours later in the front parlour of the vicarage, was dominated by the threatened imposition, and also by the report of Her Majesty's schools inspector, for the two were inextricably bound.

Having a board school in the parish, the Reverend Scrope well knew, would mean contested elections for the positions of the school managers: and he would not allow that to happen, for the simple reason that, if a School Board were ever established in Steadshall, it would allow the Dissenters a say in the running of the town's sole school – the town's Church of England school, that is.

It would also allow them a say in the appointment of the head teacher and the assistants and, as the vicar of the parish of St. Andrew's – and had been for the past nine years – he was not prepared to allow that. Never! Not so long as he was an ex-officio member of the school's management board, which he was by virtue of his incumbency, and not only that but he sat as its chairman and the unchallengeable arbiter as well.

Any decisions to be taken were put into practice only if he approved of them: and if he did not, they were not implemented – it was as simple as that. He was not going to surrender the control which the Church had over the education of the young of the town – particularly their religious education and their adherence to the Church of England Catechism – even if some scoffing souls deemed it more 'indoctrination than education.' In his view, voluntary schools and religious education were so much better than the curriculum foisted upon the children of the labouring poor in board schools. And he certainly was not going to give those powers away to a bunch of Dissenters!

The infants' and seniors' day school had been built by churchmen and was upheld mainly by subscription from churchmen, amounting to some fifty pounds per annum. For the past sixteen years, since the Act of 1870, the children of Steadshall and Bourne Brook paid weekly for the privilege: infants a penny a week, children of standards one and two tuppence a week, with scholars of standard three and above charged threepence a week. For a large family of children all attending at the same time, there were concessions to assist them: the fourth child in every family was educated free and, if three children from one family attended regularly, a penny was deducted from the fee which the third child paid. The school also had a number of 'free families' – that is, children with just a mother earning as best she could, who often had been deserted by the father and who were considered too poor: their 'penny expenses' were paid by benefactors in the town.

The Reverend Scrope was willing to admit that, with two hundred and seventy-five children in six standards, the parochial school was 'somewhat overcrowded and unsatisfactory on many points': what concerned the managers was that, if they were to meet the Department of Education's demands, they would not only require a new classroom to be built on to the present school to accommodate the September intake of infants from the town itself but they would also likely have to build a new school at Bourne Brook to accommodate all the children from there, as well as the next intake of infants.

At present, there were only two qualified adult teachers at the parochial school – Joseph Padwick, the headmaster, and Helen Dunsmore, plus a thirteen-year-old pupil-teacher, Hannah Hodgson, who had yet to attain a first-year certificate, but which she hoped to do in the near future and then go on to achieve the other certificates and, in time, obtain full qualification as a teacher in her own right. Pupil-teachers then were boys and girls of thirteen and over, who, after five years of apprenticeship, could themselves become teachers. The schoolmaster's wife also taught the infants and standards one and two their alphabets, their times tables and first reading, but she had never attended a training college so had no actual certification to do so: her forte was needlework, which she taught the girls of the four higher standards in the afternoons. Building a new school at Bourne Brook would obviously require the employment of at least one further qualified teacher and also another pupil-teacher, which would further add to the expense.

Of the school managers at the vicarage that afternoon, four just happened to be the district's biggest farmers and landowners – Charles Higgs of Sloe House Farm, Henry Bucknall of Highwoods farm, George Mott of Whiteash farm and William Eaton of Upper Beakley farm – and they were on the school management board for a reason – their own reasons. They were as much against a School Board being forced upon the parish as was their vicar, since it would mean them having to pay higher rates to fund the school, as had happened in many other places where one had been imposed upon the populace. In short, being among the principal ratepayers in the parish, they objected to people – namely themselves – being compelled to pay more simply to erect another school when the town already had one.

Of the three others present, the solicitor's clerk, Joshua Linkhorn, as its secretary-treasurer, was always swayed by the vicar and would never go against him – how the Reverend Scrope voted, so would he – while Robert Stalker, the gruff, short-tempered landlord of the Bull Inn, though at times of a more independent mind, wanted nothing which would increase the rates he and other traders and shopkeepers in the town paid. 'My rates are high enough already, I don't want any more foisted on me,' was his retort.

The Reverend Smallwood could have attended and, had he been asked, he might well have been more neutral on the matter, considering what was best for the children's education rather than the purses of the ratepayers: but at that very hour he was taking the Sunday school along with Miss Dunsmore.

The seventh member present, the elderly and benign Dr. Iveson, did not seem to be bothered one way or the other: if a second school needed to be built to ease the overcrowding, then build it. That was his thinking, but then, among them all, he was the only one who had ever visited a board school and he had discovered that they had their merits when compared with what scholars were taught at parochial schools.

Faced by necessity, the board, as rational men, decided unanimously – more an agreement of reluctant grumbles and a slow raising of hands – that there was little else they could do but accept that, if they were to ward off the imposition from the Department of Education, they would have to accept its challenge and build a small extension to the parochial school for the new infants' intake, taking up a portion of the school yard to do it, and then somehow find the means to build another small school at Bourne Brook, which would at least help to alleviate the overcrowding at Steadshall by taking away at a stroke all those who would otherwise be walking each day from the hamlet.

Cost and time were, of course, the predominant factors. 'I have already looked into the best estimate of enlarging the parochial school and building a smaller school at Bourne Brook,' Joshua Linkhorn said in a somewhat grim tone, having been tasked with the matter by the management board before the vicar's return, 'and the best I can come up with is that it would cost us about seven hundred to eight hundred pounds to meet the requirements of the Department of Education – building an extension here and a small school at Bourne Brook. That does not, of course, include the appointment of a school master or mistress for Bourne Brook, who would require an annual salary of, say, sixty pounds, and the employment of a pupil-teacher for the lower standards.'

The Reverend Scrope had always believed that what he did in the parish, he did it for his God and for the people of the parish.

'We shall have to start a subscription list among the parishioners,' he declared, 'and I shall expect everyone to give.' He meant the others on the board as much as himself: all promised that they would 'most certainly... without a doubt... in due course... of course, of course...' once they had consulted their own finances to see how much they could spare, though it was noticeable to them all that Robert Stalker, the landlord of the Bull, visibly blanched at the prospect.

To start the subscription list, the Reverend Scrope told them, he himself would donate a sum of forty-five pounds from his Living – which amounted to five hundred and forty-seven pounds per year, though he did not disclose that fact. He believed also that there were enough well-to-do people in the town who attended church that they might make 'great strides' towards raising the full sum within a year if they tried hard enough, if people were generous enough, though the actual full amount, while not beyond their means over time, was not achievable in the few months they had been given – unless a very generous benefactor came forward.

'Well, it won't be from one of the tea-drinking Baptists,' sniffed George Mott, 'or the Methodists or the Congregationalists for that matter. It'll have to come from us as usual.'

Like many other parishioners who attended church and duly paid the weekly fee to send his three young children to the parochial school, the farmer resented the fact that the Non-conformists had their children educated at the church school as well, yet, save for the weekly fee the children paid, not one farthing for the annual cost of running it came from any of their chapels. In comparison with other towns, the three denominations had come late to Steadshall, appearing only in the previous fifty years and, in the thirty-eight years of the school's existence, not one of the chapels had so much as taken up a single collection for it. The Church alone had borne the annual cost and that in itself was a cause of continual and bitter resentment among them all...

NINE

THEREAFTER, the management board's discussion turned to the school inspector's report and most particularly the parochial school's log book in which the daily happenings at the school were recorded, such as the daily attendance of the pupils in each of the six standards, along with a full record of any and all punishments meted out and also any comments the schoolmaster felt obliged to make about the performances of his staff, Miss Dunsmore and the pupil-teacher Hannah Hodgson, as well as any admonishments he felt obliged to give. While there were unfavourable comments about his assistant, Miss Dunsmore – '...*her manner is extremely tiresome at times... she is often vindictive and disagreeable... is too shrill by half and too hard on her charges...*' – and about the pupil-teacher Hannah Hodgson – '...*must work harder... has to be told everything twice...*' – unsurprisingly, there was none about his wife and her needlework instruction.

'I regret to say I had trouble obtaining the log book,' the secretary-treasurer, Joshua Linkhorn, reported. 'Mr. Padwick and his wife were most objectionable when I went into the school four days ago and asked to see it so that I might read it in advance of the school managers' meeting. Mr. Padwick was very reluctant to hand it over. He said that he had not finished writing in it and wished to retain it. I only obtained it on Friday evening by going into the school after it had closed for the day, using Miss Dunsmore's key, and opening his desk drawer.'

Why the schoolmaster and his wife had attempted to thwart him became evident when the Reverend Scrope read the log book, for, in it, too, were recorded all visitors to the school, including Her Majesty's inspector, who three weeks previously had made his annual inspection. Not only that, it also contained the inspector's full report, which the schoolmaster was obliged to paste into it, and which did not make for satisfactory reading.

'I found the children deficient in reading, writing and arithmetic,' the inspector had reported, *'and I saw no sign of any improvement in the standard of work from my last visit here. Attainments are still far from satisfactory. My feeling is that there is too much emphasis upon religious instruction and not enough upon other more general subjects. The elementary work is in a very backward state throughout. Arithmetic is almost an entire failure. The fact that not a single sum was correctly worked in the fifth and sixth standards seems to prove that the scholars are not classified according to their ability. Spelling is weak in all standards, particularly in the fifth and sixth. The grammar above the second standard was badly done. Two children were struck off for copying and a large number required constant watching. On geography and history, very few answered my questions with any intelligence, which is not surprising since I understand neither subject is taught much here. The present staff are wanting in the power necessary to control the number of children assembled and I am of the opinion that a second full-time assistant-teacher and possibly a second pupil-teacher are desirable...'*

Normally, inspectors did not bother testing the younger children of standards one and two as they were just beginning, but this time the inspector had done so, disturbed perhaps by the poorness of the upper classes: and he had come to the conclusion that the children in the lower standards were also not being taught adequately: and, though the pupil-teacher, Hannah Hodgson, had hoped to receive a certificate from his visit which would help her to qualify as a teacher when she was older, he did not find her teaching up to the standard he would have expected and so could not countenance a first certificate for her at that time: she would need to improve very greatly if she expected to progress, was his comment.

It seemed to him that much of the teaching of the youngest was being left to the pupil-teacher and two girls, an eleven-year-old and a twelve-year-old, who served as monitors: he found it deplorable that, in between the morning and afternoon lessons, the pupil-teacher was to be found instructing the two monitors on the facts of the next lesson and that they were then expected to teach them that way to the younger children.

The record of attendance kept in the log book was 'somewhat deficient,' the inspector had also recorded: too many were absent when the weather was bad, such as on snowy mornings or when heavy rain was falling. According to the log book, on one particularly bad day, of the two hundred and seventy-five on the register, a hundred and sixty-three had been absent, including every child from Bourne Brook because a snowdrift had blocked the road. Indeed, the inspector had complained, attendances had been down on the very morning of his visit, it being quite noticeable again that few from Bourne Brook were present due to the heavy rain on that day.

Payments then were by results, with four shillings paid for each pupil who attended two hundred and fifty times in the previous year, plus up to eight shillings per pupil based on their results in the inspector's examination in reading, writing and arithmetic, with extra money available for history and geography – if they were taught, which at Steadshall they were not – not properly.

However, as a consequence of his findings, Her Majesty's inspector had given notice that he would be recommending to the Department of Education that the annual grant, which helped to sustain the parochial school as much as the parish's contributions, be reduced by one-tenth, so that instead of their full grant of sixty pounds and fifteen shillings per annum, six pounds one shilling and sixpence would be withheld and they would be receiving only fifty-four pounds thirteen shillings and sixpence.

'Most unsatisfactory,' declared the Reverend Scrope as he closed the log book.

'Disheartening,' said Joshua Linkhorn, 'and after all your good work, your reverence. If children cannot read, how will they have access to the Bible – to God's word?'

'It's a damning report all right, begging your pardon, vicar,' Charles Higgs of Sloe House Farm agreed.

'These results are too poor to ignore,' snorted William Eaton of Upper Beakley farm. 'We pay rates to give these young'uns an education and they don't seem to care a darn if they get one or they don't.'

'You can't make children learn if they don't want to,' said George Mott of Whiteash farm. 'Perhaps the best thing might be to take the older ones out of school afore their time and put 'em to work on a farm. I could do with a couple of lads on my farm right now.'

'So could I. There's always work for fit young lads on the land,' echoed Henry Bucknall of Highwoods, to which William Eaton and Charles Higgs chorused their agreement.

'In the circumstances, there is only one thing we can do,' the Reverend Scrope asserted. 'We must ask Mr. Padwick for his resignation. Clearly, he and his wife are not up to the task of running so populous a school. We shall go to the school together tomorrow. In view of the inspector's report, I do not foresee any problems. We will give him three months notice or, if he wishes, a fortnight's notice and a suitable payment of, say, a month's salary to compensate. That should be time enough for him and his wife to find another position and also for us to advertise in *The Teachers' Guardian* for a replacement. We can retain Miss Dunsmore, I think. I do not see any reason to dismiss her. And the pupil-teacher, the Hodgson girl, she is quite an intelligent girl – quite a pretty girl, too...'

TEN

THE REVEREND SCROPE knew full well that there had always been mutterings from some in the town about the way he did things in the parish, about the decisions he made, the orders he gave, the expectations he provoked from them all: he was well aware, too, that there were some who even went so far as to complain of what they termed his 'imperious' conduct in dealing with those matters, or so his 'eyes and ears among the people,' his warden, Walter Crowfoot, had reported back to him.

It was acknowledged by everyone that, when it came to making decisions and getting things done, whether concerning the church or the school, the Reverend Scrope felt it his duty to ensure that they were 'done properly, done correctly and done speedily, with no procrastination,' as he put it, no matter what objection might be raised against him, which to the townsfolk meant, of course, 'things being done his way and only his way out of downright cantankerousness,' as his parishioners put it to each other, but, of course, never to him.

But then he was the vicar, the Archbishop of Canterbury's servant in residence, God's chosen shepherd among His flock – among people who were by virtue of their class and their forebears less educated than himself: if he did not control and guide the affairs within his domain, then who would? It was his duty to do so, his calling: it could not be left to the people themselves or the two wardens who administered the general affairs of the church? No, he expected and considered it only right that they deferred to him on all matters concerning God's House, and, when it came to matters concerning the school's management board, he made the appropriate decisions and the others were expected to endorse them and put them into practice.

As it turned out, come the Monday, the deputation to join him on his march up Head Street to the school to inform Joseph Padwick that he was dismissed forthwith was sadly lacking in numbers when the time came for them to gather at the vicarage. For a start, none of the farmers was present: they sent word that they were all far too busy to bother with such a trivial matter as sacking a schoolmaster. The vicar would have to do it himself: after all, it was not a difficult task: over the years, they had done it many times themselves to their own workers. One simply told whoever was being sacked to leave, paid what one owed them if one had to do so and saw them off one's property.

The Reverend Smallwood also failed to appear: he should have been there – indeed, he was expected to be there to support his vicar: his failure to join the deputation was, in the Reverend Scrope's mind, tantamount almost to a 'betrayal.

As it happened, in his parish at Bourne Brook that morning, he had called on an aged crone who was nearing her end and who had become mightily fearful that St. Peter was going to deny her entry through the Pearly Gates when she reached them because of certain indiscretions she had made during her younger life, when she was a favourite of the boys of the hamlet. The curate's unfortunate disclosure that as a penitence she would probably have to spend some time in Purgatory before she was allowed to enter the gates into heaven put the poor woman into such a state that he had to remain by her bedside and pray to God for her forgiveness till she was calmed: thus, he was delayed.

The vicar, however, could wait no longer: it was noon and that was the time best suited for what they were about to do – when the children would be on their way to their homes for their dinners. Thus, the deputation which marched up Head Street that noontime was reduced to four – the vicar and the secretary of the management board, Joshua Linkhorn, and the two most reluctant members of it that day, Dr. Iveson, who, having no sick to visit, would rather have gone fishing, and the landlord Robert Stalker, who was already grumbling about a likely loss of trade at the Bull if the business took too long, as he had customers to serve and barrels to tap.

Even so, the unexpected sight of the four men, all known to the scholars of the parochial school as members of the management board and, therefore, important people, with the vicar, the most important of them all, at their head and all with stern and solemn expressions on their faces – the sight of them striding through the school gates caused many of the children streaming out to smirk and to speculate among themselves on what 'Old Paddywack,' as they called their master, even though he was just past thirty, was about to receive.

When the four men pushed open the main door and went inside, it proved too much of a temptation for the children who had remained behind at play, those from Bourne Brook and a few others who had brought their own bread and cheese and pickled onion lunches: they hauled themselves up to peer through the high windows to see what they might see, till they were vociferously ordered down by Miss Dunsmore.

Joseph Padwick was seated at his desk at the far end of the schoolroom, writing on a sheet of paper, preparatory to going home to the cottage opposite for his own lunch. Curiously, he did not seem unduly concerned, but smiled to himself as they entered and his greeting was as much a nonchalant acknowledgement of their arrival as a query as to why they were there. He had been informed first thing by a smiling Miss Dunsmore of the vicar's return while he was away, so it was no surprise to him to see the delegation enter: it was an expectation, really.

'Gentlemen?' was all he said, looking up as they threaded their way between the serried rows of low benches and double-desks, the narrowness of the aisles between, though wide enough for children, the diminutive Miss Dunsmore and the skinny schoolmaster to pass, seeming to hinder the more portly landlord and the aged doctor: either that or they hung back deliberately, for they allowed the vicar and the secretary to reach the schoolmaster's desk well ahead of them.

'Mr. Padwick,' the vicar said in reply, in what was no more than an acknowledgement of his own.

'I am glad you have called,' went on the schoolmaster, the beginnings of a smile on his face. 'It saves me the bother of having to walk down to the vicarage – '

Puzzled frowns creased the faces of the vicar and the secretary, while, behind them, wry smiles appeared on the faces of the doctor and the publican: they had sensed something in Joseph Padwick's casual manner which the vicar and the solicitor's clerk, more intent upon bustling in and looking officious, had not. In short, they suspected something was afoot – something perhaps to do with the schoolmaster's disappearance over the weekend?

Joseph Padwick pulled open the top drawer of his desk and took out an envelope.

'I regret to have to inform you, gentlemen,' he said, the smile broadening as he handed the envelope to the Reverend Scrope, 'but I have to tend my resignation. I have been offered another position at a much larger school in Edmundsbury. I am at this very minute writing back to confirm that I shall definitely be accepting the post I have been offered. Therefore, I must give you three months' notice of the termination of my employment as the master here. Of course, it also terminates my wife's employment as a part-time assistant as well. Everything is contained in the letter.'

Doctor Iveson and Robert Stalker could not help but smile as they noted the unexpected reddening of the Reverend Scrope's cheeks: he had been pre-empted and both the doctor and the innkeeper knew from experience that it would not sit well with him: it was only with great control that the vicar was able to reply as calmly as he did, though there was still a bite of sarcasm in his tone.

'Thank you, Mr. Padwick,' he said, taking the letter and opening it to read. 'You have anticipated us, perhaps wisely in view of the fact that we are here to ask you for that resignation. It seems that will not now be necessary. You have saved us the trouble. Your resignation avoids the unpleasantness of that – '

He quickly perused the letter, keeping his face stiff and his manner formal, then handed it to Joshua Linkhorn to read. 'I think I speak for all the members of the school management board when I say your resignation is accepted,' he informed the schoolmaster coldly, not even bothering to turn around to confer with the other three men behind him, who were reading the letter together, the doctor and the publican looking over the secretary's shoulder. 'And, since you are so keen to quit this school and this town and go on your way, then perhaps we can come to an agreement which will be beneficial to us all. What do you say to an agreement that you leave the school at the end of the month – the twenty-sixth, say – and we will pay you a month's salary in lieu of your three months' notice?'

'If I am to move so soon, I shall require moving expenses as well,' Joseph Padwick informed him calmly, still smiling as he leaned back in his chair and boldly met the vicar's gaze. 'At least ten pounds? Grant me that, sirs. If I am to move before my notice is up, I shall require the funds to do it as I have very little in savings – the money paid me here did not allow it.' He now altered his gaze to look at the others. 'If it is your wish, I shall be gone by the end of the month as agreed. It will certainly benefit me to be able to tell my new employers that I can start ahead of time, for they are as anxious for me to begin as you are for me to leave.'

'To which school is it you go?' the Reverend Scrope asked, his eyes narrowing slightly as he fixed them on the schoolmaster: he knew that there were at least two large schools in Edmundsbury, one a boys' grammar school, for it was a far larger town than Steadshall, and the other a Poor School for the children of the labouring classes. Surely it could not be the former that his now disgraced master would be joining? He could not possibly have been accepted for a post at the grammar school. Could he?

'To which school in Edmundsbury I go is of no concern to you,' the schoolmaster said, with deliberate politeness, 'except to say that I shall be glad to leave Steadshall and that my salary will be higher and my classes will be far smaller and, therefore, more manageable than has been the case here.'

'You are impertinent, sir,' the Reverend Scrope exclaimed, reddening even more.

'No, sir, I am being truthful,' Joseph Padwick asserted, retaining his calm demeanour, but looking now at the other men and ignoring the vicar's bristling indignation. 'Your school, sirs,' he told them, 'is so grossly overcrowded as to be near impossible to teach in properly. The teaching staff is totally inadequate. You cannot expect satisfactory results among your pupils unless the teaching staff is increased, which you gentlemen seem most reluctant to do. You need at least one more assistant-teacher and, in my opinion, a second pupil-teacher. When I first came here, I was promised that those aspects would be remedied. I have waited and they have not been.'

Here he turned back to the Reverend Scrope. 'I know all about the ultimatum you have received, Vicar.' he went on. 'That is one reason why I have decided to go. It has nothing to do with your return. It is just a coincidence that you have returned as I have made my preparations to leave. I had hoped to be gone before you returned. What I will tell you is that the present infants' accommodation is not suitable for those you have, let alone those who are coming. Where you will put the new intake in the autumn is beyond me?' He paused, as if wondering whether to add anything further, then made up his mind. 'All this you have brought upon yourselves,' he declared. 'It is small wonder that the Department of Education has had to act. I for one would have welcomed a board school. I shall not be sorry to leave Steadshall, not sorry at all.'

It was all too much for the Reverend Scrope, first to hear the schoolteacher maligning the school and then to hear him laying the blame at the management board's door and, by inference, himself.

'I accept your terms, Mr. Padwick,' the Reverend Scrope snorted, 'One month's wages, you and your wife to leave the school and the cottage at the end of the month and you to receive ten pounds for your moving expenses. Come, gentlemen, I have heard enough. Our business here is done.'

Turning on his heel, he pushed past the doctor and the publican, giving no thought to the smallness of the space in which they stood, and almost knocked a surprised Joshua Linkhorn over one of the low double-desks as he did so. Had not the publican seized his arm, the poor man would have been sent sprawling.

Under his breath, unheard by the others as he made his way out, the Reverend Scrope vowed: 'I shall see about this new school of yours, Mr. Padwick. You will not insult me and get away with it...'

ELEVEN

THE NAME STEADSHALL was derived from the Old English 'stede,' meaning 'the site' or 'the place,' and 'hald,' meaning 'a refuge' or 'a shelter': thus, over time, Stedeshald, 'a place of refuge' or 'a place of shelter,' became Steadshall.

When Daniel Defoe rode there on his *Tour Through the Whole Island of Great Britain'* in the early Eighteenth Century, he found it a pleasantly situated market town, irregularly built on both slopes of a gravelly valley through which wound a small fast-flowing river: he had noted that a market was held each Tuesday on the High Street hill, when some business was done in corn and cattle and the like by farmers and dealers at two of the several inns: there were also, he had noted, two fairs for cattle, sheep and horses, one in May and the other in October. Apart from recording that the High Street was notable for its considerable length and for the many good houses, shops and inns which lined its long descent to the river, his only other comment, was that the town, lying forty-six miles from London on the high road to Edmundsbury, had no apparent industry and that 'its chief trade seems to depend upon the few gentlemen of any fortune who live within the neighbourhood spending their money in the town.'

Steadshall's population then comprised some three thousand five hundred souls, including the hamlet of Bourne Brook and the surrounding estates and farms: these figures barely increased over the next hundred years: prosperity had continued to elude the town.

Everything changed when an American entrepreneur named George Oldcourt, from New York State, arrived in the town in the third decade of that century to marry a local landowner's daughter, saw the potential of the river flowing along the valley at the bottom of the hill and decided to set up a silk spinning mill even as elsewhere the 'Swing Rioters' were roaming the Southern Counties smashing the machinery on farms and in factories. In five years, as the fashion for wearing silk burgeoned, George Oldcourt became a wealthy man and built two more mills at the bottom of the town.

Though, initially, the main work of the Steadshall mills was spinning a variety of silks, changes in female fashion in the middle of the century saw the latter two mills turned over to the production of crepe, which had become the main dress material worn by upper-class and middle-class women. One mill manufactured soft crepe, the thin, crinkle-textured fabric, woven in silk, which resulted from the arrangement of the weft, which was formed of yarn from two different bobbins twisted together in opposite directions, while the second mill produced a harder-finished fabric, made of hand-twisted silk yarn and typically dyed black and used for mourning: the older mill continued to weave garments of pure silk.

Over the next three decades, George Oldcourt increased the profits of his company by a phenomenal fourteen hundred per cent by installing three steam-engines to drive the rows of power looms. Except for fifty or so men and boys employed to do the heavier bulk and lifting work, the greater number of his workers, more than ninety-five per cent, were women and girls, which helped to keep down the labour costs. In those same thirty years, as his profits increased a thousand-fold, the wages of his thousand or so workers' barely doubled. Women were paid less than six shillings a week, with girl workers the cheapest of all, receiving only a shilling and sixpence a week, or just over a farthing an hour for a sixty-hour week. The few men earned eight and tuppence a week, which was barely more than the amount earned by the many other men of the town who six mornings a week trudged out to the many farms of the district for their labour, though at least the mill workers were in the dry and relative warmth of the spinning and packing sheds when the winter winds blew and the freezing November fogs and chill March rains came.

The advent of three large mills along the riverside at the bottom of the long hill meant that a greater number of houses had to be built to accommodate a rapid influx of workers from the surrounding villages: consequently, rows of cheap, hastily built, two-up and two-down workers' cottages sprang up in the lower part of the town along the narrow Factory Lane East and Factory Lane West and out along the Bromptree road.

The mills also brought the branch railway line, running nineteen miles from the Lapperchall junction to Hilvershall to the northwest and passing the town along the same river valley at the foot of the hill and this, together with the factories, was a spur for further progress and improvement which was still a wonder to the older folk that so much should have happened in so short a time.

By the time of the Reverend Scrope's arrival nine years previously, Steadshall's population had risen to more than six thousand: a new town hall had been built halfway up the High Street to replace the old moot hall and the aldermen and councillors met there every month in a spacious, oak-panelled chamber. The petty sessions were also held there every alternate Tuesday for the fourteen surrounding parishes and the county sessions bi-monthly. A Temperance Society appropriated the property every Wednesday for its Band of Hope meetings, sometimes attended by more than two hundred, while another part of the town hall was occupied by a new 'people's library,' which boasted more than a thousand books.

Of the other improvements, Steadshall's streets were by then gas-lit from a gas works in Kofemary Lane, had all been paved at a cost of some twelve hundred pounds by the local Board of Health, which had also expended upwards of five thousand pounds in providing a water supply from an artesian well. At the bottom of the town, a corn exchange had been erected so that, on Tuesday market days, the farmers coming in from the surrounding district could conduct their business in respectable and private surroundings rather than in the town's crowded and smoky inns. On North Street, a Penny Bank had been established, open every Saturday evening from seven till ten o'clock.

The growing population had, naturally, attracted the Dissenters, who now vied with the Reverend Scrope's church of St. Andrew to save the souls of the townsfolk and keep them on the straight and narrow to heaven: a church had stood on the site of St. Andrew's at the top of the town since late Saxon times, though it was not till the reign of King John that a building of any substance had been erected. The greater part of the church – the nave, the north and south aisles and the chancel – dated from the early years of the Fourteenth Century: there were minor additions of the north vestry, and north and south porches in the early years of the Fifteenth Century, but the physical look of the church remained largely unaltered until the start of the Eighteenth Century when the east end was extended and four high crocketed pinnacles were added to the corners of the dominant tower to give it a more cathedral-like appearance.

Unluckily for the Reverend Scrope and all preceding vicars, George Oldcourt had been a Unitarian and had attended their meeting house in Hamwyte: he had also preferred living in that town rather than in

Steadshall because it was more attractive and was closer to the main rail line to London. There, he had built a twenty-room mansion set in a three-thousand-acre park, travelling the few miles to Steadshall each day by carriage, with footmen standing on the back and, though like many sincerely religious men of his time he was in favour of social reform, that was only so long as it did not interfere with the operation of his business and the making of profit.

When, soon after he had set up, Parliament introduced the Factory Act of 1833, restricting and governing the employment of children – his young girl workers – he argued that it would do nothing but injure manufacturing businesses like his own, check improvement and increase the costs of production. If Parliament were so set upon passing such legislation, restricting and governing the employment of children, he suggested it should attempt to protect children only under the age of ten and that the children whom he employed, from the age of eleven onwards, did not need their protection and were not at all badly treated. 'No children among the poor of this town are healthier than those employed in my manufactories,' he pompously asserted.

It was this imposition by Parliament which caused him to put himself forward to become the Whig Member for the town: he might not live in it, but his mills employed by far the greater number of its girls and women so he had a right to look after his own interests. He served for a number of years, till the necessity of having to be so often in the House about its business interfered with his profit-making over at Steadshall, which by then had risen to forty-five thousand pounds per year, giving him a personal fortune of seven hundred thousand pounds.

When he had died aged eighty-six, sixteen years previously, the mills passed to his son, Thomas: if the Reverend Scrope had one great regret, it was that Thomas Oldcourt, knight of the realm, bachelor, by then in his sixtieth year, preferred to spend his days alone in his father's fine mansion collecting stamps, snuff boxes, and birds' eggs and left the running of the mills to a blunt-spoken Lancashire incomer from Preston by the name of Henry Horrocks, who himself lived in a fine mansion in the nearby and more picturesque town of Bromptree: no one of any importance, it seemed, wanted to live in a quiet backwater like Steadshall when there were livelier and more picturesque places nearby in which to pass their days.

The Reverend Scrope had always had to acknowledge the unfortunate fact of life that the two richest men who had ever lived in that part of the county and who could have contributed substantially to his church's coffers had they attended – George and Sir Thomas Oldcourt – had preferred always to live elsewhere and to worship elsewhere so that others rather than his church benefited. Even Horrocks, the mill's current manager, was a Wesleyan – and a tight-fisted one, to boot, his workers said – and went to the Wesleyan chapel in Bromptree, so there was no change to be got out of him either.

For that reason, what Sir Thomas or his manager, Horrocks, paid his female workers, or what he paid the men, was never the concern of the Reverend Scrope: anything involving the plight of the labouring classes in their two-up, two-down hovels of cottages at the bottom of the town he had left to the good offices of the various curates he had employed, of which the Reverend Smallwood was the third in his nine years there. As vicar of the parish, his sole concern was saving the mortal souls of his parishioners and ensuring they reached their rewards – if they deserved them – in the next world, not the price of their labour in this world.

His one tenuous link with the wealthiest man in that part was that, when Sir Thomas's mother had died, being a Steadshall woman, so to speak, she had been buried in St. Andrew's churchyard close by the wall of the tower and Sir Thomas, on his very rare visits to the town, never failed to visit her grave and lay flowers on it when the tedious business at his three mills was done and before he returned to his lonely mansion in Hamwyte.

Consequently, the Reverend Scrope always tried to make himself 'available' when the mill-owner did visit, in the hope that he might attract a donation towards the church's upkeep from him, however small – but always hoped to be substantial: but as yet none had materialised in his nine years there. Sir Thomas, like his father before him, was a staunch Unitarian, prayed at the old meeting house in Hamwyte and, like many men of wealth, was not one for giving his money away. Not that being a Christian and going to pray twice every Sunday prevented him from ordering his manager to deal harshly with the dissatisfied. For, when fifteen years before, just after he had succeeded his father, the women power loom weavers at his three mills had gone on strike, thinking it a good time to ask the new owner for 'a bigger share of the company's profits' – meaning better wages – he had ordered his manager not to negotiate with them and to record the names of 'the twenty to thirty who have been foremost in this shameful disorder for immediate and absolute discharge.' Then he went back to his stamp collection and his drawers of birds' eggs.

If there were one consolation for the poor folk of Steadshall, it was that at least the tread-wheel had been taken out of the old House of Correction and its eight wards and five day rooms were mostly locked and empty and gathering cobwebs and dust, though it now housed a police station in one part, accommodating a sergeant and two constables, and some of its twenty cells were still put to temporary use on Saturday nights and Sunday mornings by certain of the town's regular inebriates. Anyone else convicted at the petty sessions or the bi-monthly county court of more serious misdemeanours was immediately dispatched to the none-too-tender mercies of the county gaol at Melchborough…

TWELVE

THE JOURNEY by train from Steadshall to Edmundsbury in the next county took all of four hours then, from setting out to arrival. When the Reverend Scrope made the trip two days after his confrontation with the schoolmaster, he did not enjoy any part of it, not while going, while there, or while returning. Not because he questioned his reason for going, for he felt that it was an absolute necessity that he went and, when he set out he was relishing that part of it. No, his lack of enjoyment stemmed, firstly, from the fact that he had inveigled the curate into accompanying him and the Reverend Smallwood was not of the same mind as his vicar: nor was he the most talkative of fellows, so their journey, which took up the whole of the morning, was made in almost complete silence, save for the occasional observation on the weather, which that day was one of bright sunshine.

The second fact, and one of far greater perturbation to the Reverend Scrope, was that Edmundsbury had a bloody history of anti-Protestantism and, as the train finally pulled into the town's small station, he could not help but sense that he was entering the realm of the ungodly, the realm of the 'anti-Christs' even. Indeed, a shiver ran down his spine as they climbed Station Hill to St John's Street, crossed Cannon Street, went along Garland Street on to Lower Baxter and turned into Angel Lane towards the cathedral and the gateway of the old abbey: for it was there, during the attempted Catholic revival of 'Bloody Mary's' reign that seventeen Protestants had been martyred at the stake for refusing to return to the old religion – in the eyes of the vicar of Steadshall, seventeen brethren of sacred memory among thirty all told throughout that county who had been put to death in the name of Papist intolerance. Was it their ghostly presence that he sensed as they turned on to Crown Street and passed the massive ruin of the abbey gate and the Norman tower? In his imagination, he could almost hear their shrieks of pain as the first flames seared their skin and their voices calling upon him and all other Protestants to avenge their martyrdom.

Of the town's general history, the Reverend Scrope knew only that, from early times, it had been one of the cradles of Catholic Christianity in the country: its Benedictine abbey, burial place of the Saxon king Edmund, who had been tied to a tree and shot full of arrows by heathen Danes in the Ninth Century when he had refused to renounce his Christian faith – which even the Reverend Scrope acknowledged was admirable – had at one time been third only to Canterbury in Kent and Walsingham in north Norfolk as a destination for pilgrims.

Before the abbey's high altar, the English barons were said to have met in 1214 to swear an oath to force King John to accept Magna Carta. However, in 1539, Henry the Eighth had confiscated its wealth and the townspeople, who had rebelled against their abbots several times over the centuries, had pulled down many of the abbey's walls and used the stones for their own building. Catholicism, though, had not been suppressed and when Elizabeth the First came to the throne, the town became something of a bolt hole for priests, harboured by several wealthy recusant families, though, in the minds of many in other places, it paid for its adherence to Rome when a great fire destroyed a hundred and sixty of its houses during Scottish James's reign.

In the years after the Restoration, when Charles the Second returned to England, the Jesuits were quick to establish a school there till they were put to flight by the 'Glorious Revolution' of 1689, when the Catholic James the Second was deposed in favour of the Protestant William of Orange. Catholic priests, however, had continued to be active in the area throughout the Eighteenth Century and were still scuttling about its streets at the time of the Emancipation Act of 1780.

By the time the Reverend Scrope visited, it was a quiet provincial market town of some thirteen thousand souls and its only significant industry was the brewing of beer, though in the Middle Ages it had had a flourishing cloth industry. He knew that a boys' grammar school had been founded in the mid-Sixteenth Century in the brief reign of Edward the Sixth, but, apart from that, the only other major school of which he knew was the Poor School, at which four hundred boys and girls of all denominations received elementary education in reading, writing and arithmetic, some history and geography, and practical subjects such as gardening for the boys and laundering for the girls.

So, if it were not the grammar school to which Joseph Padwick was headed, then it must be the Poor School, he reasoned.

'Ought we to be doing this, Mr. Scrope?' the curate asked as they approached the gates of the Poor School. 'It seems rather petty to be seeking to taint a man's application for a teaching post in this way. I urge you to reconsider before it is too late, before we have sullied a man's character. I have no wish to be accused of slandering another's reputation.'

'It is not slander to speak the truth,' the Reverend Scrope snapped back, giving his curate a sharp look. 'Truth is a defence against slander. They have a right to know that their new master and his wife – I assume she will also be teaching there – are considered to be incompetent by Her Majesty's inspector – and by me. I intend to tell them and I shall. It is the least I can do.'

When they were still twenty yards from the school gates, the Reverend Smallwood suddenly stopped: the vicar, who was already a good two yards ahead by that time, only realised what was happening when the curate's shadow disappeared from view alongside him.

'I am sorry, vicar, but I cannot and will not go on,' the Reverend Smallwood declared.

The Reverend Scrope turned to see his curate standing stock still on the pavement some ten yards back, his arms folded firmly across his chest, his chin raised up and his head turned slightly to one side in what he supposed to be a dramatic gesture of defiance, but which the vicar took to be little more than a show of petulant boyishness, which, in his opinion, a grown man should have left behind years before.

'What we are doing is wrong, sir, entirely wrong,' the curate went on. 'It is – ' He paused, as if searching for the right phrase, before adding: ' – it is un-Christian.'

The Reverend Scrope eyed his colleague for a second or so and drew himself up to his full five-foot nine against the other man's beanpole six-foot-two. 'Nonsense, Smallwood,' he said, with as much distaste in his tone as he could muster. 'How can it be "un-Christian" to want to warn people of the fraudulent nature of someone who is about to enter their midst. The man has proved himself an incompetent. They should be warned and they *will* be warned and, if you will not accompany me, then I shall do it alone. You are a great disappointment to me at times, Smallwood, a great disappointment.'

With that, the Reverend Scrope, seething at what he considered the curate's lack of moral fibre, marched on determinedly through the open gates of the school, went up the path, mounted the steps at the front entrance and, stopping only to mop his brow with his handkerchief, knocked loudly on the door knocker. The sound of it echoing inside brought a host of inquisitive boys' faces to the windows of a classroom alongside, both curious and amused to see a perspiring, red-faced clergyman standing on their front step, till an unheard voice inside ordered them back to their desks and their faces disappeared. Presently, the front door was pulled back by a tall, grey-haired man, in his mid-forties, wearing dark clothing, over which was draped a loose chalk-dusted gown: indeed, in his hand he still held a piece of chalk from his teaching.

'Yes?' he enquired, looking the vicar up and down as if to appraise him. 'May I help you?'

When the Reverend Scrope had heard footsteps approaching, he had backed off the top step to the one immediately below, to put a little distance between himself and whoever opened the door, the better able to address them: instead, he found himself at a disadvantage, being looked down upon by a much taller man, who regarded him with a haughtiness bordering upon contempt.

'I am here to see the headmaster,' the Reverend Scrope said, removing his hat as a matter of politeness prior to entering. 'Scrope is my name, Reverend Hugo Scrope, from Steadshall. I have come with some information which I think the headmaster should hear and which I believe he will thank me to know when he has heard it.'

'I am the headmaster,' said the tall figure in the doorway, making no attempt at all to open it wider so that the clergyman might enter, and still continuing to look condescendingly down at the man below him.

'Oh, how do you do, sir,' the Reverend Scrope began, but received no acknowledgement in return from the tall headmaster. 'I have come about a master whom I believe you may have hired just recently, a Mr. Joseph Padwick, who is currently – though not for much longer, I am pleased to say – the master at Steadshall Parochial School in my parish. I am the chairman of the school mangers there, ex-officio, of course, being the vicar of the parish. I merely wish to warn you as the headmaster of this school that I have had cause to dismiss the man you have hired, Mr. Padwick, and his wife, who also taught at my school. I did so for gross incompetence in their teaching. I have given them till the end of this month. We have lately had a most unfavourable report by the schools inspector from London. It really was quite awful. I have not brought a copy with me, but I can honestly say that he was most scathing about the teaching at the school under Mr. Padwick's residency, most scathing.'

The Poor School headmaster seemed to be listening, for he had not closed the door, though there was a certain inscrutability about his gaze as he continued to look down upon the man before him.

'So, I feel it is my duty to warn you, sir,' the vicar of Steadshall went on, 'that you may well have enlisted the services of an incompetent. I will not say the same of his wife, but the man himself has brought our parochial school so low that the Department for Education is threatening to impose a School Board on the town. That is how low we have sunk, thanks to Mr. Joseph Padwick, and why I am here to suggest that you reconsider his appointment.'

There was a pause of a few seconds as the Poor School headmaster pursed his lips, as if weighing his reply, carefully forming the words in his head before pronouncing them, and still making no move to open the door wider to admit the vicar. Finally, he said: 'You say you have come from Steadshall today to communicate this to me?'

'I have, sir. I have come with my curate on the train. It has taken us all of four hours to get here.'

'Where is your curate?' the Poor School headmaster enquired, raising one eyebrow and looking along the line of the railings some thirty yards away.

'He is by the gate, sir,' answered the Reverend Scrope, turning round himself and just managing to catch a glimpse of the lanky curate's shoulder protruding from one side of a brick pillar.

'I take it he is there because he has no wish to be a part of this?' the headmaster enquired, and, not waiting for a reply to the obvious, he went on: 'He is a wise man, your curate, a wise man, indeed, whereas you, sir, you are a fool, a first-class fool! As a Church of England vicar, you should know better. Be off with you, sir! Be off with you!'

The astonished Reverend Scrope almost reeled backwards down the steps: he had never been so insulted: certainly, he had never been called a fool to his face before: and neither had he been addressed in such a cold, commanding manner before.

Without waiting for him to bluster up a protest, the Poor School headmaster continued: 'I know well the capabilities of Mr. Padwick. Given the right material with which to work, bright pupils and not country dullards and an officious, meddling set of school managers led by a mentally unstable vicar, he is a first-class master, as is his wife, whom I also know. I have no intention of reconsidering either of their appointments. Indeed, I welcome them. So your journey here today has been wasted. Of course, if you had taken the trouble to look at the plate on the gatepost where your eminently sensible curate is hiding, you would not have walked up this path and wasted my time with this preposterous rubbish. If you had looked, sir, you would have seen my name upon it as the headmaster of this school – Henry James Padwick. Padwick, sir, Padwick. I am the elder brother of Joseph Padwick, the master you seek to denigrate, and the headmaster of this school for the past twelve months, ever since I came down from the Isle of Ely, where I taught previously. It is I who has hired your schoolmaster – my brother – and I shall not be dismissing him on your recommendation. Indeed, if I decide to tell him of this conversation, I should think he would have a very good case for bringing an action against you for slander. Bear that in mind as you return. A very good day to you, sir.'

The door was slammed shut, leaving a stupefied Reverend Scrope to walk slowly back down the path, humiliated beyond measure, feeling himself once again under the scornful gaze of not only the Poor School headmaster but the scores of pupils who had come to the windows to watch him leave. As it happened, there was no one there: it was all imagined: the headmaster had returned to his classroom and the boys were still seated at their desks, but the imagined humiliation did not stop the Reverend Scrope from barking angrily at his curate when he enquired what the Poor School headmaster had said.

Even the vicar of Steadshall was not above saving face with a small lie. 'He said he would consider it and thanked me for the information,' he told the Reverend Smallwood, stony-faced.

He did not see the puzzled frown on the curate's own face as his vicar stalked off back down the hill towards the railway station: for the curate had read the sign on the gatepost while the vicar was standing at the door conversing with the tall, grey-haired man in the black gown and had noted the name of the headmaster was the same as their own 'disgraced' schoolmaster and, naturally, he had wondered about it…

THIRTEEN

THE REVEREND SCROPE returned to Steadshall, smarting but unbowed: the embarrassment was put to the back of his mind, which is what he did with most embarrassments. He was ready to press on with what needed to be done next: and that was the appointment of a replacement for Joseph Padwick and perhaps even the hiring of either another assistant to replace Padwick's wife to compliment Miss Dunsmore, which would be costly, or, better and cheaper, to hire a second pupil-teacher. He had not yet made up his mind.

The Padwicks left Steadshall two weeks after the vicar's return from Edmundsbury: he did not bother to watch them depart: that task he delegated to the Reverend Smallwood, more to take the keys to the school and the cottage off them than to wave goodbye. 'Good riddance to them both!' was the only thought which crossed his mind on the morning of their departure, their goods loaded on to a carrier's cart and themselves seated up beside the driver, huddled under cloaks, as it trundled out of Steadshall bound for Edmundsbury and its Poor School.

The process of replacing Joseph Padwick was well in hand, anyway: for immediately upon returning from the embarrassing confrontation with the schoolmaster's brother, the Reverend Scrope had gone straight to his study and had written out an advertisement, which he had posted that same evening to *The Teachers' Guardian:*

> *'Senior master urgently sought to take charge of Church of England Parochial School, Steadshall, teaching standards one to six. Immediate commencement vital. Salary £75 per annum, with rent and rates. Two hundred and seventy-five pupils approximately daily. Accommodation available. Some help with moving expenses. Reply to Rev. H. Scrope, The Vicarage, Steadshall.'*

There was no point in discussing the matter with the other school managers: what had to be done needed to be done promptly if he were to meet the magazine's deadline for advertisements: it could not be left to await a meeting of the school managers – better to get on with it: they would agree with him, anyway.

Normally, when he appointed someone to the post of master of the town's parochial school, the vicar would request an early interview with all applicants, be there two or be there twenty, usually at Wivencaster, as the nearest large town, in a room booked for the purpose at the George Hotel on the High Street, where he had interviewed Joseph Padwick and his wife three years before. There, he would ascertain the character of each applicant, view their qualifications and record details of their references with a view to writing to the referees for further information or for corroboration or explanation of what they had already written.

Normally, also, the three-month period of notice which a departing schoolmaster was expected to give allowed him the time and the opportunity to do those things at his leisure, but the current appointment was too pressing to allow such a delay: for no sooner had the Padwicks departed than Miss Dunsmore was complaining to him that she had been left in charge of two hundred and seventy-five children 'all by myself,' of which at least a hundred and fifty, she avowed, were quite likely to become unruly and unteachable no matter what she did, and that she had only a thirteen-year-old pupil-teacher and two girl monitors to help her.

The Reverend Scrope could not help her himself had he wanted to do so, which he did not: if he had done anything at all, it would have been to have the more senior pupils pass the day reading aloud from the Bible, but he had other matters about the parish which, to his mind, were far more pressing. However, he did promise that he would speed the appointment of a replacement for the 'traitorous Padwicks' and, in the meantime, he would ask the Reverend Smallwood to help her out with the teaching, to which the curate reluctantly agreed.

Meanwhile, one other influence played its part in bringing him to a hastier decision than he would perhaps otherwise have wanted to make: and that was England's perverse weather. Travellers abroad, upon returning to England after many months away in warmer and more salubrious climes, can often fall foul of the sudden drop in the daily temperatures of these islands. This, the Reverend Scrope duly did one week after the Padwicks had left. For ten days, as Miss Dunsmore and the curate attempted to tame the more unruly elements of their respective standards – the one with shouts, the other with clouts – he was laid up in bed with a chest infection, a severe head-sweating cold and a variety of other aches and pains, all of which necessitated two visits from Dr. Iveson.

The doctor's categorical instruction, more a directive really, was that he was to remain in bed and certainly not to travel anywhere, especially not just to undertake an interview when the whole matter could be conducted just as efficiently and as expediently by post: there was just no need. No, he must stay where he was, keep himself warm, take plenty of broth and drinks of hot Russian tea carried up to him by his sister and, within a week or so, the doctor promised, he would be 'as right as rain' and well enough to conduct the church services again. However, if he did not take his doctor's advice, then he could well be in bed for a fortnight or longer and he, the doctor, would not be held responsible. The doctor left it at that and the vicar duly took his advice, though he did get out of his bed each night to kneel beside it and, though not out of disrespect for the medical man's opinion: but deeming it necessary to add some influence from above, prayed for God's guidance in helping him to solve his unwanted and unsought dilemma.

So when he received a reply to the advertisement one week after it appeared – it was to prove his only reply – he decided that God must have answered his prayers and there would be no need for an interview at the George Hotel in Wivencaster, no need to run to the expense of a room, and, if the applicant appeared to be suitable, to appoint him: his judgment was sound, was it not, and guided by God?

The applicant, one William Warburton, certainly appeared to be suitable: in his letter replying to the advertisement, he stated that he held a first-class teaching certificate from the Chester Training College in Cheshire, had been the master of a National School in Stepney, East London, for the past three years, but had had to leave 'for personal reasons of health' and was at that very time looking for a position in the countryside outside of London and so was available to take up the post immediately, as required. He believed he had 'the necessary experience' and looked forward to 'the challenge' of becoming the head teacher of a parochial church school as he was 'a committed Christian.' He enclosed with his letter a reference from a Reverend Edgar Coulson, rector of the parish and secretary of the school management board, whom the Reverend Scrope did not know, stating, *'I cannot say how sorry we shall be to lose the services of so valued and trusted a teacher as William Warburton due to his need to leave the smoky atmosphere of London for the healthier pastures of the countryside.'* He also provided a second reference from one Henry Bowden, chairman of the management board, confirming the board's *'complete and utter satisfaction'* with William Warburton during his three years at their school and to say that *'he has proved himself a most excellent teacher and he will be greatly missed...'*

In a second letter to the Reverend Scrope, accepting the vicar's hurried appointment, the successful applicant, William Warburton, further stated: *'I shall be arriving on Saturday afternoon, the seventeenth, with my wife Martha, who is also a teacher, with a second-class certificate, with the ability to teach infants, (also sewing in all standards). We hope to be there round about teatime...'*

The Reverend Scrope congratulated himself upon having made a firm decision and acting upon it when time literally was of the essence: and he had done it from his sickbed, whereas, if the matter had been left to the school management board, they no doubt would still be discussing the wording of the advertisement. Now, thanks to him and in spite of his illness, there would be a new schoolmaster in place within a week or so: and, better still, one with a wife who could also teach: both at an agreed joint salary of a hundred and ten pounds per annum. He did not agree with those in other places who thought married women should not teach and that it should be left to spinsters: if employing a man's wife as an assistant-teacher were cheaper than employing another unmarried woman, then so be it: he would sanction that, just as he had with the Padwicks. It was *his* school, after all, and it was done at schools in London from where the couple were coming, so it was not so unusual.

Unfortunately, he would not be there himself to meet him as, on the actual date of his arrival, the Bishop of Wivencaster had invited a number of clergy from the surrounding parishes to tea at his palace to discuss the coming Easter services and, illness or not, now that he was out of bed again, nothing would keep the Reverend Scrope away from a meeting with his Bishop: and, since his Lordship's secretary had specified that families were welcome as well, he would be travelling the eight miles to the old Roman town with his sister Agnes to introduce her and to show that all was at peace and in order at the Steadshall vicarage. The nursemaid Sarah and the child Elizabeth would, of course, remain in the vicarage, with the new cook-cum-general-cleaning-woman, a middle-aged widow named Bertha Buck, whom he had hired from the town, looking after them.

For that reason, he had asked the curate to wait at the cottage to greet the Warburtons and hand them the key, not that the Reverend Smallwood minded: on the morning of the new schoolmaster's arrival, there was no person in Steadshall more relieved and more thankful for it than the Reverend Smallwood. Over the past fortnight, he had found it exhausting working from eight in the morning till five in the afternoon, trying to keep up with all the different standards, eating rapid and irregular meals at his lodgings along the Siblingham road, hurrying to the school and back from it, attempting to curb the incessant noise and boisterousness, and still with the care of his curacy at Bourne Brook to be done, his sermons to write, the sick to visit, the early service to take on Sundays before rushing back to Steadshall to fill in for the sick vicar at St. Andrew's. Yes, he would willingly wait at the cottage to greet them, as courtesy demanded, and hand them the key.

He would be nearby at the vicarage, anyway, for, with the Reverend Scrope and his sister out, he had asked permission to use the vicar's library in the study again: he often used the vicar's collection of religious books to help him write his sermons and had done so even before the vicar had left on his round-the-world tour and all the time during it. This time he wanted most particularly to read the Reverend Scrope's copy of 'His Sacred Breathings' in order to write his sermon for the morrow. All he had to do was to walk up to the cottage at four o'clock and wait for the new schoolmaster and his wife to arrive, hand them the key, then he could return to his studies...

FOURTEEN

ON THE AFTERNOON that the new schoolmaster and his wife were due to arrive, the Reverend Smallwood waited at the cottage opposite the school till past four o'clock, then till past five, then till past six and finally till past seven, but no carrier's wagon came rumbling into view: he even walked three times back down Head Street to its junction with the High Street to see if any vehicle were approaching up the long hill, but each time there was none.

Eventually, as the shops drew down their shutters and the High Street emptied of townsfolk, he made one last foray back down Head Street, praying to see them approaching as a steady drizzle had begun to fall and he had no umbrella with him: but still there was no one. Reluctantly, he returned to the vicarage, leaving the cottage door unlocked for them, though he could not leave the key in the lock or hanging up inside just in case someone went past who was curious enough to enter and light-fingered enough to take it. By then, the drizzle was turning to steady rain and his coat and jacket were already soaked through: he could do no more.

It was perhaps just as well that he did give up when he did, for it was near to eight o'clock before two tarpaulin-covered carrier's wagons finally rumbled over the level crossing where the Bromptree road enters the town, turned on to the bridge over the brown river at the foot of the High Street and began the long climb up the hill towards the parish church and Head Street.

A flooded stream overflowing on to the dirt turnpike had delayed them and caused a wide detour: and the two carriers, being Londoners, were unfamiliar with the narrow lanes leading to Steadshall. They had gone to the couple's London lodgings the previous day, loaded the furniture and carted it as far as Melchborough, the county town thirty-five miles from the capital, where they had stayed overnight at an inn, before making the final twenty-five-mile journey to Steadshall, setting off only in the early afternoon as they had had to wait for the two owners of the furniture to join them off the train from London.

Husband and wife William and Martha Warburton were seated together beside the driver on the lead wagon, huddled under an umbrella, staring dismally out at their new surroundings, at the closed shops with their blinds drawn down and at the empty pavements, with the only signs of life at that hour coming from the lighted lamps burning in the windows of the Bull Inn at the bottom of the town and the double-gabled White Hart halfway up the long hill.

Fortunately, the Reverend Scrope had remembered to include instructions on how to reach their destination in the second of his letters confirming the appointment: '...*from Bromptree, climb the hill through the centre of the town. At the top of the hill take the right-hand road up Head Street past the church and continue straight on up the Burestead Market road. The villa is on the left, a hundred yards farther up. It is directly opposite the school and has a blue door. My curate will be there to meet you...*'

'Here we are, sir,' called the lead carrier at last, bringing his wagon to a halt outside a small, two-storey, slate-roofed, red-brick cottage: it was a minute before eight o'clock.

William Warburton, tall and thin, in his late thirties, with light brown hair and grey-blue eyes and even when seated displaying the round-shoulders of one who had sat for years at a desk, lifted the umbrella and peered out at his and his wife's new residence. He had been told in the Reverend Scrope's second reply, accepting his application for the post, that the cottage awaiting them was, in fact, '*a villa standing in its own spacious grounds*' and that it was in '*a fairly good condition.*' It was none of those things: it was a tiny place, near to tumbling down, as far as William could see, with a small garden and did not look to be at all in a 'good condition.' It was with some apprehension that he noted its sagging roof and leaning chimney, that one of its upper bedroom windows was lopsided and that its windowpanes were grimed with dirt and stained by rain. The blue paint on the front door was faded and peeling, while at one end of the cottage the guttering had become dislodged from the down-pipe and rain was already pouring on to the earth.

'Good God, William! Is this it?' the exclamation of disbelief came from Martha Warburton, who was a few years younger than her husband and much shorter in height, with a round face, puffed cheeks, a small mouth, tilted nose and a high forehead surmounted by a band of dark hair parted in the centre, which was all that was showing under her wide-brimmed black hat.

'I'm afraid so,' was William Warburton's grim reply, delivered with an audible sigh as he climbed down: he shared his wife's misgivings about the place, but did not see what else they could do, except to turn the carrier around and head back – to where? London? He could not go back there? Melchborough? He knew no one there and it was several hours' journey away, anyway. They would have to stay – for the time being at least.

Wearily, he rubbed at himself for a few seconds to ease the soreness of his aching joints, then pushed at the small wooden gate half-hanging off its hinges and walked slowly up the short path, despondently noting the weed-strewn patch of garden either side, for the Padwicks had so disliked the place they had never tended it. It was with another apprehensive sigh that he lifted the latch, found the door unlocked and entered: to the head carrier, the schoolmaster's decision even to inspect the cottage suggested that he had resigned himself to the worst and that he and his mate could now get down and begin to unload.

Not so Martha Warburton: she had accepted nothing yet. With a curt command of 'Do nothing yet,' she rose from her seat and, without waiting to be helped, gathered up her rain-soaked skirt in one hand, jumped down and hurried up the path after her husband. She found him standing in the narrow passageway which ran through the centre of the cottage, staring up at some wide cracks in the ceiling and at the lopsided frame of one of the interior doors, as if ruminating on their possible seriousness.

One sniff was all Martha Warburton needed, for hardly had she entered than she was exclaiming: 'The place smells of damp. I can smell it.'

Through the lopsided door to the right was a small sitting room with a fireplace. 'Oh, my goodness!' Martha went on, throwing up her hands in horror as she entered. 'Look at the dirt on the wallpaper – it's filthy. It'll take a week to scrub that off.'

A finger was run along the window sill. 'And the dust! There's dust everywhere! Look at it!'

An inspection of the fireplace brought the accusation: 'Gracious me, they didn't even bother to clean the place before they left! Look at the grate, it's full of ash. They've left it just as it was…'

Across the passageway in an equally small dining room, it was: 'Dirt, dirt and dust everywhere! And damp! Damp everywhere! And grime! Grime everywhere!'

She went on like that as they went through the house – into a scullery at the back, where a dusty cobweb crossed the two lower window panes like a frayed muslin curtain, then up the stairs to the first bedroom to find dust and feathers from an eiderdown all over the floor and the walls as in need of washing as those downstairs: and the same in the smaller bedroom.

'I am not having this,' Martha declared angrily, as they came down the narrow staircase. 'This is not acceptable – not acceptable at all. It's appalling. Who do they think we are?'

The two carriers, meanwhile, had undone the ropes holding down the tarpaulin covering the furniture on the first wagon, had removed it and, more in hope than anything, had begun to unload, first, the double-bed, then the mattress, followed by a chest of drawers, a small wardrobe, a dining table, two dining chairs, one armchair and a horsehair settee.

'Do we carry it in or not, lady?' the older of the two carriers asked, seeing by the furious look on the woman's face as she came out the front door that something was clearly not right within.

'You will wait,' Martha Warburton ordered him firmly. 'You will not put one stick of furniture into that house until I say so.'

'We need to get the furniture inside, lady,' the second wagon driver reminded her. 'We have a good five-hour trip to make back to Melchborough.' That was where their overnight lodgings would be again: beyond that, they faced a further five or six hours trundling back to London.

On the second wagon were a small upright piano, for Martha Warburton taught music and was quite accomplished, a glass bookcase and multiple tea chests of books, utensils, clothing and other sundries collected in the ten years they had been married.

'You will do as I say,' was the reply they received. 'You have been paid. No furniture is to go in until I say so.' She pointed at the furniture already unloaded on to the road and ordered them: 'And be so good as to cover that with your tarpaulin. I do not want my furniture ruined.'

William, meanwhile, was trying to placate his wife. 'The place can be cleaned, Martha,' he said, spreading his hands in that gesture of a man who either cannot see why the woman has become so upset or does not want to make a fuss over the reason for it, but simply wants to get on with what they are doing. 'It will take time, but we can do it.'

'William, we cannot allow them to get away with such slovenliness,' Martha Warburton declared firmly, 'If we allow them to do that on our very first day here, before we have even begun, then who knows what other liberties they will think they can take. No, we must do something. Start as you mean to go on, that's what I say...'

FIFTEEN

THE REVEREND SMALLWOOD had not forgotten that the Warburtons were due that evening and he had genuinely intended walking back to the cottage at eight o'clock to see if they had indeed arrived: it was just that, seated in the warmth and dry of the vicar's study, he had become so immersed in the book from which he was making his notes that he quite forgot the time. It was a loud and incessant knocking which reminded him.

Normally, if he were at the vicarage when someone knocked on the front door, it was left to the new cook, Bertha, if she were still there, to answer it as the vicar had no other servants and, if not the cook, the vicar's sister, Agnes, and, if not her, the nursemaid Sarah: but the cook had gone home and the nursemaid was up in the nursery watching over the sleeping child Elizabeth and this time the knocking was so insistent and so disruptive that, in exasperation, he threw down his pen, strode out into the hallway and pulled open the studded oak door himself.

Standing on the step was the bedraggled figure of a short, slim, behatted and bespectacled woman in her early-thirties, a look of fierce determination on her face: behind her, in an equally dishevelled state, holding his hat in one hand despite the rain, stood a tall, slightly bent figure, with a long, thin nose, a tight mouth covered by a drooping moustache and high cheekbones framed by curly, untrimmed brown sideburns.

'Good evening,' said Martha Warburton politely, but with no smile to accompany the greeting, 'are you the vicar?'

'No, I am his curate,' the Reverend Smallwood answered.

'I should like to see the Reverend Scrope, if I may,' the woman said. 'Is he at home, please?'

'No, I am afraid he is not,' the curate answered, in his concern at late-evening callers holding the door only half-open as if fearful that the woman might attempt to push past him.

'I am Martha Warburton,' said the woman firmly. 'This is my husband, William. He is to be the new master at the parochial school. We have just arrived on the carrier within the last hour. I have come to complain about the cottage we have been allotted, the one opposite the school. I understand it is provided by the vicar for the schoolmaster. I regret to say it is not in a fit state for people to move into. The last tenants have left it in an utterly filthy state. The walls are covered in grime, there is dirt and dust everywhere, one can barely see out of the windows for the dirt on the glass and I found mice droppings in one of the bedrooms. The place is not fit for human habitation. It looks as though it might fall down at any moment. I want to know what the vicar is going to do about it. The place should have been cleaned from top to bottom before we came and any repairs that needed doing should have been done. It really is not good enough.'

'Oh dear,' said the curate, a little taken aback to be handed what to his mind was an unrectifiable problem at such an hour when all he was doing was trying to finish the sermon he was preparing for the morrow: had they arrived earlier, in the late afternoon, say, he might have been able to help them, though how he did not know.

'If there is a problem with your accommodation, I am sorry,' he told them, feeling a little guilty. 'That is a matter more for his reverence than for me. I am only his curate. I do not see what I can do at this time of night, except to say that I am sorry you do not approve and to apologise for not being there to meet you when you arrived.'

'We were delayed on the road from Melchborough,' the man behind the fierce-looking woman informed him with a weak smile, talking over her head. 'We got lost and then one of the wagons got stuck in a large puddle for a while.'

Seizing the chance created by the man's interruption, the curate switched his attention to him: he seemed more affable than his fire-breathing wife. Also speaking over the wife's head, he said: 'I will certainly inform Mr. Scrope of your – your – ' He searched for a neutral phrase and found only one. ' – your comments. I am afraid that is the best I can do for the moment. I can do nothing myself. I will willingly call in sometime tomorrow to see how we might deal with the matter, once I have seen Mr. Scrope and discussed it with him.'

Martha Warburton did not like two tall men speaking over her head: it made her feel even smaller than her five-foot-two height. 'When will the vicar return?' she asked, her voice maintaining its sternness.

'I cannot say,' the curate answered with a shrug, slightly closing the door so that no more than his face and his upper chest were visible.

Then with a weak, 'I am sorry, it is late. I can do no more for you this evening. I will tell the vicar that you called,' he bade them 'Good evening' and closed the door.

Had she been on her own, Martha Warburton would have banged on the knocker till the door was opened again, but her husband, knowing her temperament, took her by the arm and led her away, though she resisted him till they were clear of the gate.

'This won't do, it won't do at all,' she complained as the two went back towards the High Street. 'If this is how they treat their schoolmasters, giving them a filthy, rundown cottage, expecting us to clear up someone else's mess, then they have another thing coming. I for one will not stand for it.'

She said it more to herself than to her husband, for, as they walked away, his attention had been distracted by the movement of a curtain at an upstairs window: a face was looking down, watching the couple disappear.

'Who was it?' the Reverend Scrope called down to the curate.

'The schoolmaster's wife,' the curate called up to him.

Contrary to what the curate had told the Warburtons, the Reverend Scrope had returned from Wivencaster sometime after seven o'clock and had gone straight to his bedroom, telling the curate that he did not wish to be disturbed: the loud knocking had disturbed him, however, and he had been listening to Martha's complaints at his bedroom door.

Agnes had also gone up after their return, first to help settle Elizabeth in the nursery and then, complaining of a headache, to bed, though the Reverend Smallwood sensed that she was simply avoiding her brother's company. It seemed he had scolded her over something after they had left the Bishop's palace and she had resented what he had said: he felt quite sorry for her and a little guilty over the lie he had had to tell the Warburtons.

Saying the vicar was out when all the time he was either in his study reading or reclining on his bed upstairs was quite normal, the curate had found on his sojourns at the vicarage, especially if a caller arrived unannounced and uninvited and seemed bent on making a complaint or stirring up trouble of some kind. Before the vicar had set out on his round-the-world trip, Joseph Padwick's wife had been the worst for that, always calling to complain about something or other: and one thing the curate knew was that the vicar did not deal with the wives of his schoolmasters, no matter of what they complained: on those occasions, he had found himself making the self-same excuses as he had made to the Warburtons.

'What did she want? She did not sound as if she were very happy about something.' The vicar had not quite been able to hear what was being said, but knowing from the sound of the woman's voice that she was angry about something, he had remained where he was.

'She was complaining about the cottage, your reverence,' the curate told him. 'She was saying it was damp and dirty and in need of repair.'

There was a snort up on the landing. 'If she is so disappointed with the accommodation, perhaps we should terminate their agreement before they begin.'

'I do not think that there is any need,' the curate said quickly. 'Besides, if we did, we are duty bound by law to give him three months' notice from the present date and his salary with it, as I doubt he would accept a nominal sum to set him free at once. With your permission, I will call on them tomorrow to see what it is they are complaining about and, if necessary, I will arrange for two of the women of the parish to go round first thing on Monday morning and help them clean the place. Perhaps we ought to see Mr. Crowfoot about any repairs that need doing? They ought really to have been done – '

'Yes, yes,' the vicar interrupted him irritably. 'Perhaps we should have asked someone to clean the place after the Padwicks left and made a few repairs, but it all costs money, you know. I realise that it should have been arranged before they arrived, but I was ill at the time and unable to do so. And no one else seemed to want to do anything.'

It was an accusation aimed as much at the curate as it was at the other members of the school management board. 'No one else would have dared,' the curate muttered to himself as he went back into the study.

For William and Martha, there was nothing else they could do, except return to the cottage: unhappily, Martha had lost the battle with the two carriers: for, faced with a five-hour drive over bad roads back to their overnight lodgings, they had prevailed upon William to allow them to unload the furniture and the boxes, which they had hurriedly done while the schoolmaster and his wife were heading for the vicarage, in their frustration at being made to wait at so late an hour depositing it willy-nilly.

The furniture was in the right rooms, but simply dumped in the middle of each, leaving William and Martha to sort it out. All they could do was to lay a fire against the evening chill and boil some hot water for making tea and then begin placing the furniture where they wanted it, though their first task was to assemble the iron bedstead...

SIXTEEN

THEY WERE STILL ASLEEP when, just after eight o'clock on the following morning, there was a loud rapping at their door: Martha hurried down to open it and found the Reverend Scrope, looking haughty and put out at the same time, standing on the step: behind him was the curate she had met the night before.

'I am the Reverend Scrope,' the vicar announced breezily, taking off his hat and making an attempt at a smile: he offered Martha his hand, but did not exactly shake hers as simply allow their fingers to touch and then withdraw his own.

'I regret I was not here to welcome you,' he went on, looking boldly at Martha, who was conscious of the fact that, having leapt from her bed to answer the door, she had on only her nightgown and no housecoat.

'Goodness gracious, is the man looking at my breasts, at my nipples?' she wondered, for his eyes had settled briefly on that part, before lifting to her face again.

Without waiting for an invitation to enter, he brushed past her into the hallway. 'I was taking tea with the Bishop of Wivencaster and other clergy yesterday,' he said over his shoulder as he turned into the front parlour, 'so I was unable to meet you.'

Martha, bemused and with her cheeks flushed crimson, followed him.

Behind her, the curate, looking slightly embarrassed, removed his own hat and quietly closed the door. He had intended to call on the Warburtons sometime that afternoon to view the cottage and see how justified were their complaints – and he had hoped to do it alone. But just as he was about to set off on his walk to Bourne Brook, for he had a morning service to conduct and a sermon to preach, on turning on to the High Street off the Siblingham road, he had found the vicar waiting for him.

'We will go to the Warburtons and deal with the matter together,' he had announced. 'I wish to see for myself if there is anything in their complaints.'

'I still have to get to Bourne Brook,' the curate reminded him, 'for my own service.'

'Yes, yes,' was the vicar's airy response, for he was already striding off along the pavement. 'Afterwards, afterwards.'

In the parlour, a barefooted William was hurriedly buttoning his shirt-front, having hastily pulled on his trousers to follow his wife downstairs.

'I gather you are unhappy with your accommodation,' the Reverend Scrope began bluntly, this time extending his hand to the husband, who had no more chance to begin a reply than had his wife, for having touched fingers a second time, the vicar turned away and immediately begun examining the lower part of the walls.

'My, my!' he said with a sigh. 'I do see your point, dear lady. It is quite soiled. All I can think has caused this is that the previous tenants, the Padwicks, kept a dog, a Welsh sheepdog, a collie, I believe, which seemed to like rubbing itself along the walls. I agree with you: it should all have been washed off and the place dusted out.'

He turned to his curate with an accusing look on his face, as if to say 'Why was that not done?' but did not wait for a reply: instead, he turned and led the way across the narrow passageway into the room opposite, where he completed another examination, circling it to peer at the walls and the window sill and making noises with the tip of his tongue up against the back of his lower teeth

'I had no idea it was like this,' he lied, again looking at his curate with feigned displeasure. 'You should have told me, Mr. Smallwood – ' He turned back to the Warburtons. ' – We shall have someone from the parish call in first thing tomorrow morning to clean the place throughout – two of the women of the church. Mr. Smallwood will see to it. One really would have thought the Padwicks would have cleaned it before they left. We should have looked into it, Mr. Smallwood, should we not?'

There was little the poor curate could say, except to agree with him without protest, thereby accepting the blame for the cleaning not having been done.

'The cottage itself is somewhat old,' the Reverend Scrope informed them matter-of-factly, as if it were enough to excuse the lean of the chimney, the lopsided window and doorframe and the cracks in the hallway ceiling, 'but I do not think it will fall down just yet. Ha, ha, ha

– ' The laugh was forced and of a peculiar honking kind with which some unfortunates are saddled, of which the Reverend Scrope was one. ' – I shall have a builder call in the next day or two and take a look at the ceiling, the chimney and the gutter to see what can be done – if that will satisfy you?'

The vicar's promises were enough to placate Martha. 'If the two cleaning ladies could come in first thing tomorrow, I should be quite satisfied with that, Mr. Scrope,' she said, even forcing a faint smile of appreciation herself.

That matter settled and the Reverend Scrope apparently satisfied with the outcome, he reached into his pocket and produced the keys to the cottage and, more importantly, to the school. 'You will need these, Mr. Warburton,' he said, handing them over with a slight laugh, before his face changed again and took on a more serious look.

'Shall we be seeing you in church later?' he asked. 'It is Palm Sunday today.'

'I think not, if you will be so good as to excuse us,' William said politely. 'My wife and I would like to use the rest of the day putting things in order here. We have a lot to unpack and so little time. We arrived later than we intended yesterday evening because it took the two carriers longer to get here than we intended. Certainly, we should both be delighted to attend church *next* Sunday, especially as it is Easter. For now, though, we should prefer to get this place ship-shape, if you will excuse us? And, of course, there are things to do before the start of school tomorrow.'

The Reverend Scrope was somewhat taken aback: he had not expected a refusal. 'But you would be working on a Sunday,' he reminded them. 'You would be working on the Lord's Day – '

'I am sure the Lord won't mind, Palm Sunday or not,' William Warburton said casually, though with a smile and a raised eyebrow in an attempt to allay the clergyman's concern.

'Really, Mr. Warburton, I do not think it is your place to say such things!' the Reverend Scrope rebuked him. 'You are a schoolmaster, not a clergyman.' In the Reverend Scrope's opinion, it was highly irregular, first, to try and guess what the Lord might be thinking and, second, to express those thoughts aloud as a layman: only clergymen like himself had the ear of God: it was only to them that the Almighty communicated His thoughts. For the moment, however, since it was his first meeting with the new master, he would not press the matter: the schoolmaster had been suitably chastised and, besides, there was something else on his mind.

'One more thing before I go,' he said, rubbing his chin as if the thought had just occurred to him. 'We have not discussed the matter of the Sunday school. Miss Dunsmore, the assistant-teacher, and Miss Hodgson, the pupil-teacher, have been taking it since Mr. Padwick left us, with the occasional help of the Reverend Smallwood here – '

William was ahead of him. 'Then they should continue to do so,' he said quietly, but firmly.

The Reverend Scrope was again taken aback. 'But the teachers at the school are always expected to teach Sunday classes,' he said, straightening up to his full height as if he were seeking to impose his authority upon the other man. 'Mr. Padwick always took it, with his wife and with Miss Dunsmore, of course. The teachers have always taken it.'

'The advertisement said nothing about my having to take the Sunday school as well,' William calmly reminded him, slightly embarrassed at having to point out a matter which the other seemed to have taken for granted. 'Neither did you say anything about it in your letters to me. No agreement has been reached that I should take the Sunday school classes as well as teaching all week at the school. I have no contract.'

'An oversight on my part, a simple matter of expediency necessary at the time,' the vicar replied, his manner growing haughty again. 'Had I been able to interview you, I should have explained it then. I could not because I was ill. I should have thought, however, you would have realised it would be one of your duties, that whoever becomes master of the parochial school is expected to conduct and take charge of the Sunday school. Who else but the schoolmaster would do so?'

'Your Miss Dunsmore and your Miss Hodgson?' William suggested, his embarrassment growing, but still maintaining his politeness. 'Or perhaps your curate? As an ordained clergyman, I should have thought he is far better qualified to teach from the Bible than I or my wife. We are merely qualified to teach the subjects we know. I have never yet taught Sunday school.'

The Reverend Smallwood was quick to jump in. 'I could not possibly do it, not every week throughout the year, anyway,' he declared, adding quickly when his vicar turned to him: 'Now and again, perhaps, but I have my own church, St. Mary's, at Bourne Brook, to attend to.'

His vicar gave a loud throat-clearing harrumph: this was another embarrassment which he had not anticipated. Then, realising perhaps he had not spoken of something which the other might be expecting him to mention, he added quickly: 'There would, of course, be extra remuneration added to your salary, as there is always a good number to be taught at the Sunday school. Though we no longer insist that all of our children attend church on a Sunday, it is expected that they should all attend Sunday school if they wish to continue at the parochial school – excepting those whose parents are Dissenters, of course. They go their own way on such matters. You would not, of course, have to take it during the school holidays.'

'It is not the remuneration which interests me,' the schoolmaster replied, somewhat wearily. 'I have been a teacher for many years and I find that I need to rest on Sundays – both my good wife and I look forward to Sundays as our days when we have time to ourselves – it is for that reason and that reason alone that I do not wish to take the Sunday school.'

The vicar had not expected an argument over such a trivial matter as who took the Sunday school. 'I really think you ought to be taking it, as the head teacher at the school,' he tried again, his tone sharpening.

'And I regret, sir, I cannot do it and I will not do it for the reason I have given,' William Warburton replied, his tone also hardening.

Had he not had to return to the vicarage to prepare for that morning's special service, the Reverend Scrope would have argued it out with the schoolmaster there and then. There was a scowl on his face as he walked back down Head Street towards the vicarage a good five paces ahead of the curate, who did not hurry to catch him. He had offered the man a sum of seven pounds per annum to take the Sunday school and he had refused him point-blank. In his view, that was nothing more than blatant disrespect for the Church.

It did not help that he knew much of it was his own fault: if he had not fallen ill when he had and had been able to interview the new teacher first and present him with a proper contract, it might not have happened: he would have settled the matter of the Sunday school – or not appointed the man at all. As he pushed open the vicarage door, he could not get it out of his mind that he had been outmanoeuvred and that did not sit well with him.

With a sigh, he realised that he would have to ask Miss Dunsmore and the pupil-teacher, Hannah Hodgson, to continue teaching the Sunday school: he had already told the curate that he would have to help whenever he could. As for the new schoolmaster, he would need watching, both him and his wife. 'I hope they are not going to give me the same trouble as the Padwicks,' he said to himself...

SEVENTEEN

THE FOLLOWING MORNING, William was at the school by seven o'clock, well ahead of any anticipated first arrivals: he wanted to make a full inspection before anyone interrupted him.

Had he been able, he would have liked to have gone across to the school on the Sunday afternoon, giving himself plenty of time to make a thorough inspection in daylight. However, it had not been possible: the Sunday school was being held there from two-thirty till four-thirty and, by the time it finished, the mid-April dusk was already beginning to close in. He did look out of an upstairs window as the children gathered, surprised by their number, and watched the diminutive figure of Helen Dunsmore, come bustling up with an armful of papers: at least, he assumed it was the assistant-teacher because he saw her clip one child around the ear when he did not get out of her way quickly enough as she went through the gate.

The children who followed her through the porch door did so with unhappy faces and slumped shoulders, as if they were being forced to pass the next two hours under sufferance rather than going willingly. He did vaguely consider crossing the road to introduce himself, but decided against doing so: appearing at the Sunday school might not be prudent in view of his earlier confrontation over it with the vicar.

Martha agreed. 'Let it be,' she said. 'The Sunday school is not our concern so we should have nothing to do with it. We should not go near. We start tomorrow. We have enough to do here, unpacking everything…'

While William inspected the school, Martha remained in the cottage to await the arrival of the two women cleaners, who the vicar had promised to send to help: she would come on later, as eager to start at her new school as was he, she told him, but only after the cleaners had been set their tasks. They were due to arrive at eight o'clock so there was plenty of time for her to cross to the school before nine: that was, supposing the curate had remembered to ask two of the women parishioners in the first place. If not, then William knew full well that Martha would simply roll up her sleeves and set about cleaning the place from top to bottom herself: she was that type of a woman. Of late, she had begun to amuse him with comments about women getting the vote – 'suffragism,' she called it – and was even suggesting that it would be a good idea if women were elected to Parliament – 'to show the men a thing or two,' she said.

He had, of course, looked across at the school building when they had arrived, but there had been no time to study it properly in the fading light: having to traipse up to the vicarage on that first night and then the business of Sunday's unpacking had deterred him from looking too closely, as had the arrival of the Sunday school pupils after dinner. Now, however, he could inspect it at his leisure.

What he found was a long, single-storey, red-brick building, with a half-dozen high-arched windows along the frontage facing the road and a sizeable porch towards one end, in design not at all unlike the school in Stepney from which he had been ejected so humiliatingly a short while before, but in this case much, much longer – by necessity since its roll was far greater, two hundred and seventy-five, compared with only a hundred and ninety or so at the East End school.

The yard, however, was another matter: in Stepney, it had been laid with smooth tarmacadam, was enclosed by sturdy iron railings and had a proper drainage system installed. The yard of Steadshall Parochial School, though substantial in area, was a haphazard mixture of dirt, shingle and sand, seemingly thrown down or scattered about at random to fill its numerous potholes and puddles, though without success, for most of the puddles seemed to have returned as a result of the weekend's rain. Quite clearly, it was not at all suitable for children to run around on and play their games. It was with something of a weary sigh that William's first thought as he crossed it was that it was in drastic need of digging up and relaying: it was something which would need seeing to – eventually – he thought to himself.

In the advertisement, the vicar had boasted that there were two hundred and seventy-five pupils at the school, yet there were just four lavatories, two at one end of the yard for the girls and two at the other end for the boys, all served by buckets, which William found to his disgust were almost at the point of overflowing. He made a mental note that they would need emptying immediately – even if he had to do it himself. They were a health hazard. And there also seemed to be a shortage of paper squares.

At the boys' end, a high wall also enclosed a concrete urinal trench, which should have drained through a hole into the field beyond, but it, too, did not appear to have been attended to in the past month, perhaps longer, for it smelled badly and was clogged by extraneous matter – something else which would need correcting and which again he might have to do himself.

He let himself in the porch door and was surprised to find there was just one single, high-ceilinged room, running the whole length of the building and divided at a rough midway point by a thick, faded blue-velvet curtain, divided into two halves, each hanging from a stout brass rail which crossed from one wall to the other and was itself supported at its centre by a black-painted iron stanchion screwed to the floor. Off the main room, through a narrow arched doorway lay a smaller classroom, a fifth of the size of the main room and seemingly built as a late addition: that was where Martha would teach the infants and the juniors of standards one and two.

The first thing he realised was how cold and damp the large room was: there was only a single wrought-iron stove positioned near the door to the infants' room, which did not appear to have been lit of late, for there was no residue of coke ash inside it or on the brick hearth around it and no coke in the scuttle alongside or bundles of kindling with which to start it. The lack of a heated stove was, he thought, the most likely cause of the general mustiness of the room. While outside, he had noticed that the coke bay was empty: the supply, if there had ever been one, was exhausted and had not been replenished.

Nor, it appeared, had anyone bothered to sweep the classroom of late, certainly not in the past fortnight, he guessed: crushed chalk and dust covered the floorboards, many of which were pitted and splintered in places, and a trail of dried-mud footprints led in from the porch door. Small rush mats had been laid, but they were frayed and more of a hindrance and a danger than of use, he thought. It would be better if they were replaced by a single larger mat, coconut matting perhaps, to cover the main walking areas of the splintered floor. At least, the clock on the wall corresponded to the time on his pocket-watch – twenty minutes to eight then.

From an arithmetic example left on the blackboard, it was clear that the first half of the main room was where the pupils of standards three and four were taught by Miss Dunsmore, whom the vicar had praised quite highly in his letter to him. That would remain to be seen: he would judge no one till he had met them and observed them: and if they came up to his standards, then they would have nothing to fear. If they did not…

The room, he found, was divided into four sections, with each section taking up its own quarter area – standards three and four on one side of the curtain nearest to the infants' entrance and standards five and six – his standards – on the other side of the curtain, farthest from the door.

It was a surprise to count only twenty double-desks in the first part of the room, filling the back of one section. Those, he supposed, would be for the sixty pupils of standard four: but they could only take forty, so where did the remainder sit – the other twenty? They must sit five abreast on four low benches similarly lined up in front of the desks.

As there were no desks or benches but a large area of bare floor in the other part, the puzzle of where the other forty-eight children of standard three sat was only solved when he lifted the lid of a large box under a window at the back of the room and found it filled with small rush mats with rounded ends and straw-filled sacking 'cushions.' Clearly, the children of standard three had to sit on the floor in their own section: he made a mental note that the dirt-laden mats would require a good beating and the grease-covered cushions a good scrubbing. Another dozen benches would not go amiss either and neither would another dozen double-desks.

It was as he had feared it might be, but had hoped it would not be, not after the vicar had stated in his first letters how proud he was of the education the Church was providing for the children of the poor in Steadshall: he knew then that he would have work to do…

EIGHTEEN

TO WILLIAM, looking about him, it was as if the school's needs had either been neglected or the number of pupils had grown so suddenly that they exceeded the school's means of supply. As much through despair as frustration at what he was finding, his first action was to take a tattered cleaning rag hanging off one of the easel's pegs and vigorously rub out everything on the blackboard.

Things were no better in the second part of the main room, beyond the curtain, where the two standards he would teach, five and six, sat, in total ninety-two pupils, mostly aged ten and eleven years, but still with a few twelve-year-olds and even one or two thirteen-year-olds, who, though they had progressed through all the other standards, had yet to acquire their 'labour certificate' – the certificate of proficiency in reading, writing and arithmetic required by all scholars in standard six for them to be exempted from the obligation of attending school: in short, to be able to go to work.

An inspection of the double desks of wrought iron and wood in his part of the room, set out in seven rows either side of a central aisle, revealed that several had broken parts and, on one of them, an attempt at repair had involved tying a sawn-down table leg to one of the cracked ironwork stanchions to brace it. The floor there, too, was as dusty and dirt-covered as everywhere else and, once again, no attempt had been made to clean off the blackboard.

A tall cupboard standing along one wall revealed itself to be where the slates, boxes of chalk and copybooks were kept for standards five and six and where what few reading books they had were piled, many of them so tattered and frayed as to be almost beyond repair – and, therefore, use – with pages loose and others probably missing, while in some the pages had been disfigured by pencil or ink markings, and in one or two by crude anatomical drawings of how boys of ten and eleven imagined female parts to look.

When he opened a similarly tall cupboard on Miss Dunsmore's side of the curtain, there were no reading books at all: there were, however, a dozen well-thumbed Bibles. Clearly, the Bible was the most commonly used reader in the bigger room, a fact seemingly confirmed by a large, faded chalk semi-circle drawn on the floor in her half. Around these, he knew, it was a practice typical of parochial schools for children to stand with their toes touching the line, no fidgeting allowed upon pain of a ruler across the knuckles or a slap on the arm, and for each child to read aloud in turn from, say, the *Book of Moses* or the *Book of Job* or the *Book of Samuel* or some other prophet. From his own experience, William felt it was an unsatisfactory method of teaching children to read properly simply because many of the words used in the Bible were not words which the children were used to speaking: small wonder then that they frequently stumbled over the long sentences and understood nothing of the meanings of the words they read. He had changed all that at the school in Stepney and had introduced the children to proper story books: it was that which had led to his first serious confrontation with the vicar there – the first of many, as it had turned out.

'It might well have to change here, too,' he thought to himself.

It was as if no one had bothered to restock the cupboards as items were used up, worn, disintegrated, were broken or lost. For example, in the cupboard for the two higher standards, he counted only thirty-six pens and nibs in a small cardboard box, far too few for the number in his standards, who would more likely be the ones to use them. There was only one half-empty quart bottle of black ink and there did not seem to be many rulers: and what there were appeared to have been deliberately cut along their edges with penknives so that it would be virtually impossible to draw a neat, straight line with them. They were also worn so smooth by use and so inked in places that reading off the inches, half-inches, quarter-inches and other fractions was well-nigh impossible. At the bottom of one cupboard, he found several pots of fish-paste glue: most were empty, but what few contained anything at all the glue had long since hardened to uselessness because the cork stoppers had been left off and the air had dried out the paste.

There were, however, two quarter-inch-thick canes leaning against the back wall of Miss Dunsmore's cupboard, as if placed there to be on display every time the door was opened – as a reminder to any sluggards not to incur her wrath.

In the smaller classroom for the infants and juniors, the children sat on benches, no more than a foot high, and wrote their letters and numbers with a peg stylus on small trays of fine sand: the trays, emptied of sand, lay in an untidy pile on the floor beside a near-empty box of sand, most of the contents of which seemed to have been strewn on the floor all around it and no attempt made to brush it up and return it. He did not count the trays, but noted that there did not seem to be the seventy or so for each of the younger children to have one apiece. The teacher's desk, much smaller than the other two desks, stood in one corner: beside it was a small stool, with a dunce's cap lying upon it.

At various points around its green-painted brick walls, long banners displaying numbers from one to twenty, multiplication tables and the letters of the alphabet were hung: in between were several pictures of different objects drawn in chalk, a daffodil on one, a carrot on another, a boat on a third, a cat on a fourth, a horse on a fifth and so on, with the name of each printed underneath. For their lesson, the younger children would chant aloud in unison the name of each till they had learned to 'read' or at least to recognise the word associated with its picture: and once they had done that, they would be asked to use them in sentences, before moving on to a 'reader' of some kind months later.

Having finished his tour and been thoroughly disheartened by it, William sat at the large teak desk in what would be his half of the main room and searched through the drawers for the school's log book and what else he could find – several pens with broken nibs, two bottles of ink, one blue, one red, a large blotter, a dictionary, a hymn book, a second large well-thumbed Bible with several frayed and torn pages, a prayer book and a catapult, confiscated, he supposed.

There was also a printed copy of the rules and regulations of the school, which were much as William expected them to be for a church school:

'1, *Any child whose parents reside in Steadshall parish may become a scholar and, under certain circumstances, children from neighbouring parishes.*

'2, *The payment to be made by children will be at the rate of one penny a week for infants, twopence a week for children in standards one and two and threepence for standard three and above, but, if made in advance, it will be reduced to the rate of eighteen pence a quarter for those in the third standard and above and ninepence in the Infant School. No parent will be expected to pay for more than three children and any beyond that number from the same family will be admitted free.*

'3, The school hours are from nine to twelve-ten and two to half-past four in the summer and from nine to twelve-ten and two to four in the winter.

'4, Prayers commence precisely at five minutes past nine and children absent from prayers will, after warning, be suspended for the rest of the week. Monday is the only day of the week on which new scholars will be admitted. Applications for admission must be made to the Reverend Hugo Scrope, vicar.

'5, The elder children from both schools are expected to attend on Sunday. Continued absence on that day will be followed by dismissal. This rule does not apply to children who may be admitted from another parish or who attend other churches.

'6, The sweeping of the rooms, if required, will be done by children selected by the Master and Mistress.'

Clearly, no one had been bothering with that rule lately, William said to himself. The next rule read:

'7, Children are to be sent clean to school. A clothes club for the benefit of poorer children is opened on the first Monday in April and continues open for twenty-four weeks.

'8, It having been found that children frequently apply for leave of absence without the knowledge of their parents, each child will be furnished with a card showing their absences during the week. Parents are earnestly requested to examine the card at the end of each week and give information at the school if their children have been absent without leave.'

He was still glancing at this when the first of the children began to appear in the yard. Knowing that a new master was due to start that day, one or two small faces appeared at the windows, the bolder souls lifted up by their more timorous friends as the sills were too high for them to do it by themselves. William did not mind: it was only to be expected that they would want to know what their new master looked like. He was more concerned about how they would react to his new teaching methods.

'Start as you mean to go on,' Martha had said: well, one of the first things, he vowed to himself, would be to return the school to a state of tidiness and the second would be to press the school managers to make up the deficiencies...

NINETEEN

THE YARD had almost filled with children when finally he closed the log book and walked outside with the school's large brass bell in his hand: several of the mothers who had brought their younger children to the school that morning had gathered by the gate, as curious to see the new master as were their offspring. There was an immediate hush from the children as William exited the porch and stood by the door: they all stopped to stare at him and several crept away or turned their faces from him as if not wanting to attract his notice. He smiled to himself: it was to be expected: it was as he wished it to be.

Many of the children, he noted, were as ragged as those he had taught in London, worse some of them, with no attempt being made to repair tears in the boys' trousers or in the elbows of their coat sleeves, while the girls' dresses were patched with all manner of different-coloured materials: their footwear was mostly hob-nailed boots for the boys and homemade clogs for the girls.

Martha joined him soon after, smiling a 'Good morning' to the mothers and the silent, mournful-faced throng of children as she hurried through the gate. She seemed to perceive the dispiritedness of her husband even as she approached. 'How bad is it?' she asked, her smile disappearing and her brow creasing with concern.

'Bad enough,' William sighed. 'There are a lot of things which will need to be put right.'

Martha left him and went inside to see for herself: when she returned five minutes later, she was as grim-faced as was her husband. 'We shall just have to do our best to improve it,' she declared. 'We'll see the school day out first and give the place a good sweeping once the children have gone home. We can hardly do it while they are here. It would raise too much dust. Perhaps the assistant-teacher and the pupil-teacher will help us. By the looks of things, our first task is going to be to make the schoolroom habitable at least.'

What concerned William more at that moment was that it was almost ten minutes to nine and yet neither Helen Dunsmore, the assistant-teacher, nor Hannah Hodgson, the pupil-teacher, had yet arrived in the yard: in his view, they should have been in the school yard ahead of most, if not all, of the children: time was ticking on and he was due to ring the school bell at nine o'clock.

When Helen Dunsmore did arrive, it was just two minutes to nine – far too late, in his opinion: she was in the company of a pretty, if sulky-looking, girl, whom William assumed was Hannah Hodgson. Somewhat surprisingly, the two came through the gates giggling like two schoolgirls, even though the bespectacled, hook-nosed teacher was at least twenty years older than her companion.

William and Martha exchanged meaningful glances, both thinking the same thing – that the two had conspired to arrive together and as late as possible so as to assert some independence of action: in short, they were issuing a challenge to the authority of the new master at the outset, as if to say 'We always arrive at this time and intend to continue doing so.'

Only when the two were a few yards from where William and Martha stood did they cease their giggling, lift their heads and acknowledge his presence. The bespectacled Miss Dunsmore introduced herself first. 'Good morning,' she said boldly and not with any great politeness, 'I am Helen Dunsmore, the assistant teacher, and this is Hannah Hodgson, the pupil-teacher.'

'I am pleased to meet you,' William and Martha replied in turn, each accompanying the greeting with a smile and a handshake. As he took Helen Dunsmore's gloved hand, William somehow sensed in her eyes a certain resentment, as though his arrival had upset some aspiration of her own – he was unsure – while Hannah Hodgson took his hand still with a certain sulkiness of demeanour.

He thought of saying something about their late-coming, but decided that there and then was neither the time nor the place to comment upon it: he would do that later: he had no intention of allowing them to assert themselves in such a blatant fashion.

Since it was one minutes to nine by then, it was time for him to ring the bell: as he clanged it loudly, giving his customary six shakes, two young girls hurriedly detached themselves from a group of older girls playing hopscotch in one corner of the yard and ran forward, calling out instructions to the younger children quickly to form their respective lines: girls in one line, boys in the other, each standard forming its own line in height order, so that there were twelve lines in all, standards one and the infants combining. The two young girls were the twelve-year-old Alice Barbrook and the eleven-year-old Olive Chaplin, who acted as monitors: it was their morning task to help the infants' teacher – in this case, Martha – to herd the wide-eyed younger children into two reasonable lines, start them marching on the spot as all the children did before entering the school, and then to lead them inside. Miss Dunsmore, meanwhile, helped by Hannah Hodgson, was doing the same with her four lines comprising the hundred and eight pupils of standards three and four snaking back across the yard and also stamping out their on-the-spot marching.

The older children, those in standards five and six whom William would teach, the ten-year-olds, eleven-year-olds and twelve-year-olds and the few thirteen-year-olds, responded more sluggishly to the clanging of the bell, as was to be expected. Most of the girls had gathered in one corner of the yard, conversing together and giving occasional glances towards their two new teachers, while the older boys, having looked in their direction to see what they looked like, had then ignored them and returned to their game of football, kicking a blown-up pig's bladder they had obtained from one of the town butcher's about the yard and shooting at a goal chalked on a high wall which divided the yard from the next-door meadow.

As the boys came trotting up, not hurrying, he thought he discerned a certain resentment from some of the older ones that their game had had to be abandoned. For that reason, they gave a desultory shuffle as their example of marching on the spot. William decided that he needed to assert his authority from the outset. 'Come on, boys, get those knees up!' he barked. 'Jump to it! One, two! One, two! One, two!' Unexpectedly, the boys responded with some vigour: the first small battle had been won.

The younger children, whom Martha was to take, stamped in first, followed by those of Miss Dunsmore's two classes, girls first, then the boys, then the girls of standards five and six, who sat on one group of double-desks farthest from the main door, followed by the reluctant boys. He was pleased to see that once inside, however, the children stood in silence at their benches and desks, the boys with their hands behind their backs, their earlier obduracy having given way to caution, if not acceptance, and the girls with their hands folded demurely in front of them: they were taking no chances with the new head teacher: they would wait and find out about him first.

Once William and Miss Dunsmore had taken their positions at the front, the two monitors, Alice Barbrook, who was in William's standard six, and, Olive Chaplin, who was also in his standard five, but often helped Miss Dunsmore, drew back the two halves of curtain so that the whole room of more senior children might join in the assembly prayers. At first glance, there seemed to William to be far more boys in standards three and four than perhaps there ought to have been, as though a number of them had been held back from moving on to standards five and six, which, if nothing else, told him something of their abilities – or, more accurately, their lack of abilities – and also perhaps the teaching proficiency or otherwise of the incumbent mistress, though that would remain to be seen. If that were so, he would have to do something about it.

Having bade them 'Good morning, children' and having received their 'Good morning, sir' in reply, William turned to his assistant. 'Will you lead the assembly, Miss Dunsmore, please?' he requested. 'As it is my first morning, I wish to observe how it is done here – if you will be so good?'

The assistant-teacher did so without demurring, pleased to be given the opportunity. 'Hands together,' she commanded, 'eyes closed, bow your heads. Let us pray. Repeat after me. "Lord, teach a little child to pray, And fill my heart with love, And make me fitter every day, To go to heaven above".'

Then, taking a square of printed card from her own Bible, she gave the lesson for that morning: '*To order myself lowly and reverently before my betters.*'

'Your betters,' she told them as they stared dumbly back at her, 'your betters are the landowners, the mine owners, the factory owners, the squire, the vicar and all who provide employment for you. You come to school to prepare yourself for future work. What you learn here you apply to working life. Repeat after me: "*I must not lie or steal. I must not be discontented or envious. God has placed me where I am in the social order. He has given me my work to do. I must not envy others. I will not try to change my lot in life. It is a sin of which I will never be guilty".*'

To William, watching the children as they mumbled their reply, it was obvious from the feet-shuffling, the sagging bodies and the occasional sly glances they gave each other out of the corners of their eyes, which marked their disinterest, that they must have heard the same 'lesson,' such as it was, being said countless times before and so took little notice of it. He was to learn later that it was one of three standard morning dogmas which were repeated almost *ad nauseum* throughout the school year – designed quite clearly to ensure the children were kept 'in their place' and 'to know their place' in the scheme of life as they were 'God's laws for them' and were not to be challenged or deviated from.

That would also need to be changed...

TWENTY

ONCE THE CURTAIN had been drawn back across, William's first task of the day was the laborious matter of taking the register and receiving the weekly payment from the children for their schooling. Whatever their religious persuasion – Church of England or Nonconformist – all were supposedly equal in the eyes of the Church, though when William had first opened the register, the letters 'B' and 'PC' and 'PM,' written in red ink beside the names of several of the children, had puzzled him: it dawned on him only after a while that they referred to 'Baptist,' 'Primitive Congregationalist' and 'Primitive Methodist.' He could only surmise that they were there for the benefit of the school's management board – and, most probably and more importantly, the Reverend Scrope.

As each child came forward to drop his or her pennies into a small, black money-box he had found in the bottom drawer of his desk, William tried not to look too intimidating or too stern, smiling as each girl gave him the customary bobbed curtsy and called out their name and the amount they were depositing in the bowl to be checked against the roll on the page, for it was clear that the children were apprehensive about him and several still kept their eyes lowered.

Fortunately, most paid a week's money in advance each Monday, so there would be no need to go through the same ritual every day, which would speed things up and allow him to get on with the teaching: a few, however, still paid daily, which was usually when their parents could afford it. Those, he knew, would be the ones who every now and again would miss school if their parents did not have the money for that particular day, especially if they were from large families.

One thing William was determined to deal with was the surliness of some of the boys: for when he began to call out their roll, while the girls had answered brightly and come forward quickly, some of the older boys, those of an age who hoped soon to be leaving and going out into the world of the working day, displayed a surliness which bordered on insolence, he thought, some waiting till he made a second call before answering, pretending not to have heard him the first time. That needed to be nipped in the bud, too.

'If I call your name once, boy,' he said to one tall, lanky youth with a thatch of fair hair, named Joseph Challis, 'you will answer me the first time. If I have to call twice to any of you – ' He ranged his eyes over the pupils seated before him. ' – I shall keep the lot of you in at playtime till you learn to listen when I speak.'

Again, as Martha had said: *'Begin as you mean to go on!'*

Their surliness, he put down to the treatment which they had received in the past and which a perusal earlier of the school's punishment book had revealed: canings – boys on their backsides and girls across their hands – had been meted out for perceived infractions such as 'rude conduct... sulkiness... answering back' and peculiarly 'insolent thoughts,' as well as the more serious 'leaving the schoolyard without permission... throwing ink pellets' and 'being late.' Tellingly, one sentence in his predecessor's hand read: 'Gave Joseph Challis five strokes for being late. Cane broke.' Clearly, the children, especially the boys, thought, 'Why should a new master be any different from the one who has just left?' They expected the same hard discipline to continue.

On the other side of the curtain, he could hear Miss Dunsmore taking the names and payment from those in standards three and four, shrilly calling out each name and often accompanying it with a cry of 'Stand up. Come forward. Be quick about it, boy. Right, go back and sit down!' and occasionally 'Why not, girl? or 'Why not, boy?' the latter remark addressed to children who, he assumed, had forgotten their money that morning – or were unable to pay. He made a mental note to speak to Miss Dunsmore about it and ensure that a list was kept of any defaulters: he did not intend to be out of pocket himself because of it.

That completed and the money locked away in the bottom drawer of his desk, including that which Miss Dunsmore and Martha brought to him from their classes, he needed first to find out what his children knew and the best way to do that was to test them as might a schools inspector, finding out first what arithmetic they could do and later how they stood with their reading and writing. After prayers, he had asked Miss Dunsmore to give her pupils similar tests and then to show him the results: he had learned through his correspondence with the vicar why the previous master, Joseph Padwick, had been dismissed and did not intend to suffer the same fate if an inspector called unexpectedly.

In arithmetic, Miss Dunsmore's standard three scholars were expected to be able to do long division and understand pounds, shillings and pence and do multiplication in the giving of accurate change if they were to satisfy a visiting inspector: they were also expected to be able to read a short paragraph from a more advanced reading book than the lower standards and to be able to write out a sentence dictated slowly to them a few words at a time, say, from the same book. Standard four pupils, in addition to those, were expected to be able to comprehend the compound rules of common weights and measures, read a few lines of poetry or prose at the choice of the inspector and write a sentence slowly dictated by him from a reading book of his choice, again a few words at a time.

Standard five scholars being tested by an inspector would be expected to be able to read a short paragraph in a newspaper or a more advanced reading book, to write down a short ordinary paragraph from the same newspaper or book, again dictated slowly to them, and, in arithmetic, be able to work out the costs involving bills and parcels as well as do long division, multiplication and the rest. His older pupils of standard six were expected to be able to do all that, to read with fluency and expression from a story book or book of poetry, write a short letter or an easy paraphrase and, in arithmetic, in addition to the rest, be able to work out proportions and fractions and be competent working with decimals.

For the first lesson for his two standards, William chalked on the blackboard a half-dozen different arithmetical examples which he wanted them to complete on the slates which he had the monitors, Alice Barbrook and Olive Chaplin, give out. He was not overly pleased with what he discovered: many of the boys seemed to struggle at the long divisions, the fractions and particularly over the decimals, which they seemed not to want to comprehend, treating the sums with the same indifference he had seen displayed earlier, though he was cheered by several of the girls, who seemed a lot brighter and more eager to please.

When the morning break of fifteen minutes came at ten-twenty, the children stood up and filed quietly out standard by standard into the yard, their faces still stiff with apprehension – till they were outside, that is, then the shrieking cacophony which accompanied their brief escape from the torture of perches, rods and acres, pounds shillings and pence and ounces, pounds and hundredweights began.

At the break, Miss Dunsmore, Martha and Hannah Hodgson went out into the yard to supervise the children, particularly to guard against squabbles among the girls playing hopscotch or skipping or fights among the boys playing football or wrestling with each other, but also to ensure that none of the recalcitrant older boys went over the wall and sneaked off.

In the meantime, for the second lesson, William copied on to the blackboard in clear copperplate writing two short passage from Charles Dickens's *A Tale Of Two Cities,* which he had brought from among his own books that morning especially for that purpose, the first being *'It was the best of times, it was the worst of times, it was the age of wisdom, it was the age of foolishness, it was the epoch of belief, it was the epoch of incredulity ...'* The second was a carefully abridged version of the thoughts of the lawyer Sidney Carton, who, having led a debauched and wasteful life, in an act of supreme sacrifice, goes to the guillotine in place of the French-born aristocrat Charles Darnay, beginning *'I see the lives for which I lay down my life, peaceful, useful, prosperous and happy, in that England which I shall see no more...'* and ending with *'It is a far, far better thing that I do than I have ever done; it is a far, far better rest that I go to than I have ever known...'*

Once the children were all sitting up straight and had their hands palms down on their desk tops, he read them the two passages, explaining each and its place in the book, and then had Alice Barbrook and Olive Chaplin go round filling the ink wells and handing out the copybooks and pens to the standard six pupils, to some excitement, for it was apparent that they had not been allowed to use pens overmuch and had done most of their writing in chalk on the slates: the fifty-five scholars of standard five would continue to do so.

'Be careful not to get too much ink on your pen nibs,' William warned the lucky few once everything had been given out. 'Do not dip the nib too far into the inkwell, and give it a little shake as you take it out – like so – before you begin. And write neatly, please. Try not to smudge your work. I do not want to have to punish any of you for blotting your copybooks on my first day here. Is that clear?' It was, they chorused back.

While that was going on, he went through the curtain to observe Miss Dunsmore for a short while, just as she and Hannah Hodgson were handing out spelling scripts.

'Sit up straight, hands palms down on desks, eyes front,' Miss Dunsmore was calling out, standing behind her desk and rapping its top with one of the canes from the cupboard. She acknowledged his appearance with a frown and a nod and continued as loudly as before: 'You are now going to copy these spellings in your best copperplate writing. I do not wish to see writing which does not exactly represent the writing on these script sheets. Neither do I wish to see writing that is too large. Neatness, neatness at all times.'

The words on the script sheets all contained the vowels 'e' and 'a' together. 'Before we begin, you will sound out each letter of the word and then say the word,' she went on. 'Are you ready? Then begin.' She tapped on her desk to keep time and they all began to recite in unison: 'B-r-e-a-k-f-a-s-t... breakfast. T-r-e-a-s-u-r-e... treasure' and on through 'instead... weather... heaven...' and a half-dozen other words, all the time chanting together as the cane rapped down threateningly on the desktop.

Then the children bent to their writing in silence, not daring to look up or at each other, the chalk scratching and squeaking on their slates, the letters of each word sloping at what they hoped was the rigid angle of sixty degrees and each done with light upward strokes and slightly heavier downward strokes.

After five minutes or so, during which time he walked up and down between the desks and benches and mats to observe, William voiced his thanks to Miss Dunsmore and returned to his side of the curtains, where, as far as he could discern, the children had passed the time writing quietly and solemnly with their heads down. As he walked up and down between the desks there, he found that most had more or less completed their task: some had done it well, especially the girls, some had done it poorly, particularly two of the older boys, who he guessed by their size were hoping to obtain their leaving certificates before the summer break and be done with school forever: for they grimaced and muttered to themselves under their breath as they worked, as if to say it was not how they wished to spend their time.

That test over and the copybooks collected, he had them read individually from the same book, a paragraph or a half-dozen lines apiece, going himself along the rows, desk by desk, pupil by pupil, and when necessary spending time to get each one to pronounce some of the vowel sounds correctly, for the local accent was as harsh to his ears as had been that of the children he had taught in Stepney. He had hoped that at least the older children would be able to read with some enthusiasm, but most just read in a bored monotone.

It was still necessary to instruct them firmly: 'You, boy, what is your name?' And when told in a mumble: 'You will start. As you read, you will point out the words along each line with your index finger. This one. If you do not know a word, you will sound it out. When I say "Stop," you will stop. You will then pass the book on to the next person on your right. They will continue immediately so all of you listen to where the others finish. I do not want to punish children who lose their places on my first day here, but I will if I have to. Right, you first. Finger up. Finger down. Begin...'

From the other side of the curtain came the harsher and shriller voice of Miss Dunsmore: 'Chalk up. Chalk on desks. Slates up. Quiet!' It was followed by the normal scolding one by one for this or that demeanour incurred in their spelling or writing test: for some, despite her admonishments, had written their lettering too big, others too small, some sloping them too much, others not enough, and several not properly joining up their writing.

While William was quite ready to praise a child who did well and had already earned return smiles from several of the girls, nothing, it seemed, was done well enough for Miss Dunsmore: by this time, the children on her side of the curtain were reading in turn from the Bible – much to William's disappointment – and the shouting, commanding, scolding and cajoling rising above their low mumblings seemed to grow as dinnertime approached, as if they required always a deal of commands to achieve anything.

'Right, finish. Pass the Bibles back to me. Quickly now, quickly!' she screeched as the clock's hands finally touched ten-past-twelve. There was the dull thump of a heavy book hitting the floor, which could only have been a Bible falling from some child's nervous hands: it was followed almost immediately by the sound of a sharp slap and a pained cry...

TWENTY-ONE

THE GREATER NUMBER of the children went to their homes for their dinners, while those remaining, mostly the pupils from Bourne Brook, sat at their desks or on their benches or mats to eat bread and dripping or cold bacon sandwiches from their tin lunch-boxes, washed down with bottles of weak lemonade, cold tea or plain pump water, before going outside to play till school resumed at two o'clock.

During the dinner break, Martha had crossed back to the cottage to prepare some lunch for herself and William and so was able to report that the two women sent by the curate had thoroughly cleaned the two parlours, the stairs, the skirting-board paintwork, the inside window sills and the panes of glass inside and out and the front and back doors and were at that very moment on their hands and knees in the front bedroom, scrubbing away at the bare floorboards with brushes and pails of soapy water.

'They have worked really hard,' she enthused, as she and William ate together in the 'Big Room,' as the children called the main room, and, for the first time since their arrival, she seemed to be in a more pleasant frame of mind. It was noticeable to them both that Miss Dunsmore and Hannah Hodgson had taken their lunches into the smaller classroom, the 'Little Room,' to eat so as to be away from them, they both supposed.

William thought it prudent not to comment at that time on what he had discovered that morning regarding his own pupils or on what he had observed on his foray to Miss Dunsmore's side of the curtain. 'Walls have ears' was the saying and it would be better if they could discuss that later back at the cottage. However, on his return to his own side of the curtain, he had made a point of listening every now and again to what was happening on the other side and was particularly shocked by the stumbling Bible-reading attempts of several of the standard three boys. From what he had observed and from what he was then hearing, many of the boys of Miss Dunsmore's two standards seemed deficient in most, if not all, of the requirements a schools inspector would expect of them. He now understood why the greater number of pupils in standards three and four *were* boys – sixty-five to forty-three – and why girls predominated in his own standards – fifty-two to forty.

Promotion from one standard to the next was on merit and clearly some boys had been held back. It explained why three of the older boys, whose names were on the register under Joseph Padwick, were missing from their places, they having decided not to wait to attain a leaving certificate from a schools inspector but to leave for the world of work before the new master arrived. They would have to be hauled back: for by law, they were supposed to leave only after the inspector had passed them as fit and learned enough to do so.

For the first hour of the afternoon, William had thought to give the boys of his two standards a lesson in world geography, that they might learn not only where they lived in relation to other countries of the world but also to know the seven continents, the oceans of the world and the names of the great mountain ranges and major rivers and perhaps in time learn, too, of the lives and habits of the peoples of those countries and continents. But when he had searched the cupboards, to his despair, he had found that there was not even a half-crumpled globe or a frayed atlas or a single textbook by which he might instruct them: under Joseph Padwick, it seemed, geography had either not been taught at all or had been taught only perfunctorily and then abandoned altogether because of his own disenchantment with his position there. In that respect, Steadshall was little different from Stepney: at the latter school, William had once witnessed a whole class, as their geography lesson, chanting the names of all the railway stations between London and Edinburgh on the East Coast line and then those between London and Glasgow on the West Coast line from a map pinned on the blackboard.

The interest of the remaining boys was likely to wane daily, he knew, unless he inspired them to sit up and listen to what he was attempting to teach them and actually want to learn: unfortunately, on that first day, when they returned inside after the dinner break, unable to do as he wished and not having anything else prepared, due to the move and the state of the cottage on their arrival, very reluctantly and with a loud sigh of frustration, the best he could offer the older boys was the recommended instruction upon 'an object.'

William was adamantly of the opinion that giving object lessons upon such things as crystals or snowflakes, say, or elephants and camels or different types of trees – or even, as he had in the past, pictures of stuffed dogs and different types of snail and placing a picture of each on every child's desk so that they could talk about it and copy down facts about it – giving such instruction was useless and hardly constituted a science lesson or a general knowledge lesson as he would like to have given them. The lessons were supposed to make children observe and then to talk about what they saw: unfortunately, too many teachers found it more expedient simply to chalk up sentences describing the object which the class simply wrote into their copybooks, if they used them at all, or on to the slates if they did not, and, in most cases, promptly forgot what they had written as soon as the school day ended

That was not the way he wanted to teach and, now that he was *the* head master at Steadshall, he was determined to improve upon it or discontinue the practice altogether if he could: in that, Martha supported him: but for the present it had to be, 'Sit up straight, eyes front, hands on desks. Today you will study the potato... '

He had already drawn a potato on the blackboard and had labelled its 'eyes' and other parts, including stem and leaves. The faces of the boys – and with it their interest – slumped alarmingly when they saw it, but there was nothing else he could do.

At that time, Martha had left the infants in the 'Little Room' in the care of Hannah Hodgson and had come into the 'Big Room' to take the girls from his two standards for an hour's sewing instruction: the announcement to the boys that they would be 'studying the potato' brought titters from the girls doing their needlework and even a raised eyebrow from Martha, which made William redden even more. But he had to press on.

'The potato,' William began, giving a cough, as much through embarrassment as anything, 'the potato belongs to the nightshade family. It is part of a thick stem called a tuber and it grows above and below ground. Its "eyes" are the undeveloped buds, from which the new plants can grow to a height of one to three feet. The flowers of the potato are white or purple and when the tops of the plant wither then the farmers know that the harvest is ready. Potatoes are good for us...'

All the time he was speaking, he was slowly writing his comments on the blackboard and the boys were carefully copying them into their copy books; he hoped that he might tell them something they did not know, like '...The potato has been important for a long time in people's everyday lives. For example, people in Ireland depended upon the potato crop for most of their food. In 1846, they were so dependent upon it that, when a blight destroyed most of the potato crop, between two hundred thousand and three hundred thousand people died of famine and millions of others had to leave Ireland and emigrate to this country and to America and Canada...'

Later, for the final part of the afternoon, as the weather was still fine, with patches of blue sky showing intermittently between the clouds, almost to make up for the dullness of the earlier lesson on the potato, he decided to take them all into the yard for drill. The children marched outside with the same grim reluctance as they had marched into the school after the dinner break for the afternoon register and showed little enthusiasm for anything as they lined up in rows of fifteen each, boys on one side, girls on the other.

Once they had measured the distance between themselves in front and to the side in the usual military fashion, he put them to marching on the spot, setting them an example himself, though he found that he frequently had to call out sharper commands to the boys: 'Eyes front, boy! Straighten your back. On my first command – one – turn your heads to the right, looking along the line of your shoulder, without moving any other part of the body. On my second command – two – turn your heads to the front. On three, turn to the left. On four, back to the front again. We will do that five times each side, then we will put our hands on our hips and turn just our hips to the left, then back to the front, then to the right. Is that clear? Right! One – two – three – four...'

He was almost as glad as the children were when the clock ticked round to the end of the school day at four-thirty and his first day as the head master of a new school ended, though there were still other matters to be settled from that first day...

TWENTY-TWO

ONLY AFTER the children had gone home and Martha, Helen Dunsmore, Hannah Hodgson and the two monitors, Alice Barbrook and Olive Chaplin, had finished clearing away the slates, mats, cushions, copybooks and pens and wiping down the blackboards was William able to ask the assistant-teacher and the pupil-teacher if he could 'have a word' with them both. So that they might be alone in his part of the Big Room, he took the precaution of sending the two monitors to sweep the floor in the infants' room, which, in view of its earlier neglect, would take them some time.

It seemed to him that Miss Dunsmore came reluctantly: indeed, she had already pulled on her coat and was pinning her hat as she came through the curtain, as if signalling her wish to be away, while Hannah Hodgson, also ready to go, trailed apprehensively in the older woman's wake.

William began by politely asking each of them how things had 'gone' that day, to which Miss Dunsmore replied a little huffily, as if puzzled by his need to ask the question at all, that, naturally, they had 'gone very well.' Hannah Hodgson copied her older companion, but added a respectful 'sir' at the end.

'One thing, Miss Dunsmore,' William went on, deliberately keeping his tone level, 'I was surprised this morning that you did not arrive at school till just before nine o'clock when the greater number of the pupils were already in the yard. From tomorrow, please, I should like you to be at school by eight-thirty at the latest, so that you are not only present when the children begin to arrive but also so that you can ring the bell for them to enter school at nine o'clock. If you would be so kind as to oblige me, Miss Dunsmore? It will also give you time to ensure that your schoolroom is ready for work before the children enter. I noted that it took some time after prayers for your pupils to settle down and there was much to-ing and fro-ing between their desks and the cupboard.'

'I have always arrived just before nine o'clock,' an indignant Miss Dunsmore protested. 'I have never been late in all the time I have been here. Mr. Padwick did not mind me arriving just before nine o'clock and he always rang the bell himself.'

'Well, Mr. Padwick has gone,' William reminded her, though still maintaining a placid demeanour. 'I am now the master here and I would like things to be done my way, if you please. I shall be making certain changes and I shall expect my staff to assist me in carrying out those changes and to accept them as being for the better, which I am confident they will be. What they are will be made known to you all in good time.'

'Expecting me to arrive earlier than I need to do is not a change for the better, as far as I am concerned,' Helen Dunsmore protested.

'Nevertheless, it will be done, Miss Dunsmore,' William said firmly, his tone hardening, 'and I want no argument on the matter. I shall be here at eight o'clock tomorrow, which is my usual time for arriving at a school, and I shall expect you and Miss Hodgson both to be here by eight-thirty. Is that clear?'

'I am not standing for this!' exclaimed Helen Dunsmore, her cheeks reddening with embarrassment. 'I am a friend of the Reverend Scrope – a very good friend. I am his church organist. I assist with the church choir and play the organ every Sunday, for Holy Communion and Evensong. He shall hear of this. I shall write a letter of protest to the school managers.'

'You may do as you wish, Miss Dunsmore,' William said, almost with disinterest, 'that is your prerogative, but you *will* be here tomorrow by eight-thirty, as I require, to prepare your room and you *will* go outside and ring the bell at nine o'clock to bring the children in. You will also take the register for your standards and not leave it up to Miss Hodgson or your monitor, Olive Chaplin, as I note from the entries in the register you seem to have done previously – '

While perusing the log book before school that morning, William had noticed that corrections had been made to the attendance figures on several occasions, with first totals written in an obviously childish hand being crossed out and secondary totals inserted above them in a more accomplished flourish: an obvious correction.

' – Also, from tomorrow, Miss Dunsmore,' William went on, 'it will be your duty to ensure that the school is locked after we finish in preference to it being done by the senior monitor, Miss Barbrook, which I understand is the case at present. You will do those things,

Miss Dunsmore, because I say so. They are not requests, they are my instructions.'

The look upon Helen Dunsmore's face as she flounced out, swishing asides the dividing curtain as she made for the door, was one of absolute fury. He had not even had a chance to ask her further about the incident with the Bible just before the dinnertime break or about two other punishments Martha had reported as having been meted out while she was in the Big Room and he was outside, but decided that, in view of her obvious anger, perhaps then was not the best time.

Having witnessed the master's sternness with an assistant-teacher who was almost twenty years older, poor Hannah Hodgson approached the desk, trembling with fear and near to tears: indeed, she might well have begun to cry in anticipation of her admonishment had not Martha been standing beside her husband: the presence of another woman seemed to reassure her that nothing bad was about to happen.

There had been six incidents of 'disciplining' that day which William would have to record in the log book, five of which troubled him. In two of them, Hannah Hodgson, while looking after the infants alone during the period Martha was instructing the older girls in needlework, had rapped one of the five-year-old boys over the knuckles with a ruler and then had smacked a girl across the face for wetting the floor under a bench. Both had still been tearful and sullen-faced when Martha had returned to ask what had occurred in her absence.

'There is no need to be frightened, Miss Hodgson,' William told her, even giving her a weak smile of encouragement. 'I have asked to see you because I am filling in the log book and I need to ask why you felt it necessary to strike one of the infants over the knuckles with a ruler and also why you refused to allow another child to go across the yard to the lavatory when apparently she raised her hand, resulting in her wetting the floor and one of the monitors having to mop it up?'

Hannah Hodgson's excuse on the first was that the boy had chewed the corners of a small cardboard box she had left lying on her desk: on the second, she said the girl had got into the habit of asking to 'go across the yard' almost daily at that time and she wondered sometimes whether she did it purely as a matter of habit or simply to annoy her and she was hoping to cure her, if indeed it were a habit.

'I would have preferred it if you had allowed her to answer the call of nature, Miss Hodgson,' William quietly admonished, so that the pupil-teacher would not regard it as an actual scolding. 'I do not agree with smacking a child who wets the floor, especially, as I understand it, in this case the child raised her hand to ask for permission to cross the yard and you refused her. As for the boy who chewed the box, Martha tells me he is one of the youngest in school. Did you not think it was perhaps done as an attempt to relieve his unhappiness over something, his anxiety, his nervousness? Did you not think of that, Miss Hodgson?'

There was also the matter of the miscounted numbers during past registrations, for which Hannah was full of apologies and promised to be more careful if she were ever asked to do it again, to which William informed her that, from then on, Miss Dunsmore would be responsible for accumulating all totals. With that, he thanked her for what she had done that day and she left, her face flushed in embarrassment.

The other four disciplinary incidents all involved Miss Dunsmore: as well as the slapping the girl who had dropped Bible, she had also struck a seven-year-old dullard by the name of Peter Foulkes round the head with her own Bible, so frustrated had she become by his inability to sound even simple words from the one he was attempting to read. William had heard the child's short cry of pain: what had concerned him was that he found it necessary to ask his assistant-teacher during the dinnertime break what had happened to cause the two incidents as she did not seem about to volunteer the information. Indeed, she was surprised by his request for details of incidents which, to her, were 'normal daily occurrences,' as she put it, and saw 'nothing wrong in them.'

In the third, she had reached out, taken some hair above a boy's ear in two fingers and given it a sharp and painful twist because he had momentarily forgotten himself and had picked up his chalk to begin writing on his slate with his left-hand and writing with the left-hand was forbidden in the school. That William had seen, for it had happened late that afternoon just as he and the boys were returning inside from their drill. He had not said anything at the time, preferring to wait till after school when the matter – and his views on it – might be discussed in a sensible manner: but Miss Dunsmore's sudden departure in high dudgeon had thwarted that plan.

He could have called her back, but decided that, at that time, it would only have made matters worse. 'I shall have to take the matter up another time,' he thought to himself as he watched her bang shut the porch door: he did not fool himself that, in view of what he had heard and seen of Miss Dunsmore's teaching methods from the other side of the curtain, the time would most likely be soon.

He was less bothered by the fact that she had made another boy write out a sentence of ten words ten times on his slate for kicking the boy in front of him under the desk. That was the kind of a punishment which he could sanction, though it still had to be recorded.

All in all, William reasoned, it had been a reasonably satisfying first day, with which Martha concurred, especially as the women cleaning the cottage had finished their work by the time the two of them crossed back and the place, while not spotless, was much cleaner and had a fresher smell about it. It was at least habitable. All that was required now was for a builder to call to put right the other matters…

TWENTY-THREE

AS WAS TO BE EXPECTED at the end of their first day at a new school, there were things to be discussed, which William and Martha did as they ate supper that evening: and, not unnaturally, the matter of the disciplining of the children was a prime topic. What troubled him most was that Miss Dunsmore's method of teaching seemed unnecessarily harsh.

William was not averse to instilling a sense of discipline in his charges, but he was no believer in chastising with the birch, the cane, the paddle, the strap or the yardstick every time a child did something wrong, which at Stepney had been the most common means of maintaining discipline. Instead, he was a firm believer, as was Martha, in rewarding honest endeavour, giving encouragement to those who would benefit from it, trying to stimulate the idle into useful learning rather than repeatedly punishing them for their failures. Like a growing number of others, though still far too few, he held the view that it was better to instil in his scholars a sense of responsibility for their own learning and that way to develop with them clear rules of conduct. Only then, with the acquiescence of the child, could the teacher through his teaching provide the opportunities for their success in life and, conversely, at the same time still administer to non-compliant scholars less brutal, more moral disciplines, such as lines and detentions.

That day, during his teaching of his own standards five and six, William had deliberately conceded a certain laxity, though not letting things get out of hand: he had had no wish on his first day to overdo his sternness: that he hoped would impose itself in time by word rather than physical deed. There was another reason for it, a more devious one: he had wanted to find out who were the chatterboxes and who were the whisperers and who were the workers, willing to put their heads down, and who were the idlers, devoid of purpose.

The children, of course, saw only a schoolmaster whom they considered to be as stern in his manner as all other teachers they had met – someone to be feared and whose ire they hoped always to avoid. They did not know that their new head teacher and his wife were firm believers in the doctrine that children would never learn unless they *wanted* to learn and that compulsory learning would never stick in the mind.

William was no soft touch, however: minor infractions, such as talking or fidgeting during lessons, always drew a first warning and, if the culprit persisted, he would always punish them, not with the cane, but by giving them extra work, such as writing out a tract during the dinnertime break so that they could not play with their fellows. The cane, he believed, as did Martha, should be used sparingly and kept only for the more serious cases, such as downright insolence or insubordination or bullying of younger children or, as he once had had to use it, when a boy had thrown a heavy slate at his head.

Far better was imposing a period of detention on an unruly or insolent child, keeping him or her back in school at a specified time on a school day, say, either at the dinnertime break while the other children played outside or after school as the others all went home and he or she sat alone in the classroom: or perhaps even requiring the transgressor to attend school at a certain time on a non-school day, such as a Saturday, at which the scholar would do academic work or just stand against the wall or just sit at their desk or bench in a contemplative manner. They, he felt, were far better remedies than giving a girl two strokes of the cane across either hand or a boy three, or even six, strokes across the behind and certainly better than a slap around the head with a Bible or having the hair above one's ears twisted, as Miss Dunsmore preferred to do.

Discipline, William and Martha both accepted, was not only good for children but was necessary for their future well-being, as vital to their development as were good food, excising the brain through lessons, undergoing vigorous physical exercises, receiving praise and love and what other basic needs children required. Without discipline, they believed, as did all adults, that children would lack the self-discipline, the respect for others and the ability to cooperate with their peers, which were essential, in their view, for them to be able to meet and to overcome the many challenges of life. School children, in particular, needed to be disciplined with a firm but *fair* hand so as to learn how to manage their own behaviour: and, as they headed into adolescence and the turbulence of those years, having experienced discipline, they would be more likely to navigate their way through those challenges and temptations.

Both had long held the view that it was better to strive to interest their charges in learning their lessons, first by dispensing as far as was possible with the rote system of education and the narrowness of the subjects which the children were taught – reading, writing and arithmetic, with a little needlework for the girls and primitive carpentry for the boys. For only through obtaining as good an education as it was possible for them to receive, William and Martha believed, would the children of the poor ever make anything of themselves, particularly in an agricultural area like Steadshall, where the greater number of jobs for men and boys of the town were outside it on the farms all around it and scores walked and cycled out to them daily, along the Wivencaster road, the Bromptree road, the Siblingham road and the Burestead Market road to Edmundsbury.

If there were one thing for which William was a stickler, however, it was for neatness: in his view, there was no reason why work could not be done neatly: and, just as Miss Dunsmore did, he, too, expected the children's writing to be 'copperplate' – or as near copperplate as they were able and at least attempted. Unfortunately, among several of the boys and one or two of the girls, it was most decidedly not, as much as they had tried: some, it appeared, would have done better writing with their left hands so awkward was it. However, the insistence was general then that children must always write with their right hand, though to William it had always seemed to be an unnecessary stricture and where possible he had always tried to correct it by sympathetic understanding. In his opinion, a child ought not to be punished for writing with their left hand if that were their 'natural bent,' as it had been of the boy who had done it that morning. Others, however, disagreed, Miss Dunsmore among them, it seemed.

From what William had deduced from his first tests, most of the boys in standard six would have little hope of passing the school inspector's test as fit and learned enough to leave for the world of work. None had showed any aptitude for what he had set them to do that day and so he could not expect that they would be given their leaving certificates when the inspector next came.

All those things and others, in time and with Martha's support, William was determined to change: he would begin by writing a letter to the Reverend Scrope, pointing out certain deficiencies of stock at the parochial school, which, in his view, required attention: nothing too demanding, just a polite letter from their new schoolmaster to the chairman of the school's management board...

TWENTY-FOUR

SO AS NOT TO APPEAR too eager to criticise by pointing out deficiencies too soon after his arrival, William waited two further weeks before he wrote the letter to the Reverend Scrope. He and Martha discussed how they should approach the subject a number of times, at breakfast, at tea, at school breaktimes and once even in bed before they distracted themselves from the worry of it by making love and afterwards falling asleep. Each time they came to the same conclusion – that they must act, that they could not avoid doing so and, therefore, should not delay too long, for to delay would only make it more difficult to write the letter: as time went by, the school management board would think that they were satisfied with what they had found when they most decidedly were not.

'We cannot let them get away with such awfulness,' Martha declared on the evening William finally seated himself at the dining table to write the letter. 'The place is in too dreadful a state. We must act, for the children's sake. Do it.'

Now, as William scanned what he had written yet again, holding it up so that Martha, standing behind his chair, could read it over his shoulder by the light of the paraffin lamp above them, all he could hope was that the Reverend Scrope and the other managers would not be offended by it and consider it an affront that he should even have written it at all. He had taken care to set out things plainly and to be respectful, listing first the external improvements required and then the problems and deficiencies inside the school itself.

Even so, he was still apprehensive. 'Look what happened the last time we stirred things up,' he said ruefully. 'I found myself taken by the scruff of the neck and marched out of the yard by a grocer of all people, while a big burly policeman just stood there watching in case I took it into my head to resist him somehow.'

'I think it is written well enough,' Martha said. 'I do not see how you can improve upon it. You are respectful and it is not as if you are demanding that they do everything immediately. You are merely drawing their attention to things and you do say "over time". What harm is there in that?'

'Whether they see it that way remains to be seen,' William said with a weary sigh. 'The lavatories are appalling and we do need the pens and nibs and the other things, though, if I am honest with myself, I do not hold out much hope that we will get them. If I had known the school was going to be like this, I should not have applied for the post.'

'What else could we do?' his wife asked, laying a hand on his shoulder. 'We had to apply to somewhere and Steadshall is as good a place as any. After what happened in Stepney, no one in London would have employed us. Word would have soon got about. Seeing the advertisement for this school was a godsend to us. If the managers will only begin to supply us with a few things and correct the worse discrepancies, then we shall at least have achieved something.'

'We can but hope,' said William dourly.

'You are too much of a pessimist,' said Martha, leaning forward and placing her cheek against his. 'Steadshall seems to be a nice town. It would be nice to settle down here, out in the country, out in the fresh air – ' She hesitated, gave his hand a squeeze and went on: ' – and maybe someday raise our children here. Certainly, anything is better than the East End of London, with its smoky atmosphere, its squalor and its crowded tenements.'

Her husband gave out another long sigh. 'It's just that I did not expect to run into the problems here that we have,' he said. 'I suppose I expected things would be different. I should have known better.'

'Let me read the letter one more time,' his wife said brightly, 'and if I think it is all right, we will have it delivered tomorrow. I'll send one of the children to the vicarage with it first thing.'

'My dear Reverend Scrope,' she read aloud, *'May I respectfully draw your attention, and the attention of the other members of the school management board, to certain deficiencies which I have discovered at the parochial school in the short time I have been here and which, in my view, may require attention, some rather urgently, others perhaps less so, but all, in my view, requiring attention over time.*

'I fully understand that, with the need to comply with the Department of Education, an addition to the infants' room is considered a priority, as you set out in your letter to me on my

appointment. Bearing that in mind, I should like to point out, with respect, that on my initial tour of the school I found that the lavatories at both the boys' and the girls' ends of the yard were in a deplorable state. There was little or no paper for the children to use in either of them and the waste buckets themselves were almost full and I had to ask the curate, the Reverend Smallwood, if he would as a matter of urgency kindly ask whoever did the weekly emptying to do so before they became a foul hazard to health. This, I have had to do twice since, as the man employed to collect the sewage is very infrequent in his visits and also very careless in his carrying. I have twice had to clean up spillages. Also, the boys' urinal channel was blocked when I first looked at it and I had to clear it myself so that it would function properly. It is blocked repeatedly by leaves from the trees around the school and, to me, constitutes a similar hazard to health which needs attending.

'Also externally, the school yard itself I feel is a further hazard to children running about on it. It is badly potholed and full of puddles when it rains and in urgent need of some form of repair.

'Internally, I found the school to be fearfully cold and somewhat damp. I was surprised to find that there was no supply of coke or kindling wood by which I might light the iron stove and warm the place and that there was no stove at all in the infants' room. Today, all the pupils had to sit with their coats on, as did I and the other members of staff, which is not good, yet I hear we are not allowed coke for a fire because it is 'out of season.' Further, the floorboards by the entrance door are badly worn and splintered in places. If they cannot be renewed, then I would respectfully suggest the purchase of a roll of matting which could be laid over the worst parts.

'In standards one and two, the fine sand which the children use needs to be replenished urgently as it has nearly run out and what there is has been contaminated by extraneous matter. Also, the four benches for standards three and four are totally insufficient and I would respectfully ask that some consideration be given in the near future to supplying at least another dozen so that we may dispense with the totally unsuitable rush mats and straw-filled cushions which the

*younger pupils use, which I find unhygienic and most of which
my wife has had to wash, refill and repair.*

*'In standard five, one of the wrought iron stanchions
belonging to one of the desks is broken and in urgent need of
replacing. In addition, our cupboard stocks are also low on
several counts – jars of fish-glue, pen holders, nibs, ink and
wooden rulers, also readers of any kind.*

*'I fully understand that your budget is limited and that not
all of the school's needs can be met immediately, but I should
be obliged if the school managers could see their way to
attending to the one requirement I consider to be the most
pressing, that is the erection of at least one additional
lavatory at both the boys' and girls' ends.*

*'I would be more than willing to discuss this and other
matters with you and the other members of the management
board at your next meeting, should you so wish.*

*'I remain, respectfully, your obedient servant, William
Warburton.'*

The reply came two days later: William found it lying on the
cottage mat on the Friday morning, delivered, they assumed, late on
the previous evening after they had gone to bed: it was signed by the
secretary of the school managers, Joshua Linkhorn.

'Dear Mr. Warburton,' the secretary wrote, *'The Reverend
Scrope this week has been much taken up with various church
matters, but has asked me, as the secretary and treasurer of
the parochial school management board, to reply to your
concerns regarding the school as expressed in your letter of
the fifth instant. He wishes me to state that he and the
management board are fully aware of the stock requirements
at the school at the moment, but feel that we must press on
with the more important task of raising funds to build the
extra accommodation next to the infants' classroom for this
September and also to provide suitable premises for the
children at Bourne Brook, as requested by the Department of
Education in London. Therefore, he and the management
board feel that we shall not at present be able to spare any
funds for the replenishment of the stock you designate or the
refurbishments you also list.*

*'The Reverend Scrope also wishes me to point out that the
management board is not in the habit of allowing non-*

members to its meetings. However, the management board does agree to provide an extra lavatory at the girls' end of the schoolyard as you suggest. Yours sincerely, Joshua Linkhorn...'

It was a disappointment to William, but not unexpected: at least he had let the management board know of the deficiencies, even if they did not know before, which he was quite convinced they did, but had studiously ignored them...

TWENTY-FIVE

IT WAS THE COMMOTION from the other side of the curtain on the same Friday, just as the children were settling down after the mid-afternoon break, which alerted William to the arrival of a visitor. All of a sudden there was a cry from Miss Dunsmore of 'Stand up!' followed by an irregular clatter of desk seats being lifted and a scuffling of boots and clogs on the bare floorboards as the children rose hurriedly to their feet.

William was seated at his desk, compiling a list of words for a spelling test which he intended to give his standard five pupils the next day, while for the moment the children of both standards busied themselves working out some long division sums he had written on the blackboard. The next thing he knew was the curtain had been pulled aside and the Reverend Scrope was standing before him, a haughty look upon his face. It was his first visit to the school since William and Martha's arrival, though they had, of course, seen him in church twice and shaken his hand in the porch each time upon leaving, though without actually holding a conversation of any length or value with him.

'Everyone stand,' William called out quickly and, thankfully, the whole assembly stood with a unison which was no doubt long practised. 'Sit. Continue with your work,' he said once that respect had been paid.

The Reverend Scrope paid them no heed, but plunged straight in. 'You have had a letter from Mr. Linkhorn, have you, Mr. Warburton?' he began, giving what William took to be a disdainful sniff, such as one might give if their nose had caught a whiff of something distasteful or their eyes had lighted on a sight they did not wish to see.

'I have, thank you, sir – yes,' William replied cautiously.

'Good,' the vicar said abruptly, with another sniff. 'It is the reason I have come here. I am here to tell you, Mr. Warburton, that it really is not your place to make suggestions to the management board on what may or may not be needed at this school. The board are well aware of what is needed here, but at the present time we see no reason for spending money on the items you list. There are other considerations far more pressing, as you will be aware. The need for an extension to the infants' room is of far greater importance than the need for pen nibs and bottles of fish glue. It would not be money well spent.'

'How so?' William was puzzled.

The Reverend Scrope's brow furrowed into a frown. 'Why, because of the expectations of the children here!' he declared, seeming almost indignant, as if he could not believe that he had been asked something so self-evident. 'In a school such as this, the expectations of the scholars are at the barest minimum – the barest minimum, Mr. Warburton. The boys who receive their education in the "three Rs" here will leave and become farmhands working on the land, as do their fathers and their older brothers, who no doubt also passed through this very school at sometime or other. And the girls, when they leave, they will most likely go into one of Oldcourt's mills as spinners or machine-minders just as they have always done or go into domestic service in the large houses around the district, for which there is always a call. That is their destiny in life. There are no other expectations for them. There has been a Church school here for the past thirty-eight years and it has ever been thus.'

The Reverend Scrope had fixed his gaze upon William, intending to stare him out and that way assert his 'rightful authority' over the man whom he had employed. For a full ten seconds, the two men eyed each other, neither speaking.

Despite William's instruction for them to continue with their work, the children had stopped their writing and, though still hunched over their copybooks, were sneaking glances at the two men, sensing the antagonism between them.

William broke the silence. 'You will forgive me, vicar,' he began, a measured iciness to his tone, 'but should it not be our task in life to help the children we teach here to change their destiny? Ever since I became a schoolmaster, I have deemed it my life's goal to offer the best education that I can to the children of the poor whom I teach and to encourage them to rise above their social origins. Indeed, it was one of the reasons why I became a teacher in the first place – to help to educate the children of the poor in a better way than has been done hereto. Poverty should not be grounds for exclusion from a hope of betterment in life, rather it should be the catalyst for it. Do you not think?'

'Stuff and nonsense!' was the Reverend Scrope's answer. 'Stuff and nonsense! For what purpose would any of these children want to rise above their stations? What would they do with this greater education of yours if they had it? What would you teach them?'

They were less questions than statements of contempt: William could have answered the clergyman with a long explanation, but restricted himself to replying with the confidence of one who could claim the moral high ground.

'I should like to teach them history, for a start,' he said calmly, 'the history of their own country, the history of England, from the coming of Julius Caesar, say, through to the Tudors and the reign of Elizabeth so that they might know something of England's greatness – of Crecy, of Agincourt, of the defeat of the Spanish Armada – to give them some idea of this country's achievements, something to make them proud and to generate their interest. One does not actually have to accept as categorical and unchangeable the lines of the hymn, *"The rich man in his castle, The poor man at his gate..."* does one?'

'I know the words of Mrs. Alexander's hymn, Mr. Warburton,' the Reverend Scrope replied, a little pompously, referring to Mrs. Cecil Alexander's *'All Things Bright and Beautiful,'* and, pointedly, he completed the lines of the third verse: 'And as you well know, it goes on, *"He made them, high or lowly, And ordered their estate..."* – a clear reference, I believe, to God's ordering of all things on this earth, both the high and the lowly.'

The vicar permitted himself a thin smile of satisfaction. 'I think you dream, sir,' he added condescendingly. In his view, it was a preposterous idea even to think of teaching farmworkers the history of England. Whatever next? One might as well teach them Greek and Latin and be done with it. It was poppycock!

To William, the vicar's reply was as crass as any he had heard from others who spoke against giving too much education to the labouring classes in case it made them despise their lot in life and, in so doing, deprived their wealthy betters of their services as servants, as housemaids, as grooms and gardeners and the like, or as agricultural labourers, as miners or factory hands or others who undertook similar laborious work to which their rank in society apparently had destined them.

'With respect, Mr. Scrope,' said William, the icy edge to his tone still evident, 'I do not see it as my duty to teach working class children to "know their place," though I do teach them to respect their "elders and their betters." And if I "dream," as you seem to think I do, it is a dream that I might somehow in some way improve the educating of the poor – the children of this parish as well as other parishes – so that they might be given the chance to better themselves. And just as you must run your church how you see fit, sir, then I, as a schoolmaster with nine years of experience in teaching behind me, feel that I have the right to run my school as I see fit.'

'You are being impertinent, sir,' the vicar declared, taken aback by the deliberateness of William's words. 'This is a Church school, therefore, it is *my* school. You are merely the head teacher here, employed by me!'

William maintained his measured tone. 'It is not my intention to be impertinent, sir, just to be factual and authoritative,' he said.

'Well, I consider it an impertinence,' the vicar said brusquely. 'However, I have not come here to argue the merits of education with you. I merely came to ask if you had received Mr. Linkhorn's letter of reply. Now that I have done that, I must depart. I am on my way to Wivencaster to see the Bishop and I am due to catch the four-thirty train. Perhaps I shall see you at church again on Sunday and then afterwards we might discuss your peculiar views further. For the life of me, I have not heard the like of them before.'

William thought he might try one request. 'Could we not at least have some coke for the stove? As I said in my letter, it was very cold in here on Wednesday and the children had to sit with their coats on.'

'You exaggerate surely, sir?' the vicar retorted. 'Young children are less in need of the comfort of a warming stove than we older folk. Besides, it is the custom to discontinue lighting the stove from the first of April onwards and it is now May.' He gave a dismissive wave of the hand as if the matter, having been settled by the management board, warranted no further discussion. 'All the spare coke was taken to the vicarage and no fires can be lit in school, anyway, without the prior permission of the board of managers to save on our fuel costs.'

'Even when it is bitterly cold?' a surprised William asked.

'I doubt it is ever as cold as you describe, Mr. Warburton,' the vicar answered, without so much as batting an eyelid.

The upshot of the meeting was that William learned – if he had not learned it before – that it was as well to know your clergy and, in the Reverend Scrope, he had found a clergyman of the old type, an unchallenged authority figure in his parish, who brooked no argument or even discussion and who considered himself supreme.

There was one other thing for the vicar to do as he made his way out and that was to murmur something to Miss Dunsmore, which did not seem to go down at all well with her, for she became flushed as he left her and in a short while was shouting at the 'slackers' and 'dunces and 'idiots' among her scholars even more harshly than usual.

For William, it did not matter: ever since his admonishment of her for her lateness on that first day, she now was arriving at the school by eight-thirty, as he had asked, spent the first ten minutes to a quarter-of-an-hour each day preparing her classroom before the children filed in, as he had also requested, and then went out each morning at just before nine to ring the bell, also as William had ordered. She now was responsible for the whole of the school register standard by standard and remained behind to lock the building when everyone else had left.

Meanwhile, the Reverend Scrope, waiting on the platform for the four-thirty train, was in a better mood than he had been when he had woken that morning: he had put the schoolmaster in his place, as far as school matters were concerned, and he had also dealt with Miss Dunsmore's complaint, at least for the time being.

'We have received your letter, Miss Dunsmore,' he had told her quietly, out of William's hearing, for he had drawn the curtain between the two classes back across, 'and we can see no other way except that you will have to do as Mr. Warburton wishes, at least for the time being, perhaps till another assistant like yourself can be appointed and then you can share the duties between you.'

What he did not tell her was that there was no actual 'we,' which implied a discussion, however brief, had been conducted by the management board itself: in fact, no meeting had been held to discuss her letter or William's letter and none was due to be held till the following week: in both instances, he had taken the decisions himself.

In the case of William's letter, the Reverend Scrope had simply read it, taken it to Joshua Linkhorn and instructed him as the secretary of the management board to reply along the lines he dictated: and, in the case of Miss Dunsmore, he had decided the management board should not be troubled with such trifling matters as she had raised. Further, the likelihood of another assistant-teacher being employed just then, even with more scholars likely to be added to the roll, was so remote as to be almost non-existent: the need to extend the school must take priority, as the management board had decided.

That was one of the reasons for his journey to Wivencaster, to tell the Bishop of the difficulty he was having in raising the money for the extension to the parochial school and for an entirely new school at Bourne Brook – both of which would be very costly. Subscriptions were not coming in as they should, as he would have expected them to do: he was hoping that perhaps the Diocese might advance him some money? That was one reason for his going, though there was a second reason...

TWENTY-SIX

THE RUNDOWN Hythe area of Wivencaster late on a cold and drizzling Friday night, crowded as it was with soldiers from the town's many barracks, seamen off the grain and timber boats tied up at the riverside wharf and labourers from the town's factories, was not the place for a gentleman to be seen walking up and down – not a true gentleman, anyway.

The constable in the darkened shop doorway had been watching the man for several minutes: he certainly had the appearance of a gentleman: he was smartly dressed – too smartly dressed for the area – in a dark coat and a dark, wide-brimmed hat, with a navy blue scarf half-covering his face. Therefore, the constable decided, he must be a gentleman and the seedy Hythe area was not where he ought to be, not at that time of night.

He had seen him walk down the hill past the three women of casual virtue standing together on the opposite pavement, now he was walking back up again, his head down, as if not wanting to be recognised. It was this very furtiveness which had first attracted the constable's attention: had the man acted normally, he would have been just one of the two score passing to and fro across from him, going from one boisterous public house to another.

Experience told him that the likely reason the man was there was 'business' of a certain kind with one or other of the three women. The policeman had seen men acting that way before – many, many men – and he allowed himself a smile as the man passed the women a second time without stopping to speak to any of them, which was not unusual. Invariably, when men did that, they either hurried quickly on, having decided not to partake of what was on offer, or their needs got the better of them and they turned back, struck their bargain and followed one or other of the women down the dark alleyway between two nearby houses, emerging a half-hour later, say, a few shillings lighter in the pocket and too often with a dose of something they would later wish they had not contracted. Clearly, this poor man was wrestling with his conscience more than most – should he approach the three prostitutes or not?

At the top of the hill, he stopped, stood for a few moments, then crossed the road to the constable's side and started back down the hill again: it was a usual ploy of the undecided seeking 'business,' for it allowed them to look across at the women on offer one more time as they drew level with them and make their selection which of them to 'use' for their purposes without being pressured by an approach from the women themselves – a smile, a querying look or a crude description of what was on offer. Indeed, so concerned was the man with peering across at the women than he almost bumped into two soldiers, who had come out of a public house next to the shop where the constable was standing and had started to weave their way somewhat drunkenly up the hill. The constable saw the soldiers turn and shout something at the man – barrack-room abuse – and it was then that he decided, for the man's own safety, to put him out of his misery. Stepping out of the shadows as the stranger came abreast of him, he asked casually: 'Can I help you, sir?'

'Oh – er – what – what?' the man said, flustered, taken by surprise at the policeman's unexpected appearance. Then remembering the question, he went on hastily: 'No, no, constable, no, I was just passing, thank you.'

'Just passing, sir?' queried the constable, raising one eyebrow. Still, he decided to play along. 'You looked a bit lost to me, sir,' he suggested.

'I – I was looking for the way to the railway station,' the stranger responded quickly, staring boldly back at the constable as if determined to stand on his dignity.

'The railway stations are both the other way, sir,' said the constable, pointing in the opposite direction to which the man had been walking. 'Which one would you be wanting, sir, the North Station or the Central Station?'

'Er – the North,' the man replied, beginning to wonder whether he had been caught out and whether the constable had indeed guessed his mission.

'Ah, well, you have to go back that way, sir, past the Central Station, then up the High Street, down North Hill and up North Station Road. It's a fair way, sir, a good couple of miles. It might be better if you took one of the hansoms.'

'No, no, I'll walk,' said the stranger quickly and started to hurry off.

It took the lanky constable only a half-dozen strides to catch up to him. 'I'll walk with you, sir, if you don't mind,' he said, a polite smile creasing his face. 'A gentleman like you ought not to be seen around an area like this. There are a lot of unsavoury characters around here. They'd rob their own grannies, given half a chance, some of them. You don't mind, do you sir? You'll be safer with me.'

'No, no, I don't mind,' the man said in a somewhat strangulated voice, which indicated that he did mind very much: it amused the policeman all the more, for he looked down at the stranger and smiled even more broadly.

'On business were you, sir?'

'Yes, yes,' the other replied, the irritation in his reply confirming the lie.

'Which train will you be taking?' the policeman asked next.

'I'm going to – er – er – Steadshall.'

In the darkness, the policeman smiled again at the other's hesitation: it further confirmed his suspicions, not that he really needed them to be confirmed. 'Steadshall? Oh dear, will there be a train this late at night, sir?' He had pulled out a pocket-watch on a chain and was consulting it.

'There is one at midnight to Lapperchall Junction – the milk train. I can make a connection there on the other milk train to Steadshall,' the other answered.

The constable knew of the milk train, which ran at midnight from Wivencaster up to Edmundsbury via Burestead Market, carrying full churns of milk, sacks of mail as well as boxes of fish from the Hythe docks: it stopped at Lapperchall Junction, seven miles up the line from Wivencaster, and other stations *en route* to unload or pick up, then ran on to Edmundsbury. Clearly, the man had planned his return home carefully: having completed his 'business,' his intention was simply to walk back to the station, which would take him a good half-hour, catch the midnight train, make the change at Lapperchall, take the Hilvershall train via Steadshall on the second branch line and be home by one in the morning at the latest when the town was quiet.

'It's only ten-thirty now, sir,' the policeman said, putting away his watch. 'You'd have a long wait on a cold platform. The police station is just up here, sir. Would you like to come in for a nice hot cup of cocoa and a warm by the fire for half-an-hour or so? It'd be no bother, none at all.'

'No, no, there's no need. I am quite all right,' the other man protested.

'We have to pass the station, sir – it's on the High Street – so you may as well,' the constable insisted. 'The sergeant won't mind and it'll give me an excuse to nip in for a cup of cocoa, too, won't it?'

There was little the other could do: it was useless to protest: to have done so would only have confirmed the constable's suspicions, which, from the way he was speaking, the man sensed he already had.

They walked on in silence after that, back up the High Street, till just past the town hall, with its high clock tower, the constable turned into a lighted door under a hanging blue lamp. 'In here, sir,' he said, politely allowing the man to go first – or ensuring that he did so.

Inside, a sergeant was standing at the counter writing in an incident book, while behind him a constable, caped and helmeted like the other, was warming himself by a blazing fire preparatory to resuming his beat.

'Oh, who have we here?' the sergeant asked, looking up as the two entered, a frown creasing his forehead.

'The vicar of Steadshall,' said the constable blandly, noticing with satisfaction his companion's startled reaction. 'I've brought him in for a cup of cocoa. He was on his way to North Station when I met him coming along the High Street. I know the buffet there closes at ten, so I thought he'd like a nice cup of cocoa with us while he waits. His train's not till midnight, he says. Is that right, reverend?' He obtained the nod from the startled vicar and turned back to the sergeant. 'If that's all right with you, sergeant?'

'Yes, yes,' said the sergeant hurriedly, lifting the flap at one end of the counter and motioning a red-faced and somewhat downcast Reverend Scrope through. 'It's a pleasure to see you, sir. Come this way and warm yourself by the fire.'

He gave the constable a puzzled look, as if to ask the question: why had he brought the clergyman into the police station at all? But all he got from the constable was a sly smile of satisfaction: he would tell that story later. He had known it was the Reverend Hugo Scrope, vicar of Steadshall, the moment he had spoken to him halfway down the hill, even though he had taken off his clergyman's collar and had wrapped a scarf around the lower part of his face. His sister lived in Steadshall, went to the parish church there and had been married in it three years previously by the very red-faced man standing alongside him – and he had been at the wedding! He knew all about the pompous Reverend Hugo Scrope from what his sister had told him and he had heard enough tales of his doings in the town to note him and remember him.

In the constable's opinion, it did not hurt to let a man like that know he was being taken down a peg or two. After all, he was unlikely to complain, was he? The humiliation had been discreetly done: from the time he had first stepped out of the shadows, he had made no mention of anything untoward which he considered the other might have been – and surely was – contemplating, such as the reason the Reverend Scrope, vicar of Steadshall, was walking up and down an area well known as a place where prostitutes loitered and disappeared with their customers down darkened alleyways.

It was as he was sitting in front of the fire that the vicar sneezed, quite violently, so violently that the constable, who was about to hand him a mug of hot cocoa, held back from doing so lest the recipient spill it all over his knees.

'Oh dear,' said the constable with mock sympathy, 'it seems you have caught a cold, sir. It must have been important business for you to be out and about on such a cold, damp night as this?'

All he received in reply was an unconvincing and mumbled, 'Yes, yes, it was,' which he knew to be a lie...

TWENTY-SEVEN

NOTWITHSTANDING his embarrassing encounter with the police constable in a place he would rather he had not been seen, the Reverend Scrope's visit to the Bishop's palace had not gone well: tea and cakes had been served and the meeting had been quite cordial – till he put his proposition: after that, it had become somewhat cool. The Bishop had refused him any Diocesan money for his two projects, declaring that 'what little monies we have' were needed for missionary work in Africa – which was 'of far more importance than adding an extension to a parochial school.' Any monies the Reverend Scrope required would have to be raised by subscriptions from among his own parishioners: he, the Bishop, could do no more.

Further, his journey home was not helped by the discomfort of a wait in the rain at Lapperchall junction for the train back to Steadshall: for, when he descended from the Edmundsbury milk train, he found the waiting room was locked for the night and he had to stand on the exposed platform for a further twenty minutes till the train to Hilvershall via Steadshall steamed in from a siding. When he alighted at Steadshall, it was raining more heavily still and, as at that hour there was no carrier waiting on the forecourt, he had to walk up the deserted High Street to the vicarage, becoming ever more soaked and angrier and angrier with every step.

It was after one o'clock by the time he banged shut the front door of the vicarage and, in so doing, managed to awaken not only the nursemaid Sarah up in the attic nursery but also the child Elizabeth: Agnes, too, came to her bedroom door to half-open it and watch her brother stamp up the stairs, surprised that he should be returning so late from a meeting with the Bishop: but she said nothing to him because of his clear irritability: instead, she quietly closed her door and returned to her bed to continue reading a book she had purchased in the town that day, *Wuthering Heights,* by Miss Emily Bronte, a tale of secret passions and unrequited love involving a high-spirited, free-roving girl and a mysterious and wild gypsy boy – just the kind of book she loved.

Not unexpectedly after his soaking, by the following morning, the Reverend Scrope was sneezing repeatedly and bemoaning the start of a cold: by the Saturday teatime, he had taken to his bed, suffering from the type of affliction from which men rather than women suffer at times, the same type of affliction which had beset him on several occasions in the past – namely, a severe headache, a fevered brow, aching joints and general lassitude and despair. Then, he had been eternally grateful for the sympathy and ministrations of his dear departed wife to give him relief from it: now he had no one save his sister and she was not one for comforting an ill brother: she had seen too many of his sudden 'illnesses' in the past for that.

However, this time even she had to accept that the symptoms – aches and pains, fever and bouts of violent sneezing – were genuine: as a consequence, she had to hurry round to the Reverend Smallwood's lodgings along the Siblingham road that same evening with the news of her brother's 'worsening condition' and ask the curate if he would take Holy Communion and Evensong at St. Andrew's on the morrow as the vicar was in no fit state to take either. It meant, of course, that the Reverend Smallwood had to send a hurried note over to the sexton at Bourne Brook to cancel the morning service in his own little church there, for which, in his opinion, he had written one of his best sermons, from the *Book of James*, chapter one, verses fourteen and fifteen: '...*But every man is tempted, when he is drawn away of his own lust, and enticed...Then when lust hath conceived, it bringeth forth sin: and sin, when it is finished, bringeth forth death...*'

Indeed, so stricken was the Reverend Scrope by the Sunday morning that she sent Sarah the nursemaid to take his breakfast up to him on a tray before setting off for church herself: it was while the young nursemaid was there that the prostrate vicar persuaded her to return, once she had put Elizabeth down for her morning nap, and to sit beside his bed and read to him from the Bible so that he might remain in God's good graces while he lay 'dying,' especially as the church bells were tolling and he felt guilty that he was unable to join his parishioners in their devotions. In his terrible affliction, she even allowed him to reach out and to take her hand for comfort.

It was a blow to the Reverend Scrope that he had to remain abed, for that morning he had intended to make another appeal for more subscriptions to the school building fund: so far, he had received pledges amounting to just over a hundred and sixty pounds when he would have hoped for far more by then, having set an example himself with his own generous donation of forty-five pounds. The two Misses Iseley had promised thirty pounds jointly when he would have hoped that the wealthy spinsters would have pledged that amount each, while a further thirty pounds apiece had come from Dr. Iveson and Dr. Langham. The various smaller contributions had only trickled in, however, amounting thus far to only twenty-five pounds in all, which was hugely disappointing.

It was enough to pay an architect to draw up the plans for each of the projects and, once passed by the Department of Education, for the foundations for the extension at Steadshall to be dug, the concrete footings poured and perhaps even for the first few rows of bricks to be laid, but not much else, certainly not enough for the floor boards to be laid, the roof beams to be raised, the tiles nailed into place and the windows put in and glazed! Nor would there be any left over to purchase so much as a square yard of the meadow beside the church at Bourne Brook on which to build a new school there, which a farmer had offered to sell them at a reduced rate per acre since it was pretty much boggy ground, anyway, and not of much use to him and he would be well shot of it.

The 'final notice' ultimatum from the Department of Education in London, ordering that accommodation be found in the parochial school for a eighty-five children of the town and the adjoining hamlet, due to start school in the September, or a School Board would be formed, had come as a thunderbolt to the Reverend Scrope. Despite it, he still earnestly believed a School Board could be averted if his parishioners all 'pulled together,' as he had told Walter Crowfoot.

'I shall pray to God. The Good Lord will find a way,' he added.

So what he did not want was to lose from his congregation one of the several people from whom he still hoped to elicit a substantial subscription towards the building fund, at least fifty pounds, perhaps even a hundred, and to lose that goodwill over a trivial incident involving the new schoolmaster and his wife simply because he was in bed with 'influenza' and unable to deal with it...

TWENTY-EIGHT

WHAT HAPPENED he learned later from an abject Walter Crowfoot: just before the bells finished ringing, at about five minutes to eleven, William and Martha entered the church, smiled and nodded politely to anyone who took any notice of them, looked about them and, seeing an empty pew in the body of the church with a good view into the chancel which they recalled was always vacant, they entered it rather than going to a side pew as they had done previously. And, as was their habit whenever they went to church, before taking their seats, they knelt on the hard footrest which ran the length of the pew, closed their eyes, put their hands together and began whispering a short prayer, shaming several around them who did not bother to do such things.

They were still kneeling, with their eyes closed and their heads bowed, when a farmer named John Gardiner, the largest occupier of land in the parish, who employed fifteen of the town's men and nine of its boys on his sixteen hundred and sixty acres along the Burestead Market road, came down the aisle with his wife and two daughters, stared hard at the two in the pew for a few seconds, made a loud harrumphing noise deep in his throat and strode on into the chancel. His arrival caused something of a stir, for, having been visiting relatives on the South Coast, he had not been seen in the church for six weeks.

The curate and the choir at that moment were still in the bell tower enrobing and so had still not properly formed up into a procession: the cross-bearer, Samuel Gough, was ready at the front, the candle holders behind him were in their places and the lead chorister was waiting behind them, but the choirboys were not yet ready and neither was the curate: he was still pulling his vestments over his head and trying to find the sleeve hole for his arm. Nor would he be ready to take his place at the rear of the procession when he had done that because he would still need to find his prayer book, which one of the choirboys had hidden under a cassock lying folded on a chair. The five choirboys were smiling slyly to themselves at the hapless clergyman, while in the chancel Walter Crowfoot was laying hymn books on the choir stalls, opening each at the first hymn number: all was normal, in fact.

As Walter Crowfoot told it to the vicar: 'Mr. Gardiner came to me very excitedly in the chancel before the service began and asked me to remove Mr. Warburton and his wife because they were sitting on his bench. I said, "I cannot interfere" and he said, "You must, you are the churchwarden, it is your duty to interfere." When I refused him a second time, he said I ought to be ashamed of myself to behave in what he said was such a disgraceful manner. It was most embarrassing for me, as it was spoken loudly and I am sure that half the congregation heard him.'

William was only alerted to the argument when, unexpectedly, he heard himself being referred to as 'that skinny, lanky, damned fellow there, sitting with that dark-haired woman': looking up, he saw the farmer pointing directly at him, though he was unable to hear exactly what was being said because of the chatter of others around him and the clatter of steel-tipped boots and shoes on the aisle flagstones as the last of the latecomers scurried to their places.

Whatever, the farmer was saying, the warden appeared unwilling to agree with him, for he was shaking his head and shrugging his shoulders. The next thing William and Martha knew was that the farmer, red faced and seething with anger, was standing at the entrance to the pew, glaring down at them both.

Farmer Gardiner was known for his irascibility and now he displayed it. 'You, sir,' he said, loud enough for all the church to hear, 'you may consider yourself a gentleman, but to me and my family you have proved yourself a low blackguard!'

William, not knowing why he was being spoken to in such a fashion by a man he had not seen before, replied quietly, his words laden with sarcasm: 'Thank you for the compliment, sir,' he said, giving a mocking bow of the head.

'It was no compliment, far from it,' the farmer snorted, not understanding the sarcasm of the other. 'I repeat, sir, you are a blackguard! Are you aware, you are sitting in my pew, the pew assigned to me and my family by the Bishop himself?'

Out of the corner of his eye, William became aware of a woman in her late thirties and two girls of about fifteen and sixteen years hovering nearby in the aisle.

'Are you asking us to leave, sir?' William's question was politely put, but a keen listener would have noted a certain resolve within it.

'I am,' the farmer said as loudly as before. 'My wife and children are here with me and we are waiting to enter *our* pew. You and your lady are sitting in *our* places. You will have to move – both of you.'

'Really?' said the schoolmaster, raising one eyebrow in feigned surprise. 'I am not preventing you or your good lady or your two daughters from sitting down. There is plenty of room in the pew for all of us, is there not?'

As he said it, William rose to his feet as if to motion Martha to move farther along the bench and make room for the farmer and his family: but John Gardiner was having none of it.

'I repeat,' he said, jutting out his jaw and looking about him to ensure that there were witnesses to his 'rightful' claim, 'you are sitting in *my family's* pew. Be so good as to find yourself somewhere else to sit and be quick about it. If you do not move, I will say it again: you are a blackguard, sir! A blackguard!'

'Then a blackguard I am,' said William, amused as much by the man's use of such an old-fashioned expression as his growing temper, 'for I am not moving – not for an ill-tempered man like yourself. If you do not wish to sit with us, there are empty seats elsewhere.'

The farmer did not share his amusement. Turning to the quietly sniggering congregation, as if hoping to appeal to them for support against the injustice being perpetrated against him, he announced: 'This is an insult. This is my family's pew. We have always sat here. It was assigned to me by the Bishop.' And when no support came from them, he turned back to William: 'What have I done that you should insult me by taking my pew?'

'You have done nothing, sir,' William replied calmly. 'I do not even know you. When I came this morning, it was not my intention to argue with you or anyone. I have come to church with my good wife to pray, not to engage in argument. We sat here solely because the pew was empty and the service was about to start. I shall not turn out of it to suit you.'

There was a choking sound in the farmer's throat as William went on calmly, aware that the whole church had gone quiet. 'I will tell you, sir, I would willingly have moved if you had asked me politely,' he said, 'but, since you have been so ungentlemanly as to attempt to turn out my wife and I in an angry manner, I refuse to move. I shall sit where I like and, if I choose to sit in this seat again, then I shall do so

– I will sit here for the service today and for the service next week and every Sunday after that if I feel like doing so.'

'I will go to the law if you do, sir,' the red-faced farmer declared.

'If you go to law, sir, I warn you I shall defend myself,' was William's answer. 'If you take it up, I will spend what I have got upon it. I will not be put out of a church pew by the likes of you.'

'Very well, I shall instruct my solicitor.'

'You may do what you like.'

'I say again, you are a blackguard!'

'You are no gentleman yourself.'

It was then that Farmer Gardiner decided that force was better than argument: and, without warning, he stepped into the pew, seized hold of William's coat collar and, ignoring the cries of alarm from both Martha and his own wife, attempted to pull him from the pew. Like many a man who did manual labour when it was necessary to do it, he was strong and was succeeding till William – while attempting to regain his feet, he would say – accidentally jabbed his knee high up on Farmer Gardiner's thigh. The heavier man let out a gasp of pain, doubled over and, momentarily loosened his grip: it was enough for the younger schoolmaster to shrug off the hold on his lapels and, with one hard push, to send the farmer stumbling backwards into the aisle, where he sat down with a hard bump, right in front of his horrified wife and daughters, and much to the amusement of the astonished congregation.

His face flushed with fury, Farmer Gardiner would have made a second attempt had his wife not screeched at him to stop and to remember where he was. Then, watched by the open-mouthed townsfolk, he angrily barked at his wife and children, 'We're leaving!' turned on his heel and stormed out of the church. According to those of three score years and ten, there had not been a brawl in the church in living memory, probably not even for three score years and ten before that – if ever…

Only the appearance of the cross-bearer, the candleholders and the choir, walking in procession down the same aisle to the chancel, with the curate in their wake, subdued the buzz of conversation going on all round the schoolmaster, whose wife was looking as mortified at her husband's conduct as had been the farmer's wife at her husband's.

Not much attention was paid to the curate that morning as at any moment the congregation expected – some even hoped – that Farmer Gardiner would come storming back into the church again and demand that the new schoolmaster either move or be thrown out: it would have been infinitely more interesting than the dull sermon the curate was preaching at them about 'temptation and lust,' as they doubted he knew much about either.

Both William and Martha were conscious of the fact that, all through the singing, Miss Dunsmore repeatedly turned to look at them: she was seated in her usual place at the organ and was clearly much amused to have witnessed her superior brawling in church in front of 'half the town.' Many in the congregation were the mothers and fathers of the children who went to his school and so would look to him to set an example of good manners to their offspring. What had happened would be the talk of the town for some time to come and, better still in Helen Dunsmore's opinion, when the Reverend Scrope rose from his sickbed and heard of it, it would be a huge black mark against the officious William Warburton...

TWENTY-NINE

AFTER THE SERVICE, feeling embarrassed and marked out by the whole incident, since everyone in the church had been looking at him, William sought out Walter Crowfoot to ask: 'I understood that pews were not assigned to anyone?'

'They are not,' the vicar's warden confirmed, before adding after a pause: ' – except that one.'

'As a point of law,' he went on, 'I do not know whether I have the authority to put up such a notice, but it was the vicar's desire that that particular bench should be appropriated to Mr. Gardiner in consequence of a communication he received from the Bishop. The sole condition, as I was told it, was that Mr. Gardiner and his family had to be in their places before the commencement of divine service – ' There was a second pause before he added, as if not wanting to fall out with the schoolmaster: ' – which they were not.'

It was enough to placate William, but would not have done for the farmer. Late or early, that was his family's pew and everyone knew it, 'including your good self,' he wrote in a letter to the vicar, delivered by hand the next day by one of his boy workers. 'And, if I say the schoolmaster is a blackguard, then a blackguard he is!' he added for good measure.

The letter went on in a similar vein, a diatribe against William, demanding that his intrusion into the seating assigned to him by order of the Bishop be 'curtailed forthwith' or he would not set foot in the church again, and demanding, too, that Walter Crowfoot, as a churchwarden, be in his place the following Sunday to ensure that the seats were not filled before the proper time 'to my exclusion.'

'If the person occupying my seat wishes to come to our church, there is plenty of room for him and his wife to sit elsewhere,' Farmer Gardiner said. Worse for the Reverend Scrope, he went on to state that he had considered the vicar's request for a donation towards the school building fund, which had been sent to him on his return, and he was 'pleased to donate the sum of five pounds,' but was unable to donate more at that particular time because certain expenditures were required about the farm and he must conserve his money. It was far from the fifty pounds for which the Reverend Scrope had hoped, indeed, on which he had counted, or the hundred of which he had dreamed.

It was a somewhat angered vicar, his illness having abated, who swept into the school on the Wednesday morning and confronted William amid the same clattering of desk lids and shuffling of feet as the children hurriedly stood to attention again.

'I have to tell you, Mr. Warburton, I am most disappointed in you, most disappointed,' the Reverend Scrope began, almost before he was through the curtain. 'Everything is most unfortunate, most unfortunate. I have received a letter from Mr. Gardiner regarding the matter of the disagreement in church last Sunday in which you and he were involved. He says you have expressed an intention to repeat your conduct next week. I would very much prefer it, sir, if you did not. I have to tell you that Mr. Gardiner is the largest occupier in the parish and had applied to the churchwardens and to the Bishop for church accommodation and that pew has been appropriated to him and his family. He is, I well know, a blustering type of fellow and his conduct was inexcusable, but, from his point of view, what he saw was a stranger in possession of *his* pew. He saw it as an insult to himself, his wife and the young ladies who were with him that you should refuse to let him have his seat when he asked and when, according to others, there were unoccupied seats close by.'

'I did not take possession of the pew for the express purpose of annoying Mr. Gardiner,' William replied. 'I did not know him before I entered the church and neither did I know that it was his pew. I offered to share it with him and his wife and daughters. What more could I have done? I was given to understand that there are no appropriated seats in the parish church and I acted accordingly, having sat in it with my wife before he arrived. Would you not have done the same if you had been in my place?'

The Reverend Scrope, of course, would never have done such a thing. 'I should have apologised and moved and not stated that I intended to intrude upon Mr. Gardiner's pew whenever I liked, as I understand you did,' he answered William. 'That was foolish of you, if I may say so, sir? It only stirred the man up even more. He is not used to being thwarted.'

'Neither am I, sir.'

'I understand everything that you say, Mr. Warburton. You were not to know that that pew has been allocated to Mr. Gardiner and his family by my express wish, sanctioned by the Bishop. Therefore, I should be grateful, if, when you attend church next Sunday, you and your good lady would kindly sit somewhere else. I will see to it that Mr. Crowfoot knows of your wishes and I shall instruct him to find you a pew as befits your position in the community – to the front of the nave, obviously.'

'Obviously,' said the schoolmaster, acquiescing with a sigh. 'I am sorry to have put you to so much trouble, Vicar. Not having been here long, it was not my intention – '

'Think no more of it, sir,' the Reverend Scrope interrupted, waving one hand dismissively. 'It was an unfortunate misunderstanding, no more than that...'

It was still a misunderstanding which had cost him a substantial subscription towards his building fund – an amount which, to his chagrin, was unlikely to be forthcoming even after the matter of the appropriated pew had been settled. Quite frankly, he blamed the schoolmaster's impetuosity for the disaster, though he did not say so: it was another black mark against him – another black mark to add to the business of the Sunday school and the infernal letter he had written about 'deficiencies' at the school. Goodness gracious! Then was not the time to worry about so-called deficiencies at the parochial school when the Department of Education was breathing down his neck.

Come the following Sunday and William and Martha found themselves put across the aisle by the churchwarden, in 'reserved seats,' one row behind Farmer Gardiner and his wife and daughters, so that only by turning his head could the farmer look back at them, which he did just the once, smugly eyeing the schoolmaster, savouring his victory for 'common sense.' He quickly turned back to the front, red-faced and angry, when the schoolmaster did something which, out of the corner of his eye, he had seen his pupils do on occasion, particularly if he were walking away from them after giving them a scolding and they thought they could not be seen. What William did, however, he did in open view to the farmer: he stuck out his tongue at him.

On the following Tuesday, he had another visitor at the school and, though William instructed the pupils of his two standards to rise as usual at his entrance, he noticed that Miss Dunsmore did not bother to instruct hers, merely shouting loudly, 'Get on with your work!' when heads lifted to look at the newcomer. This time, it was the somewhat red-faced curate who pushed aside the curtain.

He had come on a special errand, he said, concerning some pupils who sang in the church choir: he was to conduct a funeral service the following day and the relatives of the dear departed had specifically requested that a dozen of the school's older children sing as a choir during the service to send the deceased 'on his way to heaven happy,' as he had always loved to hear children sing. The children had done it several times before under the previous master, the curate said in a wheedling tone, as if expecting William might refuse, and they were quite happy to do it again since each was paid tuppence for their time. Would he kindly allow them to do it again as he did not want to fall foul of the Reverend Scrope and, also, could Miss Dunsmore kindly be excused for the afternoon, too, as she usually conducted the choir at such events while someone else played the organ?

'The vicar expects it,' the Reverend Smallwood added, as if that were all that was required, 'and I darest not go against him. Miss Dunsmore is quite willing. It will not take more than an hour. If you would be so obliging…?'

William was not at all happy that a dozen of the older children should be taken out of school at the whim of the Reverend Scrope: he was already missing seven of the older boys from Bourne Brook. 'They did not come to school yesterday and are missing again today,' he told the curate. 'I have to ask whether you know anything about it, Mr. Smallwood?'

'Oh, that will be for the start of the rhubarb-pulling,' the curate nonchalantly replied. 'Monday and yesterday were both fine days after the rain at the weekend so they will all be helping with the pulling, the same as today. The older Bourne Brook boys always take a few days off school at this time of the year to help out on the farms there. The vicar knows. The women pull the rhubarb and the boys help to cut off the poisonous leaves and bundle-up the stems. It is more work for boys and women than for men, I am told. I am afraid the farmers at Bourne Brook rather insist on the older boys helping them. We cannot go against them. After all, there are four farmers on the school management board so we must all help each other, must we not? And Bourne Brook rhubarb is quite a delicacy in London.'

'In my opinion, those children should be in school, learning, not pulling rhubarb in some farmer's field,' William retorted. 'Such things ought not to be tolerated and will not be tolerated by me in future. I will allow it this time, but I ask you to kindly inform the vicar that, in future, I shall expect all children who should be in school to be in school and not working in a field somewhere!'

'I am afraid that will do no good,' the curate replied, his face reddening a little. 'The vicar has already agreed to it – as the chairman of the management board, that is. If the fine weather holds, they should be back in school on Monday. It generally takes only a week.'

Having confirmed something which William had already been told by the other pupils and which he had not wanted to believe, the curate departed, leaving behind him a schoolmaster in some despair vowing that he would put a stop to such callous practices…

THIRTY

HE GOT HIS CHANCE one week later. On the very day that the first group of absentees returned, a second similar incident occurred, which served only to heighten the tension between William and the Reverend Scrope, not to mention the four farmers who served as school managers.

While the children were playing in the yard during the mid-morning break, a farmer strode through the gate, pointed at four of the older boys whose fathers he employed and, with a jerk of the thumb and a curt 'You four, you're needed in the hayfield,' he ordered them out on to the road where his trap was waiting.

The farmer just happened to be Charles Higgs, of Sloe House farm, one of the school's managers, so Miss Dunsmore, who was outside supervising the children, made no move to stop him.

Such happenings were normal in small towns and villages from which farmers drew their workers: farmers needing short-term labour – a week of picking gooseberries or strawberries, say, or three or four days helping with the hay-turning – often walked into a schoolyard and took out boys to help them with whatever job of work needed extra hands: and the boys always went, especially if the farmer employed their fathers or their brothers: they dared not refuse.

William was inside the schoolroom at the time and so did not know what was happening outside till the rest of standard six filed back inside. Tellingly, when they were all seated, four of the desks were empty.

'Where are Billy Foulkes, Henry Sayers, Thomas Cudmore and Charles Horner?' William asked, thinking perhaps that they had sneaked off somewhere.

The other boys all looked at each other: none of them wanted to tell. 'Farmer Higgs has taken 'em out to go haymaking, sir,' one of the girls said eventually.

'Has he by God! Well, we'll see about that,' declared William fiercely, incensed that, because a farmer was one of the school's managers, he thought he could simply walk into the school and call out four of his boys to work as cheap labour.

'Did you know of this, Miss Dunsmore?' he asked, grim-faced, pulling on his coat and jamming his hat down upon his head.

'Farmer Higgs has always done it,' she replied, unconcerned, indeed surprised that he did not know of such happenings and surprised, too, that he seemed to be upset by it. 'Most of the farmers do it at sometime or other in the country.'

'Well, those days are over,' William declared, brushing past her, angered as much by her attitude as he was by the farmer's attitude.

By rights, he knew that he ought first to call on Walter Crowfoot, who as the nominated attendance officer was hired to chase down absentees: for, as far as William was concerned, by taking the four boys out of school without his permission, the farmer had turned them into 'absentees' – absconders even. The churchwarden was supposed to call in at the school regularly each week to receive a list of those not at school, then visit their homes to find out why. As such, he was paid so much per head for their return: but he had not called at the school once since William and Martha had begun there and more than likely, William thought, he would be in sympathy with the farmer, anyway, and thus unlikely to carry out his mission, particularly if the farmer slipped him a few coins to turn a blind eye. No, William decided, it would be better to do it himself.

He delayed only long enough to ask Martha to take over the temporary teaching of his pupils in standards five and six and to direct Hannah Hodgson and the two monitors to look after the smaller children, then he was striding determinedly down the High Street, over the bridge at the bottom, up Mount Hill and out along the Bromptree road towards Sloe Hill farm, which lay a good two miles from the town.

The boys had been gone for at least a quarter-of-an-hour before William had learned of their disappearance and it took him almost three-quarters-of-an-half-hour of fast walking to reach Sloe House farm, for he twice had to pause to mop his brow in the broiling early summer heat so that, by the time he found the field in which they were working, down a long, pot-holed track, they were already raking at the hay which a team of other workers had cut as they passed down the field. Hay-raking was steady, monotonous work, the movements being repetitive and rhythmic, and, when doing it, one can fall into something of an unthinking trance: so when William first saw the four boys, it was difficult to tell whether they were disconsolate at being taken out of school and forced to work or pleased. They all looked up guiltily, however, when they heard his first shout.

'You four,' he cried on his approach, 'back to school this instant! Put down those rakes and get back to school, all four of you! You do not have my permission to leave school when you think you will.'

As was to be expected, the four boys hesitated, unsure whether they ought to obey their schoolmaster, whom they liked and feared a little, or the farmer, whom they disliked intensely but feared far more and who, after all, employed their fathers and, for two of them, their older brothers as well.

'Farmer Higgs took us out,' said Thomas Cudmore, a little plaintively, as if to excuse the fact that they had followed the farmer out of school without protest. 'He usually does at this time of the year. We worked for him last year and the year before.'

'I don't care how many years you have worked for him, you will not do it any more,' William ordered them, 'not while you should be in school. Farmer Higgs has no right to recruit you as cheap labour. Your place is in the classroom, learning, not out here turning hay.'

'It's money and it means we're earning,' said Billy Foulkes, a little grumpily, shrugging, as if to say, having made the move, he would rather be left as he was and it would be too much of an imposition to be forced back to school.

William knew what he meant and sympathised – up to a point: the four boys were indeed earning money, much needed money for their families, and the work they were doing was the very same work they would go to in time, perhaps in only a few months if they obtained their leaving certificates, but he still could not allow it.

Their expectations in life may be, as the vicar had chillingly told William, so limited that they viewed having to sit in a classroom from nine till four-thirty for five days a week as something of a chore, to be endured till they obtained their release, rather than seeing it as a hopeful pathway to something better, something beyond their narrow experience. Their prospect was simply to idle their way through school, then follow their brothers, fathers and grandfathers on to the land.

'You may be earning,' William snapped back, annoyed by the boy's indifference to his prospects, 'but at the moment getting an education is more important than tossing hay for some farmer. You need an education if you are ever going to be able to achieve anything.'

'You don't need an education to do farm work,' Thomas Cudmore scoffed back.

It was an argument to be expected, though he was surprised it had come from Thomas Cudmore, one of his brighter scholars, a boy with hope, in William's eyes, of achieving something better than farm-labouring all his life, even if it were only a clerking job somewhere. To him, the boy's attitude was out-and-out defeatism.

'You need an education so that you don't have to become a farm worker,' William told him tersely and, crossing to him, he seized his hay rake and threw it to the ground. 'Good God, boy! There is more to life than becoming a farm worker! If you can read books and write sentences, count and multiply and divide and do long division and fractions – the kinds of things you are learning with me – you don't have to settle for being just a farm worker all your life! Where is your ambition, boy? Is that the highest you can aspire to – working on the land?'

The boys seemed to be embarrassed by the schoolmaster's passion and looked sheepishly at each other, as if unable to think what to say next, their argument already exhausted. One by one, reluctantly, it appeared to William, the other three dropped their rakes rather than have them snatched from their grasp, walked back to where they had left their jackets and began pulling them on. William followed, ushering them towards the gate.

While all this had been going on, Farmer Higgs had been in the far corner of the same field, directing the his men: now, seeing William addressing the boys and seeing them pause in their work, then drop their rakes and start to walk off, he went running across the field to them.

'What the hell is going on here?' he demanded. 'These boys are here to work.'

'These boys are going back to school,' William countered, continuing to usher the four towards the gate. 'I am their schoolmaster and they obey me.'

'The hell they do!' shouted the farmer. 'Those lads work for me, it's haymaking time! You're not taking my lads off.'

'I am,' retorted William, positioning himself between the boys and the farmer. 'I don't care whether it is haymaking time or harvest time, these boys will be in school learning and not in your field working as cheap labour. That is the law and you know it!'

Without waiting for the farmer to reply or make a further protest, he gave Thomas Cudmore and Henry Sayers a hard push to ensure they kept moving.

'You've got a damned nerve, schoolteacher!' the farmer exploded. 'How am I supposed to get my hay in on time? They're here to turn it to dry it before we cart it. I need them. There's a good three days' work here for them. Damn the law, I say! What if the weather breaks?'

It was an opportunity which William did not want to miss and he took advantage of it. Slowly, almost with a studied indifference, he turned, eyed Farmer Higgs for a second or two, then said quite calmly: 'I suppose you will have to do it yourself, Mr. Higgs, you and your men. I am sure your men would be more than glad to get your hay harvest in on time before the weather breaks were you to pay them a little more than the measly pittance I am told you do pay them.'

The farmer could only blaze at the schoolmaster's insolence: fancy it, a schoolmaster telling him – a farmer for twenty years, one of the parochial school managers no less – how to run his farm! The damned cheek of the man! But by then, William was thirty yards up the track and all Farmer Higgs could do was to stare angrily after the retreating boys. With cheap labour available – or once having been available – at the parochial school, the schoolmaster's suggestion smacked of socialism to him: to pay his men more would set a precedent and the other farmers would not thank him for it, not when there was cheap child labour not a mile off sitting in the parochial school's classrooms, by God!

'You'll hear more of this,' he shouted after William. 'I'm one of the school managers. I'll have words with the vicar...'

'I have no doubt you will,' was William's last thought as he followed the four grinning boys out on to the main road.

It was all great fun for them, to hear their school master taking on one of the farmers – something to tell their friends about at dinnertime...

THIRTY-ONE

WHEN THE REVEREND Scrope swept into the school for a third time the very next morning, William was expecting him and so was neither surprised nor disconcerted by the rapidity of his visit. He guessed that the vicar had come in response to his confrontation with Farmer Higgs and that his intention was to reprimand him in some way: and he had no intention of allowing him to do that.

Trailing in the vicar's wake and looking even more apprehensive than usual, as if he wished everyone to know that he had been forced into accompanying his superior, was the Reverend Smallwood. Briefly, as the two men appeared through the curtain, he caught William's eye as he stood by the blackboard and gave a wearied shrug, as if to say he had tried to talk his vicar out of coming, but had failed miserably.

'A word with you again, Mr. Warburton,' the Reverend Scrope said brusquely, still paying no heed to the scholars who had all hurriedly risen yet again to chant their 'Good morning, Vicar' to him. On the other side of the half-drawn curtain, William saw Miss Dunsmore smirking to herself: she had guessed what was about to happen and was delighting in it.

'One moment, vicar,' William said and pointedly went across and closed the curtain to the wall before returning to the blackboard: it was a futile gesture really, for, though Miss Dunsmore would not be able to see, she would, of course, be able to hear and it was noticeable that during the length of the exchange which followed, silence descended in the other half of the room: indeed, the only sound to come over the top of the curtain was that of a single slap as some child suffered Miss Dunsmore's annoyance for moving and making a noise as they did it.

'I have received a complaint from Mr. Higgs, of Sloe House farm,' the vicar began, eyeing William closely, as if hoping perhaps he would admit at the outset to having made an error of judgment, seek his forgiveness and so spare him having to issue his admonishment.

'He informs me that you prevented him from taking four boys out of school yesterday to help him with his hay harvest.'

'I did not *prevent* him,' was William's calm answer. 'He took the boys without my permission and I brought them back. I do not expect and nor shall I ever allow any farmer, even if he is a school manager, to walk into any schoolyard where I am the master and take away boys to go labouring on their farms. These boys are *my* pupils, they are not serfs.'

The scholars of standards five and six, realising that, before their very eyes, a row was developing between the vicar and their master, raised their heads from their work to smirk at each other.

'You are a town person, are you not, Mr. Warburton?' the vicar went on, the condescension in his voice clearly apparent. 'Perhaps you do not understand how important haymaking is for the farmers of this region. They depend upon it to feed their livestock – their cattle and their sheep and their horses. It is imperative, when there is a break in the weather and we have several fine days together, as of now, that they get in the hay harvest. The older boys have always helped with the hay harvest at this time of the year. It is a fact of school life, of country life.'

'I fully understand the need to get in the hay harvest during periods of fine weather, Vicar, such as now,' William answered him, still maintaining his politeness of manner, 'and I fully understand, too, its importance in the farming calendar. But these boys are scholars. They are here to learn, to be educated as best I can educate them. They are not a pool of cheap labour for any farmer who finds that he is short-handed and wants them to do a few days' work for him.'

'But it is good experience for them,' the vicar protested, the extent of his irritation at William's unexpected intransigence beginning to show. 'Next year, all four of the boys will most probably be doing the very work you sought to prevent them from doing yesterday. They are paid for their time – a shilling or two shillings per week, not much, I grant you, but it all helps their families put the daily bread upon their tables. The people of this town are poor enough without you denying their sons the chance to earn a little extra. The managers have always sanctioned it. We see no harm in it. It is a fact of life.'

'It has not escaped my notice,' William said quietly, 'that four of this school's mangers are farmers themselves and so are bound to agree to such practices. Indeed, I should not be surprised if that is the very reason they serve on the management board – to look after their own interests. What I fail to understand – something I find quite deplorable and quite wrong – is that you, the vicar of this parish, should readily acquiesce to it, indeed, that you should encourage it.'

The vicar was more than exasperated now, he was growing angry. 'It is you who are wrong in encouraging these children – these boys – to imagine possibilities that are well outside the horizons of their limited hopes. Following their brothers and their fathers on to the land is all they have ever done. It is all that is expected of them. That is all they expect of themselves. It is the sum total of their existence – '

'My answer to that,' William declared, his anger also rising, 'remains the same as I gave you before. I say that, if a boy can read the kinds of books I intend he shall read, if he can write good sentences in a more than legible hand, if he can count and multiply and divide and do long division and understand fractions, if he knows the capital cities of Europe and, indeed the whole Empire – if he knows all of those things and much else besides – the kinds of things I hope they will learn here with me – then I say he is justified, in my opinion, in setting his sights higher if he so wishes. You, of all people, should be encouraging the children of this school to broaden their horizons rather than willing them to settle for what they have – for what they have always had.'

'How dare you, sir! You overstep yourself,' the vicar retorted, clearly affronted. 'Kindly remember that I am your employer. I do not need to be instructed on my duties on this earth by anyone. I look to the good Lord for that. His word and no other's is my guide. Your task, I will tell you, is to teach the children of this school to read and to write and to count well enough whereby they may receive a leaving certificate and be allowed to begin their working lives, as God intended they should. That is all we ask of you. Goodness gracious what do you wish to make of them – clerks and schoolmasters like yourself?'

The tone was scoffing and William was determined to put the man down, vicar or not, his employer or not – because he considered him wrong! 'Why not? Why should a boy not become a clerk in a business office if he has the intelligence for it?' he demanded. 'Why should he not become a schoolmaster, too, or even a priest, a man of the cloth, like yourself? The boys I teach I hope will go on to better things – some at least – anything other than standing out in the wind and the rain doing farm work for the rest of their lives, trudging behind a horse and a plough till they are too old and too worn down to continue and find themselves in the very workhouse not a half-mile from here along the Siblingham road where the grandfathers and grandmothers of many of them now reside. Why not?'

The Reverend Scrope was not really listening: William's last remark had simply brought a contemptuous smile to his lips. 'The country needs farm labourers, Mr. Warburton,' he said, a little wearily, as if he thought William were unaware of so salient a fact. 'We should have no food if it were not for them. Did you not think of that? The country would starve. Just as some men must work in factories all their working lives, some men in mines and others as fishermen who must daily brave the perils of the sea, so others must labour on the land. It is God's ordering of things – His hand in everything. These boys will, in future, provide the very food you and I eat to keep ourselves alive and keep this nation fed. That is why I find your argument so misdirected, Mr. Warburton, so foolish, so unnecessary.'

With that, he gave a curt command to his curate, who had remained silent, though apprehensive, throughout and the two of them left: he had said what he had gone there to say and he was satisfied that he had inflicted a suitable chastisement on the presumptuous schoolmaster.

The one concession he made as he walked away was to turn at the curtain to say: 'You will hear no more of this from me, Mr. Warburton. Now that I have spoken, it is an end to the matter. If you are so set against the boys in your charge helping the farmers of the district with the hay harvest, then so be it – none will be taken from you. They will remain in school as you wish them to do. I have told Farmer Higgs that and I have no doubt the matter will be discussed at the next school managers' meeting.'

William allowed himself a smile, especially when he pulled back the curtain again and saw the sour look on Miss Dunsmore's face as she realised it was the vicar who had given in: for all his bluster, he had been the one.

William was still smiling to himself as a worried Martha came through the curtain: she had heard the raised voice of the vicar and had feared that her husband was about to say something – or perhaps even do something – which he might regret: she was relieved, however, to see that he was smiling to himself.

'A small victory for us,' he said, his smile broadening at the memory of what had just occurred. 'I think it is time, Martha, that we changed a few other things round here!'

Which he did the very next day, exacerbating an already fraught situation at the school when he revealed those changes…

THIRTY-TWO

UNDER PREVIOUS masters, including Joseph Padwick, the scholars of standards three to six had customarily read passages from the Old Testament Books or from the New Testament Gospels for at least an hour each day as their reading practice: and only occasionally was that bane of their lives lightened by reading from another book. As much as William would have liked to have abolished the use of the Bible altogether, he felt he could not yet do so entirely: it would have been too drastic a measure so soon after his arrival: so he had allowed Miss Dunsmore some leeway on the matter and she had continued to use the Bible extensively – solely, in fact – whether out of laziness or a belief that the Bible and only the Bible should be read in a parochial church school he was not sure.

He could, however, improve the children's interest in reading by every now and again substituting the Bible-reading 'for something far more interesting to them,' as he said in discussing it with Martha. Several years previously, he had come across a story which had been serialised in the *Young Folks* magazine and he had purchased the various copies for just such a purpose: though a little dog-eared, as he had used them extensively at Stepney, they were still quite useable.

For his own use, he had purchased the same story in book form three years previously. It was a tale by a certain 'Captain George North' entitled *Treasure Island or The Mutiny of the Hispaniola*. His pupils' interest, he noted, had perked up from the moment they began reading from it and the narrator, one 'young Jim Hawkins,' began his tale: it increased as the pirates 'Black Dog' and then 'Blind Pew' appeared at the 'Admiral Benbow Inn' to give the old drunken seaman 'Billy Bones' the dreaded 'black spot,' for this was a story to grip their imagination. He also noted the jealousy which spread among the lower standards when they heard of it, particularly among the boys. Now was the time to make a further change, a more far-reaching change, he decided, and he was under no illusions that it would be a contentious one, too.

That day he had asked Martha to bring her copy of Charles Kingsley's *The Water Babies*, which he wanted the children of Miss Dunsmore's two standards to begin reading as a relief from their interminable Bible-reading: the book, though subtitled by its author as *A Fairy Tale For a Land Baby,* was, he well knew, a story rich in moral lessons and religious parallels which he hoped the children of Miss Dunsmore's two standards might appreciate more readily than the fire and brimstone of the *Book of Isaiah* or the two *Books of Samuel.*

'I do not see any value in children being forced to intone long, meaningless passages from the Bible and attempting to pronounce words half of which are no longer in common use and most of which they do not understand, anyway,' he explained at a dinnertime meeting with his assistant, Martha and Hannah Hodgson. 'From now on, there will be less reading from the Bible – from now on, the children will also read from proper books, which Martha and I will provide.'

There was an audible intake of breath from Helen Dunsmore: she appeared to be visibly shocked and outraged. 'You cannot do that,' she declared. 'The vicar will not like it. One of the founding principles of this school is that the children are educated thoroughly on the religion of the Church of England. The Reverend Scrope will not allow it, I am sure. I shall tell him the first chance I get. You have no right – no right at all. We cannot abandon the Bible.'

'I have every right because I am the senior master here,' William asserted, determined to put his assistant in her place. 'This may be a Church school, but we do not have to use *only* the Bible – there are other books. I want to interest the children in reading those, not kill their interest altogether by making them read long, dreary passages from the Old Testament. The children need to be educated better than they have been and reading proper books is one way to do it.'

Miss Dunsmore immediately took his comment as a personal affront. 'Are you saying that the children here are not receiving a proper education under me?' she demanded haughtily and, before William could answer, she had added: 'The education they get here is as good as they get anywhere else. It is enough for what they do with their lives. I defy you to tell me where they get a better one – '

William's anger was up now. 'Almost everywhere else that I have been,' was his answer. 'The children here are weighed down with your Bible-teaching and it has to finish. We can use the time we save to teach them other things – history and geography, in particular. I want to increase their knowledge of geography, to know more of other countries – India, America, the Cape, Canada, Australia and New Zealand. Most of the children in the higher standards cannot name either the seven continents or the seven seas and know nothing at all of other countries and other peoples. Starting from Monday, I intend to rectify that.'

'Whatever do children want to learn about the other countries for?' Miss Dunsmore retorted. 'None of them will go to any of them!'

'They need to know of the world they live in,' Martha interjected sharply. 'They cannot remain ignorant of it all their lives.'

'Most of them are ignorant because their fathers and their mothers are ignorant,' the assistant-teacher retorted, even more put out by Martha's support for her husband. 'They follow them. It is only to be expected in a place like this.'

'Nevertheless, we shall teach them as I say and we shall begin on Monday,' William told her. 'I have prepared all the information in the order you will require it and I have revised the timetables accordingly. I am quite sure it will only be a matter of you reading it to refresh your memory,'

He handed Miss Dunsmore the revised schedule and the first sheaf of papers he had prepared for the history lesson which she was to give – an account of the arrival of Julius Caesar in Britain and, for the first geography lesson, a map he had drawn of the British Isles, naming all the counties and the major cities and rivers, as well as the principal mountain ranges like the Pennines, the Cheviots, the Grampians, the Black Mountains of Wales and the Highlands of Scotland, with Ben Nevis and Snowdon pinpointed.

William knew that she was not protesting because she would be unable to teach the two 'new' subjects – from her teacher training, she would be quite competent to teach both – it was just that she just saw no reason for it.

'I will teach my two standards history each Wednesday and geography each Thursday from two o'clock till three,' he informed her, 'and you will instruct standards three and four in history for one hour each Monday, from two o'clock till three, and in geography for one hour each Tuesday from eleven-ten till dinnertime. Furthermore, as an incentive for the children to learn, not just to sit and listen, each Friday afternoon after the first week, you and I will conduct a factual test of our separate standards – ten facts on history and ten facts on geography which they should have remembered from what we have taught them during the week – a test. At the same time, each standard will also be given a spelling test of ten words which they have come across in their reading that week – devised by us, you and I, Miss Dunsmore, you and I. I want the children of this school to be able to spell correctly and, as an incentive, those who get all their spellings correct will be allowed to leave school at three-thirty, one hour earlier than usual. Those who misspell any of their words will have to write out all their mistakes five times before they are allowed to go...'

None of it met with her approval: it was too much of an upset, too much of a change: and she went off in something of a flounce to eat her lunch with Hannah Hodgson...

THIRTY-THREE

WILLIAM COULD ONLY surmise that Helen Dunsmore carried out her threat to complain to the Reverend Scrope that very day, for he later saw her writing a note and supposed she delivered it to the vicarage herself on her way home. The outcome was that the very next morning, before the bell had even been rung, the Reverend Scrope again came hurrying into the schoolroom as William sat at his desk, preparing for that day's lessons. This time there was no clatter of children rising from their desks, no chorus of 'Good morning, Vicar' to warn him: the curtain was swished aside and the Reverend Scrope was confronting him before he realised it: and he did not look at all pleased.

'All this is really becoming too much, Mr. Warburton,' he began, even before he had reached William's desk. 'Yet again I find myself having to confront you for a fourth time over school matters. Is my information correct? Am I to understand that you are proposing to stop the children reading the Bible and that you intend to teach them history and geography instead? I have to tell you most strongly that this school prides itself on the religious education it gives its children. It supports the Anglican foundation of the school. I deem it essential that they learn all about the Church, that they believe in God the Father Almighty, and in Jesus Christ, His only Son, Our Lord, who was crucified, died and was buried, and yet on the third day rose again and ascended into heaven and is now seated at the right hand of God, from whence he shall come to judge the quick and the dead...'

William allowed him to finish his creed: the poor man was purple-faced and almost breathless and gasping with indignation when he concluded: to him, to the three 'Rs' of 'Reading, wRiting and aRithmetic' must always be added a fourth 'R' – Religion, which was why it did not sit well with him that he had had to come to the school yet again to argue a point with his new schoolmaster.

'I am not ending reading from the Bible, I am merely reducing the number of times we use it for reading exercises, that is all,' William calmly replied. 'I just feel too much of our time is taken up in reading just from the Scriptures, which the children do at Sunday school, anyway, so they know them well enough. My intention is simply to introduce more varied reading – popular novels, for instance – Charles Dickens's *Oliver Twist* or *David Copperfield* for the boys, say – and for the girls, one of the Bronte sisters – Charlotte Bronte's *Jane Eyre* perhaps? I would like them to read some poetry as well at times – Lord Tennyson's *Charge of the Light Brigade* perhaps or William Wordsworth's *Daffodils* or John Keats's *Ode to Autumn* – '

Here he recited the opening lines of Keats's poem – *"Season of mists and mellow fruitfulness, Close bosom-friend of the maturing sun..."* – in the hope that they might stir something in the vicar's breast, but drew instead only a snort of disdain, which was what he had expected, anyway.

'It is my conviction,' he went on, ignoring the vicar's obvious derision, 'it is my conviction as the master here, that some of the time the children usually spend reading from the Bible could be spent teaching the older children, in particular, about England's early history – and also the geography of these islands and the world, the geography of the British Empire, in fact. I feel the children will be better off learning history and geography rather than learning about Job and his plague of boils or Jonah being swallowed by a whale, which are most probably myths anyway!'

He could hardly have said a worse thing. 'The teachings of the Bible are not myths,' the vicar retorted. 'They are the word of God given to us mere mortals through the teachings of the prophets from the time of Abraham through to the teachings of Jesus – '

He would have gone on in the same horrified, hectoring tone had William not raised his hand to signify that he accepted all upon which the vicar was berating him and, therefore, he had no wish to start an argument on the merits of the stories in the Bible. 'Yes, I understand all that, Mr. Scrope, and I have no wish to argue on Biblical matters with a man as learned as yourself – '

'I should think not,' snorted the Reverend Scrope.

' – I merely wish,' William continued, 'to add to the school's revenue, for it occurred to me that, if we were to teach history and geography and the children were tested on them both at the next school inspection, it would bring in extra revenue – six shillings per scholar is added to the annual grant, I understand, if they answer the inspector well on those two subjects. They will need to be taught properly, of course, which, in my opinion, they seem not to have been in the past, which is why I need the extra time that less reading of the Scriptures every day will give us. The last master seemed content simply to adhere to the three Rs. The Bible will *continue* to be read, but less so than before. That is all I propose.'

At this, the Reverend Scrope's mood changed perceptibly: the prospect of more grant monies being earned if the children were taught history and geography properly and then successfully tested on it by a schools inspector was a sensible enough argument: he did not like the changes the schoolmaster was proposing, but so long as the Bible continued to be read regularly in some form or other, he was less inclined to oppose it. In the end, he coughed and said almost apologetically, or as near to an apology as he would allow himself to make: 'Oh, I had not thought of it like that. Any increase in the grant is to be welcomed, I suppose – '

William interrupted him to press home his advantage, even giving him an estimate of the total extra revenue they could expect if the children inspected on the two subjects answered well: and he was determined they would answer well. Thereafter, while not actually fully acquiescing to William's reduction of the Scriptures, he did not query his plans further, nor did he stay for the special assembly planned for that morning, which upset Miss Dunsmore, for she had arranged a half-hour of hymn-singing by the older children and had thought the Reverend Scrope had come to listen to them, especially as it was, in effect, a practice for the church's forthcoming fund-raising concert in the schoolroom on the following Saturday. William had agreed to the hymn recital in the hope of placating his assistant-teacher and putting her in a good humour for once: the vicar's departure, without even acknowledging her presence, put an end to that.

The vicar's unexpected arrival to confront her husband yet again was too much for Martha's nerves, for it was after that, uncharacteristically, she reduced Hannah Hodgson to tears. While Martha joined William and Miss Dunsmore in the Big Room to conduct the half-hour of hymn-singing in preparation for the coming concert, the pupil-teacher was sent into the Little Room to supervise the infants' assembly. For some reason, she decided that it would be a good idea to light a candle as the youngest children recited the Lord's Prayer with their eyes closed and their hands pressed together: then, when the children had finished, she blew out the candle and told them quite confidently that the rising smoke was carrying their prayers up to God.

When Martha went back into the Little Room and saw the smoking candle, she was indignant and even angrier when she heard the girl's rather simplistic explanation for it. 'Don't be absurd, Hannah!' she scolded. 'The smoke does no such thing. It is just smoke. From now on, no candles will be lit where there are small children. I want no naked flames in this room. In future, they will say their prayers as normal and then begin their lessons.'

'But I was always told that is what happened when I was in the infants,' the girl protested, bursting into tears, 'and it made the children happy. They liked me doing it.'

'It is still nonsense,' Martha said. 'I will not have children misled in that way.'

'I shall tell the vicar on you,' Hannah cried, rubbing at her eyes.

'Do as you wish, I do not care,' was Martha's curt answer.

Foolish as the girl's idea was, it was unlike Martha to snap at anyone in such a manner. However, it seems the pupil-teacher did not tell the vicar, for nothing came of the incident: instead, Hannah Hodgson brooded upon the matter and bided her time and, when the chance came sometime later, she took her revenge in a different way...

THIRTY-FOUR

THE REVEREND SCROPE did not stay for Miss Dunsmore's hymn-singing because he was hurrying back to the vicarage for a reason: and that was to lock his study and deny its use that day to the Reverend Smallwood, who, of late, seemed to be finding more and more reasons to present himself at the vicarage, ostensibly to consult one or other of the vicar's books from which to pen his sermons, though the Reverend Scrope, being an observant man, suspected that there was more to it than that.

That day he was due to sit as the chairman of the magistrates' Bench at the petty sessions held in the town hall council chamber, having resumed his role as a Justice of the Peace: and, as most sessions began at nine-thirty in the morning – hence his early call at the school – and seldom finished before six or seven o'clock in the evening, a long day was in prospect. He wanted to ensure that, if the curate did call while he was out, he would have no excuse to stay and the way to do that was to lock his study and take the key with him as it was the only one there was.

He had considered refusing the Reverend Smallwood the use of the study and his library altogether, in case people gossiped about the frequency of him being at the vicarage and also his being 'alone in the house' with Agnes when he was out, but had decided against it. Besides, they were not 'alone': Bertha the cook was usually in the kitchen till either six or seven o'clock most days and the nursemaid Sarah Pockett was either in the nursery with Elizabeth, playing with her in the garden if the weather were fine, often with Agnes in attendance, or the two of them together were wheeling her about the town in the perambulator which Agnes had bought. All he could do at the present was to suspect.

His suspicions had first been raised a month or so earlier when he had returned late one evening, had pushed open the front door and, as he stepped into the hallway, to his surprise, he had seen Agnes coming out of the study where the curate was still working. There was something about his sister's manner as she hurried away from him towards the kitchen, as if she had been caught unawares and was flustered at being seen coming out of a room where she was alone with a man, even though they were not 'alone' in the house as the nursemaid was upstairs. He had not challenged his sister or the curate out of sheer tiredness.

His suspicions had been further aroused the very evening he had taken to his bed with 'influenza' and Agnes had gone round to the curate's lodgings along the Siblingham road to ask him to take the services at St. Andrew's on the Sunday. She had been away much longer than he had anticipated: he had heard the door click shut at six o'clock as she left and, though it was only a fifteen-minute walk there and fifteen minutes back, she had not returned till a quarter after seven, which meant she had been away for a good hour-and-a-quarter – though she had returned in time to help Sarah put Elizabeth to bed.

He was sure, too, that he had heard a man's voice bid her 'Goodnight' when she had returned: and that could only have been the Reverend Smallwood, who must have walked back with her to the vicarage. Now why would he do that? She was quite capable of walking back on her own! It had not been dark at the time and there were still people about. Unfortunately, he had been too ill to get out of his bed to look and now wished that he had, for then he would have known for sure.

Come to think of it, the curate had stared at his sister when they had first arrived at the station on his return to Steadshall: and when he was driving the carriage up the High Street, he had twice turned to look at her and, at the school, had jumped down from his seat just to help her down: and when they were returning to the vicarage, he had again pushed forward to help her into the carriage and each time he had insisted upon driving them when he could have done it himself.

The matter, the Reverend Scrope decided, merited him keeping an eye on both of them and, if there really were 'anything between them,' as others might put it, a liking, say, or – God forbid! – an actual physical attraction, he would quash it before it began, certainly before it went too far and they started to dream of other things!

He had brought Agnes from Somerset to be the caretaker of his house and to be 'a mother' to young Elizabeth and, in time, when the child was old enough, to be her governess, not to begin a flirtation with the beanpole of a curate! For goodness sake, Agnes was thirty-two, six years older than Smallwood! A man of twenty-six would not be attracted to a woman of thirty-two, would he? Surely not! It was almost repugnant!

It had been a different matter between himself and Jane: older men like himself often married younger women, much younger women if they had spent their earlier years in the service of others: in the service of their country, say, or as businessmen keeping the wheels of industry turning while they accumulated their fortunes, or perhaps as politicians helping to govern the nation and keep it safe against the nation's enemies – or, like himself, were clergymen, helping to keep the masses on the true moral path in the Lord's name, Amen. Such men often did not 'find time' to marry when they were younger, just as he had not till he had 'rescued' Jane from a life of spinsterhood in the service of her father: at least, she had 'known a man' before she had died, so there was some comfort for her in that.

Come to think of it also, Agnes had spoken several times about the curate, asking at breakfast only the previous week if he were coming to work in the library that day and looking somewhat crestfallen – though attempting to hide it – when he told her, 'No, he is not, he is elsewhere today.'

As it happened, that day he had sent the Reverend Smallwood to visit the parents of a fourteen-year-old named Walter Moon, who had left the parochial school two years before and the previous day had somehow contrived to fall down dead leading the trace horse while helping a farmer to drill late seed. It turned out that the two had been drilling for three days in three fields: on the fateful day, they had begun work at six o'clock in the morning in a roughly ploughed field and had worked on till nine at night, as dusk had allowed, just as they had the previous two days. Then, just as they were finishing, the boy had fallen down and died in less than four minutes, before help could be got to him. He did not appear to have been kicked by one of the horses or to have suffered a blow and Dr. Iveson had come to the conclusion that the cause of death was likely *cardiac syncope* caused by over-exertion. The curate had gone to the boy's home to talk with his mother and father about arranging a funeral for him at the new cemetery and particularly to ask if they would need any parish help towards the cost, so he was unlikely to put in an appearance at the vicarage that day. 'Oh,' was all Agnes had said, before continuing with her breakfast.

Then there was the Sunday when she had said that, for a change from attending Holy Communion at St. Andrew's, she would like to visit St. Mary's at Bourne Brook, the curate's small church, to give him some 'moral support' at his service, as well as seeing something of the countryside in-between, which she had heard was 'quite pretty' and had not as then seen any of it. She would take the pony and trap herself as she was quite competent to do so. Again, at the time, the Reverend Scrope had not thought much of it, thinking that she was just being interested or curious about the other church: it had not even bothered him when she had mentioned that she had given the curate a lift back to Steadshall after the service.

Yet, strong as his suspicions were, he did not wish to say anything without obtaining absolute proof that something 'untoward' was, indeed, 'going on' between the two of them. He was quite certain that his powers of observation were not wanting: he had seen what he had seen and had interpreted it: in his reasoning, he was still as astute as anyone, but he needed to prove that he was right: as a matter of pride, nothing else would do.

At least the day spent dealing with the miscreants of the town allowed him to push his suspicions to the back of his mind and, despite there being a further twenty-eight cases brought before him and the two other clergymen who sat with him, he was actually in a good mood when the day ended. That day, as fate would have it, he was able to repair some of the damage to his fund-raising cause which that fool-of-a-man the new schoolmaster had caused by his argument with Farmer Gardiner: for, it turned out, one of the cases brought before him involved none other than Farmer Gardiner himself.

The dispute between the schoolmaster and the farmer over the seating in church had rankled with the Reverend Scrope ever since it had occurred, particularly because of the loss of money which had resulted. In his opinion, the Reverend Smallwood should have sorted the matter out and not allowed the argument to develop as it had. Walter Crowfoot had said that he had not seen him at all while it was going on: but he had been there, had he not? So what was he doing while the two were scuffling in the aisle and costing him anything up to forty-five pounds in a lost subscription?

In the court case, Farmer Gardiner was charged with assaulting two labourers in his employ, while he in turn cross-summoned them for assault upon his person: and, as was to be expected of one of the largest landowners in the district, he appeared before the Bench, most unwillingly, complaining all the time he was there that he had better things to do than 'waste my time in a court o' law.'

The two defendants had worked all day cutting and shoring up a dangerous bank, for which Farmer Gardiner had said he would pay them a daily piecework rate of sixpence a rod, but, when they went to his mansion of a farmhouse and asked for the five shillings apiece they were due, he told them he had paid them too much for work already done and would not pay them any more than half-a-crown each, which they refused. An argument ensued and, when the farmer ordered them out of his house, the two labourers refused to go, so he pushed one man out and struck the other several times with his stick to get him out.

According to Farmer Gardiner's evidence, he had only done it when one man seized his scarf and the other wrestled him to the ground, so the Reverend Scrope, as chairman of the bench, had no difficulty in persuading his two colleagues to dismiss the case against the farmer and to convict the two labourers of assault, whom they fined fifteen shillings apiece.

The farmer nodded an acknowledgement to the vicar as he left the court, but whether it was one of thanks the Reverend Scrope was unsure and whether it would lead to him restoring his largesse to a hoped-for fifty pounds donation remained to be seen. However, he lived in hope.

The only dispiriting note that day came as he was on his way back to the vicarage and he stopped Dr. Iveson, who was walking back to his house halfway down the hill: he intended to discuss the matter of the slow rate of subscribing with him and so taken up with thinking about that and his hoped-for revival was he that he failed to notice that the doctor was in a particularly grim mood.

Even as he began to bemoan the slowness of the subscriptions, he was cut short by the doctor. 'Now is not the time, Mr. Scrope, if you please. I am not in the mood to discuss school management business at this moment.'

When the Reverend Scrope attempted to ignore him, saying somewhat light-heartedly that there was no time like the present and that he might have 'some good news to tell everyone on the management board soon,' the doctor simply turned on his heel and walked off in disgust, leaving the previously elated Reverend Scrope standing upon the pavement, looking perplexed.

The doctor had just come from the house of a family grieving for their sixteen-year-old son, a 'half-lad' named Charlie Griggs, who had been fatally injured while emptying sacks into a hopper in a farm barn. The sacks were being lifted from below by means of a wheel and pulley and it was thought that the boy slipped and fell and was dragged by the wheel into the machinery up to his waist: and, though the machinery was stopped and the boy was told to remain quiet while a man working with him ran for assistance, he had died by the time the man returned with help. The unnecessary loss of a second youth less than a fortnight after the first had been a blow to the good doctor, particularly as he had delivered both into this world.

Two days later, the curate was given the task of conducting the sixteen-year-old's funeral at the cemetery along the Wivencaster road, at which there was a fair turnout, Dr. Iveson among them, still looking very downcast. It would keep Smallwood busy for another day, the Reverend Scrope told himself – and away from Agnes.

He, meanwhile, had another matter which required his attention, one concerning another's loyalty or, as he perceived it, their disloyalty...

THIRTY-FIVE

IF THERE WERE anything which the Reverend Scrope disliked most of all, it was 'disloyalty' – disloyalty to himself, that is, for he never considered himself capable of being disloyal to others: people could only be disloyal to him: anything he did was just his pragmatism. But Robert Stalker, the landlord of the Bull Inn at the bottom of the High Street, had shown himself to be 'disloyal' by tendering his resignation from the management board in the middle of a crisis, that is, the trickle of subscriptions towards the school building fund.

On receipt of the landlord's letter, the Reverend Scrope had flown into a rage the like of which Agnes had not seen in a long time: a door had been banged shut, a chair had been kicked in the study and a threat made: 'How dare the man! How dare he! I will make him rue the day he has crosses me! See if I don't!'

It was enough to send Sarah the nursemaid scuttling out of sight back up to the nursery with the child Elizabeth in her arms and for Agnes to go up to calm her: it was not the first tirade she had witnessed from her employer.

What had actually precipitated it was the Reverend Scrope's response to the amount the landlord had pledged to donate towards the school extension: 'a miserly ten pounds,' as the vicar had cried on receiving the landlord's letter, but which to Robert Stalker amounted to several days' trade.

Soon after, while walking down the High Street, and casually acknowledging the doffed hats of the men and the curtsies of the women, the vicar had come upon the landlord's wife standing in the butcher's queue: and the Reverend Scrope was nothing if not direct.

'Ah, Mrs. Stalker,' he began in a somewhat tactless manner, 'I am glad I have caught you. Your husband has pledged a donation for the school fund, but he has pledged only ten pounds. Surely that is a mistake on his part? It is not very much. Could he not afford more? I should have thought twenty pounds at least from a member of the management board? We do, after all, need all the funds we can get.'

The other women in the queue looked at the landlord's wife: some sympathised that she was being unnecessarily embarrassed in front of them for her husband's presumed parsimony, while others sniggered quietly to themselves that she was being chastised by the most important man in the town: that would bring her down a peg or two: and one or two even shifted away from her, not wanting to be associated with the target of their vicar's displeasure.

'Oh, oh,' was all the poor flustered woman could gasp out, 'I did not know. I will speak to him about it, vicar, and try to get him to give more.' Which she did: but Robert Stalker was man who stood no nonsense from anyone and certainly would not allow an insult to pass unanswered and, to his way of thinking, the Reverend Scrope had insulted him as much as he had insulted his wife, practically calling him a skinflint in front of other people. It was that which riled him the most: so the reply the vicar got to his plea was a terse letter stating that the landlord was withdrawing his pledge entirely. *You will get nothing from me,* were his words, *'and you can accept my resignation from the management board as well.'*

He made one concession: before he delivered his letter, he walked up the High Street and knocked on Dr. Iveson's door and informed him of his anger at the way the vicar had embarrassed his wife.

'The man's a fool,' was the doctor's assessment of the clergyman. 'He has as much tact as a bull in a china shop! I wish I had your courage, for I would willingly resign myself so irritating do I find our vicar at times ...'

It was good enough for the landlord, who went up the street whistling as he headed for the vicarage: after all, he was saving himself ten pounds. But all actions have consequences and for the landlord of the Bull Inn it came the very next morning when the Reverend Scrope climbed into his pony and trap and went over to the divisional police headquarters at Shallford, a larger market town six miles distant on the road to Hamwyte: he had some information for the superintendent.

Some time before, a rumour had reached him, passed on by his warden, Walter Crowfoot, that there was a certain amount of gambling going on after hours in the Bull Inn: a number of men 'in the know' – four of them shopkeepers and churchgoers, who ought to have known better, and the others known chapelgoers – were staying behind after the other customers 'not in the know' had left and were continuing to drink and play crib and dominoes for money, at sixpence a game.

Worse, the town's three policemen – the sergeant, Charles Tucker, and the two constables, Edgar Lowther and Henry Trott – appeared to be turning a blind eye to it and, according to the rumour Walter Crowfoot had heard, they were not above going to the backdoor of the Bull themselves late on Friday nights, to be let in for what they hoped would be an unobserved session of drinking – except they had been observed by him. The gambling seemed to be taking place solely on Saturday nights and was continuing into the small hours of Sunday morning – which meant that they were gambling on the Lord's Day. So he would do as Jesus had done to the moneylenders and hawkers in the temple in Jerusalem: he would *'turn them out and throw over their tables'* or, more precisely, he would ask the superintendent at Shallford to see that the town's sergeant and two constables 'did their duty,' especially as neither of the constables seemed to be 'out and about' as much as they ought to be out and about 'after hours' on a Saturday night. Indeed, he would not have been surprised to hear that they were tucked up in their beds when, in his view, they ought to be patrolling the town's streets to deal with the 'drunkards and other nefarious characters' skulking home in the early hours. He would see that, in future, they were.

It was a pure coincidence that, just as the Reverend Scrope was preparing to set off, the Reverend Smallwood should arrive at the vicarage yet again and ask yet again if he might use the library in the study yet again: it was not on the church's business, he admitted, but was work he was doing privately, a small piece of historical research on the *Bounty* mutineers and the subsequent history of them and those who were not mutineers but had been left on Tahiti and were taken as prisoners aboard the Royal Navy ships sent to search for them. The Reverend Scrope had a book on the very subject in his library and the curate wanted to read it and to copy from it.

The Reverend Scrope's first thought was to refuse him, but to have met the curate's request with such bluntness might have alerted him to the suspicions he held concerning him and his sister: he quickly calculated that he would be away for most of the morning, with the time taken to get to Shallford at one hour, the time there possibly a further hour, and another hour for the return, so he should, he hoped be back by one o'clock at the latest, when it was quite likely that the curate would still be at the vicarage.

So as not to alarm the Reverend Smallwood if his intentions were, as he suspected, to spend less of his time concentrating on his 'private work' and more of it 'talking with Agnes,' he thought it prudent to inform him of where he was going and what he intended doing.

'Would it not be better to wait awhile?' the Reverend Smallwood suggested hopefully. 'To interfere now would only be to stir up unnecessary antagonism against the church at the very time we are hoping to raise more money for the school building fund. If indeed gambling does go on after hours in the Bull, or at any of the other inns, for that matter, would it not be better to let the landlords know that there is a rumour abroad of what is taking place and warn them that way. After all, it is the landlords of the inns and the shopkeepers of the town who are likely to be among the best givers to our cause, as they are the ones with the funds, they and the farmers.'

'*First Timothy, chapter six, verse ten,*' retorted the vicar, more than a little put out by the curate's casual acquiescence to what he considered a sin, even if the Bible did not specifically forbid or condemn it. '*"For the love of money is the root of all evil: which while some coveted after, they have erred from the faith, and pierced themselves through with many sorrows".*' And if that were not sufficient to correct his curate, he added in an equally reprimanding manner: '*Let your conversation be without covetousness; and be content with such things as ye have: for He hath said, I will never leave thee, nor forsake thee. – Hebrews, chapter thirteen, verse five".*' And with that, he climbed into his trap, called out 'I shall be back sometime this afternoon,' flicked his whip about Flora's ears and set off.

His journey to Shallford was not wasted, for the superintendent promised to 'look into the matter,' though he could not promise anything other than that as he was not in possession of the full facts, he said, and what the vicar had told him was only rumour, so far. He would, however, make enquiries and act upon what he had been told. Not having given a witness statement to a senior police officer before, the Reverend Scrope was disappointed, first, that he was not asked more questions than he was and, second, that he was not asked to sign a statement of any kind, especially as he was a Justice of the Peace. As it was, the whole business took no more than ten minutes, though he left reasonably satisfied to know that a higher authority than Sergeant Tucker and Constables Lowther and Trott had now been informed of the matter and, it was to be hoped, was preparing to act.

He returned to Steadshall and turned into the lane beside the church just as the church clock struck noon, thus the clink of the pony's hooves and the rolling of trap's iron-rimmed wheels on the metalled road were drowned by the chimes for the brief distance from the High Street to the vicarage: and, by standing in the trap as he came along by the high wall surrounding its garden, he was able to see over it.

What he saw was what he expected to see, what he hoped to see: Agnes and the Reverend Smallwood were standing together in the corner of the garden farthest from the house, where anyone standing there would be out of sight of Bertha the cook in the kitchen or anyone else for that matter, save for someone who went up to the attic nursery to look out, as he himself had once done to keep an eye on the gardener's boy, William Upson, when he had doubted whether he was working as well as he should for the money he paid him.

It was not just that the curate and Agnes seemed unnecessarily close, but – goodness gracious! – they might even be touching or holding hands. He could not quite tell because of the angle he was at, but she was looking up into Smallwood's face and smiling and he – the blackguard, the scoundrel! – he was looking down at her and smiling as well. Laughing! It was just as well he had come home when he had – another few moments and they might have put their arms around each other and started kissing!

She was holding a small fork in one gloved hand and there was a pile of pulled weeds on the lawn beside her, so it was clear she had been working for most of the morning: but how long had it been before Smallwood had walked out through the French windows and joined her? More than likely, he had been standing watching her work and talking to her ever since he had left! So much for his wanting to do 'private work' in the study: that had been no more than a blatant deception, a blind to deceive him. Well, he was not deceived and neither was he going to be deceived!

The last of the church clock's chimes faded away as he turned in through the side entrance and William Upson came out of the stables to lead the pony and trap off: he entered the house quietly through the front door and crept through his study and out through the French windows, noting the opened books spread upon his desk which signalled that the curate had indeed been doing some writing. The question was: for how long?

The guilty expression on the Reverend Smallwood's face and the flushed cheeks of his sister as he crossed the lawn to them were all he needed to tell him that something had, indeed, been going on between them. However, now was not the time to let on: instead, he asked brusquely: 'Have you finished your work in my study, Mr. Smallwood? If you have, I shall need my desk to do some work of my own.'

'Er – yes, yes,' the curate stuttered, turning away from Agnes the moment he heard the vicar's footfall on the grass. 'I have all the information I require, thank you.'

'Then you had better be about your business, Mr. Smallwood, had you not?'

'Yes, certainly, Mr. Scrope. I was on the point of leaving. I was saying goodbye to Miss Scrope.'

'Then do not let me keep you, Mr. Smallwood,' the vicar told him quietly. 'I have a matter which I wish to discuss with my sister, if you would be so kind as to leave us.'

The curate bade Agnes good day and walked slowly back across the lawn, giving one last lingering look before disappearing through the French windows into the study to retrieve his papers…

THIRTY-SIX

THE REVEREND SMALLWOOD could not help himself – he was smitten and had been since the day the Reverend Scrope had returned and Agnes had first alighted from the train with her niece Elizabeth in her arms. The vicar had been the first to descend and, despite the shortness of the time he had had to prepare the welcome, the curate had been genuinely glad to see him – even if their initial meeting was somewhat soured by the vicar's irritability. It at least meant the burden of looking after two parishes was lifted from his shoulders – and he could return full-time to the smaller parish of St. Mary's at Bourne Brook.

What he had not expected was for Agnes to be accompanying her brother: he had heard the Reverend Scrope talk about his younger sister in the West Country, where she had remained after the death of their parents, but he had never expected to meet her. He had noted immediately how small she was, only coming up to his shoulder, that she was several years older than him and that she was wearing spectacles: nevertheless, he thought she looked quite pretty in her blue dress and cape and she seemed to be very tender towards the child she was holding and considerate enough to turn and warn the nervous young nursemaid to be careful stepping down from the railway coach before he could reach her to do the same. When she spoke her greeting to him, it was in a pleasant voice which he had found instantly agreeable and, quite unexpectedly, for no reason he could fathom, when she had extended her hand the first touch of her gloved fingers on his had caused a most queer empty sensation in the pit of his stomach which he had never experienced before.

Over the weeks, he knew, he had been calling at the vicarage more times than he perhaps should have done and certainly more times than he would have done in normal circumstances: for, in normal circumstances, he would have stayed well out of the Reverend Scrope's way and communicated with him face-to-face as little as possible and mostly done it through the churchwardens, Walter Crowfoot or Samuel Gough, as he had done before the vicar had left on his round-the-world trip. But these were not normal circumstances: there was someone there who drew him to the place, someone whom he liked to see, with whom he liked to talk and who seemed to like to talk with him: he found it the easiest and most natural thing in the world to talk to Agnes Scrope: they got on so well together. Being with her, conversing with her, laughing with her took away all his shyness, all his nervousness: it gave him a hitherto unknown confidence. Indeed, her very pleasantness towards him had begun to nurture within him the hope of something better than what he had at the moment – a lonely existence in somewhat dismal lodgings, relieved only by his work, rewarding as that was.

The friendship and companionship of a woman was something to which he had given little thought until he had met the vicar's sister – now he found himself constantly thinking of companionship, lifelong companionship – in other words, marriage, marriage to Miss Agnes Scrope, if he ever plucked up the courage to ask her and she did not refuse him: and so far the signs were that she was as pleasant to him as he was towards her, so there was hope...

He might not have been so full of hope, however, if he had witnessed the Reverend Scrope's questioning of his sister which followed his departure.

'What does that man mean to you, Agnes?' the vicar had asked, bluntly, taking hold of his sister's wrist as she prepared to resume her gardening.

'Nothing,' she lied, for what was to be one of the few times in her life. 'He is a good friend, nothing more. We were just talking about things, that was all.'

'What things?' he wanted to know and, at the same time, he tightened his grip on her wrist and twisted it a little to give her 'the burn,' which had been one of the 'tortures' he had perpetrated against his younger sister when he was a young man down from Oxford for the holidays and she was a child irritating him.

Agnes gave a grimace of pain and, just as she used to do before, she allowed her knees to buckle and her body to sag so as to relieve the pain. 'All sorts of things,' she gasped, 'books, music, poetry. Mr. Smallwood loves poetry. He reads Keats and Wordsworth. He has even written some himself and has shown it to me. He also loves paintings and was telling me about Mr. Holman Hunt's *Light of the*

World. He has seen it and was telling me about it, how it was painted at night, outdoors, in the moonlight – '

This was a reference to an allegorical painting by the William Holman Hunt, which some considered a painted text, a sermon on canvas, a representation of the figure of Jesus knocking on an overgrown and long-unopened door, taken from *Revelation three, twenty: 'Behold, I stand at the door and knock; if any man hear My voice, and open the door, I will come in to him, and will sup with him, and he with Me."*

'He was telling me,' went on Agnes, bending even lower as her brother gave her wrist a further twist, 'he was telling me that he had noticed that the door in the painting has no handle and that the artist's interpretation must be, therefore, that it can only be opened from the inside – by us – by us letting Jesus into our lives. That was what we were discussing.'

It drew a suspicious harrumph from him: it had not looked like that was what they were discussing when he had seen them, but it was enough of a plausible answer to make him think and for him to release her.

'How long had you been talking before I came?'

'He had only just come out, not ten minutes before,' his sister assured him, at the same time rubbing at her pained wrist and wiping the tears from her eyes. It was a second lie: she had been talking with the curate for a good hour before her brother's return, but she could not tell him that.

'I hope you are not harbouring any feelings for the man?' the Reverend Scrope declared, giving a snort of contempt that she should even contemplate such an idea. 'You know what I mean. You are thirty-two years old, for goodness sake. You will be thirty-three in November. He is twenty-six – he is six years younger than you!'

'I am not harbouring any "feelings for him," as you put it – never,' an indignant Agnes cried and lied for the third time.

'Good,' was her brother's brusque response. 'I cannot forbid you talking to Mr. Smallwood, but I can and will forbid you from having any feelings for the man. It is quite absurd. I did not bring you all this way from the West Country to make a fool of yourself by running after a younger man.'

'I am not "running after him" and I would not consider it making a fool of myself if I did,' she snapped back, finally summoning up the courage as she moved away from him, still nursing her sore wrist.

'I sincerely hope not,' was his riposte. 'Now be so good as to go inside and ask cook if she will bring my lunch to the study. I will eat it there. I am too angry at this moment to sit with you in the dining room.'

She did as she was bade, as much to get away from him as anything else, and certainly not out of meekness: afterwards, instead of sitting in the dining room, she took her own meal on a tray up to the nursery to sit with Sarah Pockett and the child: better to be out of his way at the top of the house than downstairs where he was.

Sarah was in the process of feeding Elizabeth and noticed her mistress's sadness and her reddened eyes. 'Are you well, Miss Scrope?' she asked, genuinely concerned.

'Yes, yes,' replied Agnes, wiping some lingering moisture from her eyes: it occurred to her that the young nursemaid might well have seen what had happened while looking out of the nursery window, but she could not let her know how wretched she felt. Instead, she concentrated upon helping the young nursemaid spoon the food into Elizabeth's mouth, playing a game of trains and tunnels and trying to make her laugh as she did so.

The thought suddenly struck Agnes that, were she to meet a man and become engaged to him – 'the right kind of man,' naturally – within the next year or two, she might well have a child of her own someday – before it was too late – if she allowed the man, whoever he was, to do to her what other women allowed their men to do to them: but then, that was only natural, was it not? She would get used to such a thing over time: women did, she had been told: some were even said to enjoy it, though she did not see how, but it was the expected thing and all married women did it – allowed it. Goodness gracious, there she was thinking about 'that' and she had not even been kissed by a man – never mind that 'other thing' that they liked to do!

Henry Smallwood had never attempted to kiss her or even asked for a kiss, not even when they had been alone together in her brother's study: the man was too shy for that: he was as shy of women as she was shy of men. He had always restricted himself to polite conversation: indeed, sometimes when she had looked directly into his face while he was talking to her, he had blushed crimson and had looked away: and he had such a nice face, with bright blue eyes, a high intelligent forehead, an aquiline nose, well-formed lips and good white teeth: she had noticed all that. Really, he was quite handsome, in his way, though very thin, bony actually, as though he could do with a few good meals inside him, which she was sure he was not getting at his lodgings, since he was always out and about doing something somewhere and probably missed half his meals. He was a good foot taller than herself, she readily acknowledged, but that would not be a deterrent – 'should not be a deterrent to a woman,' she corrected herself in her thoughts – as most men were taller than women, anyway. Besides women liked their men to be taller: she would not want a man who was shorter than herself – he would be only five foot!

Want a man? Agnes smiled to herself at the thought that had come into her head. Was Mr. Smallwood the man she wanted, the 'Mr. Right' which some women writers suggested her sex should always be seeking? To be sure, he had a pleasant nature – she had deduced that the first time she had spoken to him, when he had turned to her while driving her brother's cumbersome carriage from the railway station to ask if she were comfortable – and he was always courteous when he came to the vicarage or met her in church. He was well spoken, too, and quite learned and very hard-working: but then, as her brother's curate, knowing Hugo, he would have to be.

While Agnes sat with Sarah and the child Elizabeth, the Reverend Scrope was eating his dinner in the study and reading a letter which had arrived that morning: the Department of Education in London had approved the architect's plans for the extension to the parochial school and had also approved the plans for a school at Bourne Brook: all that was needed now was the money from the subscriptions so that work might begin in earnest...

THIRTY-SEVEN

A SECOND VISIT by a schools inspector within six months of an earlier inspection was not unusual, especially if a school had had a dismally unfavourable report the last time, if a new head teacher had since been appointed and if the school were a parochial one known for its emphasis on Bible-reading and hymn-singing. The Reverend Scrope's application for approval for an extension to Steadshall's parochial school served to remind the Department of Education in London of its existence again and, therefore, of its previous inadequacies: so they decided to see for themselves what improvements, if any, there were.

The inspector arrived unannounced, as was to be expected, walking into the Big Room just after prayers one Wednesday, unfortunately, on a particularly bad day when it was very wet outside and only a hundred and eighty-seven of the two hundred and seventy-five pupils on the school's nominal roster were present and none at all from Bourne Brook because the stream there and all the ditches in between had overflowed after a week of rain and the dirt road from the hamlet was so flooded it was impassable for the youngest and those poorly shod: it was also an excuse for the parents to keep their children at home and save a penny or two.

Things began badly when the inspector decided first to take a head count of those in school that day, making the usual allowance for several from the town who genuinely were ill with mumps or chicken pox and had sent in notes. Whether out of sheer spite or just utter carelessness, knowing an accurate register was a matter of importance, particularly if an inspector were to arrive unannounced – as this one had – Miss Dunsmore had again contrived to have present in the school more pupils than the inspector himself could count, even after two attempts.

'Even allowing for the weather, all children marked present should be present,' he declared somewhat flatly. 'Consequently, I may have some hesitation in recommending the grant be approved in full for next year if this is an example of how the attendance roll is kept.'

There was little that William could say in reply: he had been caught out through no fault of his own: he was particular annoyed with himself for not having checked the register that morning, as he had done surreptitiously several times as a precaution since handing the task over to Miss Dunsmore, especially as he had still found errors, which he had duly pointed out to her. Each time he had received a huffed excuse for her 'miscounting,' which, of course, always erred on the favourable high side – such as a group of boys were 'outside in the yard at the time and were counted twice' or 'I was told the four Smith children would be late so I entered them, anyway, and put them down a second time by mistake when they did arrive.' But then he had to hand over some duties to his assistant.

Looking at the writing of the numbers that morning, he guessed what had happened: after taking the roll in his two standards, Miss Dunsmore had disappeared behind the thick curtain and, though against his express wishes, had allowed Hannah Hodgson to do the count of standards three and four, before doing it herself again in Martha's class so as not to arouse suspicion.

It was with some disquiet that William followed the inspector into Martha's room. Normally, school inspectors did not bother with the smaller children, but concentrated upon the four higher standards. However, the previous inspector, finding little that was good about the older children when he had visited, had tested the youngest as well and had been equally as disappointed in what he had found there.

In view of that, the latest inspector decided that he would like to take a look at those in Martha's room as well 'to see if there has been any improvement of the younger ones,' as he put it. Fortunately, Martha's teaching had begun to improve matters and the inspector appeared quite impressed by her older children as they copied in manuscript characters a line of print and then wrote out a few words of no more than four letters each of which he dictated to them. Since she had taken over, Martha had also concentrated upon their counting abilities and so the four picked out for testing were able quite competently to recite the five-times and seven-times multiplication tables and to do the simple additions and subtractions of not more than three figures which he set them.

Things went well, too, in William's own standards. He was relieved to see that the five chosen to read a short paragraph from a newspaper which the inspector had brought with him did so competently, then all wrote out two paragraphs from the same newspaper which were read to them and all seemed to manage it without too much trouble, including several of the boys of whom he had previously been somewhat doubtful. Those selected to answer the inspector's arithmetic questions also did so without faltering, though there was one awkward moment when one of the older boys, through sheer nervousness, struggled to divide a tonnage figure even though he had been doing similar, but more difficult, sums for the past fortnight and doing them correctly with ease. He got there in the end, again much to William's relief.

In fact, so complimentary was the inspector at the finish that he had no hesitation in recommending leaving certificates be granted immediately to nine of the scholars, four boys – the same four whom William had brought back from the hayfield – and five girls: the boys, he knew, would most likely go to work on the farms and the girls would go to work in Oldcourt's mills: it delighted them, but saddened him.

It was in Miss Dunsmore's two standards that the inspector seemed to find progress was still wanting: the four boys in standard three who he asked to read a short paragraph from a book he had brought with him, to William's shame, could barely stutter out the first few words and comprehended nothing of the meaning of what they were reading.

In the writing test, too, more than half the pupils in that standard were found wanting in both neatness of hand and correct spelling: the look of weary disdain upon the inspector's face as he viewed their efforts was like a body blow to William after the compliments he and Martha had received.

Fortunately, the situation was redeemed somewhat in the arithmetic test when, unbeknown to the inspector, the girl and boy he selected for his two questions just happened to be the daughter of one of the town's three greengrocers and the son of one of the town's publicans: both often served behind the counter and the bar of their father's premises and so were used to dealing with purchases and giving change, which were the problems he set them. The long division and multiplication tests he set the whole of the standard three pupils, however, were less successful and brought the same sad shake of the head as had their reading attempts.

The reading abilities of standard four were little better than their younger counterparts: though by introducing proper story books and curtailing their use of the Bible, William was hoping to improve the reading abilities of all Miss Dunsmore's pupils, the inspector's test had come too soon: they would improve, but only eventually. They had begun to improve, but progress was slow: children whose ears are boxed regularly or find themselves shouted at daily or have their ears pulled or their knuckles rapped with a ruler or books thrown at them are less likely to bother absorbing what a teacher is telling them and more likely to sit and sulk and pray for the end of the school day, which is what most in Miss Dunsmore's standards still seemed to do.

For instance, the two boys and two girls from standard four chosen to read a few lines of poetry and prose struggled to pronounce properly the longer words of eight or nine characters and seemed to have no proper comprehension of what the poem itself was about: nor was their any expression in their reading: and, as the inspector remarked somewhat sarcastically, children who do not understand what they read are less likely to remember it so the poetry test was counted as another dismal failure.

It was the same when he asked them all to write out a few dictated lines from the prose: some spellings of longer words were simply guessed at, some sentences were written without any punctuation whatsoever and the knowledge of when a capital letter should or should not be used appeared to be entirely unknown to most of them.

The arithmetic test on common weights and measures and areas and distances – ounces, pounds, stones, hundredweights and tons and inches, feet, yards, poles, rods and perches, as well as chains, furlongs and miles – was also a disaster, for such was the lack of knowledge of some of the pupils that suggested answers could clearly be heard being whispered from one to another at the back of the room and invariably they were wrong, anyway.

All of it was utterly disheartening for William, standing beside the inspector and listening to the stumbling of his scholars – or more rightly, Miss Dunsmore's scholars – but for whom he was ultimately responsible.

Miss Dunsmore, however, was not to be deterred and made blatant excuses for the failure of those who had been chosen, saying, as each pupil floundered, 'Oh, you have chosen one of my backward ones, the others are better...' or 'He is not the brightest among them...' and 'She has had too many absences so she is behind the rest...' as well as 'The two brighter ones from that group are not present today. They live at Bourne Brook and have been unable to get here because of the rain and the roads...'

The inspector, however, had seen enough and later, in handing his written report to William, he said quite firmly: 'I can say that there has been a marked improvement in four of the standards since my colleague was here some months ago, that is, the oldest and the youngest of the children, but there seems to have been no progress made in either of standards three and four. The results there were very poor. That will certainly need addressing before I or one of my colleagues comes again. I understand you have only been at the school for a matter of weeks, so I do not think the blame for the lack of progress in those standards can be laid at your door. It is your assistant, Miss Dunsmore, who, like my colleague earlier, I find so lacking. Myself, I would recommend you engage a new assistant-teacher and get an extra pupil-teacher from somewhere…'

THIRTY-EIGHT

IT WAS NOT for William but for the school management board to act on the inspector's report:, though he doubted that the Reverend Scrope would allow the other managers to do anything about either of the inspector's suggestion at a time when all monies were being conserved for the proposed extension and, if they ran to it, a school at Bourne Brook.

Nevertheless, he wrote a letter to them, pointing out the inspector's general satisfaction with the school's progress and included a copy of his report, though, as a precaution, after he had he pasted the report in the log book, he kept it under lock and key in the bottom drawer of his desk.

Somehow, however, the inspector's recommendation that a new assistant-teacher should be hired was communicated back to Miss Dunsmore by one of the managers – William did not know which, but suspected the secretary, Joshua Linkhorn – and, as a result, her hostility towards him and Martha increased.

In particular, the exchanges between himself and Miss Dunsmore became ever more barbed and, while she would always answer his queries, it was done each time in a tone of great weariness, as if she should not be being asked such things: and, when it came to a discussion on some matter, a simple correction or revision of some kind, he found her disagreeable, often impolite and, on one occasion, downright rude, airily waving a hand at a change he had suggested and walking off without a further word as if to say, 'If that is what you want to do, then you must do it, but you will have to do it by yourself.'

Despite the inspector's censure over the miscounting for the register, he found it necessary to caution her yet again on her carelessness in marking it and also on her slackness in relation to her general duties, such as not clearing up properly after all the children had gone home and one day 'forgetting' to lock the school properly so that it remained open to thieving all night. Fortunately, no one knew that it was open and so nothing was missing.

When William discovered it early the following morning and reprimanded her, she chided him in return for 'making a fuss over such a trivial matter,' adding sarcastically: 'Who would break into a schoolroom? There is nothing here to steal, anyway.'

Not only did William find his assistant careless but also lazy. Of late, in the final part of the afternoons, she had got into the habit of setting the children something to copy off the blackboard while she sat at her desk and wrote letters, mostly concerning the church choir and its practice evenings, but occasionally personal letters: then she would call out one of her least favourite pupils and send him to the post office or even to deliver the letter by hand, one time sending him to deliver several letters to several addresses in the town at one time.

Further, she was still in the habit of giving the monitor Olive Chaplin instruction during the dinnertime break so that she could look after a group of slower learners in standard three, who would have been better overseen by a qualified teacher, but, it seemed, Miss Dunsmore had effectively given up on them.

She was also becoming more short-tempered with her charges, if that were possible. William had noted from the very first day that the children in her two standards were petrified of her and he had seen them visibly flinch and bow their heads and brace themselves in expectation of a cuff or some other form of correction when she had walked down the aisle between the benches and the desks, especially if she were carrying a ruler or a book in her hand.

Recently, a mother had called at William's cottage to complain that Miss Dunsmore had thrown a slate at her daughter's head: he had heard the clatter himself and had quickly pushed the curtain aside, but had been told quite blandly by his assistant that the slate had only been 'dropped' and, of course, none of the children had dared to contradict her. A few days later, Martha noticed one of the girls was wincing and holding her upper arm stiffly while playing in the morning break and was told that the assistant-teacher had pinched her so hard on the fleshy part of her armpit, twisting the flesh, that the bruise was still showing when she undressed for bed three days later: it was her punishment for not being able to complete a short division sum.

Miss Dunsmore also slapped another girl around the cheek who pronounced a word incorrectly while reading aloud from one of William's new story books and, the same day, she gave a boy three raps across the knuckles with a ruler for failing to know his twelve times table. Fortunately, William had ordered that the cane be used only with his authority, which meant sparingly, though he had twice used it himself to punish three boys – one from Miss Dunsmore's standard four who, when she flung one of the new wooden blackboard dusters at him, which William had bought out of his own pocket, he had picked it up and flung it back, just missing her – and William could not allow that. The other time was when he had caught two boys fighting in the yard: as he separated them, still struggling violently, one of them kicked him on the knee and he could not allow that to go unpunished either, especially as he was limping for the rest of the day and had a sore knee for days afterwards. Like the first, each boy received three hard strokes across the backside and the punishment was duly entered in the log book.

One afternoon he heard a shriek of pain from behind the curtain and, jumping up, he found that Miss Dunsmore, in her fury, had struck a nine-year-old girl standing by her desk for not being able to do what she had been asked. The girl, caught off balance, had fallen against the nearby stove, striking it with her head and badly bruising her forehead and her cheek: fortunately, due to the time of year and the parsimony of the management board, the stove was not lit: but had it been wintertime and red-hot, as William would have wished it to be, the girl would undoubtedly have suffered severe blistering to one side of her face, for she lay dazed with her cheek pressed against the stove's cast-iron side for several seconds before recovering.

'If that stove had been lit, the girl could have been very badly burned,' William reprimanded his indifferent assistant.

'Well it isn't and she isn't and it would not have been my fault if she had,' Miss Dunsmore protested. 'It was an accident. If she had fallen normally and not staggered backwards like she did, she would not have banged her face against the stove.'

'You really must curb these flashes of temper of yours, Miss Dunsmore,' William told her firmly. 'They are becoming far too frequent.'

Which they were and, as a result, he ordered the curtain between the two sections to be pulled partway back so that he could see what was going on: it did not please Miss Dunsmore and at times made for a confusion of voices.

Matters came to a head, not the other side of the curtain but one afternoon in the yard when Miss Dunsmore and Martha were supervising the playtime together. William was seated at his desk, entering the morning's happenings into the log book, when suddenly he heard Miss Dunsmore's voice raised to a high angry shriek, followed almost immediately by an angry shout from Martha.

He was on his feet in an instant and, when he reached the scene, he found his wife and the assistant-teacher wrestling for a cane in Miss Dunsmore's hand. It seemed that one of the infants running across the yard had run straight into Miss Dunsmore as she came out of the porch holding the cane, having fetched it from the cupboard to poke at a blocked drain. She had raised it against the five-year-old almost involuntary, though whether she would have struck her with it was a matter of conjecture, for Martha, who was a few yards off, had rushed forward and seized hold of her arm before she could bring it down. The two were still struggling for the cane when William reached them.

'Stop! Stop this! Martha! Miss Dunsmore!' he cried and wrenched the cane out of Miss Dunsmore's hand himself. By then, almost every child in the schoolyard had halted in their play to gape at the two flustered women. The whimpering five-year-old, meanwhile, had run off to hide in a lavatory.

'Inside, this minute,' William commanded: and, nose in the air, convinced that she had done no wrong, the imperious Miss Dunsmore obeyed, followed by a red-faced, almost penitent Martha, who had acted instinctively to protect the child and now realised what an embarrassing exhibition she had made of herself.

'She was about to hit the child,' Martha declared as the two stood before William's desk.

'I was not,' Helen Dunsmore snorted. 'I would not hit a child so young with a cane. The child ran into me, I was merely getting the cane out of the way.'

'You were angry. You were about to hit the child,' Martha insisted.

'Yes, I was angry, but I would not have hit a five-year-old,' the assistant-teacher countered again, her manner one of offended persecution: she, a trained assistant-teacher, was not going to be accused by an infants' mistress, even if she were the senior master's wife.

'You would,' Martha shot back angrily.

William, not having seen the beginning of it, could only appeal for calm. 'Ladies, ladies,' he sighed, knowing that his wife would regain her demeanour, but expecting that Miss Dunsmore would continue with her haughty protestations of innocence.

'This cannot go on,' he told his wife when they discussed the incident over supper. 'I think the only answer is for me to write to the

Reverend Scrope...' which he duly did, delivering the letter himself the next evening, though finding that the vicar was not in and only his sister and the nursemaid were at home.

'*Reverend, sir,*' he wrote, '*I write to inform you that I sincerely believe Miss Dunsmore's conduct against her charges in standards three and four and against other pupils at this school has become such as to be intolerable and that it may have become necessary to remove her from the precincts of the school for their protection and to engage another more competent assistant in her place. As you will remember, such a course of action was specifically recommended in the recent report of Her Majesty's schools inspector...*'

Two days later, he received a letter in reply from Joshua Linkhorn:

'*I write on behalf of the vicar, who wishes me to inform you that Miss Dunsmore is, and always has been, considered to be a thoroughly competent teacher at the parochial school and, as such, the school managers have no intention of terminating her position with us. We, the school managers, wish to point out again that we do not consider it your place to suggest such things. Any engagements and dismissals at the school are and always have been the prerogative of the management board. Also, in future, would you kindly address all communications concerning the school or its staff directly to myself, rather than to his reverence, who at this time has other more pressing matters to deal with. I can then, as secretary, bring those matters before the full board, if necessary...*'

Clearly, the Reverend Scrope could not even be bothered to deal with the matter and had merely handed it to the secretary: all William and Martha could do was to sigh with frustration, confide in each other and try to ensure that the assistant-teacher's irascibility was curtailed as far as was possible, though Martha would gladly have ejected her from the school herself...

THIRTY-NINE

WHAT THE SECRETARY of the school managers meant by the vicar having to deal with 'more pressing matters' was that, despite the Reverend Scrope's repeated appeals from the pulpit, actual donations towards the parochial school extension fund were still only trickling in, a few pounds here and a few shillings there.

Promises of money to come *were* being made and there were enough farmers and landowners in the district and shopkeepers and others in the town who were regular attendees at St. Andrew's for the fund to have advanced rapidly. But, whenever one or other of them was cornered by the vicar in the church porch after Holy Communion or accosted on the High Street on market days by Walter Crowfoot, it was always, 'Yes, yes, Vicar...' or 'Yes, yes, Walter, I have not forgotten.' But it was followed always by the excuse, 'I cannot give just at the moment, Vicar (or Walter). It's a bad time for me, being just after haymaking (or just after the pea-picking) and just before the corn harvest. Wait till the harvest is in, then I'll know better how much I can give...'

Unhappily, too, despite the vicar favouring Farmer Gardiner's cause at the magistrate's court, he had not deigned to increase his donation by so much as a single shilling, though he continued to attend church each Sunday and to expect 'his pew' to be kept free for him and his family. It was as if none of them realised that the money was required there and then and, if the men from Elijah Crowfoot's builder's yard were ever to begin digging the foundations for the extension, if not actually to begin laying any bricks, they would need to know that they would be paid for the two months it would take them to do the work.

The Reverend Scrape's hope was that, once the foundations were dug, the walls would rise rapidly and, if all went well, that the roof would be in place by the beginning of August and all work internally and externally completed by the end of that month, in time to meet the September ultimatum set by the Department of Education. For, once the roof was on and the floor laid, as the architect had drawn it, the old lower bricking of a window in the old room was to be knocked away to create a doorway into the extension to match the other doorways in the school and a new separate entrance and porch built for the infants and juniors. But all that would happen only so long as they had the money to keep Elijah Crowfoot and his men working, for the builder was as ready as any builder, if continued payment were doubtful, to take them off somewhere else halfway through a job where payment was more assured.

It was all most puzzling and most worrying and the Reverend Scrope was beginning to have sleepless nights over it: even Walter Crowfoot had noted how hollow-eyed he was becoming, though he did not dare to comment on it. Indeed, if the Reverend Scrope had not had such faith in the goodness of the townsfolk and the farmers, that they were ever ready and willing to contribute to any good work carried out in their name, he might well have thought that they were resisting him for some reason.

Thus, the last thing the vicar of Steadshall wanted was for the top ten feet of the fifteen-foot crocketted pinnacle on the north-western corner of the six-hundred-year-old church tower to plummet to the ground in the middle of the day when there were enough townsfolk about on the High Street to hear the crash and to see the cloud of dust which rose up and billowed across the gravestones into the road. Unlike three smaller stones which had fallen from high up on the tower's south and west faces eighteen months previously, just before the Reverend Scrope had left for his trip around the world, the ten-foot length of pinnacle could not be discreetly collected by Walter Crowfoot and Samuel Gough and hidden in a remote part of the churchyard: it was too heavy.

Why Walter Crowfoot and Samuel Gough should have thought to deceive the people by hiding evidence of the tower's decay, no one understood: for it was evident to anyone who walked along Head Street in the shadow of the ancient church or walked up the path to the north and south porches that a considerable part of the tower was in an unsound condition and had been for some time. Indeed, even the bell ringers going through the main door at the foot of the tower were in the habit of ducking their heads as they hurried inside, just in case something fell on them from on high. The whisper was that the two churchwardens could only have done it with the connivance of the vicar before he left, as neither man was considered daring enough or smart enough to have done it by themselves – they could only have been told to do it and to say nothing while their vicar spent the next eleven months touring the world, which, of course, had only made matters worse, since no one had dared to do anything about anything while he was away.

That there was no one passing below when the pinnacle section crashed down was a blessing of a kind, for it would have killed them instantly, though it was whispered about the town that that would have been less of a mortification to the Reverend Scrope than the fact that the plummeting block had entirely destroyed the ornate ironwork railing enclosing the grave of none other than the mother of the owner of the town's three silk mills, Sir Thomas Oldcourt. Such a happening could not be hidden, for Sir Thomas might visit his mills at any time and subsequently the graveyard to lay his usual wreath of flowers on his mother's grave – his mother's now damaged grave!

Ever since the launch of his subscription fund for the school, the Reverend Scrope had been, and still was, hopeful of eliciting a 'substantial' donation from Sir Thomas – even if he were a Unitarian living in another town – so he could not allow anything to jeopardise that hope – especially a plummeting pinnacle. Hardly had the dust settled, than he was calling on one of the town's two blacksmith's to commission a replacement railing incorporating the same rising pillars at each corner and the same praying angel above a heart at the head end. Then he jumped into his pony and trap and drove over to Hamwyte to call personally on Sir Thomas at his rambling mansion in order to tender his profuse apologies for the damage that had occurred and to assure him that the ornate ironwork surround would be speedily replaced exactly as it had been, the whole work to be completed and installed at the parish's expense, of course.

In the meantime, fully cognisant of their own ignorance but recognising that the tower was in dire need of renovation, the vicar and the churchwardens decided that they required the best opinion they could possibly get on what steps should be taken as to the material to be used in any restoration of God's House and to what extent the repairs should be effected. After consulting certain persons in the parish, the mayor, the town clerk and the town surveyor himself, they settled upon the eminent London architect, Sir Arthur Bloomingfield: he would be five times more costly than employing the town's own surveyor, but Sir Arthur was, after all, the son of a bishop, born in the next county and one of the country's most prominent architects, known for designing fine churches and other buildings all over England, and known, too, to the town surveyor as a man who had a reputation for giving good value for money. In short, it might be worth the outlay, even if it could scarcely be afforded in the present circumstances.

In due course, the Reverend Scrope wrote to him at his London office, requesting that he visit the town at his earliest convenience to inspect the tower and give a written statement of what work he thought should be done. Sir Arthur duly arrived in his carriage on the following Wednesday and put himself and his assistant up at Robert Stalker's Bull Inn, much to the chagrin of the Reverend Scrope, who did not want the 'traitorous landlord' to benefit one penny piece from 'church matters.' Sir Arthur, though, was delighted to find himself with a choice of sixteen bedrooms amidst a maze of rambling nooks and crannies, old oak beams and open fires, dating back to Tudor Times – so delighted, in fact, that that evening he joined the drinkers in the taproom and treated them to round after round. Unsurprisingly, their number seemed to swell quite considerably as the clock ticked on, till Sir Arthur was finally helped to his bed and Robert Stalker rang the bell for closing with a broad smile on his face.

On the following morning, refreshed and sober, Sir Arthur and his assistant made their way to the church on its knoll at the top of the town, where they made a two-hour-long inspection of the tower, first walking backwards and forwards across the front of it, all the time peering up at the stonework, gesturing and making notes and talking between themselves, before calling for a long ladder – 'the longest you have,' they told Walter Crowfoot. Each then mounted it in turn to inspect the stonework at various places around the tower, paying particular attention to the mortar binding the stonework and, also to the double buttresses at the north-western corner.

Then, despite his fifty years and his revels the previous evening, the moustachioed Sir Arthur climbed the steep stone steps to the belfry, where he forced open one of the small leaded casement windows on the front edifice and leaned out to inspect the stonework above and below, chipping away small parts of it and catching it in his hand. After that, he and his assistant climbed the rickety perpendicular ladder to the top of the tower, forced open the hatch and squeezed through on to the leaded roof, where they spent some considerable time inspecting the three remaining pinnacles, tapping at them with their hammers and making yet more notes. Then Sir Arthur and his assistant each took it in turn to lean well out over the battlements to look down at the stonework below, secured only by a rope tied around their waists and held in turn by each other and the people's warden,

Samuel Gough, since Walter Crowfoot, having no head for heights, refused to go any higher than the belfry.

Sir Arthur looked somewhat grim when he and his assistant and the people's warden eventually descended and joined an anxious Reverend Scrope and an embarrassed Walter Crowfoot in the rope chamber: what Sir Arthur told them was enough to make the two churchwardens groan inwardly and the Reverend Scrope's face to lose much of its pallor: for when giving a client bad news, Sir Arthur believed that there was nothing to be done except to state the facts bluntly and honestly: after all, it was what he had been hired to do.

'It's the double-buttress at the north-western corner,' he told them, with a brusque professionalism. 'It has subsided by at least eight inches. The whole of it is moving away from the tower wall and has opened up a serious vertical crack at its junction. It is that which has brought your pinnacle down. The base of the buttress will have to be underpinned or there is danger of it falling bodily at no distant date. The higher part of the tower's west elevation above the line of the belfry has also suffered severe weathering and is in a loose and crumbling state. All those stones will have to be replaced. I would urge the substantial and thorough repair of those parts be undertaken as soon as possible. In the meantime, for safety's sake, the north-western buttress must be shored up or I cannot vouch for the tower's safety.'

The Reverend Scrope's question was only to be expected and the architect's answer to the same question wherever and whenever it was asked usually induced groans from whoever asked it.

'How much would the cost be – for the repairs and the restoration?' the vicar asked hesitantly, stealing himself for the worst.

Sir Arthur cleared his throat: he did not like giving estimates before he had worked out the costs of materials and labour and time: but, since he had been asked, there was no sense in beating about the bush.

'It is not an accurate figure,' he told them, 'but I would envisage the cost of repair and restoration could amount to several hundred pounds in total, including materials and labour. Say, six hundred. I will prepare a fuller report this evening and my assistant will bring it to you tomorrow.

Knowing that he was stating the obvious, but feeling it necessary, Sir Arthur added: 'The church has been much neglected over many years. If repairs had been made thirty or forty years ago, you would not be in the position you are in now.'

It did nothing to soften the blow, but at least it ensured that the crestfallen trio fully comprehended that fact was fact as sure as decay was decay, and Steadshall St. Andrew's old church tower was in an advanced state of decay.

When Sir Arthur and his assistant returned to the Bull Inn to prepare their report, the vicar and the two churchwardens retired to the vestry. Their dilemma was immediately apparent: should they abandon their plans for the extension to the school and direct the monies donated thus far towards the repair of the church tower or should they continue with the extension at the school and trust in God to keep the church tower upright for the time being, at least till it could be repaired properly?

'Which should come first,' the Reverend Scrope asked his two wardens, 'the church or the school – God or the people – God or the poor?'

'God,' said Walter Crowfoot adamantly, a little surprised that the vicar should even put the question.

'God,' echoed Samuel Gough. 'He always comes first. It matters less about the school.'

The Reverend Scrope rose from his seat and began pacing up and down, pulling at his nose and rubbing his chin, deep in thought: then, after a minute or so, preceded by a great sigh, he turned to them and declared, to their astonishment: 'It would be too costly to repair the tower at the present time. The parish cannot afford to pay for the tower to be repaired and for an addition to the school. It must be one or the other. I have decided. We shall press on with the extension to the school. As for Bourne Brook, we shall have to find some other accommodation for the children there. We shall not be able to build a school for them there. We shall have to settle for renting a barn or something...'

God would understand his decision, he told himself. 'Your House will be repaired, O Lord, and properly and be better than before,' he told heaven in his prayers that night. 'But six hundred pounds is just too much to find at present. I sincerely believe the school must come first. I cannot – I will not – have a School Board imposed upon me here. What I do, I do it for the future, O Lord, in Thy Name, so that Church will continue to educate the children of this town and ensure they will follow the true Protestant path and not be led astray by the "heathen religions" which surround us. That must not be put in jeopardy. I will fight the good fight because they are your children, O Lord...'

FORTY

THE VISIT of such an eminent personage as Sir Arthur Bloomingfield could not be kept a secret: indeed, the antics of the famous London architect and his assistant at the Bull Inn had been the talk of the drinkers of the town ever since, while their antics while inspecting the tower had been watched throughout by a curious crowd of onlookers ranged along the churchyard wall. Thus, it was not surprising that the famous architect's inspection and the state of the tower should become the subject of an article in the *County Gazette* the following Friday.

However, reporters being reporters, when not given the full facts because the churchwardens they ask are too reticent to give them the answers they seek, and the vicar has deemed it beneath his dignity even to speak to a member of the Press, the article which appeared in the *County Gazette* was concocted from rumour, comment and certain fears expressed by the ordinary folk of the town when spoken to on the High Street. That was: that to engage so eminent an architect as Sir Arthur to inspect their crumbling but picturesque old church tower could mean only one thing – that its complete demolition and replacement by a new tower was being contemplated and that the vicar and the two churchwardens were complicit in it, since all three had been present during the inspection!

It was just unfortunate that, following his inspection, Sir Arthur should be seated in the parlour of the Bull and happen to say a little too loudly to his assistant: 'It would be easier if they pulled the whole damned thing down and started again and this time built it of reinforced concrete!'

It was overheard by the landlord, Robert Stalker, who told his wife, who told her acquaintances, who told their friends… and within two days the rumour had gone round the town, causing consternation among the good people of Steadshall, that the vicar and the churchwardens intended to have the old tower pulled down and a brand-new one built in its place, not of ancient stone as the previous one, but of reinforced concrete.

A concrete church tower! There was no way the God-fearing Christians of Steadshall wanted a concrete church tower, no matter which eminent London architect designed it: they wanted to retain their picturesque old tower – even if it did have only three pinnacles! To them, standing on its knoll overlooking the long descent of the High Street and its line of shops and houses, it was a graceful landmark pointing directly up to heaven and, therefore, a constant reminder to them that God above was looking down upon them and watching over them.

The article in the *County Gazette* did not actually state as a fact that a new tower was to be constructed of reinforced concrete: it simply stated in the body of the report that Sir Arthur Bloomingfield, who had been called in to inspect it and to advise, was a prominent London architect who was known to favour reinforced concrete as a building material and had even designed and built a house for himself of that material in East Sheen.

Such a plan ought not to be countenanced, the people growled: no one was in favour of it and the only ones who would gain by it, they grumbled, would be the architect who proposed it and was paid to draw up any plans and the builder who was contracted to carry out its demolition and reconstruction – and it did not escape the notice of the growlers and the grumblers that Walter Crowfoot's brother, Elijah, who was even then about to 'line his pockets' from the construction of the school extension, was the town's main builder, who ten years previously had erected the town hall and made a good profit by it.

It was perhaps only to be expected that the unfortunate Walter Crowfoot and the bemused Samuel Gough should find themselves assailed on the High Street by people opposing the destruction of their graceful old tower. One overly-exuberant woman, coming out of Fred Norton's bakery halfway up the High Street with a loaf of bread in a basket, on seeing Walter Crowfoot going past, spat in disgust at his feet, then followed him up the hill towards the church haranguing him all the way and, when she could get no proper answer from him, for he was hurrying on to get away, she hurled her still warm loaf at the back of his head. 'Don't you dare knock our church tower down!' she shouted, adding as an insult: 'I remember you when you came to this town with no shoes on your feet, you and your brother, and not two brass farthings to rub together either! Don't think you are so high and mighty that people forget such things because they don't!'

It was a truth that forty or so years before, during the decade which people still remembered with a shiver as the 'Hungry Forties,' young Walter Crowfoot and his sibling Elijah had indeed walked into Steadshall behind their father and mother, the parents pushing a handcart upon which were loaded all their worldly goods, having come all the way from Norfolk looking for work. That they had prospered since and settled into the life of the place mattered not one jot when loyalties and feelings were at stake and the greatest loyalty many of the people of Steadshall had was to the imposing edifice of their parish church and its tower rising majestically amid its ring of statuesque elms and luxuriant horse-chestnuts.

Therefore, it was perhaps not surprising also that, the very next Sunday, a great number of parishioners, many waving placards pleading for the tower to be saved, should collect by the church gate – but not too close to the tower – to await the arrival of the two churchwardens for the morning service and to hiss and to boo them as they passed through, along with the bewildered sexton, Amos Rowley, who had played no part in anything. That done, they filed dutifully into church behind them to hear the Reverend Scrope scornfully condemn their animosity towards the two churchwardens from the pulpit, but his seeming to take sides with the wardens against the people only resulted in an anonymous cat-call from the larger-than-usual congregation, demanding: 'Why are you knocking down our church tower? It needs repairing, not knocking down.'

Instantly, other voices were raised, sparking a hub-hub of discussion till they were silenced by the vicar's angry cry: 'I will not have this kind of behaviour in God's House. If you have objections to this, then let us call a parish meeting…' Which they all agreed to do.

The meeting was convened by the mayor, Alderman Wilkins, in the town hall's council chamber on the following Wednesday afternoon at which the hundred and eighty who crowded into the room included the deputy-mayor, the town's other aldermen and its twelve councillors, plus the Reverend Scrope himself, the solicitor, Hubert Sparrow, the town surveyor, the town clerk and the two churchwardens, who, for the sake of their own safety, were desperate to dispel the rumours. Indeed, so many turned up who were equally as interested in the outcome of the meeting that fully two hundred others had to stand outside under their umbrellas and shawls in the light drizzle that fell all afternoon.

Among those who did get inside was a bloc of a dozen or so shop-owners, Dissenters to a man, Primitive Congregationalists, Baptists and Primitive Methodists, who, all being ratepayers, deemed it important enough to close their premises for the afternoon or to leave their wives in charge because they feared more than anything that some extravagant measure might be adopted in favour of Church over Chapel. The fortune or otherwise of the parish church was of no concern to them – they were there to ensure that no temporary levy was imposed by the council on the town's traders, Protestant and Dissenter alike, to pay for the demolition of the tower and the design and erection of a new one or, equally as bad, that the council did not decide that a substantial part of the cost of any work should be paid from the town's current rates. They did not want that either.

So when the mayor rose to open the meeting, they had their gaze fixed firmly upon him, as if to warn him that there would be uproar if he so much as hinted at anything which they considered untoward. Wisely, the mayor, fully conscious of their opposition, simply reminded the gathering that the meeting had been convened because 'the tower of our ancient parish church is in an unsafe and unsound condition, so far as one of the buttresses and the outer coating is concerned, and it is clearly evident that something must be done to prevent such an occurrence as had happened recently happening again – ' He meant, of course, the falling pinnacle, not the hounding of the two churchwardens...

FORTY-ONE

WALTER CROWFOOT rose quickly to provide the answer, a prepared speech in one hand, though it was noticeable that he kept his eyes lowered and avoided directing his gaze towards the Dissenting shopkeepers, aware of the hostility emanating from them. They distrusted his every word before he had even begun to speak and were more inclined to believe the reporter for the *County Gazette* than the warden of the parish church. Walter Crowfoot, however, was determined – by hook or by crook – to extricate himself, his vicar and, to a lesser extent, the people's warden from the predicament in which they now found themselves.

'The reporter from the *County Gazette* was wrong to suggest that the tower is to be demolished,' he declared with an unexpected firmness, as if by it hoping at the outset to convince all present that any rumours which they may have heard were nothing but other people's concoctions and misinterpretations. 'That is a very wrong impression which has got abroad. The Reverend Scrope and the churchwardens have never said that it would be better to knock down the whole edifice and build a new one. Nothing could be further from the truth – '

There were several present who considered that nothing would have been closer to the truth had they not protested, but they did not say so there and then.

'The Reverend Scrope, Mr. Gough and I,' Walter Crowfoot went on, 'have always been fully appreciative of the beauty and nobleness of our parish church tower – and will remain so. What *is* proposed is to make the structure of the present dilapidated tower safe by replacing any loose stones on the west front which are in a dangerous condition, rebuilding the fallen pinnacle, making sure the other three pinnacles are safe and raising up the buttress at the north-western corner. That is all.'

The shopowners, and the many others present who felt that they had had to attend to ensure that no penalty was attached to their rates either, had their eyes fixed upon the speaker, so no one noticed the vicar and the second churchwarden, Samuel Gough, exchange uneasy glances.

'Could we not just knock it down and start again?' had indeed been one of Samuel Gough's questions when the three men had sat in the vestry with heavy hearts, mulling over Sir Arthur's initial findings.

'It might be cheaper in the long run, your reverence,' the people's warden had added.

'I should be in favour,' Walter Crowfoot had quickly suggested, anticipating that the vicar was about to say the same – which may have accounted for the fact that his cheeks were flushed red and he was perspiring freely as he addressed the assembly in the council chamber, though kinder people would have put it down to the embarrassment of a man unused to speaking publicly doing just that.

'It has always been our desire to maintain as much as we can of the antique appearance of the tower,' he blatantly told those present, 'without allowing it to remain in a dangerous state or in such a condition as would destroy its artistic beauty by allowing all the ornamentation to flake away or disappear by decay.'

Surprisingly, no challenge was raised to this statement, so Walter Crowfoot paused to mop his brow and rambled on, apprising them of the details of Sir Arthur's inspection, in particular the painstaking attention he had paid to the north-western buttress and the west face: how he and his assistant had taken several photographic plates of those areas which showed quite clearly the condition of all the stones: and that they had even mounted a ladder to examine individual stones and test, so far as they had been able, the condition of each, before ascending to the belfry and the top of the tower to inspect the higher stones of the west face and the remaining pinnacles. From the plates, Sir Arthur and his assistant had made a scale drawing of the tower, numbering all the courses from the base to the top, and marking those which had decayed and needed to be replaced: that drawing he now presented to the meeting.

'Sir Arthur was adamant,' Walter Crowfoot told them, 'that, if the tower is to be maintained, the substantial and thorough repair of those parts marked should be undertaken as soon as possible – '

He again caught the Reverend Scrope's eye, but found him sitting as impassively as before, his arms folded across his chest, his chin in the air in the classic pose of obstinacy: it was as if he had come to believe that nothing could be imminent, no catastrophe could befall them, because *he* had made his decision and had prayed to God for His understanding!

Walter Crowfoot was not so sure. 'If I could make a bargain with Father Time not to have to do anything, I would,' he added wistfully, 'but Time does not stand still and, if the parish does nothing, Time will tumble the stones eventually. The feeling of his reverence and myself and Mr. Gough is that Sir Arthur's recommendations should be followed literally once we have raised the money to undertake the work.'

The one good piece of news that he could give, particularly as far as those who were concerned by the estimated six hundred pounds cost of the project, was that Sir Arthur did not wish to undertake the work himself – it was not a job in which they should be put to the expense of employing him, he had said, but he thought any local architect would be quite able to superintend and carry out the work referred to in his report.

'How are you going to raise the six hundred pounds?' one of the Dissenting shop owners shouted from the back, an almost gleeful edge to his voice. 'We don't want our rates used for your church repairs.'

The vicar now rose and waited for his presence to quieten the hubbub around him. 'The money will be raised by subscription,' he said quietly.

There was a snort from the same direction as the question had come. 'You can't even raise enough for your school extension, Vicar,' the grocer Silas Bentley, a sometimes Baptist lay preacher, chided. 'I hear you're still short of a few hundred pounds for that and that you 'on't be building a new school over at Bourne Brook either. Seems to me you don't have the money for neither the church nor the school. Seems to me the whole danged thing is going to fall down about your ears afore you lot are able to do anything about it.'

They were hurtful facts, but, unfortunately, possibly true facts.

'Six hundred pounds is a great sum, I admit,' the Reverend Scrope resumed, 'and I am fully aware that it is unlikely we shall get the six hundred pounds we require for the church repairs immediately. We have never anticipated being able to do that. However, if we can raise a mere hundred pounds, say, to begin with, we should be well satisfied. With a hundred pounds, we could begin some work on the tower, even if only to shore-up the buttress until it can be repaired properly, while at the same time continuing with the extension at the school.'

Here, with reason, he took a breath before continuing: 'In order to achieve that, the school's management board are in the process of planning another concert in the schoolroom a month from now to raise the rest of the money for the parochial school extension and we are also planning to hold a second concert later in the year to raise money towards the repairs to the tower – '

They were not: no meeting to discuss either had ever taken place: he had just thought of the idea and announced it simply to silence the questioner – a little white lie, if you will – which was why Walter Crowfoot and Samuel Gough were looking at him in surprise: it was the first they had heard of it.

' – Miss Dunsmore will be arranging the music,' the Reverend Scrope went on.

She might if she knew about it, if she were asked, which she had not yet been, but no one knew that. The Reverend Scrope simply cleared his throat of the lie and went on as boldly as before: 'We would hope to raise a good sum from that. And the Diocese will, I am sure, also be contributing to our cause – '

Though he said it in as offhand a manner as he could muster, as though it were a foregone conclusion, in his heart he knew that it was highly improbable that the Diocese would donate even one ha'penny: the Bishop was still far more interested in saving the souls of black Africans and building them mud huts in which to live than he was in paying for the renovation of the more solid bricks and mortar of England – God would be more pleased with him for doing that, he reasoned, and it would more likely smooth his path into heaven. Besides, there was only so much money to go around and his palace roof needed re-leading and re-tiling: it was starting to leak when it rained too heavily...

A practised and patronising slyness entered the Reverend Scrope's words. 'My experience of Steadshall people,' he said quietly, as though it were the most acknowledged thing in the world, 'is that, they will readily contribute towards the cost of saving the tower. I do not think there will be any difficulty in raising the amount needed to repair God's House.'

There were one or two cynical snorts along the row at the back where the Dissenters sat together, but from others there were nods in agreement: the vicar was right: they were charitable people: each knew of someone who had given to some charity or other at some time or other, even if it were not themselves.

For himself, the Reverend Scrope had said what he had said, but none knew that, at that moment, he was wrestling mightily with his conscience over his decision to continue with the extension to the school ahead of the repairs to the church tower. Had he made the right decision? More and more, it was keeping him awake at night, so much so that he was beginning to dread going to his lonely bed…

FORTY-TWO

WHEN THE REVEREND SCROPE realised late on the Saturday evening that he was standing in the darkness outside Helen Dunsmore's cottage, he did not actually know how he came to be there. To be sure, he had walked to the small, neat cottage along the Burestead Market road, but he could remember nothing of the actual journey.

He had set out from the vicarage a half-hour before merely intending to take a late evening stroll around the town in the hope of clearing his head of the turmoil within: but, as he walked, the anxieties of life had welled up and engulfed him, so much so that, though several of his parishioners tipped their hats to him and bade him 'Good evening' as he passed them on the road, he neither heard them nor was aware of them.

His mind had been in turmoil all day: he could not think clearly: he had been unable to finish his sermon for the Sunday and it lay a quarter written on his desk top. He had made the decision to continue with the extension to the school rather than sanction the repairs to the church tower – to God's House – to ensure that religious instruction would continue at the parochial school as before.

All the time, one thought was uppermost in his mind: that was, he had heard, some board schools were indifferent to religious instruction and, if a board school were ever set up in Steadshall, then there might be no learning of the Catechism at all for the children of the poor, no morning prayers, no reading of the Bible – even if it were now somewhat curtailed under Mr. Warburton from before – and no occasional services in the church especially for them either, at Christmas, Easter and Michaelmas, say. That was why he had done what he had done – to ensure that God's word was preserved among the children of the poor, so that they should know and love their Maker, attend Sunday school regularly and say their prayers before bed each night – worshipping the Lord.

But would God understand? Would God forgive him for what he had done? And by doing it, had he compromised his own reward in heaven? He could find no answer that satisfied, for when he found one, his mind dredged up one which did not.

'I am a man in turmoil, Miss Dunsmore,' were the first words he spoke when the spinster teacher opened the door to his knock, 'a man in turmoil. May I come in?'

'Oh, dear, poor Mr. Scrope,' she had said, stepping aside and watching him pass in some consternation.

He sat at the dining table with his shoulders slumped and, as people sometimes do when confused and in some distress, began rubbing vigorously at his forehead as if to ease a pain or an ache.

'I feel somehow God has guided me to you this evening, Miss Dunsmore,' he declared, without so much as a glance at her, 'for I know nothing of how I came to be here. I remember nothing of the walk to your cottage. I just found myself here, knocking on your door. It can only be God's will. Why, I do not know.'

Miss Dunsmore had passed enough evenings alone in her cottage not to welcome the distraction of a visit by someone as important as the vicar: if God had 'guided' him to her cottage, there must be a reason for it, she thought to herself.

She had spent the earlier part of the evening gardening till the light had faded, then she had returned inside to light the solitary oil lamp, intending to read one of the novels she had taken out from the town library that day, passing the time, waiting to go to bed, waiting for the first yawn which would tell her it was time to go up. Now the vicar himself had knocked at her door and, for the first time since his return from his trip around the world, *he* was sitting in her parlour: she felt honoured. To have the vicar on her side against the presumptuous Warburtons was something for which she had always hoped, but which she had never quite been sure that she had: it strengthened her cause at the school just to have him there.

When she had opened the door to him, she had thought he had perhaps come to discuss what music she had chosen for the forthcoming concert – the one the vicar had announced so casually at the town hall meeting and of which she had only just learned. It was the only reason she could think why he was sitting in her parlour, looking as though the weight of the world were upon his shoulders. That he just wanted to talk about his troubles did not enter her head till he mentioned it: she guessed straight away what those troubles were.

'You have made the right decision, Mr. Scrope,' she said sympathetically, seating herself on a chair on the same side of the table so that the two faced each other no more than three feet apart. 'You had to save the parochial school from being forcibly pushed aside by the Government. I cannot see that you could have done anything other than you have.'

She thought briefly of leaning forward and placing one hand on his arm, purely as a gesture of sympathy, nothing more: she was close enough, but resisted: just as no man had ever put his arms around her, so she had never offered that type of affection to any man, save for her father when she was very small.

'The church tower will be repaired in time,' she went on. 'The Lord knows you will do that and will not neglect it. You should not worry so. You did your duty as you saw fit and a man can do no more.'

'Ah, duty,' he said with a long sigh. 'Duty is a heavy taskmaster for the likes of parish priests like myself who do not have a good woman in whom they can confide. I miss my Jane, Miss Dunsmore. I will be honest, I miss my Jane. I miss her comforting presence,. She was someone in whom I could always confide. It is a lonely life being a widower – '

'You poor man,' said Miss Dunsmore and this time, unable to help herself, she did reach out to lay a consoling hand upon his sleeve. 'You can confide in me, Mr. Scrope. I have always regarded you as a dear friend. I would be happy to help you. You have such a heavy burden to carry – the town, the school, the souls of every one of us. '

'Yes indeed,' he said quietly, as if ruminating. 'Yes indeed, Miss Dunsmore, I have. I have, indeed.'

She did not understand that what he needed at that moment to ease his troubled mind was the kind of distraction which only a woman can give. Sitting and talking with a woman was one thing, but what he required at that moment was to be able to touch her – to be *allowed* to touch her! Not in the way she was touching him – but in a different way! The thought came leaping up from somewhere deep within his mind's recesses: it was no good just thinking about it: he must tell her – he must ask her.

'I have to tell you that, right at this minute, Miss Dunsmore,' he said, lifting his head to look directly at her, 'that at this moment I am in need of the kind of comfort that only a woman can give – the kind of comfort that only a wife can give when a man is troubled.'

Her hand left his sleeve and he saw her stiffen visibly in her chair: she was staring at him, her mouth partly open in surprise, as if unable to believe that she had heard what she had heard and struggling to accept that she had interpreted his meaning correctly.

'Oh Mr. Scrope,' she gasped. 'Do you mean? – ' She could not bring herself to articulate what he was implying – what he was asking. Did he really mean *that*? Did he really mean he wanted to lie with her?

Be bold, he told himself. Now is the time! Now is your chance! She is a woman and, therefore, there to meet your needs: it only requires a few more words, a few more soothing words.

The ache, the undeniable ache, spurred him on: he wanted to lean forward and place his hand on her breast, just to fondle it, to appease his need to fondle the softer parts of a woman, to test her reaction: for, if she allowed him to do that, if she encouraged him to continue by doing nothing to prevent him, he would do so – he needed to do so! Had not God made Eve to comfort Adam? And if he were allowed to continue, depending upon how much she welcomed his attentions, how responsive she was to his touch, he might even suggest that she permit him to do other things – unbutton the front of her blouse, for instance, and reach inside her camisole and fondle her breasts in the flesh, even to ask her pull up her dress and petticoats so that he could reach down inside her drawers as he had liked to do with Jane all those months before – and perhaps after a while the two of them might go up to her bedroom, close the curtains and indulge in a full coupling, he the widower and she the lonely spinster unlikely ever to have had a man lie on top of her with his roused manhood working to a climax inside her...

'God would bless you for it,' he told her. 'He would reward you in heaven. You would be in His good graces. You would be doing His will if you allowed me, I am convinced of it.'

To ask her such a thing! She jumped to her feet and was backing away from him, her mouth still open in utter shock.

'My dear Miss Dunsmore,' he said, quickly, rising to his feet, but making no move to close the gap between them, 'I mean you no harm, no disrespect. It is just that I am a lonely man who has been denied the physical solace of a woman – my Jane – for over a year now. I am denied everything that is associated with holy matrimony. Tonight I need someone who will help me, who will relieve me of this ache this ache in my soul.'

The ache was not in his soul, it was elsewhere. She nodded dumbly and remained a few feet from him as if frozen to the spot.

'But I do not know how,' she said. 'I have never – I have never done anything like – like that before!'

'There is no need to be afraid, Miss Dunsmore,' he said, moving closer to her so that he could put one arm about her shoulders: he felt her whole form quiver as their bodies touched.

'It is such a little thing, I ask,' he assured her. 'It is done every night by wives with their husbands. It is an act of love. Does not Jesus say, "Love thy neighbour as thyself."? You would be like the Good Samaritan helping the man beset by thieves on the road to Jericho. If you wish, I will say a little prayer for the both of us before we begin. Have no fear, Miss Dunsmore – Helen – I will guide you. I am a man of experience. You need not be afraid...'

'Be gentle with me, you are the first,' were her final words as he led her up the stairs to the bedroom.

He promised that he would. Even so, she was totally unprepared for the physical assault he made upon her: she had never lain naked with a man or seen a man's full nakedness: nor had she been touched by a man, had her legs gently prised apart, allowed anyone to do what he did, not knowing how to respond to his kisses or his hands which cupped and squeezed her breasts and invaded her secret parts. And she was startled, shocked even, by the desire his touching engendered in her and by the passion he displayed as he lay on top of her, the weight of his body crushing her, feeling the boniness of his hips moving rhythmically against hers. The hairiness of his chest, the hairiness of his legs and his loins, the hardness and the heat of him, the brief pain of his entry and the unexpected joy of what followed – all of it was new to her, as she had often dreamed it would be...

When he had finished and she lay in the semi-darkness amid a tangle of sheets, stunned and exhausted by all that had happened, she asked him, somewhat plaintively: 'Will you be needing to do this again, Mr. Scrope?'

'No, I think not, Miss Dunsmore,' he said casually, swinging his legs off the bed and standing. She had served his purpose: he had been satisfied: he was calmed again in his mind and his body. 'I do not think I shall need to bother you again. You have served God and I bless you for it.'

His back was to her so he did not see the look of disappointment upon her face. After he had dressed and left her, she lay a long time on the bed, wondering – if that was what it was like to lie with a man, then perhaps she could entice him to return somehow, someday, to repeat it. Men in such 'need' were always susceptible to the wiles of a woman, she had heard. Given time and encouragement, she might even induce him to change his widower's status…

FORTY-THREE

THE VERY NEXT DAY, Sunday, heavy downpours and violent thunderstorms – the worst seen in that part of the county in living memory, some of the older folk said – struck that part of the county, causing ditches to overflow, fields to flood and leaving the dirt road between Bourne Brook and Steadshall impassable to wagons, carts and coaches alike. The Reverend Smallwood vainly attempted to reach his congregation by walking through the downpour, but in the end was forced to turn back when confronted by a fifty-foot-long 'lake' where the road should have been.

At Bourne Brook itself, the stream overflowed its low banks and a number of cottages built close by on the flood plain were inundated by two feet to three feet of brown, foul-smelling water, which had drained off the cow meadows and out of the farmyards further upstream. When the waters receded, the people brushed the brown scum left behind out of their cottages and swilled down their floors, thinking everything would be all right: but, two days later, a mysterious fever and violent retching sickness struck the inhabitants of the hamlet, particularly those living in the flooded cottages, of whom more than forty were children. Not unexpectedly, come the Tuesday morning and the number of children walking to the parochial school at Steadshall was down drastically and come the Wednesday it was zero.

That the fever was extremely contagious was brought home to William when Martha walked over to Bourne Brook on the Wednesday evening to ascertain how serious the outbreak there was: she returned in good health, but by mid-day on the Thursday was feeling poorly and by the evening was quite feverish herself and retching also: and, by the Friday morning, after a sleepless night, she was too debilitated even to walk across the road to the school. Young Dr. Langham was sent for and he ordered that she drink only water sweetened with sugar which had been boiled first and recommended at least a week or maybe even two weeks of bed rest, which was a blow, for it left William with just his assistant-teacher and the pupil-teacher Hannah Hodgson, plus the two monitors.

Then, on the Monday of the second week, Miss Dunsmore herself sent in a note to say that she, too, was 'feeling unwell,' followed on the Tuesday by one from Hannah Hodgson and on the Wednesday by a third from the monitor, Alice Barbrook, though she complained only of a painful septic foot, which made it difficult for her to stand: it meant that only William and the second junior monitor, Olive Chaplin, were present to run the school.

All William could do was to pull back the heavy curtain which divided the Big Room and teach all four standards together and, before each assembly and during each dinnertime, instruct Olive Chaplin on what lessons to give the infants, what sums to set them, what lettering or numbers they should be copying on their slates and what stories she should read to them, at the same time appointing two other girls from standard six as temporary monitors, one to help him and the other to help Olive in the infants' class.

The Reverend Smallwood visited midway through the morning on the second Wednesday, sent by the vicar to find out what was going on and how bad it was, for the usual numbers from Steadshall itself continued to attend. He stayed to help out, giving standards three and four an unexpectedly eloquent and passionate declamation of the twenty-two verses from *'The Wreck of the Hesperus'* by Henry Wadsworth Longfellow, several from memory, and then writing them on the blackboard for the children to copy out:

> *'It was the schooner Hesperus,*
> *That sailed the wintry sea;*
> *And the skipper had taken his little daughter,*
> *To bear him company.*

> *'Blue were her eyes as the fairy flax,*
> *Her cheeks like the dawn of day,*
> *And her bosom white as the hawthorn buds,*
> *That ope in the month of May...'*

However, he had other duties to fulfil, namely a funeral, and after the dinner break excused himself for the rest of the afternoon: nor did he return the next day, put off, William surmised, as much by the prospect of teaching a hundred and more unreceptive, smirking children as by the constant noise from Elijah Crowfoot's men, who that very day had finally begun work on digging the foundations for the extension to the infants' room and were clattering about outside.

Before he left, however, the Reverend Smallwood did promise that he would report the seriousness of the situation to the vicar, but the Reverend Scrope made no appearance: instead, on the Thursday morning, when William just happened to glance out of the window of the Big Room, he saw the vicar and the curate driving past in the vicar's pony and trap, heading out along the Burestead Market road. The Reverend Scrope did not even bother to turn his head to look in the direction of the afflicted school, as though what was happening there was nowhere in his thoughts: the curate did cast a sideways glance towards it and then somewhat guiltily lowered his eyes, as though he were regretful for some reason.

Where they were going that day, William had no idea, but it so infuriated him that, while all four standards were copying down a passage from Charles Dickens's *David Copperfield,* which he had written on the blackboard, he sat at his desk and wrote an angry note to the Reverend Scrope:

> '*Sir, For the past two days, the school has been in the charge of just myself as the head and a single monitor, Olive Chaplin, which I find most unsatisfactory.* (He omitted to mention the other two.) *My own wife has been struck down by the same fever which has also laid so many low in Bourne Brook. I have no idea how long this situation may continue and the doctor says it could be a further fortnight before my wife is well enough to return. Miss Dunsmore and Hannah Hodgson are also off ill and I have no knowledge of when they will return.*
>
> '*I wish to know immediately if you are going to supply me with help or am I to take the responsibility of supplying myself? Two of us, a child monitor and myself, are now doing the work of four. Unless I hear from you by the end of this day that you are willing to supply me with proper help next week, I shall be obliged to close the school tomorrow and every day thereafter till either my wife or Miss Dunsmore or Miss Hodgson returns or I am given the help I require.*'

No reply was forthcoming from the Reverend Scrope that evening and when William went up to the bedroom and found that Martha was utterly inert, her fever even worse, too stricken even to eat the beef broth he had left her, he decided he must carry out his threat. 'Quite frankly,' he told himself, 'I need to stay at home and look after my wife.'

The next morning found him standing at the school gate, waving away all the pupils as they arrived – and receiving happy smiles for it from them and even thanks from some of the parents, for some were beginning to worry about possible contagion if their children were all closeted together: till then, thanks to Dr. Iveson and Dr. Langham and the town's Health Board, the fever and accompanying retching were confined to Bourne Brook.

Still, neither the vicar nor the curate visited: all that happened was that Joshua Linkhorn sent a terse reply, pushed through William's letter box late on the Saturday evening:

> '*Sir, I have already mentioned to you that all communications regarding the parochial school should be sent to me as the secretary of the school management board and that the Reverend Scrope is not to be troubled. I can assure you that the management board are fully aware of the situation regarding the staffing at the school and, if the current situation persists for any length of time, we shall endeavour to supply the gap caused by the illness of your wife and other members of your staff, namely Miss Dunsmore and Miss Hodgson. An approach is being considered regarding the recruitment for a limited period only of an assistant-teacher from the parochial school at Bromptree, where they are fully staffed. In the meantime, in view of our need to keep up the attendance register so as to secure a maximum annual grant from the government, we insist that you reopen the school forthwith, utilising whatever resources you have…*'

Fortunately, the board's endeavours to recruit an assistant-teacher from outside were not required, for Miss Dunsmore and Hannah Hodgson both returned to the school on the following Monday. William was at least glad that it could now be run properly again: he reopened it that same day and made a point of thanking young Olive Chaplin for her help by buying her a pen, a bottle of blue-black ink and a small pad of flower-framed writing paper.

Her diligence was in contrast to the demeanour of Miss Dunsmore, who had not been seriously affected, saying only that she had been sick several times in the morning during her time off, fortunately without the fever associated with it.

Hannah Hodgson, meanwhile, openly admitted that she had not actually had any illness, but had been kept at home by her widowed mother when she had suffered a stomach ache following the onset of the kind of bleeding which afflicts young females of her age. She said it almost with a smile upon her face, as if to say, 'I don't care. My being off pays you back for making me cry.'

'Goodness gracious, girl! My own wife has been struck down by the fever and is still ill,' William cried, his anger rising. 'She has been in bed since last week and I have had to close the school and all you had was a tummy ache! God, girl! I despair of you, I despair of you! That was very irresponsible of you, do you know that?'

'I do not and you have no right to talk to me like that,' she retorted, but not with any bravado, for her lower lip was trembling as tears began welling in her eyes 'My mother told me to stay at home. She knows when I am ill or not. If you have anything to say about it, you will have to talk to my mother and not to me.'

'I will address you how I see fit, Miss Hodgson, because I have that right as your head teacher,' William snapped back. 'By your selfish action, you let me down and you let the school down. Away with you, girl! I am too angry. Go to your class before I say something I might regret.'

'I'm not going to any class,' the young girl shouted, the tears streaming down her cheeks. 'I'm not going to stay here any longer and be told off for nothing. All I ever do is get told off! I'm going to tell the vicar on you! That's what I am going to do.' And with that, she ran out through the door, her fists balled up to her eyes, crying pitifully. Neither did she return for the rest of the week or the following week...

FORTY-FOUR

THE REASON that Hannah Hodgson did not return was because, when she knocked on the door of the vicarage, she found herself confronted by a full-blown crisis in that household: the nursemaid, Sarah Pockett, had gone missing during the night.

She had gone to bed as usual the previous evening, but sometime during the early hours she had slipped out of the house and vanished, taking a small suitcase of clothes with her: a small amount of money was also missing.

A note propped against a clock on the mantelpiece in the nursery explained:

> '*I do not wish to stay here any longer. I am going back to Somerset. I have taken only what I think is owed to me from Miss Scrope's petty cash box in the kitchen. I hope she will forgive me. I thank her for everything she has done for me while I have been here and I am sorry to let her and baby Elizabeth down. I shall continue to go to church regularly as I am a good Christian.*'

For some reason, there was no mention of her employer, but perhaps that was only to be expected of a young girl of sixteen who for the past few months had been living in the same house as the man who was not only the vicar of the town, the shepherd of his flock, as she understood it, the most respected personage in Steadshall but an anointed servant of God Almighty – and also one who could be cantankerous in the extreme, often hurtfully condescending when asked anything, pedantic and overbearing most times, irascible without cause at any time, childishly petulant on occasion and always demanding, always demanding, expecting strict obedience from others and their indulgence without demurral at whatever peculiarities and foibles he had.

Enquiries by one of the constables in the three hours since the letter had been found had ascertained that she had bought a ticket for Steymarket junction from the clerk at the railway station and the station master had seen her waiting on the platform with her suitcase as the first train of the day came in, the five-thirty from Hilvershall en route to Lapperchall junction, where it would meet a down-train from Edmundsbury to the Steymarket junction with the main line to London. From there, she could take an up-train to the capital and, since she had been gone several hours already, there would be no bringing her back: she would already be in London and quite possibly even on a train from Waterloo back to Somerset.

Agnes opened the door to the tearful Hannah Hodgson, hoping that it was the nursemaid returning: the Reverend Scrope was standing behind her in the hallway, not looking at all pleased by anything.

'Oh, tell her I have no time to deal with her now,' he began, when his sister announced that the pupil-teacher was asking to speak to him: but then he stopped, the anger upon his face vanished and he turned towards the thirteen-year-old with an unexpected beaming smile.

Hannah Hodgson's arrival at that precise moment was the answer to his prayers, or it would have been had he stopped to say any since the discovery of the nursemaid's disappearance. However, for the past two hours he had been seated in his study, muttering to himself, seeming to be somewhat shocked by what had occurred and not really wanting even to reply to his sister when she asked him, somewhat rhetorically, why had the nursemaid done such a 'cruel thing' as leaving a small child who adored her, over whom she cooed day long, and fleeing as she had, without even asking for a reference or giving any period of notice? To all this, her brother had simply shrugged his shoulders and his only comment was that she was 'an ungrateful girl, a very ungrateful girl.'

'Ah, Hannah, my girl, come in, come in,' the vicar said, motioning for the pupil-teacher to step inside. 'You may be the answer to my prayer. Come – come with me. I have a proposition to put to you...'

A slightly bewildered Hannah Hodgson, still sniffing back the tears – she had begun crying again as soon as she reached the vicarage gate – dutifully followed her vicar into his study, the door was clicked shut and she was motioned to a black, horsehair couch.

The Reverend Scrope seated himself beside her: a handkerchief was produced to dry her tears, an act of kindness for which she thanked the vicar in a sulky mumble, before blowing her nose loudly: and when he placed an arm around her shoulders, he was only doing what a consoling gentleman would do in the circumstances when faced with a tearful young girl seated on a couch beside him: it was not at all the irritation it might have been if it had been done by others.

He began by asking what had brought her so expedientially to the vicarage and, when she frowned to hear the word 'expedientially,' he repeated his question more simply: 'What brought you here, Hannah? You seem upset?'

She told him and did not mind that his arm tightened about her shoulders as he pulled her briefly to him in a hug before releasing her.

'Never mind Mr. Warburton, Hannah, I shall deal with him,' he reassured her, giving her another gentle squeeze. 'After all, I am his employer. I am the chairman of the school management board and also the vicar, so I am able to deal with things like that. He shall not shout at you again and upset you. I promise you that.'

The girl sniffed her thanks and again she did not mind when he hugged her a third time. 'Tell me, Hannah,' he said, quietly, 'do you have any brothers and sisters at home?'

She did, one older sister of sixteen, who was in service somewhere and whom the vicar vaguely remembered, and three sisters all under school age, the two youngest twins aged four, born just after her father had died or pneumonia. The outcome of his questioning was that a quarter-hour later, when Hannah emerged from the study, her tears had dried, though she was still looking a little apprehensive, while beside her the beaming vicar announced to his waiting sister, sitting on a chair in the hallway: 'My dear, our problem is solved. Hannah has agreed to be our new live-in nursemaid. She has younger sisters at home and is used to looking after them. She will be perfect for looking after Elizabeth…'

That was, of course, once the matter had been settled with her widowed mother, but that would come down to what sum the mother would accept for her initial loss and what wage he would pay the girl, after deducting her board and keep, of course. As for the schoolmaster, he would send a note round in due course to tell him that she would not be returning and that, in due course also, he would see to it that a new pupil-teacher was appointed.

But that could wait – he had other matters on his mind. The previous Sunday, the Bishop had made his biennial visitation and the church had looked unsightly with the ugly wooden props already in place against the tower to hold up the unsafe north-western buttress – erected by Elijah Crowfoot's men before starting work at the school and yet to be paid for from money which, strictly speaking, he did not have.

The Bishop had pulled a face at the disfigurement. 'I hope this will be seen to soon, Scrope,' he had said, with a scowl.

The Reverend Scrope assured him that it would – in time – but had to tell him that it was with 'great sorrow' that he did not think they would have enough money to begin the actual work on the repairs to the tower before the New Year at the earliest, still five months away, that was, always supposing enough came in by subscription in the meantime to allow it. The subscription fund for the school extension was still advancing by dribs and drabs, while that for the tower's repair had barely begun.

To start the latter fund and to shame the townsfolk into giving more quickly, he had given a further fifty pounds from his own Living. His hope was that, on seeing the problem first hand, the Bishop would promise him some diocesan funding, but he did not: his missionary work in Africa was still more important, it seemed, than the people of his own country.

Even Dr. Iveson had become somewhat of a grump of late, the Reverend Scrope had noted. When he had asked him a week previously if he could possibly see his way to doubling his contribution by giving the same amount towards 'the repair of God's House' as he had already given towards the school extension fund, the doctor had replied somewhat caustically that he needed what money he had to repair his own house as the recent heavy rains had dislodged the guttering at the front and the water pouring from it had soaked through the brickwork and ruined the plaster and the wallpaper in his parlour.

Sometimes, it seemed to the Reverend Scrope, that the good doctor was losing interest in the management board, the fund-raising and the church.

There was also another worry – Helen Dunsmore. Ever since the night he had called at her cottage, he found himself forever trying to avoid catching her eye while he was giving his Sunday sermons, for when she was not playing the organ, she was forever turning to look up at him when he was in the pulpit. She had done it even in the presence of the Bishop: it had been most disconcerting: he only hoped that his Lordship had not noticed. She had even followed at his heels when he and the other members of the management board had showed the Bishop the work already completed on the extension, as though she were a member of it, too, and not just an assistant to the head master who just happened to teach there. He might have to have another word with her – thank her again for her kindness, but inform her that he was not looking for a repeat.

The continual letters from the school were also proving to be tiresome: there had been five in as many months since the new schoolmaster and his wife had taken up their posts and the latest lay on his desk at that very moment. If the schoolmaster were not complaining about the dankness of the place or the shortage of this or that, it was that this or that needed to be repaired or the boys' urinal channel was blocked again, the emptying of the toilet buckets was still irregular or, as he had in his most recent letter, that he himself was being overworked and needed more help. The man's complaints were endless…

FORTY-FIVE

WILLIAM WAS NOT too put out by Hannah Hodgson's failure to return: for, in the mid-August, he was able to close the school for the traditional three-week 'harvest holiday,' when most of the boys and girls of the higher standards did go willingly into the fields around the town to help with stooking and carting the sheaves of wheat and barley on the farms, whiles others went into the orchards which lay to the south and west to help pick the plums, pears and apples.

While the school was closed, work on the extension pushed on apace and, once it was completed in the last week of August, William arranged a thorough cleaning of the whole school, for which several of the parents volunteered to work over two evenings. The sawdust, brick dust and wood shavings left by the builders in the extension, were swept up, the grimed windows were cleaned, the two new doors and a new window were painted and the walls were distempered green and cream. In the Big Room, the old frayed mats and cushions were washed again, the benches and desks were all polished and the cupboards cleaned, while outside the drains were cleared of leaves and other detritus, the worst of the playground potholes were filled with sand and shale, donated by a benefactor, and two of the fathers, of their own volition, even whitewashed the lavatories so that all would be spick and span for the start of the new year on Monday, September the sixth.

The Reverend Scrope and Joshua Linkhorn made a tour of inspection of the completed extension and announced themselves thoroughly pleased by everything. Martha, too, was pleased that the days of overcrowding in the Little Room would finally be over, though the problem now was that someone other than her would be required to supervise the smallest of the children in their new room.

At the same time that Steadshall's extension was being readied for opening, a disused 'cow byre' at Bourne Brook was being cleared of its stalls and detritus and swilled out and swept out by some women of the congregation there: it was the only place they could find for the new school. A loose brick floor had been laid over the dirt, its walls had been whitewashed, its beams creosoted and a window knocked in one wall to provide daylight: several dilapidated benches had also been acquired *gratis* along with an old cast-iron stove and two large cupboards, one for each department. No longer would the children of Bourne Brook have to walk to Steadshall through wind and rain and hail and snow and gales and floods, for which their parents were heartily thankful. It would, however, still come under the auspices of the Steadshall management board, of which the Reverend Smallwood remained an ex-officio member.

On the day that the Steadshall extension was opened, the remaining pupils from the town attended a special morning service at St. Andrew's church, conducted by the Reverend Scrope, to give 'thanks to God' for providing them, first, with the additional classroom at Steadshall and, second, with the 'new school' at Bourne Brook – even if the full amount for both was not yet fully 'gathered in.' At least, the old 'cow byre' was on higher ground than many of the dwellings around it which had been flooded so disastrously by the swollen brook only weeks before.

In the early afternoon, on what was a bright Indian summer day, the Steadshall children, with William, Martha and Miss Dunsmore in attendance, marched a short distance along the Burestead Market road to Wood Hall, the home of the two aged Misses Iseleys, who received them with smiles of delight, particularly the younger children, and conducted them to long trestle-tables set out on the lawn and laden with buns, cakes, jellies and orangeade.

However, before the children were allowed to sit down to eat and certainly before they prayed to be made 'truly thankful' for what they were about to receive, the Reverend Scrope spoke a few words, though few detected the sarcasm of his tone as he told them how heartily glad he was that they had built the extension 'on time.'

'Had we not,' he said, 'we should have had a School Board imposed upon us, for you must remember that our duty as citizens is always to do what the Government of the land tells us to do. So it is with great pride and thanks be to God that I say, here and now, the threat of the Government's imposition of a School Board upon this town is banished forever. We shall continue to teach our children as we have always taught them – to fear God, to love God and to believe in God. There will be no heathens in my parish…'

There was a smattering of applause from the three score or so of adults present to assist and the children cheered, though without knowing exactly why.

'And we are pleased to announce also,' the Reverend Scrope went on, 'that a Miss Rose Cockle has been appointed the teacher at the new Bourne Brook school at a salary which is reasonable to the school management board – ' It was to be fifty-nine pounds per annum, far more than most of the children's fathers earned, but he would not tell them that.

The appointment was a surprise to William and Martha: they had expected that Helen Dunsmore would be given the post: indeed, they had not only thought her appointment to be a foregone conclusion, given her repeatedly declared 'friendship' with the Reverend Scrope, but were both hoping for it – praying for it, in fact, as it would mean that William could say farewell to his grouchy assistant-teacher and, he hoped, welcome a new assistant, perhaps even two, who would be more amenable and more industrious.

'The strength of a school,' the Reverend Scrope went on, adopting his sermonising mood while the children fidgeted and eyed the cakes and jellies, 'the strength of a school does not by any means depend upon the number of scholars attending it, but in the proficiency of the scholars themselves – in the way they pass the Government's examinations, the way in which they learn to fulfil the duties of this life and prepare for the life which is to come. That is the whole basis of National Schools like Steadshall Parochial School, which are and shall ever remain the glory of England for which the clergy of the Church of England have worked so hard in order that every family in the land might have the advantage of its own parish school.'

He finished to loud applause and then went inside the Hall, for that day another gathering was taking place to celebrate the elder Miss Iseley's sixty-eighth birthday and the tea for the children was a special treat from her. William and Martha remained with the children, for neither they nor Miss Dunsmore had been invited 'inside,' which William and Martha, for their part at least, put down to the machinations of the Reverend Scrope and the recent troubles with him. Indeed, as he walked to the house, the vicar passed within twenty feet of them, but did not so much as nod in their direction to acknowledge their presence or even give them so much as a glower, which they might have expected of him. More of a surprise was that he did not look towards Helen Dunsmore either: she was standing at the end of one of the long trestle-tables and the vicar passed within five feet of her and either did not see her or deliberately ignored her. It seemed to cause her some confusion, for William and Martha saw her redden and turn quickly away and give a sharp reprimand to some child who was about to reach out for an iced bun before they had been given the order to 'tuck in.'

There was little time to dwell upon the matter, anyway, for, after the children had finished their tea, which they did in double-quick time, hundreds of little hands snaking out to seize cakes and buns, holding up mugs and glasses for drinks of lemonade poured from what seemed to be a never-ending stream of jugs and bending to spoon in mouthfuls of jelly and trifle – after they had eaten all and left nothing, they went into the meadow behind the house where swings and other amusements such as a seesaw and a small hand-turned roundabout had been provided for the youngest, while running races, three-legged races, egg-and-spoon races and sack races were organised for the older children. And while that was going on, the adults sat listening to a small brass band from Wivencaster playing selections of hymn music and popular pieces of the day, which they did till the early evening, before ending the day by striking up *God Save the Queen* as three hearty cheers rang out and the company made for home...

FORTY-SIX

SOLELY IN VIEW of the non-return of Hannah Hodgson when the new school year began and due to the lack of communication of any kind from the vicar on the matter, William, requiring a replacement pupil-teacher, decided it might be a good idea to have two pupil-teachers. The two obvious choices were Olive Chaplin and Alice Barbrook, who were both bright and resourceful and quite prepared to boss the older children, even the boys, into obedience and to coax the younger children to do what was wanted of them. They would make ideal pupil-teachers, he thought, as he turned the key on that first morning.

The drawback was that both had left the school at the beginning of the harvest holiday, having received their leaving certificates, Olive Chaplin to become a maid in one of the big houses in the district and Alice Barbrook going into one of Oldcourt's mills.

In William's scheme of things, Olive Chaplin would return to assist Martha with the smaller children and Alice Barbrook would help Miss Dunsmore in place of Hannah Hodgson. Both girls were willing to return and, indeed, the parents of both thanked William for the 'wonderful chance' he was proposing to give their daughters, even if their salaries as pupil-teachers would be even less than the pittance they were already earning. It mattered more to them to have their daughters become pupil-teachers rather than having them continuing to work as a maid and a mill hand.

That was William's plan, supported enthusiastically, even thankfully, by Martha, and, surprisingly, also supported by Helen Dunsmore, who, having got over a second bout of sickness during the harvest holiday, was looking altogether more pleased about something: William even caught her singing quietly to herself one time, as if a great worry had been lifted from her shoulders and she was relieved by it. 'All is now well again, thankfully,' she replied when he enquired and she even smiled as she said it.

Of course, any appointments at the school would have to be approved by the management board and so William wrote to Joshua Linkhorn, as he had been instructed by earlier replies from the secretary, informing him of his idea:

'Sirs, With the start of the new year, I am in urgent need of supplementing my staff at the parochial school. In view of the fact that I have received no communication regarding the likely return of Miss Hodgson, who I understand has been seconded to other duties at the vicarage, I should like to propose to the school management board that Olive Chaplin and Alice Barbrook, two former monitors whom I regard as both entirely competent, be indentured forthwith as apprentice pupil-teachers...'

There was a delay of several days before his communication was raised at the next management meeting in the vicarage: that he had the temerity to write to the board requesting their approval on such a matter drew the vicar's ire, as did what he considered to be a pointed reference to his own lack of action.

'It is none of his business, tell him so,' he instructed Joshua Linkhorn. 'Does the board approve of this, for I do not?'

Surprisingly, the other members of the management board thought it a reasonable idea – or at least they did not object outright or see it as controversial a matter as did the vicar: the four farmers attached no importance to it at all and shrugged away the vicar's objection, while the Reverend Smallwood bravely thought it an 'an eminently sensible decision, in view of the shortage' and Dr. Iveson added with a weary sigh: 'The man is only suggesting what I would have suggested, faced with the same problem.'

'...If you would agree' William's letter continued, *'I should propose setting an hour a day aside to prepare the two pupil-teachers for their later examinations. At present I would give them lessons in the morning before school begins, though in the coming winter, since they both have to walk a mile daily to school through any and all inclement weather, their lessons would probably have to be taken after school from 4:30 to 5·30 in the afternoon instead of from seven to eight in the morning.*

'Respectfully, I would also like to apprise the members of the management board of the fact that a female teacher training college, run by a former qualified teacher, has been

opened in Wivencaster and is recruiting pupils. In addition to full-time studies, the college plans to hold special training classes for pupil-teachers on Tuesday and Thursday evenings from 6.30pm to 8.30pm and on Saturdays from 9am to noon. They will be taking entrants for the latter from the end of this month. Therefore, I should like to request the management board consider allowing both nominees to attend lessons there. The fees are not excessive. Pupil-teachers attending such classes are also allowed two half-day holidays per week and would be available to help at the parochial school on all other days.'

While the vicar was adamantly against the schoolmaster's suggestion *per se*, it was the latter part of the letter which caused the greater discussion among the lay members of the board, for it meant that extra expense would have to be incurred if the two girls were to travel by train to Wivencaster on the days in question. Unsurprisingly, when the vote was taken, only Dr. Iveson and the Reverend Smallwood were in favour of an arrangement being made: the secretary-treasurer, the four farmers and the vicar were not.

'We cannot afford to pay for these girls,' the Reverend Scrope protested. 'Mr. Warburton asks too much of us yet again. I have something different in mind...'

The secretary was instructed to write a reply, stating:

'...As regards your suggestion concerning the sending of the two former monitors, Chaplin and Barbrook, to Wivencaster to receive instruction in pupil-teacher duties, the board discussed the matter at length and saw no need for such an expense to be incurred. We understand that both are presently in suitable employment. His reverence wishes it to be known that he will be proposing an alternative to you in due course...'

William read their rejection with a sigh: he had put what he considered a very reasonable proposition to them and had hoped that they would see the sense of it, but they had not. Meanwhile, he had to inform Olive Chaplin and Alice Barbrook of the rejection, which he and Martha did with heavy hearts and much regret that same evening: both girls were in tears when they left them: Alice remained in the mill and Olive continued with her maid's duties.

The news of the Reverend Scrope's 'alternative' came the next day when Joshua Linkhorn walked into the school just after the start of assembly with a flabby, puff-cheeked youth in tow. The vicar had 'found' William a new pupil-teacher of his own choice – one Edward Crowfoot, the fifteen-year-old son of the builder, Elijah Crowfoot, and nephew of Walter Crowfoot and, by all accounts, not a particularly bright lad: but his father and his uncle wanted him to better himself and so the churchwarden had suggested he might be a suitable replacement at the parochial school for Hannah Hodgson.

William was incensed: it was, to him, an intolerable imposition: he knew nothing of the youth or his appointment till he entered the school.

'This is Edward Crowfoot,' Joshua Linkhorn announced, almost apologetically as the scowling youth sauntered in behind him and gave a menacing stare towards some younger children. 'The Reverend Scrope has sent him as the replacement for Miss Hodgson as, I understand, she will not be coming back.'

'I must protest,' William wrote in another letter the same day to the management board – and, consequently, to the vicar. *'While I accept that the management board is fully entitled to make such appointments, I should have thought they would at least have considered asking for my advice on the matter as the head teacher of the school and even to have allowed me either to sit in when the replacement was being interviewed so that I might express an opinion, or otherwise, upon his suitability. I find your action something of an imposition. I know nothing of the youth, save he attended a boarding school at Witcheley and left it two months ago. Now he has been foisted upon me solely upon the recommendation of one of your churchwardens, seeking a position for his nephew who has returned to live in the town...'*

The secretary wrote back: *'I hope you will understand that it is for the school management board and only the school management board to take such decisions. The applicant, Edward Crowfoot, has spent seven years at a highly respectable school in Witcheley, where he was regarded as an apt pupil. His term reports have been viewed by us and are perfectly acceptable. It is our unanimous opinion that he is admirably suited to joining you as a pupil-teacher...'*

It did not matter that the vote at the management board had not been unanimous – Dr. Iveson and the Reverend Smallwood voting against – the vicar was adamant that the appointment be confirmed and so it was...

FORTY-SEVEN

AS HE HAD done since his arrival, William continued to record the happenings at the school in the log book: over the weeks which followed, he was to note, in particular, the slackness of the new pupil-teacher and also his continued exasperation with Miss Dunsmore...

'Monday, September 6th – Start of new school year. Total on roll 218. At insistence of the vicar, have admitted fifty-three more in Infants, who are put in the extension. Have appointed two new monitors – Sarah Barnes and Elizabeth Smith, both twelve, from standard six. Barnes to help Mrs. Warburton and Smith to assist Miss Dunsmore. Still feel the school overcrowded, despite opening of new school at Bourne Brook. Hear they have almost a hundred scholars crowded in there. Introduced to new pupil-teacher Edward Crowfoot today, who is to help me. He begins properly tomorrow. Not impressed. He is very sulky-looking. We shall see how things turn out.'

'Tuesday, September 7th – New pupil-teacher Edward Crowfoot's first full day. Had not arrived at start of lessons – walked in at 10.30. Excuse, overslept – not used to getting up early.'

'Wednesday, September 8th – Sadly, learned Robert Hubble, aged six, one of Mrs. Warburton's class, died of diphtheria fever yesterday. Seven other children in same row of cottages at lower part of town have same fever and have been isolated. Said by Dr. Iveson and Dr. Langham to be progressing favourably and hope to return to school eventually.'

'Monday, September 20th – Reproved pupil-teacher Crowfoot for not having learned 20 lines of Keats, which he was to recite to standard five as example of poetry.'

'Wednesday, September 22nd – Crowfoot not at lessons. No note of illness received. Very poor.'

'Tuesday, September 28th – Crowfoot asked leave of absence from 11 o'clock. Agreed reluctantly, but told him this time only.'

'Friday, October 1st – Had dinnertime errand about town with Mrs. Warburton, so told Crowfoot to have school reopened for afternoon by two o'clock. Miss Dunsmore taking children's choir in church for another funeral. Crowfoot absent, talking with older town boys. Had to open school myself on return at 2.15. Crowfoot reappeared at 2.30. Spoke strongly to him.'

'Tuesday, October 5th – Mary Green and Sarah Bunting suffering from measles. Rest of children from same row of houses have to stay at home, eleven in all.'

'Thursday, October 7th – Complaint from Robert Tucker, standard five, that he was slapped about the ears by Crowfoot. Took Crowfoot aside and told him strongly not to cuff the children.'

'Monday, October 11th – Crowfoot absent from morning lessons. Excuse: illness. Twenty-two children also absent – mostly with measles.'

'Wednesday, October 27th – Disagreement between Robert Stebbings and Thomas Dollery. Gave both Milton passage to learn by heart by Monday. Twenty children still absent.'

'Friday, November 5th – Confiscated ten rook scarers from Crowfoot. Told him they are not to be brought into school. Suspect he was hoping to sell them to younger boys. Found Miss Dunsmore's afternoon register for standards three and four inaccurate again. Third time of late. Sheer carelessness. She made excuse some children going home at lunchtime and not returning as expected. Told her, if in doubt, count them again – only way. William Burton most persistent offender. Went myself to his home and brought him back for three o'clock. He was collecting for Guy Fawkes bonfire. Could not find other absconders – John Day, George Timpson, Robert Walker and Hubert Beard. Will deal with them Monday.'

'Monday, November 8th – Vicar took assembly prayers for first time. Wanted to hear Miss Dunsmore's choir. Mentioned to him

afterwards Crowfoot's persistent late-coming and sloppiness and also Miss Dunsmore's sustained attitude of hostility towards me and Mrs. Warburton. Was told to put any complaints I had in letter to school management board and they would consider them. Will do, but expect nothing to come of it. Miss Dunsmore looked highly pleased with herself. Punished Day, Timpson, Walker and Beard with three strokes of cane for Friday's absence.'

'Thursday, November 11th – Miss Dunsmore ten minutes late. No apology. Very unsatisfactory. Rang the bell myself. Took top standards all together myself for prayers.'

'Monday, November 15th – Miss Dunsmore sent note, saying she was temporarily 'ill' so managed the four upper classes all by myself. Crowfoot supposed to help, but more of a hindrance. Had less noise and felt quite satisfied with the result, feeling no one else (save Mrs. Warburton) could have done it or would have been able to do it, certainly not Miss Dunsmore, who was seen by one of the farm children on way to school standing outside her cottage. Everyday I feel the uselessness of her as my assistant.'

'Wednesday, November 17th – Had to speak sharply to pupil-teacher Crowfoot again for cuffing Robert Beale about the head. Beale's nose bled as a result. Talked very seriously to him about conscientiously discharging his duties to me and the school. Gave him Lord Palmerston's speech on education and teaching of three Rs to read.'

'Monday, November 22nd – Pupil-teacher Crowfoot ten minutes late. Feel disgusted with his irregularity. Mrs. Warburton had occasion to reprimand Miss Dunsmore for hitting a girl about the ears. I had to intervene to pacify both.'

'Wednesday, November 24th – Pupil-teacher Crowfoot's exercise (comprehension) shamefully done. Feel most discouraged and dissatisfied with the tone of him and the way he works or rather 'passes the time' in school hours.'

'Monday, November 29th – Pupil-teacher Edward Crowfoot absent all day without my leave. I firmly believe the school would be better off in every way without him. I am completely tired of trying to awaken him to a sense of his duty.'

'*Tuesday, November 30th – Told pupil-teacher Crowfoot I thought it high time he gave notice to leave. Reprimanded Miss Dunsmore for twisting ear of Billy Shuttleworth and throwing book at Rose Amiss.*'

'*Wednesday, December 1st – Vicar sent special request via Miss Dunsmore to choose twenty-four of older children who attend Sunday school (no Non-conformists) and form a choir to sing at vicar's Christmas Eve carol service in the church as fund-raiser for tower repairs – especially as bells cannot be rung. I agreed, but with reservations. Found singing practice in school all afternoon while others at lessons very disruptive. Feel children's singing less important than receiving education, particularly when there is a good church choir who could do it.*'

'*Monday, December 6th – More disruption from carol practice in Miss Dunsmore's half. Again took up whole of afternoon, from two till four-thirty. William Shuttleworth cut Rex Hull's head by throwing a stone at him. Hull's mother came. Made Shuttleworth apologise. Boys actually good friends, she said!*'

'*Tuesday, December 7th – More disruption. Miss Dunsmore asked and obtained half-holiday to take carol singers into church to practice. Carried on at school very quietly with help of monitors Barnes and Smith.*'

'*Thursday, December 9th – Have closed school early for Christmas holiday on advice of Drs. Iveson and Langham together. Many children suffering from scarlet fever. Outbreak serious. Thirty-three absent from school yesterday. More cases expected, both doctors say. Five of sufferers are among Miss Dunsmore's carol singers. Have advised her to close Sunday school and abandon carols practice. Gave notice to parents no children to attend school or Sunday school for next three weeks till after New Year.*

'*Vicar arrived in high dudgeon this afternoon and protested strongly about early closure and especially abandonment of carols practice. Told him it would be folly for carol singers to practice together. Reverend Smallwood present and surprisingly concurred. Very grateful to him. Said it was only thing to do in circumstances and best for children's health. Regret, he was rather rudely told off by the vicar and I told Reverend Scrope so. Said we had to close the school or we could have a number of deaths of children on our hands. Vicar left in angry mood...*'

FORTY-EIGHT

WILLIAM was unrepentant about closing the school: he knew that he had done the correct thing: he had the support of Martha, he had the support of the town's two doctors and he had the support of the town's health committee. He even had the support of the four farmers on the school management board, to which he had sent his letter announcing the closure: and the mayor himself had called at his cottage to commend his prompt action.

But best of all were the grateful notes from the many parents, slipped through his letter box during the night, thanking him for his prompt action once the first diagnoses of the disease had been made, for within a matter of days it had been followed by four more cases, then six more, then ten more, till more than fifty cases were reported among his young charges.

No, the school would remain closed whatever the Reverend Scrope demanded. Scarlet fever was the leading cause of death among children, William knew: though it might seem to go away for a while, for years sometimes, inevitably it would reappear without warning from no source of which he knew.

The rapidity of its assault was the startling thing: it took only two to three days after the initial infection for a child to develop the characteristic symptoms – sore throat, high fever, the bright red tongue and scarlet rash spreading over the body, starting on the chest or under the armpits or behind the ears and then moving elsewhere, particularly in the folds of the skin and the groin.

William had seen the devastation an epidemic of scarlet fever could cause within a family. Only fifteen years previously, when the disease had last swept through the whole of England, causing thousands of child deaths – more than thirty thousand, it had been said by some – forty thousand, by others – he well remembered the hushed whispering among the members of his own family at the news that a family not two doors from his had lost five of their six children within a matter of three weeks, one child after another being struck down, none older than nine years of age, and no one knowing from where the fever had come or why it fastened so viciously upon the young.

It seemed to William that the very proximity of two hundred and more children in what was still a crowded – if not an overcrowded – school, with all the coughing and sneezing and breathing upon each other that went on, the disease could not help but be spread between them, as surely as it was spread within families, perhaps by the sharing of a towel to dry themselves, by wearing each other's clothes and by sleeping together in the same bed.

These were the believed causes, according to Dr. Iveson and Dr. Langham, but, whatever the causes for the contagion, William was adamant – one did not take the risk with scarlet fever: sufferers needed to be isolated, for weeks on end if needs be, and their clothes and bedding burnt to prevent contagion. He was not prepared to risk the life of a single child at the school for the sake of the Reverend Scrope's carol service, even if it were for his tower fund. He liked to sing carols himself and loved to hear children's voices singing them – assuming that they were being sung in tune, that is.

For the Reverend Scrope, the cancelling of the children's carol service was the last straw, more so even than the closure of the school without his authority being sought first or the schoolmaster's repeated complaints to the management board about his assistant-teacher and his new pupil-teacher.

How dare Warburton do such a thing? Simply informing the secretary of the management board by a hand-delivered note and not even letting him know first – or even asking for his permission. Just standing at the school gate and telling the children as they arrived to go home again and that the school would be closed at least till the first or second week in January, as he had done in the summer – all because a few of the children had caught scarlet fever!

There had been scarlet fever outbreaks before and they had never closed the school once in his time in Steadshall. Yes, he knew it was a highly contagious disease and that sometimes a few poor mites died from it, but that was not in his hands. That was all in the hands of God, was it not? If God called them to His presence, then they must go.

Did the foolish schoolmaster not realise what it did to his plans regarding the carol concert? He had hoped that the singing of the children would draw a good crowd: he had even seen the printer about printing the tickets – six hundred at sixpence a time: now all was lost because a few of the children had caught scarlet fever and the 'blackguard' Warburton had closed the school and told the parents their children should avoid attending Sunday school as well, which meant there would be no carol practice and, therefore, no carol service on Christmas Eve. And that fool of a man Smallwood had agreed with him! The damned impertinence of him!

That something had upset her brother more than usual – more so even than when he had questioned her about the Reverend Smallwood – was clearly evident to Agnes Scrope as she and Hannah Hodgson sat in the nursery, playing with Elizabeth. When he returned from the school, first, the street door was banged shut with a force enough to make the walls and widows shake, then she heard her brother's voice cursing 'Damn the man! Damn the man!' as he strode down the hallway to his study. The door of that was then banged shut in the same manner as the street door, again with enough force to cause a vase to jump on a table in the hallway.

Her brother did not emerge for well over two hours, during which time, after a long period of silence, certain other sounds of anger emanated from the study, shouts which she discerned to be cries of 'God would not allow it! God would not allow it!' followed by more banging as if the desk or a chair were being kicked, then other dull thuds as if books or other objects were being thrown about.

What had particularly irked the Reverend Scrope about the schoolmaster's 'arbitrary' cancellation of his carol concert was that he had thought long and hard about the list of carols the children were to sing before giving the music sheets to Miss Dunsmore. For example, he did not want them singing any carols composed by Dissenters and yet so many carols seemed to have their roots in Non-conformism – either that or they had Catholic influences, with many of the hymns and carols sung in other churches (though not his own) stemming from translations from Latin and Latin was the language of Papist priests.

For instance, he had had to rule out the fine old popular carol *'Joy to the World,'* written by Isaac Watts in 1719, based on *Psalm 98* in the Bible, because he knew that the author's father, John Watts, had been a Non-conformist with views so extreme that he had been imprisoned for them twice. He had also had rejected *'Good King Wenceslas,'* which, though written by an Englishman, John Mason Neale, and published thirty or so years previously and a favourite with children, it peculiarly contained no reference whatsoever to the Lord's birth and, besides, the so-called 'Good King Wenceslas' was a

Catholic monarch of Bohemia, martyred in the Tenth Century following his assassination by his brother Boleslaw.

Hence his annoyance when the practices had been cancelled, for he had compiled a list of 'good Protestant carols' – some English Protestant, some American Protestant, others German and Austrian Lutheran – which had taken him quite some time and he had been well pleased with his work. He had even written to the Bishop, inviting him to the service. Now it had been cancelled and with it his chance to raise money to pay off the rest of the amount he owed Elijah Crowfoot, not only for the school extension but also still for buttressing the tower – which was why he kicked the chair and his desk and threw several of his books about the room, till one flew straight through a pane in the French windows.

In his temper, he also made another decision and sat down to write a letter, one he had long thought about writing...

FORTY-NINE

WHEN THE ARCHITECT Sir Arthur Bloomingfield had inspected the church's tower, one the other things he had told the Reverend Scrope and the churchwardens was that all bell-ringing must stop: the bells must remain silent till the tower was properly repaired or he would not be responsible for what might happen. Thus, the bells of St. Andrew's had been silent ever since and, though the six bell-ringers continued to attend the church, they no longer had a Thursday evening practice and they grumbled much about the length of time it was taking even to begin the repairs.

Word of their grumbling in the vault of the double-gabled White Hart halfway down the High Street, to which by tradition they had always retired after practice, had somehow reached the ears of the Reverend Scrope: and nine days before Christmas, the six bell-ringers found themselves 'sacked' – tersely informed by letter from their vicar that their services were 'no longer required.' What irked many was that their crime was not so much that they sat in the White Hart and grumbled but that, according to the vicar, they had failed to contribute to the last fund-raising concert.

'*The bell ringers, as a group,*' the Reverend Scrope wrote in the letter to them, *'have not in any way been seen to be supportive of the fund-raising efforts for the tower repairs, most particularly when the concert was held at which eighty-two pounds four shillings and tuppence was raised. They were not seen to be present...'* They were not – at the time, they were sitting in the White Hart, grumbling as usual.

Also held against them was the fact that only three of the six ringers had made actual individual donations of a shilling or two to the tower fund from their own meagre earnings, which was considered overly harsh by those who read the letter since two of the three who did not give were quite aged, one seventy-three years, the other seventy, and neither had the means.

The vicar went on to state that his decision followed on from the bell-ringers' '...*apparent unwillingness over past years to help raise funds to improve access to the bells by the provision of a better ladder. This was a matter to which I and the churchwardens had looked to you for assistance, but without success. Now, due to other considerations, it remains an outstanding matter to which we feel unable to commit funds at this time. As your vicar, I would, therefore, be grateful if you would deliver the keys of the tower to the vicarage at your earliest convenience. Although we shall possibly be recruiting a new team of bell-ringers once the tower repairs are completed, I cannot foresee that we shall be employing any of the former ringers...*'

Saddened as the bell ringers were by the high-handedness of the vicar's action, seventy-three-year-old John Chalkstone, who had rung the bells for nigh on sixty years and was by far the most experienced bell-ringer for fifty miles around and one of the best treble-ringers in the Eastern Counties, was the most distraught.

'I don't know what I shall do with myself on a Sunday morning and a Sunday evening if I can't ring my bells!' he wailed, near to tears as he sat in the snug of the White Hart on the Thursday evening that the vicar's letter was delivered. 'And what'll I do on Thursday practice nights from now on? I'm an old man. I've been ringing the bells since I were a lad. I'd have liked to have gone out still ringing 'em and maybe had my "thank you" from God himself when I gets up to heaven. Now I won't ever be able to ring my old bells again afore I dies...'

The poor man finished his drink and shuffled out: two days later the news spread around the town that he was dead – of a broken heart, some said – and the villain of the piece was undoubtedly the Reverend Scrope. Indeed, feeling against the vicar was running so high that, when the funeral was held on the following Wednesday and the old man was conveyed to the cemetery on the hand-pulled cart, several of the rougher elements in a crowd numbering more than three hundred hooted their vicar on his arrival to conduct the ceremony. Fortunately, the town's police sergeant and his two constables, anticipating trouble, had turned out, but they still had to appeal to the crowd to keep order out of respect for the deceased or they might be forced to set about them with their nightsticks. Even so, some mourners more bold than others did not shy from shouting sundry hints to the vicar of what they would like to do to him as he walked to the grave, of the variety 'We ought to bloody bury you with him!'

None of it seemed to affect the Reverend Scrope, if indeed he heard any of it above the hissing and booing: and, as the committal concluded and the men began shovelling the earth on to the coffin, he walked briskly back to his pony and trap tethered by the gate, mounted, wheeled it around and, with a brusque crack of the whip, plunged through the crowd without so much as a 'Make way!' or a 'Move yourselves!' Fortunately, all in his path managed to leap aside.

Once the police had satisfied themselves that the vicar was out of danger, they mounted their bicycles and rode back to the station, thinking they had done a good job. However, some of the more exuberant youths had been angered not only by the old man's death but also by the vicar's perceived indifference and his overly hurried reading of the burial service, as if keen to get his former bell-ringer underground and gone from sight and memory and himself away from what was clearly a hostile crowd.

In consequence, three of these youths went into a farmer's field across from the cemetery and seized an old straw-stuffed scarecrow, fashioned a parson's white collar from the folded half-page of a hymn book, then, on two other pages torn from the same hymn book, drew on one a face caricaturing the Reverend Scrope's and on the other printed his name in bold capitals, before pinning it to the scarecrow's front. To raucous cheers, the effigy of their despised and sanctimonious vicar was hoisted up on a pitchfork someone had fetched and the whole three hundred mourners marched back into the town, where they flooded into the churchyard and lined the whole length of the low wall across the lane from the vicarage, baying for the Reverend Scrope to come out.

That the Reverend Scrope did not appear was because, when he had returned to the house, he had discovered to his annoyance that the Reverend Smallwood was there yet again and was deep in conversation with Agnes in the hallway, except that he was not so sure it had been just conversation which had drawn them so close together. They were facing each other, almost touching, it seemed, and she, silly woman, was blushing a beetroot red when he pushed open the front door, having left it to Old Thomas and the Upson boy to stable the pony.

The Reverend Smallwood had drawn quickly away and his sister had disappeared into the kitchen at the back of the house, but the lanky curate had not been quite quick enough: he had seen what he had seen! It was clear by the embarrassment showing on both their faces that they had been talking about something they did not wish to share with him. What exactly, he had no idea, but he would find that out in time, he would find out.

'Why are you here?' he demanded of the curate, and was non-plussed when the curate handed him an envelope with an almost pained smile, which, upon opening, he found to contain a cheque for fifteen pounds towards his tower fund from 'the grateful parishioners of Bourne Brook St Mary's.'

He had to concede that it was a legitimate enough reason for the man to be in his house, though it was not reason enough to find him talking to his sister the way he had been: he thought he had put that one asunder with his warning to Agnes. In the end, all he could do was to ask the curate to thank his parishioners at Bourne Brook and send him on his way as he wished to do some work in his study.

It was a half-hour later, after the Reverend Scrope had completed the work that, being disturbed by the continuing noise outside, he went to the front parlour window and looked out. As he pushed aside the curtain, a great roar went up from the three hundred gathered opposite. And what was that thing they were holding aloft? A scarecrow? A scarecrow dressed to look like a vicar, with someone's name upon it. His name! And they were setting fire to it! Setting fire to an effigy of him!

With an angry snort, the Reverend Scrope tugged the curtain closed. 'Barbarians!' he snorted. 'Barbarians! Heathen idolitors1 Half of them are Dissenters, anyway. They are not my people. They would not do such a thing...'

FIFTY

CHRISTMAS DAY that year fell on a Saturday, with an extra Bank Holiday declared on the Monday and the Tuesday. In the vicarage, the whole celebration of present-giving revolved around pleasing the toddling Elizabeth: she was the centre of everyone's attention from the moment she was brought down from the nursery in her new clothes – fawned and cooed over by her Aunt Agnes, by Bertha the cook, who was in for the day to prepare the midday meal, and also by her 'new friend Hannah,' whose name she had just learned to pronounce.

Even her father managed to give her a 'Good morning, happy Christmas' kiss and a smile at breakfast before setting off for the church in order to obtain some peace away from the feminine squeals of delight and also to give himself time to prepare for his usual Christmas Day service – for he could not neglect the day on which the Lord was born: that would have been a sacrilege.

His Christmas Day service was always based upon the first two chapters of *The Gospel According to St. Luke,* which he read to the congregation, small as it was. The reading was followed by the singing of three carols, all three having been selected initially for the children to sing at the now abandoned carol concert – at least the assiduous research he had mounted would not be wasted, after all – and damn the schoolmaster! Damn him!

Unfortunately, his first choice, *'Christians Awake, Salute the Happy Morn,'* well liked by him for its reference to the Archangel Gabriel's *'Behold, I bring good tidings of a Saviour's birth…'* fell a little flat as not many of the town's Christians had awakened that early morning to attend the service – little more than a hundred, Walter Crowfoot estimated. It was followed by *'Good Christian Men Rejoice,'* which the Reverend Scrope understood to have originated in Germany and so was safe even if it were a very old Latin Christmas song, called *In Dulci Jubilo,* though that morning there were not many good Christian men in the congregation to rejoice, the majority present being female as their husbands and sons were all refusing to attend following old John Chalkstone's funeral. They finished with another 'safe' early Eighteenth Century hymn, *'While Shepherds Watched...'* written by Queen Anne's Irish-born Poet Laureate Nahun Tate, and sung to the anonymous Sixteenth Century tune *'Winchester Old'*: until just over a hundred years before, it had been the only Christmas carol officially sanctioned by the Church: if the Reverend Scrope had been given reign, it would still have been the only carol sung in his church at Christmas.

Helen Dunsmore, as the organist, had suggested *'Hark! The Herald Angels Sing'* as a rousing finale – 'to send the worshippers home happy to their Christmas dinner,' she had said – but the Reverend Scrope was not going to have a carol written by a Dissenter like Charles Wesley, the brother of John Wesley, sung in his church, not while there was breath in his body, even if what was sung was a revised version of Wesley's original lyrics, with Felix Mendelssohn's more uplifting cantata replacing the Methodists' solemnly sung first version.

Nor could he allow Edward Caswall's *'See Amid the Winter's Snow'* for, even if the writer were the son of a vicar, a Brasenose man at Oxford and, for a while, an Anglican curate, he had turned 'traitor' in his early thirties after the death of his wife and converted to Catholicism: to have that carol sung would have left a bad taste in his mouth and spoiled his Christmas dinner. And there was not much point either in putting up *'Once In Royal David's City'* for any children in attendance – as, due to the scarlet fever outbreak, there were none in the congregation, as he saw when he mounted the pulpit to give the lesson.

After the service, the Reverend Scrope and the two churchwardens spent a half-hour or so to delivering small hampers, paid for by a long-standing bequest, to the residents of the ten almshouses along the Siblingham road and then he returned to the vicarage at two o'clock for his Christmas dinner. On the way back, he called at the Reverend Smallwood's lodgings and the two walked back to the vicarage together: he had felt obliged to invite him, not so much through any altruism that the bachelor curate would be alone in his lodgings on Christmas Day after taking the service at Bourne Brook, but simply so that he could observe how he and Agnes continued to react when together. He was convinced that, despite what she had avowed earlier, 'something' was still 'going on' between them: what he needed was confirmation that the curate was indeed rekindling his 'interest' in her and that she was reciprocating: and one way to obtain that information was to observe them closely when they were in close company, such as across a dinner table.

One thing he did not intend was to lose his sister, his housekeeper, the aunt and unofficial 'mother' of Elizabeth, in marriage to Henry Smallwood. If he were to accuse her again before he had his proof and it were to turn out that she was not 'flirting' with a man years younger than herself, as she said she had not been, but was just being her usual friendly self, smiling at Smallwood because she smiled at most people, talking with him because she had to talk to someone and there were not many she could talk to on the same level as herself – except himself, of course, and he was usually too busy – if that were the case, then what...?

It was a dilemma and he must tread carefully: his great fear was that if he upset his sister again, she might take it into her head to decamp back to the West Country. She was a free woman, after all, and could be strong-minded when she needed to be – certainly strong willed enough to do just that and he did not want to give her the excuse. Would she leave Elizabeth or would she stay for Elizabeth's sake? Really, his daughter was his trump card in the whole affair: but then again, anything was possible where love and passion were concerned – anything – as he was beginning to realise from Miss Dunsmore's unwanted, attention.

During the dinner, out of the corner of his eye, when he turned momentarily away from the table as Bertha the cook was about to carry some dishes from the room, he thought he saw a look flash between the two of them when they thought he was not looking, and he saw, too, Agnes's cheeks flush bright red when he turned back to the table: he also saw the curate gulp and almost choke on his forkful of goose and saw Agnes smile brightly at him because of it.

He also noted how upset Agnes appeared when he suggested to the curate that, now that the new school had opened in Bourne Brook, albeit in a whitewashed cow byre, perhaps it might be a good idea if he were to look for lodgings there so that he would be on hand in the hamlet at all times and need to return to Steadshall only when his assistance was required at St. Andrew's. He also noticed how relieved Agnes seemed when the curate rejected the idea, saying he was too comfortable in his present lodgings and his landlady was used to his coming and going at all hours, something to which another landlady might not take.

Later that same evening, when Hannah Hodgson left them to put Elizabeth to bed, he went into his study across the hallway to fetch a bottle of port, leaving Agnes and Smallwood together in the front parlour. He was only away for a minute or so and, as he re-entered the room, he called out to ask the curate whether he would like another glass of port? It was a simple question, the answer to which was either 'Yes please' or 'No, thank you.'

Yet, as he pushed open the door, the curate sprang back from his position close to Agnes like the proverbial scalded cat, and Agnes herself turned quickly to the fire and dropped something discreetly into it. He had seen it sizzle briefly as she stabbed at with the poker, as if wanting to burn it quickly. He could not be exactly sure, but it looked like a piece of a plant, a piece of holly or something, something with green leaves, anyway.

And he was certain that it was not the heat of the fire which had flushed both their faces...

FIFTY-ONE

THERE WAS ONE way of ending it all, of course: he could write to the Bishop and ask him to withdraw the curate's license: he would need to give reasons which he could defend legitimately, reasons which Agnes would not suspect as having anything to do with her, but which he could argue were motivated by nothing other than the curate's inability, in his opinion, to fulfil his duties satisfactorily in helping him to run the two parishes. That and his growing disloyalty!

Even before he had gone to Australia, he had wondered about the Reverend Smallwood, whether he was even up to the job of looking after a parish as large as Steadshall, whether he was competent to act as the caretaker and whether he might not be overwhelmed by the importance of his task in doing it week in and week out for a whole year, which was how long he had expected to be away. That he had returned earlier had been due solely to circumstances – the fair wind which had borne the clipper on the last stages across the Pacific to San Francisco and the vastly improved crossing of the United States coast to coast.

Before setting off around the world, he had actually gone so far as to visit the Bishop and intimate to him that he would prefer a temporary incumbent to be appointed to oversee the parish while he was away, a retired vicar, say, looking for a short-term position to bolster his finances: but the Bishop had been adamant. 'The Reverend Smallwood has to learn the ropes somehow and the sooner the better,' he had said, 'and what better way than being thrown in at the deep end.'

The curacy at St. Mary's was Smallwood's first outside the shaded cloisters and lawned quadrangles of Cambridge: he was the son of a friend of the Bishop and had been foisted upon him three years previously. If the reports of the sexton-cum-churchwarden at Bourne Brook and his own churchwarden were to be believed, he had generally performed his duties well enough since he had been licensed. If he had a fault, it was that, at only twenty-three years of age when he arrived, he did not seem at all informed about certain aspects of life which a man of his age perhaps ought to have known, such as the rise in the numbers of illegitimate births among the many girls working at the crepe mills, the drunkenness which was often prevalent among the labourers in some of the ale houses around that area on Saturday nights and the amount of petty larceny with which he himself had occasion to deal all too frequently at the magistrates' court.

His curate sometimes seemed to be more concerned with the health of the folk at Bourne Brook, supporting the parish council there in calling for the erection of a second water tower and dispensing with the hamlet's three pumps which had served them to the present – at times preferring to talk more of things like that than Godly matters. And if it were not the needs of the people in Bourne Brook about which he had fulminated in the final days before, mercifully, he had escaped him by setting off on his round-the-world trip, then it had been the lack of a proper sewage system for certain of the properties at the lower end of Steadshall itself, where the greater number of the labouring classes lived, or the dilapidated condition of many of their cottages, things which the Reverend Scrope considered should best be left to others, to the health board, say, or the town's two doctors or the owners of the properties themselves rather than men of the cloth.

As it happened, the Reverend Scrope's mind was made up for him during the very first week of January, when he set out one morning for Wivencaster in his pony and trap, intending to visit the library there to seek out a particular book which the small library in Steadshall did not possess. The library in Wivencaster was much larger and with a greater variety of books, whereas the town's library hardly ever stocked the kinds of books which he liked to read, books on history, on old wars, as well as faith.

A mile out along the Wivencaster road, he suddenly remembered that he had left his purse on the chest of drawers in the bedroom. Wearily, exasperated at his own foolishness, he turned the trap round and drove back to Steadshall: on reaching the lane leading to vicarage, he slowed the pony to a walk, so that he might jump down on to the pavement outside the vicarage and tether the reins to the low wrought-iron railings in front before entering with his key.

He heard their voices in the small back parlour alongside his study as soon as he entered, a man's voice and a woman's voice – unmistakably Agnes's and Smallwood's – murmuring together and barely audible through the stout wooden door unless one paused outside and held one's breath to listen. That it was the Reverend Smallwood was the surprise: he had not been near the house since they had said goodbye to him at the door on the evening of Christmas Day, so what was the curate doing at the vicarage? At that time of the morning, he was supposed to be in Bourne Brook doing his pastoral work.

The only person who knew of his intended trip to the library at Wivencaster that day was Agnes, so it was either her doing or the greatest coincidence that the curate should turn up within minutes of his departure. He was less inclined towards the coincidence and more inclined to believe that a message must have been sent to Smallwood somehow and the curate had simply waited till he had set off before sneaking into the house, knowing that Agnes would be unconcerned about compromising herself because Bertha was in the kitchen as usual and Hannah was up in the nursery. No one would think anything on seeing the curate knocking at the front door: they would think he could only be calling on church business as usual. Damn the man! He should have got rid of him long ago.

His first thought was to push open the door and confront them when an idea came to him just as the tinkling notes of a piano started up: they could only be on the far side of the room where the piano stood, which accounted for his difficulty in hearing what they were saying.

It was an matter of moments to place a chair carefully in front of the door, step up on to its soft covering and peer in upon them through the fanlight: they were just as he expected them to be, just as he had envisaged they would be, she at the piano, he leaning over her, both with their backs to him and so caught up in each other that they did not even notice the slight change as his head blocked the light filtering into the room.

The piano-playing was just a ruse for them to be close together, to brush against each other, to press against each other, Agnes seated on the single stool, playing some melody he did not recognise and Smallwood bending over her, one hand upon her shoulder, his face bent close to hers as he reached across to turn the page of the musical score, perhaps even his hand lightly brushing across her front, touching her where she had not been touched before – as far as he knew, anyway. No, he was sure of that: no one had touched Agnes as yet: she did not have the looks to attract other men as other women attracted him, the prettiness of features, say, of the nursemaid Hannah. Now there was a pretty young girl!

He watched only for a few seconds, just to assure himself in his own mind that what he was seeing was what he understood it to be, then he quietly stepped down, noiselessly replaced the chair and retreated, taking the stairs quietly, retrieving his purse off the chest of drawers and exiting the front door all within a minute so that the murmuring, smiling, laughing pair in the back parlour neither heard anything nor suspected anything. Once outside, he carefully and unhurriedly wheeled the trap round, nodded an acknowledgement to a passing parishioner, walked Frederick to the junction with the High Street, mounted there off the old mounting block and trotted off back towards Wivencaster.

A letter to the Bishop was now definitely called for: he would write it on the morrow, locking himself in his study so that he would not be disturbed, so that Agnes would not suspect anything: she would never know why he had written to the Bishop. She had attempted to keep her attraction to Smallwood a secret and could only have thought she had done so by the way she was behaving, so she would not suspect that he had done it for the reason he had.

The curate deserved what he was about to receive: had not the ungrateful man supported the damned schoolmaster, saying that, in the circumstances, cancelling the carol concert was for the best!? Very well, if the curate would not support him, then the curate would have to go: he did not want traitors in his midst. He was not going to have that long streak of lean named Henry Smallwood making overtures to his sister: no other man was ever likely to want to embark upon a courtship of her, not at her age, not with her looks, which was why Smallwood was such a threat: he was the first man who had ever paid her any attention.

He would write to the Bishop and demand that he be moved. Yes, that is what he would do, demand that he be moved…

FIFTY-TWO

THE REVEREND Scrope was seated once more on the black horsehair couch in his study when there was a gentle tapping at the door and Hannah Hodgson called out that she had brought his afternoon pot of tea and plate of ginger biscuits. Somewhat wearily, he rose to his feet, crossed to the door and unlocked it: at that precise moment, he would rather he had not been disturbed, for the house was peaceful – peaceful enough to be able to hear the ticking of the grandfather clock in the hallway – but afternoon tea at four o'clock whenever he was in the vicarage was a tradition and one which he enjoyed.

The girl entered and padded across to the small table beside the couch, keeping her eyes downcast: though her previous shyness had long since gone, she still paid her master the respect due to him, due to one whose place in the hierarchy of the town was far above her own.

The vicar returned to the couch and waited as the girl poured the tea and added the milk: she would leave to him the number of spoonfuls of sugar he added to sweeten it. That day, he was feeling particularly apprehensive: he had written the letter he had intended to write and had posted it earlier that afternoon: then he had returned to the vicarage to relax. He expected that the letter would reach the Bishop within the next two days: he had set the wheels in motion: the die was cast: he could only await the outcome.

'Tell me, Hannah, do you enjoy your work here?' he asked, seemingly casually, as the girl turned towards the door.

Hannah Hodgson paused, blushing slightly, not expecting to be asked such a question, one which was not, as other 'questions' from the vicar usually were, framed as a command or a chastisement.

'Oh, yes, sir.' She waited in case he wished to ask her something else.

There was a place beside him on the couch. 'Come and sit here beside me, Hannah,' he said, patting the vacant spot. 'I would like to talk to you about something.'

The girl dutifully crossed to him, sat down timidly beside him and placed her hands upon her lap.

The Reverend Scrope added his usual two spoonfuls of sugar to his tea, stirred it slowly for a few seconds, took a sip and then returned the cup to the tray on the small table before him. 'What I meant, Hannah, was, do you find your work here rewarding?' he asked, leaning slightly towards her as a display of friendliness. 'Looking after a small child, I mean? Looking after Elizabeth?'

'Oh yes, sir,' the girl replied politely, not knowing of any other answer she could give: she was in the presence of her employer, a respected man, a man of authority, one whom it did not pay to upset. 'I like children, sir,' she told him truthfully. 'I have always got on well with my three younger sisters.'

'Do you go to see your sisters?' There was genuine interest in his voice.

'Oh, yes, sir, on my afternoons-off. I also give my mother some of my money from my wages.'

'That is very good of you, Hannah, very good of you, indeed.' The vicar moved his hand across to give her knee four gentle pats, almost as if he were doing it absent-mindedly.

'You don't miss the school, you don't miss being a pupil-teacher, I mean?'

'A little, sir,' she answered, keeping her eyes on the hand still resting upon her knee, but making no attempt to shift away. 'I liked being a pupil-teacher. I was hoping to become a real teacher one day, sir, like Miss Dunsmore – perhaps even go to a proper training college once I had got my three certificates.'

'Would you like to become a pupil-teacher again?'

It was an unexpected question and it surprised her. 'If I could, sir,' she answered hopefully.

'Well, there might be a way that you can, Hannah. There just might be a way you can.'

The girl waited expectantly: becoming a pupil-teacher again would mean she would have what her mother called 'prospects': it would be better than being just a nursemaid: she did not want to remain a nursemaid forever, changing babies' or toddlers' soiled clothing, bathing them, playing with them, attending to them day after day and with only one afternoon off a week. As much as she liked children, there were no 'prospects' in being a nursemaid: to her, it was like being a mother without the happiness of caring for one's own.

She had heard that Edward Crowfoot had left the school, so there was a vacancy. 'I wouldn't want to go back to the school while Mr. Warburton is there?' she said. 'He shouts at you and tells you off for doing things wrong, even when I haven't. I should like to start again, but not under Mr. Warburton, if I can help it.'

'Quite, quite.' The Reverend Scrope removed his hand from her knee, lifted the cup, took another sip of tea, replaced the cup and replaced his hand on her knee, gently patting it again. 'Tell me, how old are you, Hannah?' he asked finally.

'Thirteen, sir,' she told him proudly.

'And when will you be fourteen?'

'In April, sir.'

'I take it that one day you will want to get married? You say you like children, so I suppose that one day you would like children of your own?'

'I expect so, sir.' The girl was puzzled: why was he asking her such questions?

'You would have to be married first, of course,' he informed her, 'find a husband, meet a nice young man, get married in church – my church perhaps.' The latter was said with a smile.

She remained puzzled: everyone she knew who had children was married: it went without saying, did it not, that you got married to have children? Or so she had always assumed. All girls she knew wanted to get married some day and have children: in that, she was no different to them, though it was true some girls started 'making babies' with boys before marriage, but all got married eventually, before their babies came.

'I was wondering,' the Reverend Scrope began, then paused as if contemplating whether to keep the thought to himself, before finally deciding. 'I was wondering, Hannah, the schoolmaster, Mr. Warburton, tells me a very good teacher training college has opened recently at Wivencaster. They give instruction to aspiring pupil-teachers twice a week, on Tuesday and Thursday evenings and on Saturday mornings. What I was thinking is, there is a young ladies' college attached to the school for full-time day pupils. If you wished, I could send you there – not at the moment, of course, but when you are a little older, in a year or two, perhaps, when Elizabeth is older. You could stay in lodgings and you would get a good education, become a proper schoolteacher, trained properly with other young ladies, like Miss Dunsmore. You would become a young lady yourself.'

'Oh, I would like that very much, sir,' she said, her eyes widening in surprise. Then the obvious thought struck her: 'But I could not afford to pay for it, sir. I could not afford to pay for the lodgings or the lessons.'

'That can easily be arranged,' the vicar replied, airily waving one hand as if it were a matter of no consequence.

'Oh, sir!' the girl said, unable to believe her good fortune: to be sent to a ladies' college, to study with young ladies to become a teacher – it was beyond her wildest dreams. It was the most natural instinct in the world for her to throw her arms around her benefactor as a gesture of thanks for his offer: she did not even mind when his arms enfolded her and held her tight. Though her mistress and Bertha the cook were out shopping on the High Street, the door was unlocked, so she had nothing to fear.

There was silence for a few seconds, then he murmured quietly: 'Did you – did you like the Christmas present I gave you, the sewing box?'

Strictly speaking, it was Agnes who had chosen the whitewood sewing box, containing a variety of needles and reels of coloured thread: it was she who had wrapped it and addressed it: all he had done was to hand it to her on Christmas morning before going to church: but then she did not know any of that.

'Yes, sir. Thank you, sir?'

There was a pause, as if he were again thinking of what next to ask or say, before he suddenly requested: 'Would you do something for me, Hannah – would you stand up?'

The girl stood up.

'Would you now do me the honour of sitting upon my lap, Hannah? I have not had a young girl such as yourself sit on my lap for such a long time and it is such a pleasant thing, such a comfort to a man like myself.'

Gently, he reached out, put one hand lightly about Hannah Hodgson's waist and pulled her to him: she went unresisting. Once she was settled on his lap, his arms enfolded her again. When he had pulled Sarah Pockett on to his lap, she had jumped up straight away and fled the room near to tears: the next morning she had gone.

'You know, Hannah,' he said, lowering his head on to her shoulder, 'I sometimes feel very lonely, especially since my dear Jane departed this life for a better life in heaven. Do you ever feel lonely, Hannah? I mean living here. Do you not sometimes miss your mother and your younger sisters as I miss my Jane?'

'Sometimes, sir,' she said, frowning down at the bald patch upon the crown of his head, 'when I am in bed at night. But then I have Elizabeth with me.'

'Yes, you are good to Elizabeth,' he said. 'She dotes on you, you know. You are a little mother to her, an older sister, too.'

The girl blushed. It was unexpected praise.

'I think for that, for being such a good nursemaid to little Elizabeth, you deserve a good kiss from me, Hannah. May I?'

'If you wish, sir,' she answered, again surprised by the request

He kissed her, not on the cheek as she had expected he would, but firmly on the mouth: and, as he did so, his right hand came up to cup her right breast, not to squeeze it, just to cup it gently.

'My, what are these little beauties, Hannah?' he asked, feigning surprise, moving his hand across to her right breast, then back again.

The girl blushed, not because his hand was upon one of them, but because he had noticed them at all: she had observed in the mirror when she washing herself that they had begun to grow, but she did not think anyone else would notice them yet: they still seemed so small.

'My breasts, sir,' she said, her cheeks reddening with embarrassment. 'They have begun to get bigger.'

'They have indeed!' he exclaimed. 'I shall have to tell my sister to have a word with you. There are things you will need to know – women's things – about what happens to young girls' bodies as they grow up. She knows – she will help you.'

Then unexpectedly, he said: 'May I see them, Hannah, may I see your breasts? They seem so small. I have never seen a girl's breasts so small as yours. May I have a peek at them?'

He was already beginning to unbutton the front of her dress. She wondered whether she ought to say 'No,' to push his hand away, but then he was her employer, the vicar of the parish, her elder and her better: how could she? Before she could think what to say, even to refuse him, he had undone all ten buttons and was sliding his hand inside her camisole, running his fingers tips over her nipples, repeatedly pressing the small mounds and sighing to himself in a way she had not heard before. It was most strange to hear him…

FIFTY-THREE

THREE SUNDAYS into the new year and the morning and evening congregations at St. Andrew's were no better: they had declined steadily ever since old John Chalkstone's funeral and that morning the turnout was even worse, as Walter Crowfoot and Samuel Gough discovered when they again counted together and made it no more than eighty-nine, a very poor showing scattered among the rows of pews. A dozen farmers and their wives – but not their children – were seated in the usual pews at the front: but, since they all resided outside the precincts of the town proper, but within the parish, they were mostly unaware of the true anger against the vicar and would not have cared, anyway. The rest, the two wardens noted with a sigh, were mostly the aged and the declining, who came to church less to receive the vicar's words of wisdom and more to ensure that, when their time came to approach Saint Peter at the Pearly Gates, they would not be turned away because of a lack of attendance down below.

The Reverend Scrope had finished his sermon: he was not so sure how many of them had understood the lesson, but for the present he would let that matter go: after all, he had an important announcement to make.

The previous evening he had received another letter from the schoolmaster, asking quite bluntly: '*Are you going to do anything about replacing Edward Crowfoot or am I to do it myself? Things cannot go on this way. If you will not act, I will...*' The outbreak of scarlet fever, while not yet over entirely, had subsided as quickly as it had broken out and the school had reopened on the previous Monday.

What peeved the Reverend Scrope was that the letter had again been addressed to him personally and not to Joshua Linkhorn, as he had specifically requested: the schoolmaster was being obnoxious again and, by sending the letter to him, he was clearly blaming him for the lack of action. That might well be true, but over Christmas and the New Year, his time had been taken up with other more important things and he had quite forgotten about needing to replace Edward Crowfoot: someone should have reminded him. Even so, that was no reason for the schoolmaster to get on his high horse about it and no reason at all for his lack of manners.

He had spent much of the previous evening mulling over what to do, then he had come to a decision, just like he had over the curate. Be bold and God will be with you! His only disappointment was that the person concerned was not seated amid the congregation: it seemed he, too, had joined the protest against him, a further insult.

The faces which stared back up at him as he mounted the pulpit to begin reading the parish notices were not eager faces, he recognised, more ones wanting to be released: but they would have to wait till he had told them what he was about to tell them: then they would have cause for a good gossip…

'Many of you will know that I am a patient man and a lenient man,' he began, expecting that such a statement went without saying, but he said it anyway, 'but there are certain things I cannot tolerate – ' A pause here to allow the words to sink into their befuddled brains. ' – The first of those is disloyalty and the second is insubordination. I, therefore, have no hesitancy in announcing that, the management board of Steadshall Parochial School has unanimously agreed to request the resignation of the schoolmaster, William Warburton, and also of his wife, Martha Warburton.'

In the stunned silence which followed, the one thing which everyone remembered was the angry exclamation from Dr. Iveson in his pew to one side of the nave. Of them all, he had not blamed the vicar for old John Chalkstone's death, as he had attended the old man on his deathbed and put it down to old age and years of over drinking.

'I know nothing of this!' the doctor shouted, rising to his feet. 'When was this decided and by whom? I am a member of the management board for the school. I have attended no meeting at which this was discussed. You do not do this in my name. If that is the way matters in this parish are conducted, as of now, I am no longer a member of the school board. I resign. I am done with you and your shenanigans! I have had enough of them. Good day to you! Good day to you all!' With that, he signalled to his stunned wife to follow him and stamped out of the church, banging shut behind him the five hundred-year-old oak door in the south porch.

What the congregation did not know and were not told was that an extraordinary meeting of the management board had indeed been convened in the vestry a mere half-hour before the service was due to begin – part of the management board, that is, for only the Reverend Scrope, Joshua Linkhorn and two of the farmers – Charles Higgs and Henry Bucknall – were present. At it, a certain letter which the Reverend Scrope had received a few days previously in reply to one he had written a month earlier was shown to them and, in consequence, a proposition was made and accepted by all with shrugs of their shoulders: it was the only thing that could be done: they could see no other way. The decision had been taken before Dr. Iveson had even left his house to walk the fifty yards up the hill to the church with his wife: he would only have voted against what was proposed, anyway, which was why he had not been sent for to join the meeting.

The Reverend Scrope waited for the murmuring to subside. 'Be that as it may,' he went on, as if referring to the noise made by the doctor's angry departure rather than the accusations, 'a letter will be sent this very day to Mr. Warburton, asking him to resign, which means that, within a few months, when he has served his notice – we are suggesting three months – we shall have a new head teacher – a new headmistress, in fact. The school managers have not allowed the grass to grow under our feet – ' He permitted himself a smile at his use of the idiom. ' – and we have taken the unanimous decision to appoint Miss Helen Dunsmore as the new head of the school – '

Helen Dunsmore was in her usual place at the organ glowering at the boy who pumped it to ensure that he kept up the instrument's pressure: the appointment was an utter surprise to her and she could think only that it was the vicar's way of saying 'thank you' for the selfless service she given him that day he had called at her cottage needing 'comfort': at that moment, she would willingly have given him the same comfort again if he had requested it. All she could think to do was to beam back at the many pairs of eyes that had turned to look at her, hoping that none noticed how much she was blushing and at the same time wondering whether any knew of the reason, as she perceived it, for of her sudden promotion?

'We shall also be employing two new assistants to Miss Dunsmore,' the vicar continued, 'and we shall also be requiring a new pupil-teacher...'

In fact, unbeknown to those who heard him, he had already drafted an advertisement for two assistant-teachers, declaring that the Steadshall Parochial School Board was willing to accept '*a satisfactory second-class certificate from a respectable college...*' and that way be able to reduce the salary he paid them: forty-five pounds per annum was quite sufficient, he felt, for what qualifications they would possess: and, if they were competent, there might not be a need for a new pupil-teacher after all – well, not for a while.

By the Monday morning, the news of the Warburtons' dismissal – for that was what it was, a 'request' for his resignation or no – was known to everyone in the town, pupil and parent and interested parties alike. None could believe it. People gathered in small groups to discuss it: it was the topic in all the shops where the women met, in the inns and ale houses where the men sat drinking and even among the girls minding the machines at Oldcourt's mills – one and all condemning the high-handedness of the vicar in dismissing a second schoolmaster, one whom everyone respected and who had not even completed a year in the post.

Even the Reverend Smallwood was dumbfounded by the arbitrariness of the vicar's act. 'I am sorry, but I cannot support you on this,' he told the Reverend Scrope, confronting him in the vestry that same Monday morning. 'I just cannot. Neither will the people stand for it. They will turn against you – ' He meant 'even more,' but could not say so. ' – The school inspector's last report alone militates against your decision. Mr. Warburton is a first-class teacher. In the short time he has been here, he has imbued even some of the lost causes of our school with at least the beginnings of learning. Really, Mr. Scrope, I cannot believe that you have done this thing! It is a monumental folly on your part, a monumental folly!'

It was the first time that the Reverend Scrope had been spoken to in such a fashion by his curate: indeed, the first time he had been spoken to like it by anyone. So the vicar fell back on his authority if nothing more than as a means of retaining his dignity. 'I am the vicar of this parish,' he declared firmly, trying to control his own anger. 'I decide such things. I am the chairman of the school management board. It is up to me to make decisions and for the board to agree with me. We cannot have the schoolmaster declaring himself in that way – demanding this and that, closing the school of his own free will and cancelling my carol concert without so much as a by your leave. He and his wife have been nothing but trouble since they came, what with his interminable letters of complaint to the board: *"We have not enough slates... We have not enough abacuses... We need more benches... The school is too dark and dank... We need more reading books... Why cannot we light the stove?"* Miss Dunsmore is a sound replacement and she believes in the principles in which I believe – the proper religious education of the children of this parish. The children will learn as well with her as with him. His treatment of Miss

Hodgson when she was a pupil-teacher there was diabolical. Let the people talk. I am the vicar of this parish and I decide what is right and what is wrong…'

What happened next was, on the Tuesday, the town crier, an aged resident in his eighties, took up his brass bell again after an absence of twenty years and went round the streets announcing that an 'indignation meeting' of ratepayers and inhabitants would be held on the Wednesday evening in the town hall council chamber. Come the start of the meeting at seven o'clock, the place was so packed that, while two hundred were squeezed inside the chamber, a further two hundred stood outside, some hoping for a chance to go inside if others left, willing to risk the crush, but others just prepared to stand outside and wait to hear what was to be done.

It was no surprise to those inside to find Dr. Iveson seated at the front with Dr. Langham: the real surprise was that seated with them were the three Non-conformist pastors – the tenant farmer and Primitive Methodist preacher Hezekiah Coker, the carpenter and main Baptist lay preacher Thomas Chiddup and the blacksmith and Primitive Congregationalist preacher Gabriel Grout.

By unanimous acclamation, on a proposal by Thomas Chiddup, seconded by Hezekiah Coker and supported by Gabriel Grout, Dr. Iveson was immediately nominated as the chairman, which he accepted with a reluctant sigh, and immediately motioned for Dr. Langham and the three Non-conformist pastors to join him up on the mayoral dais, where a long table and a half-dozen chairs had already been set. The good doctor was chosen because, at that moment, after his angry walkout from church, he was the most respected man in town: he had stood up to the vicar and told him what he thought of him and, as a result, had been applauded on his entrance. Besides, with his quiet yet authoritative manner, he was the only one liable to be able to control the known hotheads among them, one or two of whom, standing around the walls, were already suggesting some form of physical retribution be taken against the vicar, most of it involving a rope and a tree branch or tar and feathers and a hurdle – and the meeting had not even started.

Finally, the chairman rose and raised his hand for quiet. 'I find this a painful meeting over which I have been asked to preside,' the doctor said. 'It is one I would not have chosen for myself. You call this an "indignation meeting" – well, the very word "indignation" implies something about which you are very indignant. You are being asked to express sympathy with Mr. Warburton and to protest against his arbitrary dismissal as headmaster of the parochial school, a move with which, as many of you will know, I do not agree. We are gathered here to receive more light on what is a very painful subject for us all...'

The subjects of the meeting, William and Martha, were not present: they had thought it best to stay away to allow people to express their opinions for or against them – though, it was to be hoped, in favour – in a free and honest manner, without having to hold back on what they might say because of their presence.

Dr. Iveson had only just settled himself back in his chair and was banging his gavel to quieten the ensuing hubbub when the Reverend Scrope of all people began pushing his way through the throng, shouldering aside any who were too slow to give way. As far as he was concerned, it was a meeting 'open to all' and he intended to have his say to it and 'put them straight on a few things,' as he had told Agnes before leaving the vicarage. He was not going to be kept out of a meeting which was called against himself.

Behind him, looking apprehensive, as if he were wishing he were not there and certainly not having to accompany the vicar, came the Reverend Smallwood. The furore which had erupted outside at their appearance was immediately repeated inside as they began pushing through to the front: shouts and curses, boos, catcalls and crude workmen's epithets greeted them. 'Throw the buggers out!' from one. 'Kick 'em out!' from another. 'Judases!' and 'Clergy bastards!' from others and 'Bloody clergy!' from yet more.

'I wish to speak,' the vicar cried, ignoring it all and coming to a halt before the dais upon which the chairman, Dr. Langham and the three pastors sat. 'I wish to address the meeting. I know it is against me, but for what purpose has it been called?' He airily waved one hand, as if to dismiss whatever was about to be said was of no consequence, anyway.

The Baptist Thomas Chiddup had already risen to his feet to speak. 'This meeting is being held in support of Mr. Warburton and his wife following their unwarranted dismissal by you from the parochial school,' he told him, staring hard back down at the vicar and his nervous curate. 'We are here also to consider what future educational arrangements this town may require.'

'And what might those "future educational arrangements" be?' the vicar asked in a scoffing tone. 'What further arrangements could you possibly need?'

'The provision of a second school, for one,' Thomas Chiddup told him forcefully, 'with a schoolmaster and a schoolmistress whom the people respect, an independent school, one that is not overcrowded and not beholden to the Church either, most of all one that also is not subject to the capriciousness and the contrariness of a meddling vicar.'

'The Church provides all the educational requirements that the children of this town need,' the Reverend Scrope retorted pompously, reddening a little at the Non-conformist pastor's clear insult, but determined not to be disconcerted by it. 'There is no need for a second school. The very idea of it!'

'There are some of us who think that what we have might be bettered by an independent school,' Thomas Chiddup snapped back. 'There are some of us who think the parochial schools of the Church of England are more interested in Anglican indoctrination than real education and that vicars and bishops and the like have too much of a say in the running of them – '

He would have gone on had not Dr. Iveson jumped to his feet in an attempt to keep tempers in check.

'Gentlemen, gentlemen,' he admonished, 'we must not argue the merits of different schools among ourselves. The purpose of this meeting is, first and foremost, to support Mr. and Mrs. Warburton. For myself, I am here to tell you that a resolution has been handed to me – ' He had actually scribbled it out himself. ' – that *"We, the parishioners of this town, in a public meeting assembled on this day at the town hall, do hereby express our satisfaction with, and perfect confidence in, Mr. William Warburton as the schoolmaster, and also in his wife as his assistant, and our respect for them as residents among us".'* A loud cheer went up at that. 'We shall speak on that.'

It was met with a snort of derision from the vicar. 'Then you will be supporting a liar and a charlatan!' he declared loudly...

FIFTY-FOUR

THE WHOLE ROOM went quiet: the doctor's forehead creased in a frown: it was as if he could hardly believe what had just been said.

'That is a monstrous allegation, Mr. Scrope,' Dr. Iveson protested. 'Mr. Warburton came to this town with a good character from a respected clergyman in London and the chairman of the management board of his previous school. I have seen the references. You showed the letters to me at the meeting at which we endorsed his appointment.'

'Yes, it is true that I was presented with two letters which *purported* to be references from two gentlemen in London as to the good character of Mr. Warburton,' the vicar said, a sneering edge to his words, as if he were relishing the moment, 'one from a clergyman, the other from the chairman of a school management board. Unfortunately, I have since discovered they are both – for the want of a better word – forgeries! Forgeries! They were not written by the clergyman in London or by the chairman of the school management board whose names they bear. They were most probably written by Mr. Warburton himself – and perhaps even by his wife collaborating in a wicked forgery!'

All around, there was a sudden buzz of voices as the import of what the vicar had said was taken in, digested and whispered back to those in the doorway and outside.

'I have my proof,' the vicar shouted above the noise, holding aloft a sheet of paper, 'a letter signed by the very clergyman who is supposed to have provided one of the references. At the time of Mr. Warburton's appointment, no check was ever made on his references. An oversight on my part, I grant you, but at the time he was hired I was unable to do so because I was too ill to travel, as Dr. Iveson himself will confirm, and the appointment was made more quickly than perhaps was wise, due to the previous master leaving before his notice had expired.'

How did all this affect the proposal before the meeting? The chairman was at a loss as to how they should proceed, as was everyone else.

'You are here, Vicar, and Mr. Warburton and his wife are not,' he tried. 'They are not here to defend themselves.'

'Perhaps we should inform Mr. Warburton of these charges and ask him to come here so that he might do so,' Thomas Chiddup suggested, biting his lip. The last person he wanted to put one over on him was the sanctimonious Higo Scrope.

A vote was taken and it was accepted unanimously that someone be dispatched to fetch the schoolmaster: in the meantime, the meeting was adjourned, though the buzz of chatter continued: the people had heard nothing like the vicar's accusation before and few of them could even believe that he, despicable and disliked as he was, had made it.

Cheering began outside a quarter-hour later, surged in through the door and then echoed around the room: William had arrived, though he made his way with some difficulty to the front, for he was slapped upon the back thirty times and had his hand shaken twenty more before he reached the front.

While they had been waiting, the five men on the dais had been handed the letter and each had read it. 'An accusation has been made against you,' the doctor told William in a distinctly grave tone. 'You are here to refute it. You have the floor, sir. Give your defence.'

To their surprise, William did not seem the least fazed at being called to answer the vicar's charge: he waited for the same buzz of voices to subside, cleared his throat and then, facing them, he said quite matter-of-factly: 'The charge is true. I do not refute it. The two references which I presented to the Reverend Scrope *were* written by me, one with my left hand and one with my right – ' He allowed himself a brief smile at his own duplicity. ' – I did it for a reason: my previous employers would not provide me with references and I required a post as a teacher to keep body and soul together. It is as simple as that.'

'You deceived us!' cried the vicar. Having moved to the side of the chamber on William's appearance, he now stepped forward to confront him directly and also to place himself before the gathering as the victor of the argument, the upholder of truth and honesty.

Again, the many voices had to be silenced by the chairman's gavel.

'You were dismissed from your previous post?' the vicar cried, an evident note of triumph in his voice.

'I was. I do not deny it,' the schoolmaster calmly answered him. 'My deception was only in obtaining the post here. I am a certificated teacher. I spent five years as a pupil-teacher myself before attending a teacher-training college. I am a qualified teacher. I possess a first-class certificate, but I was dismissed from my previous post and refused a reference. So I wrote my own. That is all.'

'That is all!' The vicar was almost beside himself with joy that a man should condemn himself so openly.

'Yes, that is all,' William continued. 'Being dismissed is no crime – the crime that was committed was not mine or my wife's – the crime was committed by a member of the management board of my previous school and it was for that reason I was sacked.'

'How so, Mr. Warburton?' the doctor asked, somewhat puzzled by the teacher's calm demeanour in making his revelation, as were the two hundred others in the chamber.

'The school where I taught before I came to Steadshall was in the East End of London, a place called Stepney Green,' William told them. 'There are many poor people living in that area – many of them foreigners – immigrants.'

'Jews, you mean,' snorted the Reverend Scrope.

'Yes,' said William calmly, 'Jews – Jews from Poland and Russia – refugees from the tyranny of the Tsar, driven out of their own homes – their towns, their villages, their own countries – and come to England to find sanctuary. I had taught at the local parochial church school for two years before we began to take in young Jewish scholars. Not many at first, just a few. But as their numbers grew, so certain people began to complain. Unfortunately, it did not suit everyone that their sons and daughters had to sit next to Hebrew children – children who were not Christians – '

'Children of the Christ-killers!' the Reverend Scrope snorted again.

'If you will,' William said quietly, unfazed by the malevolence of the comment and prepared to allow the man to reveal his own bigotry if he so wished. 'But these same people who objected to their presence, the good Christian parishioners, were still quite prepared to exploit them, to force them to live in rat-infested, disease-ridden tenements, a hundred and more people on each floor, in rooms divided and divided again as more and more arrived, so that a family of ten or more lived in what was little more than a cubby hole. Sometimes in the one tenement building there might be up to a three or four hundred people, young and old together, husbands and wives, grown girls and grown men, with all the horror and squalid living that that entails –

and the "good Christian men" of the parish charging them exorbitant rents to live like animals in buildings which should have been pulled down years ago. My crime – the reason for my dismissal and the refusal of the rector and the chairman of the school management board to give me a proper reference – was because, when a group of younger Jews organised a rent strike to get their Christian landlords to repair their properties and reduce the numbers they were taking in, I supported them! That is all. I wrote two letters and three pamphlets for them which were presented to the authorities because their English was not good enough. That was my crime, sir – I was a pamphleteer, supporting some poor foreigners who were being exploited by greedy, uncaring landlords, of whom one was the Church of England no less, for the Church owned four of the tenement buildings in which these poor people were forced to live. I was ordered by the reverend gentleman who employed me to stop helping them – to stop writing pamphlets for them. I refused and that is why I was given three months' notice and refused a reference – for refusing to stop helping poor people when ordered to by a Christian bigot.' He was looking directly at the Reverend Scrope as he said it.

The whole room was listening in quiet astonishment, but William had not finished.

'One of the reasons for my dismissal from here,' he went on, 'appears to have been because I have had great difficulty with one of the assistants whom the vicar has been anxious to keep – Miss Dunsmore, who, I hear, is now to be promoted in my place – ' He paused briefly, as if allowing those who knew of the teacher's friendship with the vicar to arrive at some conclusion of their own thinking. ' – Since I came to Steadshall, I have persistently had to correct Miss Dunsmore over certain school matters which I ought not to have had to do and, I understand that, because of it, she has complained to the vicar on numerous occasions – ' He shrugged, as if to say that was only to be expected of her. ' – I also had cause to complain to the management board over the insubordination of the pupil-teacher, George Crowfoot – the churchwarden's nephew – who was foisted upon me without so much as my being consulted as to his suitability. I simply recommended that he be let go because, in my opinion, he was totally unsuited to the work. Yet all the while he was there, he, like Miss Dunsmore, was supported and encouraged by the vicar, so much so that I found it almost impossible to rule my own school. Crowfoot was on several occasions also extremely cruel to the children in his charge, yet I was powerless to dismiss him. To do that,

I required the say-so of the management board and the management board is ruled – with respect to you, Doctor – ' The doctor harrumphed and waved a hand dismissively, for he had already quit that body. ' – ruled by the Reverend Scrope. No decision can be taken by the board unless he sanctions it. That is how tied they are and how tied are the hands of any schoolmaster who comes here.'

William was going to have his say whether it did any good or not: even if he had condemned himself by his admission at the start, he intended to ensure that they knew of everything which had occurred between him and the Reverend Scrope.

'The vicar and I also disagreed over Sunday school,' he continued. 'When I was appointed – hired – I was not given a contract and no mention was made in the letter of appointment that I was expected to take the Sunday school as well as the day school. I am a religious man – my wife and I, as many of you know, go to church. For reasons of my own, I did not want to take the Sunday school and I told the vicar so right at the beginning. Unhappily, it has been a sore point between us ever since. He has said several times that, as the head teacher at the school, I ought to be taking it. I said I would not do it because I needed to rest on Sundays. That was my only reason, yet I am told that when the managers asked the vicar what fault there was to find in me for not doing it, he said only that, in refusing, I had spoken disrespectfully of the clergy. I did not. I merely pointed out that perhaps the Sunday school would be better taken by a churchman than by a lay person like myself.'

There were murmurs of surprise and some indignation: William paused again and the murmuring quickly subsided under the glare of the doctor.

'One thing more,' William said, 'I was told by the vicar himself only yesterday that, if I did not stop this meeting from going ahead, I should be reported to the Government inspector and to the Department of Education. My assumption on that was that the inspector would act against me and that I should somehow be prevented from obtaining another post. I consider that a blatant attempt at coercion, which is unfitting for a man of the cloth.'

'That is true,' the town hall's caretaker, Albert Tonkin, a stoop-backed man in his late sixties, called out from amid the crowd. 'The vicar himself come to me and asked me – implored me, he did – not to let you have the council chamber for this meeting and to make up some excuse for it – that I'd lost the keys or something. He also told me, if I allowed you in, he would not say any more prayers for my dead wife, which I pays him to do, just like everyone else.'

From the looks many of the men around gave him, very few, it seemed, would be as conscientious as he about the memory of their dead wives to want to follow his example.

At that, there were cries of dismay and angry shouts against the vicar, which the chairman quickly silenced with several more loud raps of his gavel and a stern call for 'Silence! One at a time! There will be no shouting! This is not a cattle market! Who wishes to speak now?'

The Reverend Scrope just could not understand why the whole mood of the meeting was against him, rather than against the schoolmaster, who had admitted to deceiving them, who had confessed to forging two letters of reference. It was beyond his comprehension...

FIFTY-FIVE

THOMAS CHIDDUP indicated that he would like to speak again and was given the floor.

'It is a fact, I am told,' the Baptist pastor began solemnly, 'that four of the school managers were not at the meeting at which it was decided to give Mr. Warburton his resignation notice and so knew nothing of it. Doctor Iveson was one, the Reverend Smallwood was another and George Mott and William Eaton were also not present. The meeting, as I understand it, was called in the vestry before the morning service on Sunday and Doctor Iveson was not informed of its being held. And of those who were there – Mr. Linkhorn, Mr. Higgs and Mr. Bucknall – I am given to understand that two said they did not care one way or the other about the vicar's information but would go along with whatever he said, while the third always votes the same way as the vicar, anyway. I will not say which one of them that was, for I think we all know already – '

Everyone knew, of course, that he referred to Joshua Linkhorn: from the vicar, there was a just a further snort of defiance, but, tellingly, no denial.

'However,' the Baptist preacher went on, 'we are not here to criticise the managers of the school. It appears the lead in this whole movement has been taken from first to last by one person and one person only and that the members of the management board who were present were simply asked to rubber-stamp one man's arbitrary decision, that man being the prime mover in all of this. The purpose of this meeting is to correct that misinformation and I think, by his explanation of what has occurred, Mr. Warburton has done that.'

The eyes of everyone in the room swivelled towards the vicar: from whom there was another indignant snort, followed by a huff of annoyance.

'I have it on the word of Dr. Iveson,' the pastor continued – again there was a polite bow and a smile between the two – 'I have it on his word that no fault has ever been found with the teaching at the parochial school at any of the meetings of the school management board at which it has been discussed. At the last examination, I am told, twenty-six children were presented to the inspector, of whom twenty passed in reading, nineteen passed in writing and fourteen passed in arithmetic. I think I speak for all when I say that, since Mr. Warburton's arrival, the people have come to respect him greatly and, as our schoolmaster, he has the confidence of us all – save for one who stands here – ' A great cheer went up at that: they all knew at whom the metaphorical finger was pointed. ' – the same one, I understand, who even denied him the right to speak in his own defence at the meeting which voted for his dismissal. Even common criminals are allowed their say in the courts of law before they are sentenced, yet Mr. Warburton was allowed no say whatsoever.'

An observant onlooker would have noticed that by this time the curate, perhaps becoming fearful of something happening, had quietly separated himself from the vicar and had allowed a number of others standing alongside to interpose themselves between the two.

'According to the last inspector's report,' Thomas Chiddup announced, 'the teaching at the school has shown a marked improvement in the very short time that Mr. and Mrs. Warburton have been here and yet Mr. Warburton has had to cease because he cannot agree with his vicar. I very much would like to see a poll taken as to how many in this town – in his own congregation – do agree with the Reverend Scrope. I doubt whether there are sixty out of six thousand in the parish who would agree with him on most things.'

He waited while the laughter and cheers died: he had one final flourish to make. 'Some of us in this town have long campaigned for the introduction of a School Board,' he said. 'If we now get one, then you might all like to thank the Reverend Scrope for it.'

The Baptist sat down to more cheers and the Congregationalist Gabriel Grout stood up. 'I, too, have never heard a word of complaint said against Mr. Warburton. The master has been so successful in getting the children on that a good number of them have been able to leave school and get work. I say, if children are properly taught, they should all be able to pass the leaving standard when they are old enough. Our Mr. Warburton has got more up to the leaving standard in the short time he has been here than any other master before him has ever done – ' There were smiles and sarcastic cheers at that, which he accepted with a mock bow and waited for quiet to descend again.

' – I do not know in what newspaper one advertises for a new teacher for a school – '

'*The Teachers' Guardian* usually,' he was told by the chairman.

' – but I do know that an advertisement for *two* assistant-teachers for our town school has already been posted to the *County Standard* in Wivencaster, to appear this Friday. It was sent by post on Monday morning and arrived at their offices yesterday. I know because one of the printers at the paper is a member of my congregation and he came to me and told me that he had set it in type that morning. It seems to me that a deliberate attempt has been made by one person in particular to negate the whole purposes of this meeting – to express our satisfaction with Mr. Warburton as our schoolmaster and to keep him in his job! It seems to me that whoever wrote that advertisement – ' He was looking directly at the Reverend Scrope now. ' – wishes to present us with a *fait accompli* – in short, to deny us our rights!'

At that, there was uproar as people stood to shout abuse towards the vicar and the sound of chairs crashing over echoed around the chamber. The Reverend Scrope stepped forward again and held up his hands as if, like Jesus quelling the waves on the shore of Lake Galilee, he could with a single gesture quieten the tumult of jeering directed at him.

But the people did not want to hear him. 'Vote! Vote! Vote!' they shouted and, faced with the fact that the tumult was unlikely to cease unless he took firm action, the chairman quickly rose, banged his gavel again and called for one. As far as the chairman could see, every arm save the vicar's was raised in favour – in jest, some even raised two – and, despite the Reverend Scrope's refusal to lift his hand, the resolution declaring the people's confidence in their schoolmaster was passed 'unanimously' amid great cheering, to be followed immediately by a second proposal and a second 'unanimous vote' – save for the same solitary unraised hand – that a copy of the resolution should be sent not only to all the school managers but also to the Department of Education in London, along with a petition, calling for a 'searching inquiry' by them. Amid the melee, no one thought to record how the curate voted – whether he voted at all or abstained – tucked away as he was amid the crowd: in fact, hidden by the throng, he raised his hand with the rest both times, though it was timidly done, with his head down and his shoulders hunched.

Someone amid the uproar shouted that, as the vicar had sacked their schoolmaster, they should send a petition to the Bishop requesting the vicar's removal. 'Get him out!' the voice shouted.

It was too much for the Reverend Scrope: he immediately sought the centre of the room one more time. 'Friends, friends,' he shouted, raising his hands again in the hope of commanding their attention and their silence, 'it is the Baptists who are stirring up this trouble for their own ends. They want a School Board here. They want to see the closure of the parochial school – *your* Church school. That is why they are doing this. Do not let them! Do not let them!'

However, no one wanted to hear any more from him: boos and cat-calls rang out and a half-dozen of the rougher element surrounded him and, mouthing crude insults, began pushing him towards the door. In the interests of fair play – six against one – the Reverend Smallwood attempted to interpose himself between them, but was himself seized by three of them and sent stumbling out of the same door after his vicar, pitching forward on to the hard pavement as he did so and winding himself badly.

Ahead of him, the Reverend Scrope, not having fallen, merely straightened himself and strode off indignantly up the hill towards the vicarage without so much as a backward glance and so he did not see the Reverend Smallwood climb to his feet, brush himself down and then, after a brief conversation with those who had thrown him out, shake hands with two of them as if an apology were being made and be slapped upon the back by the third, before re-entering the meeting.

In that short time, the long table had been lifted down, sheets of paper had been produced and a snaking queue had formed to sign the petition calling for the school management board to withdraw their notice demanding that the schoolmaster resign.

'My hope is that all ratepayers will sign it,' Dr. Iveson was calling out from the dais.

Standing in the line waiting to do so, though not a ratepayer himself, was the Reverend Smallwood...

FIFTY-SIX

THE PETITION calling for the school management board to withdraw their notice to the schoolmaster, signed by more than three hundred of those who had attended the 'indignation' meeting, both inside and outside the town hall, was delivered to the secretary of the school managers the next day. But it was a second petition, got up after the town hall meeting by a five-man committee comprising the three Dissenting pastors and two lay members, which prompted the Reverend Scrope to call an extraordinary general meeting of the school managers at the vicarage on the very next Saturday afternoon. For that petition was to be sent to the Bishop and called upon him 'to remove the Vicar of Steadshall from his incumbency because he has lost the trust of the townsfolk.' Copies of it had been left in all the town's shops and inns and even at Oldcourt's three mills and, by all accounts, it was being signed by the greater number of townsfolk, churchgoers and chapelgoers alike, whether ratepayers or no.

Those who sent the first petition to the management board were under no illusions that it would be acted upon and so it proved: the petition was merely passed from hand to hand by those who were seated in the vicar's front parlour – namely, the Reverend Scrope, Joshua Linkhorn, the four farmers and, the seventh and last to peruse it, the Reverend Smallwood. Not present, of course, was Dr. Iveson, whose name was at the top of the first page: by then, he had sent in his official letter of resignation.

On the proposal of the Reverend Scrope, seconded by Henry Bucknall of Highwoods farm, the petition was rejected and the fifteen sheets of paper dropped into the waste basket alongside the vicar's chair.

'In the interests of democracy and fair play, its receipt ought to be recorded,' the Reverend Smallwood protested from his place at the end of the table: no one noticed his signature on page eleven because no one read it and he did not enlighten them.

'I am not having a petition against me recorded in the minutes of the management board!' was the Reverend Scrope's indignant response. 'We have already made our decision on the schoolmaster. The man deceived us by claiming the support of referees he did not have. In my opinion, we have been generous in giving him three months' notice. We should have been within our rights to dismiss him on the spot. I think it is very magnanimous of us to keep him on at all – him and his wife. We cannot go back on it now. His stay with us will terminate at the end of April. Until then, he will remain at his post.'

The worry for him was not the petition calling for the schoolmaster's reinstatement but the one to be sent to the Bishop. How to counter that was his problem and, for that purpose, he had already primed Joshua Linkhorn.

'I propose,' the secretary declared when the matter was raised as the first and only item on the agenda, 'I propose the school management board draw up a petition of our own, declaring our unstinting support for the vicar. We can ask all churchgoers to sign it as they enter the church porch on Sunday and also any ratepayers about the town whose support we can garner. It will need to be done quickly so that we can send it to the Bishop to counter the petition drawn up by the Warburtons' supporters. We need to get it in ahead of theirs, if possible.'

'You could organise that for me, could you not, Mr. Smallwood?' the Reverend Scrope said in the manner of one who expected his request to be met without demurral. 'You could also get the ratepayers at Bourne Brook to sign it, too.'

Henry Smallwood took a deep breath and clenched both fists to steel his nerve. 'I could,' he said, 'but I will not. I regret I cannot oblige you, Mr. Scrope. I still firmly believe you and the board are wrong in asking for Mr. Warburton's resignation. In view of that, I feel it would be hypocritical of me to then manage a petition for you on a matter which is the subject of a profound disagreement between us.'

The Reverend Scrope could hardly believe his ears. 'Do I understand that you refuse to help your vicar, Mr. Smallwood?'

'You do, Mr. Scrope. I am sorry.'

'Sorry? Sorry?' the vicar exploded. 'I have never heard anything like it in all my born days. You are my curate, sir. If you will not support me, then I think you had better leave this meeting.'

The Reverend Smallwood rose, politely bade good evening to the others and, with as much dignity as a man can muster when he has to shuffle around behind chairs to reach the door, he departed with his head held high, glad to be leaving, for in the vicar's eyes he had seen a malice which he had never expected to see upon the face of a man of his own calling towards another, a man who every Sunday expounded from the pulpit the lessons of the Scriptures – love, tolerance, forbearance.

It was four days later, on the following Wednesday evening, when the curate returned to his lodgings along the Siblingham road, that he found a large, bulky envelope addressed to him lying on a tray in the hallway: it was from the Bishop's secretary at Wivencaster: enclosed with it were eight pages which as he unfolded them he knew to be in the Reverend Scrope's handwriting. He read the secretary's letter first:

> '*My Dear Reverend Smallwood, His Lordship has asked me to write to you to inform you that some time ago he received a letter from the Reverend Scrope in which, somewhat surprisingly in his Lordship's view, the Reverend Scrope asks His Lordship to grant him permission to request your resignation from the curacy of St. Mary's, Bourne Brook, or, failing that, for His Lordship to withdraw your stipend and instigate your removal from the parish to a position elsewhere in the county. Further, I am asked to inform you that the Reverend Scrope accuses you of not supporting him on certain matters involving the functioning of the parish and he claims that, because of it, his influence for good in the parish has been diminished. His Lordship views all these matters as a very sad and distasteful state of affairs. He wishes you to know that at present he is not minded to take a decision on the matter concerning yourself, but includes the letter sent to him by the Reverend Scrope so that you may know of it and reply to His Lordship upon it. An early response would be appreciated...*'

The vicar's letter, when he read all of its eight pages, was damning: and such was the anger rising within the curate that his eyes recorded only those phrases which seared themselves on his consciousness: '*...is defiant, argumentative and headstrong... has openly and wantonly opposed me on several occasions... is lacking in humility... falls well short in the performance of his duties... is somewhat deficient in his knowledge of certain aspects of life about which a man* *of his age ought to know… excuses the laxity and libertinism of the labouring classes by saying it is a result of the social conditions in which they exist rather than a natural tendency of such types to indulge in licentiousness…'*

There were many others, such as the request that the vicar would be obliged if *'…respectfully, Your Lordship would kindly keep this communication a secret between us as it would undoubtedly upset the Reverend Smallwood to know that he has been found so wanting in the performance of his duties…'*

For what reason had the vicar done this? For what cause? He knew of none: he did his work diligently, he visited the sick, he prayed for the dying, he baptised the babies, he joined Miss Dunsmore at the Sunday school at least twice a month and he ministered to the non-believers with the same fairness as he did to the believers. His parish books were in order: no monies were missing or withheld: all collections were recorded and delivered to the two churchwardens at Steadshall within a day or two. He had supported the vicar over the extension to Steadshall's school and on the opening of the new 'cow byre' school at Bourne Brook: he also supported the parish council there in its endeavours to provide a better water supply. There was no cause of which he could think.

The curate replied, refuting all the vicar's allegations:

> *'My Lord, No one has a greater desire to be loyal to the vicar than I, but he has to act honestly and fairly. For refusing to comply with his wishes, because I consider certain aspects of them unjust, I have suffered most keenly and only last week was asked to leave a meeting of the school managers against my will. I could make a number of other revelations, but I hardly think that necessary. His letter to you speaks for itself. Finding that I would not be his henchman in all things, he simply asks in the most clandestine way that Your Lordship have me removed from the parish. I state to Your Lordship that I will not resign because I do not believe that I have done anything which requires so drastic an action from me. Also, if I were to resign, another curate would come, only to be victimised in the same way as I have been…'*

As it was, it was only by chance that the curate learned that a further extraordinary meeting of the school management board had been called…

FIFTY-SEVEN

MOST UNUSUALLY, the meeting was being held mid-morning on a Friday when the usual gatherings of the management board were held on Saturday afternoons so that all could attend, particularly the four farmers, who had business about their farms all week and took Saturday afternoons off only to ensure that nothing was decided at any meeting which might cost them money. It was also held then so that there was no carping about 'unnecessary absences' from Joshua Linkhorn's employer, the solicitor Hubert Sparrow, who for five-and-a-half days of the week preferred his senior clerk to be at his desk copying out depositions rather than drinking tea in the vicarage parlour.

How the curate got to hear of the second extraordinary meeting was that, at ten-forty-five on the Friday, just as he was preparing to set off on his usual walk to Bourne Brook, one of the minor clerks at Sparrow's solicitor's ran up the path of his lodgings along the Siblingham road and pushed a note through the letter box: it was to inform him that a meeting had been called for that morning and was due to start at eleven o'clock – in a quarter of an hour.

By having the notification delivered so late, Joshua Linkhorn could say that he had fulfilled his duty by sending it, but clearly the expectation was that the Reverend Smallwood would be well on his way to Bourne Brook by then and the note would have dropped on to the hallway mat, to be picked up later by his landlady and left on a side-table for him to read when he returned in the evening. In short, though still entitled to attend all meetings as an ex-officio member of the board, despite what had happened at the last gathering, they would have preferred that he missed this one, which, he supposed, could only have been at the instigation of the Reverend Scrope.

Fortunately, the curate had been delayed and was still at his lodgings when the note was pushed through. There was no time to inform anyone where he was going: he simply rushed up to his room, stuffed the Bishop's bulky package inside his jacket and ran the half-mile or so to the vicarage: he intended to confront his vicar in the presence of the other members of the management board and have it out with him once and for all.

The nursemaid, Hannah Hodgson, let him in, holding the hand of Elizabeth, who stared up at him with smiling eyes, pleased to see someone whom she recognised as having once been a frequent visitor and who had always greeted her with a smile and a friendly word. There was, however, no sign of Agnes.

'The mistress is in her room,' the nursemaid informed him, closing the door. 'Shall I tell her you are here, sir?'

'No thank you, Hannah,' he said, his very determination to carry things through acting to calm his nerves. 'I am here for the meeting.'

'They are in the front parlour,' the girl said over her shoulder as she led the toddler away.

He waited till they had disappeared up the stairs, then, taking a deep breath, he pushed open the parlour door. Joshua Linkhorn and the farmers George Mott, William Eaton and Henry Bucknall were already seated at the parlour table: the only one absent was Charles Higgs: the vicar was also not in the room.

Joshua Linkhorn looked surprised and reddened visibly when the curate entered, but still managed to greet him cordially, if a little diffidently, as he handed him a hand-written agenda: thereafter, the secretary-treasurer kept his head down and concentrated upon his papers. The three farmers, knowing nothing of the Reverend Smallwood's mission or the attempt to keep him away, greeted him pleasantly enough, but, remembering the last time, said no more to him and talked among themselves of farming matters while they waited for the Reverend Scrope.

He soon appeared, smiling a greeting to everyone as he came through the door – that was, till he saw his curate seated on one side of the table next to the secretary: at that, the smile froze on his lips to one of displeasure, confirming the curate's suspicions that he had indeed not expected to see him there. There were even quick glances exchanged between him and the secretary, as one asked angrily 'How is he here?' and the other expressed an embarrassed 'I do not know!'

Generally, the Reverend Scrope made it a point on his entry to go round the table, shaking hands with everyone at it: that he proceeded to do, first with the three farmers on the one side, then with the secretary facing them and finally, as brazenly as any innocent, he offered his hand to the Reverend Smallwood, though, unseen by the others, his lips were twisted into a thin smile.

The Reverend Smallwood had made up his mind what he would do even before he had reached the house. 'I would rather not,' he said coldly, staring at the hand extended to him, but making no move to take it: then he calmly turned back to the table, acutely aware that the eyes of everyone else at the table were upon him.

There was no way he was going to shake hands in friendship with the man who was trying to have him removed from the parish and who was hoping it would be done in secret, as he had asked, and that the blame for it, if blame there were to be, would fall on the Diocese and that way he would avoid any unpleasantness towards himself from his own parishioners. What the curate himself might think of his underhand method, it seemed the Reverend Scrope had not bothered to take into account, since he had expected that his part in it would remain unknown, which it might well have done had the Bishop not sent the letter which the Reverend Smallwood carried in his pocket.

The vicar made no comment or protest: all he did was to feign surprise and incomprehension, as if to rectify his own dignity, shake his head slowly for the benefit of the others and take his seat on the other side of Joshua Linkhorn, clearing his throat as he did so to show that he was unfazed by what had happened. The vicar, the secretary and the Reverend Smallwood now sat in that order on one side of the table, with the three farmers facing them.

The Reverend Smallwood waited till the vicar had finished the usual short prayer and the 'Amens' had been said: then, before anyone could say anything, he asked quite casually: 'Why has this meeting been called so hurriedly?'

'It has not been called "hurriedly," as you put it,' the Reverend Scrope responded with a snort. 'It was set at the last meeting. Had you been present you would have known.'

Since he had been asked to leave the previous meeting, it was a cynical remark, but he chose to ignore it: that was an old quarrel: the new one was far more important.

'Then why was my notification delivered to my lodgings less than a half-hour ago?'

'A mistake on my part,' Joshua Linkhorn interrupted quickly. 'I should have sent it round yesterday evening, but it was mislaid. I apologise.'

It was an unconvincing answer. 'Why today?' the curate asked. 'Why on a Friday morning? Why not on a Saturday afternoon as usual when everyone is usually free to attend?'

The secretary seated between them was ignored and the question was put directly across him to the Reverend Scrope, but he was ready with his answer. 'A Friday is as good a day as any,' he said. 'I have found, of late, that doing things on a Saturday tends to upset my preparations for Sunday. I find that I prefer quiet on a Saturday, so I have decided that, in future, meetings will be held at other times.'

'Now is my time!' the curate told himself: and, reaching inside his coat, he produced the Bishop's bulky letter for all to see, noting the vicar's consternation as he did so, as if he recognised the envelope as one emanating from the Bishop's palace.

The Reverend Smallwood rose to his feet, unfolding the various pages as he did so. 'I have here a letter sent to me personally by His Lordship's secretary,' he said. 'In it, he asks me to comment on a letter His Lordship has received from the Reverend Scrope, which is nothing but a blatant attempt to ruin me with the Bishop. I would like now to read both letters to this meeting so that you may all know what is going on – '

'No, you may not read either of them here,' the Reverend Scrope cried, jumping to his feet. 'This meeting is about school matters. We are here to discuss the appointment of two assistant-teachers at the school. Neither of those letters is about school matters.'

'Part of your letter to his Lordship refers to school matters, therefore, I have a right to read it,' the Reverend Smallwood retorted, which it did, since the vicar had stated as part of his criticism, *The curate's sympathies seem to lie more with the new schoolmaster, William Warburton, than with me and, on certain matters over the past few months, he has supported him against me...'*

'I know for a fact that the letter in your hand is not about school matters,' the vicar asserted, stepping away from the table so that he now stood behind the bewildered Joshua Linkhorn, the better to confront the curate, 'because I have not written to the Bishop about school matters.'

'I say you have!' the curate replied, his tone hardening. 'It is in this letter and the other members of the management board have a right to hear it.'

'That is a lie,' the vicar shouted. 'If you do not stop this, I shall be forced to take you by the scruff of the neck and eject you from this meeting.'

'You will not,' the curate shouted back. 'I left last time to spare the others the embarrassment of our disagreement. I shall not do so a second time. I am here as a legitimate member of the board and neither you nor anyone has the right to put me out of a legally constituted meeting.'

'I can do what I like in my own house,' the vicar shouted again, stepping forward so that he was within touching distance – seizing distance really – of the curate: the two were so caught up in each other that they were oblivious to the bemused faces of the other members of the board, unused to seeing two clergymen arguing in such a manner.

'Pah!' was the curate's contemptuous response: and, to show his contempt further, he began reading aloud: ' *"My Dear Lord Bishop, I should like to draw your attention to a matter in my parish concerning my curate, Reverend Henry Smallwood, which is causing me much concern and displeases me greatly..." –* '

The Reverend Smallwood got no further, for at that point the vicar lunged forward and attempted to snatch the letter from his grasp: but the younger man was too quick for him: he jumped aside and, still holding the pages aloft, continued to read aloud: ' *"...For some time now, he has, I regret to have to inform you, resisted my endeavours..." –* '

With an angry shout, the vicar lunged forward again, intending to seize the curate by his collar and carry out his threat to eject him, but his intended victim simply took a step backwards to give himself room to continue reading. The result was the vicar lost his balance and grabbed at the curate to prevent himself falling: as a consequence, the two men crashed to the floor together, knocking a chair sideways. They ended up with the curate lying on his back, all breath knocked out of him, and the Reverend Scrope sprawled on top of him, the one underneath still attempting to hold the pages of the letter out of the reach of the other and he still attempting to seize them.

Shouts of 'Give me those!' from the vicar were met by equally firm retorts of 'No, I will not!' from the curate, who, in kicking his legs in a desperate attempt to wriggle free of his assailant's weight, appeared – at least from the pained gasp the vicar gave out – to drive his knee upward and accidentally to catch the Reverend Scrope in a most sensitive place.

So stunned were the other board members by what was happening that it was several seconds before they thought to react: then, the burly Henry Bucknall came swiftly round the table and, wrapping his muscular arms around the vicar's middle, he pulled him unceremoniously to his feet, while George Mott seized the curate in the same way, though such was the anger between the two clergymen that, even when erect, the two farmers still had to hold them apart.

'Leave this house!' the vicar shouted, his face still creased with the pain of the curate's kick. 'I will not tolerate your presence here one minute longer. Go! Go!' His finger was pointing to the door: he was almost apoplectic with rage.

'I think it would be for the best, Mr. Smallwood,' Joshua Linkhorn said somewhat lamely from the far corner of the parlour, to which he had retreated to avoid being kicked himself by the curate's flailing feet.

'Whatever you say, you have not heard the last of this – or of me!' the curate cried, straightening himself to maintain his dignity, before marching round the table to the door.

So incensed was the Reverend Scrope that he could not resist following the Reverend Smallwood to the street door to make one last remark.

As the curate walked down the path, the vicar limped to the gate and hissed angrily after him: 'You are no longer my curate! If you so much as attempt to set one foot in this house again, I shall slam the door in your face. Agnes and I will have nothing more to do with you – ' Pained scorn entered his voice here. ' – Oh yes, I know all about you and her. I have seen you creeping around. I am not blind. I am not a fool. She is my sister, so whatever you had in your mind, you can put it out. I forbid you even to talk to her and she will no longer talk to you. I shall see to that. Your friendship with her – if that is what it was – is finished. Finished! Now go! I do not want to see your face near me again. And you certainly have not heard the last of this from me.'

He did not realise that, above him, one of the bedroom windows on the second floor was open at the bottom so that the occupant might have some air: the vicar's angry words carried easily up to it and inside. Standing behind the fall of the curtain was Agnes herself: she had retired to her bedroom when the three farmers had arrived in order to escape the smell of their pipe tobacco, for they always smoked at the meetings. Now she was peering down at the Reverend Smallwood and her brother and tears were trickling down her cheeks…

FIFTY-EIGHT

WHEN MARTHA answered a polite knocking at the cottage door the following Saturday evening, she was surprised to find the town's three Non-conformist pastors standing on the step. They enquired politely if they might speak to her husband and, after showing them into the small front parlour, she went to fetch William, who was standing by the vegetable patch at the bottom of the small, rear garden, gazing somewhat forlornly at the first signs of his potato plants poking up through the soil, potatoes he would likely never lift.

When he joined the three men in the parlour, they each rose to shake his hand and Thomas Chiddup's first act was to invite Martha to remain as they wanted her to hear the reason why they had called.

'We have a proposition to put to you,' the Baptist said, reseating himself and giving the schoolmaster and his wife an affable smile. 'We have been considering for some time whether there ought to be two schools in Steadshall – a second school, a British School, one not beholden to the Church or to the Reverend Scrope, if you will – to help relieve what, I am sure you both will agree, still is unacceptable overcrowding at the parochial school, despite the opening of the new school at Bourne Brook.'

'That is why we are here, to ask if you will stay and educate our children,' the Congregationalist Gabriel Grout chipped in, unable to hold back their reason for calling, which drew a sharp glance from the Baptist, as if to say 'I thought we agreed that I should do the talking.'

'That is what we are here to ask,' Thomas Chiddup confirmed, regaining his composure. 'We were hoping that you would become the headmaster of a new independent school. We have thought it all out and all three chapels are together on this. The population of our town grows every year and a second school will be needed sooner rather than later. We say, "Why not now? Why not a new independent school free of the Church?" We are all agreed: our new Baptist chapel along the Wivencaster road would serve very well as a schoolroom.

There are good storage cupboards and a curtain could perhaps be hung down the middle between the two sets of children, the older ones and the younger ones and there are nigh on a hundred of them from our three chapels who go to the parochial school at the moment. They would all come over to us, so, if you were to take up our offer, you would have a decent attendance from the off, so to speak. The chapel has a good-sized scullery at the back for hand-washing and face-washing and there are already two bucket lavatories in the grounds, one for the boys and one for the girls, and we could soon build two more if they are needed.'

'Thomas here is a carpenter,' Hezekiah Coker, the Primitive Methodist, chipped in this time, pointing to his companion, though it was a fact which William and Martha already knew. 'He could soon knock up three or four extra lavatories, if they are wanted, couldn't thee, Tom? It would be no problem to him.'

'It is our opinion – and the opinion of many in the town,' the Baptist pastor resumed, wanting to keep the conversation on more decorous lines, 'that no better schoolteacher is to be found in the whole county than your good self, Mr. Warburton. If we opened a school, we would need a good head teacher and we are all agreed on you – ' He reddened slightly and looked across at Martha. ' – Two good teachers,' he corrected himself, 'if you and your good lady would take up the posts?'

'The chapel would only be a temporary school,' the Congregationalist Gabriel Grout interrupted again. 'We have plans – big plans. We have a half-acre of land in mind which we hope to buy and eventually to build a proper school on it.'

He paused under the further withering gaze of the Baptist and Hezekiah Coker jumped in again. 'Mr. Chiddup has already written to the Department of Education to ask them: if we were to open a proper school, would we be put on a level with the other school in the town – the parochial school? If we had two hundred scholars, say, just as a likely number, all in a school built for purpose, and, if they were under the Government, would we be entitled to the same yearly grant as the Church school gets now?'

'Aye, I have done that,' Thomas Chiddup nodded, 'but, as yet I have received no answer. We should, of course, take scholars from Chapel and Church – we would not discriminate. Anyone who wanted to come to us would be allowed to come. We firmly believe that, once we were up and running, under your stewardship, sir, and your good wife's, that quite a few of the church children who presently go to the parochial school would quickly come over to us. If you would take charge, we should pay you both the same salary as you have been receiving at the parochial school. All we need to begin, sir, madam, is your positive answer.'

William rubbed a finger under his nose, sniffed and scratched his scalp above his ear, as men do sometimes when ruminating upon something. 'It is a very tempting offer,' he said, turning to look at his wife. 'I should be willing to take up your offer, if Martha is willing, too.'

'Oh, I should be willing,' his wife said cheerfully. 'Apart from the Reverend Scrope, I have found life in Steadshall quite pleasant. If that man could be got rid of, I should be a happy woman – a very happy woman indeed. I do not want to leave Steadshall and move again just because of that man, but there are things which would have to be settled before we could agree – for a start, where we would live. We are due to leave this cottage when our notice ends and we shall need somewhere to live. And how would the school be financed? Who would pay our salaries? Who would pay for the slates, the copybooks, the blackboards, not to mention everything else a school needs?'

'There is no need to worry about the cottage or the funding, Mrs. Warburton,' the Baptist pastor said with a reassuring smile. 'The assistance of several influential gentlemen in the district has already been promised to get us started and we would hope, too, to receive the support of the British and Foreign School Society. The society funds all our British Schools by subscription from prominent Non-conformist Christians – not only our schools but our teacher training institutions as well. As for accommodation, Mrs. Warburton, Mr. Grout here tells me he has a small cottage which he owns and which is vacant at present and which is yours to rent – for a nominal sum, of course – should you say yes.' Here he gave what was intended as a disarming smile. 'And you would not be expected to attend his chapel any more than you would be expected to attend mine or Mr Coker's.'

He thought for a second or so, as if wondering whether to add anything else, then said: 'We should, of course, have to form a board of management, with a majority of Non-conformists to serve on it to manage the school and you would be expected to act entirely as the board directed.'

Neither William nor Martha could see anything wrong with their plan or the latter statement: it was only to be expected of them if the school were to be run as other British Schools were run. The news that the British and Foreign School Society would support their endeavour, backed as it was by several prominent evangelical and Non-conformist Christians, was enough to persuade them. As the founders of British Schools throughout the country, the British and Foreign Society had long been in conflict with the National School Society, which had founded the Church of England parochial schools: so the opening of yet another British School in opposition to the Church would be a minor triumph for the former society.

After a bout of handshaking to seal the deal, the three men left the cottage with smiles upon their faces. Behind them, the schoolmaster and his wife hugged and kissed each other as they celebrated their good fortune before suddenly Martha seized her husband by the hand and, with an impish smile, tugged him towards the door and up the stairs to the bedroom, intending another form of celebration...

A quarter-mile away in the vicarage, the Reverend Scrope was seated alone in his study, reading a communiqué which had arrived that afternoon via a special messenger from the Bishop's palace in Wivencaster. He was not in a good mood as he read it, not because of the kerfuffle involving the curate – he could deal with that – but because the Bishop had declared himself *'deeply disturbed to have received a most surprising memorial, signed by many townsfolk in Steadshall, requesting that His Lordship remove you from your benefice.'*

Further, they had pronounced themselves to be *'...deeply grieved by the fact that, after being vicar of the parish for nine years, the Reverend Scrope has lost all spiritual influence and that his residence among us is wanting in influence for good. Therefore, very respectfully, we pray Your Lordship to recommend him to resign...'*

'In consequence,' the Bishop's secretary had written at the end of his letter, *'you will be required to attend an inquiry...'*

FIFTY-NINE

THE INQUIRY was held on the following Thursday morning, in private, in the assembly room of the Red Lion Inn, halfway down Wivencaster High Street and a short carriage ride from the Bishop's palace: the old inn was chosen because the Bishop did not want the many lay persons summoned to attend 'cluttering up' his palace while they waited and tramping mud across the polished oak floors and pile carpets.

No reporters from any newspapers were allowed to attend, though both the *County Weekly* and the *Wivencaster Standard* had their scribes waiting outside in the hope of gleaning a few unguarded snippets about the proceedings inside, possibly from one of the laymen present. They obtained neither and no details of the Reverend Scrope's humiliation appeared in the local weeklies other than a reference to the fact that the inquiry was held because *'the ratepayers and inhabitants of Steadshall have expressed their dissatisfaction with their vicar.'*

William was one of just twelve laymen from Steadshall in opposition to the vicar invited by the Bishop's secretary to give 'evidence of the Reverend Scrope's general conduct,' as far as it concerned themselves: they occupied one room in the old inn, while those speaking in favour waited in another. The latter included a previous curate at Steadshall, several clergymen from other parishes around the district, a former assistant schoolmistress at the parochial school who had left before Joseph Padwick had arrived, Joshua Linkhorn, the farmers Charles Higgs, Henry Bucknall, George Mott and William Eaton and – only to be expected – the two churchwardens, Walter Crowfoot and Samuel Gough.

The Reverend Smallwood was called first before the Bishop and a panel comprising the archdeacon and two other senior clergymen, with the Bishop's secretary seated at one end of the table taking notes in impeccable shorthand. Surprisingly, the Reverend Scrope was allowed to sit-in at a small table set to one side of the room, with the obvious outcome that he would hear all that was said about him and be more able to refute it.

Not unexpectedly, the curate was greeted on entering by a glowering look from him, which was sustained throughout his twenty minutes of testimony and cross-examination, especially during his account of the tussle and his failed attempt to read the Bishop's letter and the subsequent struggle on the floor.

'At the beginning,' he began, 'I was loyal to the Reverend Scrope, but found myself turning against him because I was upset by his antagonism. In particular, I took exception to measures he adopted to avenge himself on those who displeased him. Against my will, I accompanied him to Edmundsbury once solely to speak to the headmaster at the Poor School there in an attempt to prevent Mr. Padwick from obtaining a post there, which, I am glad to say, we failed to do. Another time, the Reverend Scrope went to the police superintendent at Shallford in an attempt to cause trouble for the publican of one of the town's inns after he resigned from the management board, claiming that gambling was going on in his establishment after-hours, and when the town's police sergeant and two constables failed to act as he wished, he claimed they were turning a blind eye to it and that they did not seem to be "out and about" as much as he thought they should. Our final disagreement – save over the reading of your Lordship's letter to me – concerned my outright opposition to the notice given to the schoolmaster, Mr. Warburton. I disagreed intensely with the Reverend Scrope and told him so and was slighted for it. Those and other occasions were the ones which made me turn against him and begin to support those who wanted him removed from the parish – just as he attempted to have me secretly removed.'

There was an unmistakable bitterness in his words: the poor man was becoming emotional and had to pause to blow his nose and wipe his eyes with his handkerchief. 'It appalled me,' he went on, recovering himself, 'to see that things had come to such a pass in Steadshall that our own vicar should be burnt in effigy by his own townspeople – by his own parishioners – like a Paris mob during the French Revolution.'

'That was not an effigy of me!' the vicar interrupted, leaping to his feet and glowering even more fiercely at his curate.

'And I say it was,' the curate responded, equally as firmly, staring him down. 'It was your effigy I saw being carried on a pitchfork through the streets for all to see on the day I brought some money to you. The effigy was made of hay and straw, with a turnip wrapped in sacking for a head, and had a face drawn on a sheet of paper pinned to it – your face, complete with sideburns and a moustache so no one could mistake it. It was you and no one else. I have never witnessed the like of it before – nor a mob congregating in the churchyard across from the vicarage and shouting and cat-calling in a very rude manner and even knocking over several of the older gravestones near the wall so little did they care for their own church and their own clergy. When I left the house, I watched them and I saw the Reverend Scrope's effigy doused in paraffin and covered with tar, given a mock funeral service by the mob and then set on fire. Everyone cheered as it burned and cheered even more when it fell to pieces. Later, I saw boys and youths and even women kicking the head about the High Street. I could not believe that the good offices of the Church had been brought so low. The whole business was an utter disgrace to the Church.'

He paused and took a sip of water from a glass standing on a small table beside his chair. 'Your Lordship once asked me for my opinion on matters in Steadshall,' he went on calmly, 'and I wrote a long letter to you giving my opinion. I will add one thing which I did not write at that time: It is my opinion that Your Lordship should find some means to put an end to this scandal caused by the attitude of the vicar and his parishioners towards each other in Steadshall. I must leave that to your wiser judgment. What I will say is that such outrages on decency as have occurred in Steadshall should not be allowed to continue, for religion and morality alike are injured and the Church is brought into contempt in the eyes of its enemies.'

He rose, bowed to his Bishop and the other clergy and walked out without so much as a backward glance towards the Reverend Scrope: he no longer cared what the man thought of him. Agnes had written a letter and sent it via Hannah Hodgson, saying that he must stay away from the vicarage at all costs and let things calm down: there was in Steadshall then no more embittered or distraught man than Henry Smallwood, licensed curate of St. Mary's Church, Bourne Brook.

Dr. Iveson was called next and confined his evidence to matters concerning the school management board and his reasons for resigning from it and for willingly acting as the chairman of the very meeting at the town hall from which the memorial sent to the Bishop had emanated. He made no apology for it and neither did he mince his words.

'A great number of church people are downright ashamed of what the vicar has done in dismissing Mr. Warburton,' he told the Bishop and his panel. 'Both he and Mrs. Warburton are popular with the children and their parents. The standard of learning at the school has risen remarkably under their administration – which begs the question: why did the Reverend Scrope consider it necessary to dismiss him if the school was performing so well? The reasons he gives are, in my opinion, ridiculous. If Your Lordship requires it, I could give you a hundred examples of the Reverend Scrope's vexatiousness which Mr. Warburton and others, myself included, have had to suffer over the years.'

Thankfully, the Bishop did not, though he did permit one example. 'The Reverend Scrope's general attitude towards others was the principle reason why I resigned my seat on the school management board,' the doctor told the panel. 'Late last year, to help raise more funding for the school, I suggested to the vicar that, by having more people on the management board, we might bring in more funding – by having more benefactors. Yet when I asked him if he would appoint more school managers and named three who were willing to stand, he refused me quite vehemently. He did not like any of them and would not have any of them except "over his dead body!" When I persisted, he told me quite forcefully that it was not a matter he wished to discuss with anyone. It was his decision and his alone. Till then, I had always thought that the management board were simply the trustees for the people, spending the money raised by subscription and by parish events for the benefit of the school, and as such should they not be used as a weapon by which the Reverend Scrope gratified his own private animosities.'

There was a snort from where the vicar was seated, but the doctor ignored him. 'In my three years as a member of the management board,' he continued, 'no decision could ever be acted upon without the express sanction of the vicar. Nothing could ever be done without his say-so, whether it be the purchase of new writing slates for the children to designating the day after which the school's stove could no longer be lit or the date after which it could be lit again. It was an intolerable situation. In my opinion, his attitude towards the schoolmaster, William Warburton, was exactly the same as his attitude had been towards the previous schoolmaster, Joseph Padwick. If anyone disagrees with him, if anyone challenges his authority on any point, he will simply take no notice of them – or, as in the case of Mr. Warburton, declare that they should be dismissed for not acting entirely as he, the vicar and chairman of the management board, directs. As a result, I decided I would align myself with any cause attempting to have him removed...'

William was among the last of those in opposition to be called: he began by conceding his deception over the references – he could hardly do otherwise – and apologising to the Bishop for it, adding, however, that it did not make him an incompetent schoolmaster, which he considered the Reverend Scrope was inferring by dismissing him and his wife. Then he gave a full account of his troubles with the vicar over the past year, including his problems over the conditions in the school, its shortages, its other problems, his own troubles with Miss Dunsmore and the pupil-teacher foisted upon him, Edward Crowfoot. He explained also why he and Martha preferred not to teach Sunday school – because of his need and his wife's need to rest on Sundays – and he complained also of the lack of staff at the school over the months he had been there and the board's refusal – or the vicar's refusal – to hire an assistant-teacher in addition to Miss Dunsmore and Martha, which he had mentioned to him several times.

'My letters should all be detailed in the minutes of the management board,' he informed the panel. 'As a teacher, I feel myself committed, through education, to encouraging children to imagine possibilities they never imagined they might have. Sad to say, it appears to be a sentiment with which the Reverend Scrope profoundly disagrees.' The statement was, in fact, a subtly changed version of an earlier comment from the vicar himself, which caused the Reverend Scrope to glower at him as he left.

When later the Reverend Scrope seated himself on the chair before the panel to give his reply to all that had been said against him, he decided that the first thing he must do was to damn the curate once and for all in the Bishop's eyes.

'The curate is a very ill-behaved and ill-mannered man,' he declared, shaking his head slowly as if he regretted having to say it. 'Besides being disloyal to me, his vicar, he is a person who, I regret to have to say, cannot conduct himself as a gentleman. On the occasion I found it necessary to eject him from my house during the management meeting, he behaved in a manner which was a disgrace to the cloth. He stood up and shouted that he wished to read a letter. Quite reasonably and quietly, I told him I did not wish the letter to be read because it had nothing to do with the subject under discussion at that time. I tried to reason with him in a quiet manner and my refusal, politely and calmly explained to him, ought to have been conclusive, but Mr. Smallwood persisted and when I, reluctantly, very reluctantly, went forward in order to enforce my right as the chairman of the meeting to eject him, which I did myself rather than ask others to tackle him in his highly agitated state, he threw himself to the floor, shouting and behaving in a very absurd manner.'

He paused here, ostensibly to allow the secretary to finish taking down the shorthand note, but in reality so that the members of the panel could exchange glances between themselves.

'I have to add, Your Lordship,' the Reverend Scrope continued, adopting a tone of the utmost gravity, 'that if anything is stated by the curate to the contrary outside this room, I shall not hesitate to begin an action for malicious slander against him. I find that I cannot trust the man or work with him. I fear that the year he was by himself while I was away has been too much for him – the strain of work, I think, for which, sadly, I blame myself for going and leaving him – ' The implication was clear: there was no blame attached to the Bishop, who had made the decision to allow it: that was best not mentioned. ' – I fear it has all been too much for him, running two parishes. Therefore, I would respectfully urge Your Lordship to withdraw his licence – temporarily, I should add – till he is better.'

The whole inquiry took seven hours, with a break for luncheon, and at the end of it the Bishop announced that he would reserve judgment while he discussed what had been said with the other members of the panel. His finding was posted on the parish notice board at the top of the town by Walter Crowfoot one afternoon a week later, addressed *'To the townspeople of Steadshall.'* A large crowd gathered to read it and many emitted groans when they did. The reply stated:

> *'As a result of the inquiry held on Thursday last at the Red Lion Inn, Wivencaster, by myself, supported by the archdeacon and two other clergymen, I have to intimate to you that, although I am far from satisfied with the state of the parish, as revealed by the witnesses whom we examined, I can find no sufficient reason to take any further steps with a view to removing the incumbent.*
>
> *'I trust, therefore, that you and your friends will endeavour as far as possible to promote a better feeling than at present exists in the parish, although I am bound to admit that events which have recently occurred are sufficient to have produced a feeling of distrust and uneasiness on the part of the parishioners and I cannot deem unreasonable the application*

which you made to me with a view to inquiries being instituted.

'Further, so that the obvious antagonism between certain parties might be eased, I have arranged for the Reverend Henry Smallwood to leave his curacy at St. Mary's, Bourne Brook, forthwith and to take up a new post at Saffron Walden, where he will assist the rector of St. Mary the Virgin.'

Not unnaturally, there was a satisfied smile on the face of the Reverend Scrope when he discovered that he had been 'vindicated' – what others thought did not matter. He was in church on his knees, thanking God for not forsaking him and so did not see his sister Agnes slip out of the house later that evening and stand before the notice board at the top of a near-deserted High Street: nor did he hear the terrible cry of anguish she let out – Saffron Walden was almost fifty miles from Steadshall…

SIXTY

NEVER IN ALL her born days did Hannah Hodgson ever expect to be asked what she was asked that evening by the Reverend Scrope, her vicar, her employer, the most important man in the town, more important in her eyes even than the mayor and all the aldermen on the town council: she could hardly believe her ears.

She had just got little Elizabeth off to sleep in the attic nursery when the vicar returned from the church: that he was in a good mood was obvious, for he was humming a hymn tune, which he did only when he was in a good mood: and, in all the time she had been at the vicarage working as the nursemaid to Elizabeth, she had not heard many tunes being hummed by him.

She heard him go into his study and then a few minutes later he rang the bell three times, which was a signal that whoever was available, the cook, his sister or Hannah herself, should bring him a pot of tea and some biscuits for his supper.

As it happened, the mistress was upstairs in her bedroom again, claiming to have a headache again, though Hannah doubted that that was the true reason: she had been having a lot of headaches lately, especially since the vicar's argument with the curate by the gate, and a strange atmosphere had descended over the house, a hostility even between her and her brother which Hannah did not understand. They did not exactly argue, there was just an unmistakable coldness between them, an abruptness in their exchanges, which were few, except for any necessary remarks concerning the running of the house or whether he would be in or out for his dinner or his supper.

When the vicar was in during the day, Miss Scrope seemed to prefer the company of either Old Tom the gardener or Bertha the cook, and sometimes Hannah and Elizabeth on their daily strolls around the town – anything to be out of the house, it seemed, to be out of her brother's way, rather than sitting in the parlour where he might come across her. Several times of late Hannah had seen her standing outside talking with Old Tom – once all afternoon – not even minding the inclement weather at the time, just content to watch the old gardener and the Upson boy digging along the borders, discussing with the older man where to weed, which flowers she might pick, which ones ought to be dead-headed, where to clip the rose bushes. And, if she were not with Old Tom, then she would be found sitting at the kitchen table talking to Bertha, sometimes for as long as an hour or two hours at a time, discussing things with Bertha, the next week's meals, what groceries were to be bought, whether the milk was off – that kind of thing – using the kitchen as a sanctuary, for the vicar hardly ever went into it, but would always ring the bell in his study to summon someone to bring him something from it.

She had always joined Hannah at the appointed hour to help put Elizabeth to bed, but now she came earlier and stayed longer, especially if her brother were in the house, sometimes staying as long as two or three hours, first playing with her niece, then helping Hannah undress her and put her in the cot. As the child lay on her pillow, she would recite nursery rhyme after nursery rhyme to her and often sit there long after Elizabeth had gone to sleep, only leaving when Hannah herself yawned and intimated that she, too, wished to sleep.

At one time, she would have gone down afterwards and sat in the parlour, to do her needlework or her sewing or to read one of the books she obtained from the new library: but, ever since the row between her brother and the curate, she would retire to her bedroom, sometimes making an excuse and hurrying out of the nursery if she heard the front door being banged shut, announcing *his* return. Of course, she never spoke to Hannah of it, or tried to explain herself, but just hurried away in case *he* came up the stairs to the nursery himself, which he did, for the vicar was not a neglectful father, Hannah had to acknowledge. It was just that he was a very busy man and left the day-to-day care of Elizabeth to his sister and to her.

He had always on occasion climbed up to the nursery to kiss Elizabeth goodnight if he were in the house and it was not too late: but, lately, ever since she had sat on his lap in the study and allowed him to fumble inside her camisole, he had been climbing the stairs more often to see his daughter as she lay sleeping and had even taken to giving Hannah a kiss – just a quick soft kiss on the mouth or the cheek and perhaps a squeeze of her bottom with one hand before he went back down again, but no more than that. The kissing and touching were of no consequence to her – she felt nothing – it was just something the vicar did and then he was gone, though she now found herself sighing with relief if the footfall on the attic stair were the lighter one of Miss Scrope rather than the heavier tread of her brother.

That evening her mistress had gone out rather unexpectedly, without a hat and with just a shawl over her shoulders, and, though she had returned soon after, she had gone straight to her bedroom without even coming up to the nursery. Hannah had wanted to ask her something about her own underclothing – there had been some blood on her nightgown two days previously – and she wanted to ask the mistress about it: she would have to wait till morning if the mistress were about, though even that was not always guaranteed now. Everything within the house was most peculiar indeed at the moment.

The summoning bell rang five minutes after the vicar returned from the church: when Hannah entered the study, she found her employer standing by the French windows, seemingly staring absentmindedly out on to the rear garden: he turned as she laid the tray on the small table beside the couch and it was only as she turned to go that he said almost absent-mindedly: 'Don't go, Hannah, I have something to ask you.'

Unexpectedly, before turning away from the widow, he pulled the curtains across, throwing the room into half-darkness, then crossed to the door and turned the key in the lock. Hannah waited patiently.

'I have had some good news today, Hannah,' the vicar said brightly, 'and I would like to share it with you.' He did not go to the couch to sit, but sank into an upholstered, walnut-framed armchair beside his desk.

'Come nearer, Hannah,' he said, motioning her to cross to him. 'Now sit on my lap again, will you, please, I have something to ask you.' His hand was around her wrist as he gently pulled her down. 'I am in a happy mood today, Hannah. I have had some good news from the Bishop – very good news – and I am very pleased by it – very pleased indeed – so pleased, Hannah, that I have bought you a little present. Would you like a little present?'

The girl said nothing, but waited while he reached down beside the chair and felt around one of the legs: when he lifted his hand again, there was a long, elegant pencil case in it, with a posy of forget-me-nots painted on its top.

'This is for you, Hannah,' he told her, 'for being a good girl – for looking after my lovely Elizabeth and being so nice to me.'

She took the pencil case, let out a small murmur of pleasure at its painted top, slid it open and gave a louder exclamation of delight at its contents – a layer of different-coloured pencils, a six-inch ruler, a small protractor, a shiny brass compass and a two-tone rubber.

'Do you like it?' he asked. 'You may give me a kiss if you do – as a thank you.'

The girl found her head being pulled down as he kissed her firmly on the mouth: she did not protest or try to jump away, but allowed him to do it: it was just like he had done before: his breath smelled the same and she felt his hand come up the same way and begin caressing her breast.

'I like kissing you, Hannah,' he said and kissed her again, his hand moving from one breast to the other and gently squeezing each in turn as he did so.

'Remember the last time you sat on my knee and I spoke about you going to a young ladies' college in Wivencaster and I said I think there might be a way we could send you so that you could become a proper teacher?'

'Yes, sir, I remember,' she said, nodding and flinching at the same time as he squeezed her left breast too hard. In fact, she had forgotten his promise, simply because she had not expected anything to come of it.

'Well, I promised I would and I am going to make enquiries about it all,' he said, 'because I would like you to go there for a reason, Hannah, a very good reason. I would like you to become a young lady, a proper young lady, an educated young lady. And when you have become a young lady, Hannah, you could become my wife. You could marry me – ' The girl's mouth fell open in utter surprise, but he did not wait for her to answer or to protest.

'– Will you marry me, Hannah?' he asked, now caressing each breast in turn and pulling her face down to kiss her firmly on the lips again. 'Say you will marry me. Say you will, Hannah. Please. Make me a happy man. You will be my wife, won't you? I'm a very lonely man, Hannah. My sister is upset at the moment and I don't know why. I have no one to talk to, no one to share my life with. You are a very pretty girl, Hannah, a very pretty girl indeed, and I am greatly attracted to you. I would like to make you my wife someday when you are older, when you are a proper young lady, an educated young lady, and perhaps you will even become the mistress of our school one day? Will you marry me, Hannah? Will you?'

Somewhat to her surprise, the nursemaid found herself saying yes – 'Yes, if you want me to, sir.'

She suddenly felt very sorry for her vicar: he could be very sharp at times and bad-tempered and she was quite frightened of him when he complained about Elizabeth's crying, such as when she threw a tantrum because she could not fathom a toy or fell and hurt herself or found some other reason to scream, or just cried through tiredness when she could not get to sleep, as all children do. She not only felt sorry for him but she did not mind at all his hands doing what they were doing.

'Oh, bless you, Hannah, bless you, my dear, dear girl,' he cried and, as she looked at him, he seemed to be smiling and wiping a tear from his eye. 'If I could, I should marry you now, make you my wife. Then you would be the most important lady in the town.'

'More important than the mayor's wife or the doctor's wife?' she asked, a little incredulous.

'Oh, yes. You would be *the vicar's* wife.'

He kissed her again, longer this time, harder than before. 'Will you do something for me, Hannah, please?' he asked, gently easing her off his lap, for which she was thankful because something disturbing had been happening while she sat there: something hard had begun pressing against her buttocks: she could feel it through her thin dress.

'What do you want me to do, sir?'

'Would you show yourself to me, Hannah? Let me look at you? After all, you are going to be my wife one day, Hannah – someday we are going to be married and men and women who are married often show themselves to each other. God allows it and even blesses it. It is all a part of His great plan. I used to look at my dear departed wife. '

The girl was standing before him now. 'You mean, lift my dress, sir?'

'Yes, if you would, please, Hannah. It would make me very happy if you did that. You want me to be happy, don't you?'

She was not sure how to answer him. 'Yes, sir,' she said eventually, then reached down, picked up the hem of her dress and lifted it to her chest.

'That's nice, Hannah,' he said, leaning forward and staring closely at her, while she peered back at him over the top of her dress, wondering what he found about her that was so interesting: after all, she was not wearing her best drawers and really ought to have changed them that morning, but had not.

'Will you do one more thing for me, please, Hannah,' he said, 'will you take your drawers down so that I might look at you properly? Just drop them down around your ankles. That's a good girl. There is no need to take them off completely.'

She bent down and did as he asked, but decided to step out of them, anyway, rather than stand there with them around her ankles in case she moved unexpectedly and they became entangled and caused her to fall.

For more than a minute or so, he continued to look at her, to inspect her, pulling her closer to him so that she was standing in between his long legs, one hand caressing the smoothness of her inner thighs and then moving slowly up to stroke the soft down of her pubic hairs and the swell of her stomach. Suddenly, he bent forward and fell to his knees before her. She could not see exactly what he was doing because the dress and her petticoats were covering his head, but she felt his cheeks brush the insides of her thighs and she was aware that something hard was nuzzling her – his nose! He was kissing her *there!* Before she could pull away, his hand was between her legs, pushing them farther apart and the tip of one of his long fingers was hooked inside her, touching parts no one had ever touched.

She knew that what he was doing was wrong, that she ought not really to be letting him do it because her mother had warned her against boys – and men – wanting to do such things to young girls, but when she attempted to take a step back, she found he had hooked one arm around her waist and she was held there: for some reason, too, her legs would not move back and, indeed, she found herself moving forwards to him, so as to allow him to do what he was doing.

For almost a minute she stood there: then suddenly he sat back on the chair, twisted her round and pulled her on to him, lifting her dress at the back so that her bare buttocks were exposed. There was something different about sitting on his lap now: for he had opened his trousers at the fly and pushed them down a short way to bare his legs and something warm– and hard – as hard as a boy's arm – was nestling between her legs.

'Do not be afraid, Hannah,' he said, closing his arms more tightly around her, 'I shall not hurt you. I just want you to sit on me...'

It was a good five minutes before he stopped moving under her: suddenly, his whole body shuddered and he gave a loud gasp, as if of pain, followed by a long drawn-out sigh before his head fell against her shoulder and stayed there. Something wet and sticky was on the inside of her thigh – something from him.

'It's all right, Hannah,' he said, lifting his head to kiss the back of her neck, still a little breathless, 'there is no need to worry about what has happened. It is something that just happens when men do this. I have finished now. You may go, if you wish – you have been most kind to allow me.'

As he released her and she stood up to look for her drawers, he took her by the hand again and said almost plaintively: 'You won't tell anyone about this, will you, Hannah? I wouldn't want anyone else to know about this. This is just between the two of us, isn't it – between me and the pretty young girl who one day is going to become my wife? Wipe yourself between your legs before you go out. Oh, and don't forget your pencil case...'

SIXTY-ONE

JUST HOW MUCH his standing in the community had indeed suffered as a result of the unfortunate business concerning old John Chalkstone and the dismissal of the Warburtons was brought home to the Reverend Scrope the very next day when he went down the High Street. People, who only months before had been loyal churchgoers, now turned to stare into shop windows and pretend not to see him, while others crossed the road to avoid him, some making no attempt to hide their actions and their indignation towards him: others still, if he stopped them and attempted to begin a conversation, looked about them in embarrassment, made weak excuses and hurried off at the earliest convenience.

It was something of a shock and a disappointment to him, for till then he had been firmly of the belief that those who had taken it into their heads to send a memorial to the Bishop complaining about him had all been 'meddling' Dissenters and their opinions of him could be discounted: also, that it was they more than his own parishioners who were refusing to accept that the Bishop had exonerated him at the subsequent inquiry.

If further confirmation of his unpopularity were needed, it came on the Sunday when he found that the numbers attending church had dwindled yet again, with the consequence that the collection was most definitely down. The subscriptions for the yet-to-be-started repairs to the tower had by then almost dried up entirely and there was still an amount of sixty pounds outstanding to Elijah Crowfoot for the school work, which the management board would have to settle soon somehow: he might even have to pay it out of his own money, which did not please him. It was a town school, after all.

However, despite the continued slowness of everything, the Reverend Scrope remained buoyant: having seen off the Government's threat to impose a School Board on the parish, he was determined that, in due course, he would achieve his target of the estimated cost and repair of God's House as he had promised in his prayers before attending the Bishop's inquiry. God had answered him then by instructing the Bishop, the archdeacon and the two other clergymen on the panel to absolve him: he could not now let God down.

So he sent Walter Crowfoot to see his builder-brother, Elijah, to discuss when work might start on the tower: he was eager to begin, despite the lack of money: that he still believed would come in God's good time.

Elijah Crowfoot, however, was not so sure. 'I'll start when the vicar can guarantee the money. Till then, he can bloody well wait!' was his reply to his solemn-faced brother, who then had the unenviable task of returning to the vicar to tell him of it. There were enough other jobs on Elijah Crowfoot's books to keep his men busy till mid-May at least, so he was in no rush: brother of the vicar's warden or no, he did not intend to get 'burned' a second time.

Meanwhile, the town surveyor had been making regular – almost weekly – inspections of the tower and had warned that preliminary work at least ought not to be put off too much longer – it should certainly begin within the next month or two, he had said, for during the more severe weather that winter, water had seeped down between several of the upper stones on the front elevation and the expansion and contraction of the ice had caused yet more damage, which now would also need to be repaired.

There was one way, the Reverend Scrope decided, by which he might improve his standing in the town again, at least among those who were still regular churchgoers, and that was by arranging yet another 'concert and tea' in the schoolroom. His parishioners seemed to enjoy the entertainment provided, or so it seemed to him looking on as an observer: a tea and entertainment would at least give the townsfolk something to which they could look forward, for there was no theatre in the town and the Whit Monday fair, their only annual celebration of any moment, was still a way off. It might also bring them back to the church.

The tea and concert was held on the Saturday after the Warburtons' term of notice had expired so that he would not have to deal with them, and most particularly with 'him.' Instead, Miss Dunsmore, as the new head teacher, was in charge of all the arrangements in the schoolroom, along with a small group of 'loyal ladies,' comprising the church's rota of cleaners and flower-arrangers: the new head teacher seemed quite pleased when her vicar complimented her on her work, for she smiled at him most pleasantly and seemed most disappointed when he made his excuses at the end of the concert and left before she could talk to him again.

It was also a convenient gathering at which to introduce the two new assistants to Miss Dunsmore: the first, Miss Margaret Sawyer, a twenty-one-year-old from a training college in Derbyshire, with a second-class certificate, had already started at the school the previous week, taking over standards three and four from Miss Dunsmore, who, as the senior, naturally took standards five and six. The second teacher, a nineteen-year-old Miss Hilda Bird, had arrived only the previous day to begin on the Monday: she was just out of a teacher training college in London, also with a second-class certificate: she would be in charge of the infants. The recruitment of a pupil-teacher had still to be discussed by the management board and the Reverend Scrope was in no hurry to propose it.

As it turned out, the concert and tea was reasonably well supported, with a hundred and fifty parishioners, young and old alike, attending to applaud the songs, recitations and varied instrumentalists: in consequence, sixty-two pounds, eighteen shillings and fourpence-halfpenny was raised by donations and ticket sales towards the final bill for the extension, enough at least to pay the remainder of the money owed to Elijah Crowfoot, with the hope that he might soon see his way to beginning work on the tower.

It was also a thankful task at that same gathering to be able to introduce the new curate at Bourne Brook, the Reverend Thomas Wyndham, just out of theological college, whose licensing service was due to be held at Bourne Brook on the following Tuesday. The tall, bespectacled, twenty-three-year-old, with an overly prominent Adam's apple, a long nose and protruding teeth, had been nominated as the Reverend Smallwood's successor by the Bishop himself and the Reverend Scrope, personally, had had no say in the matter.

At the licensing service, he was at least able to speak to the Bishop for the first time since the inquiry and he was pleased to find that His Lordship made no mention of the matter: indeed, he seemed quite affable, especially when told of the success of the concert and tea and the number of parishioners present, not to mention the amount raised. It was almost as if all were well between parish and Diocese again.

Watching the nervous young curate walking in procession down the aisle at Bourne Brook with his patron on the day he was to be licensed as the priest-in-charge there, the Reverend Scrope's mind went back over the years to the day he, too, had walked in procession with his patron, led by a choir, with a dean and an archdeacon following and a bishop and his chaplain bringing up the rear.

The images of his own licensing service twenty-three years before had stayed with him simply because it had been so memorable – the most memorable day of his life, he still thought, the symbolism of the moment and the rich poetry of the text being spoken to him as he stood before his bishop causing tears of happiness to well in his eyes. Indeed, on rising on the morning of his licensing, the certainty that God had put him there in his first parish to do His bidding had so overwhelmed him that he had performed an involuntary jig of happiness around the bedroom of the vicarage in which he was lodging.

If there were one thing which marred the day at Bourne Brook and increased the Reverend Scrope's frustration, it was that, at the Bishop's suggestion – which was tantamount to a direction – the very generous collection taken at St. Mary's was shared, half to assist the victims of the early summer's flooding in the hamlet and half to go to famine relief in some remote part of Africa of which he had never heard – Bechuanaland or somewhere – but none of it was to go to the tower fund.

'The tower will not fall down just yet, Hugo, I have God's word on it,' the Bishop joshed after his third port. 'My chaplain has it on good authority from the town surveyor that it will hold for a month or two more. We can use half of the collection for my cause and the rest to go towards the poor people of Bourne Brook. They will be pleased that the arrival of a new curate has brought them better fortune.'

It was particularly irritating to the vicar, for he had sent out invitations to several prominent landowners and their wives throughout the north of the county, not only to attend the service as privileged guests but afterwards to take tea with the Bishop at the vicarage: and, as he had hoped it would, it had resulted in several generous donations towards the tower fund, which ordinarily might never have been given. The extra money from the collection would have been the 'icing on the cake.'

'You are getting there, Hugo,' he had said, 'you are getting there. I told you that you would and that you would not need the Diocese's money.'

If the Reverend Scrope had anything for which he could be thankful that day it was that Agnes put on such a show of smiling pleasantness in hosting his guests that none could have guessed that brother and sister had barely exchanged more than a couple of dozen words during the whole of the previous week. However, once the Bishop's carriage had set off back to Wivencaster and the other guests had departed, after instructing Bertha the cook about the meals for the following day, ensuring that Elizabeth was safely tucked up in bed and read a bedtime story, Agnes had retired to her own bedroom again 'to read.' Indeed, so much of her time seemed to be spent 'reading' in her bedroom when her brother was at home, she had even requested her lunch be taken up and occasionally her supper, though she would sit at the dining table if he were out: for his part, the Reverend Scrope still preferred to take his meals alone in his study, carried to him on a tray by Hannah.

Thus, for Hannah life went on much as before: every now and again, she took a pot of tea or coffee or jug of cocoa and a few biscuits into her employer for his supper – and, every now and again, he would ask her to stay and he would draw the curtains and lock the door. He still requested to 'see' her and asked her permission to 'touch' her and, unnerving as it was to have an older man rubbing his hands over her breasts and thighs and buttocks, inserting his finger between her legs, it was soon over, the whole thing never lasting more than a half-hour at the longest, so she could close her eyes while he did it and think of other things.

Of late, he had begun to ask her to 'touch' him, to grip his hard 'thing,' which he dropped his trousers to show her, and to rub it between her fingers: he said it was what husbands and wives did before they 'made babies together.' She had done what he asked, not happily because she did not like doing it, giving in only because of his persistence and because he always let her go straight afterwards.

He still gave her presents – red ribbons one time, some pink gloves another time, a silver bracelet, a garnet ring and other things which lay at the bottom of her chest of drawers – not every time, but most times. He was still promising to send her to the ladies' college at Wivencaster once little Elizabeth was old enough not to need a nursemaid full-time and saying, too, that they would be married once she had qualified and become 'a proper young lady,' as only then would it be right for them to marry. 'How pleased your widowed mother will be for you to marry a gentleman and become a proper lady,' he had told her as he pulled her on to his lap yet again.

One time, he had said he would 'like to make babies' with her when she was grown up, but for the moment he would make no such demands on her as it would not be right: she was just past her fourteenth birthday, for which he gave her an illustrated Bible as a present...

SIXTY-TWO

ON THE DAY that the British School opened in the Baptist chapel along the Wivencaster road, a hundred and forty-nine scholars waited at the gates: for, in addition to ninety-four chapel children, a further fifty-five from the parochial school had decided they would rather be taught by William and Martha than by Miss Dunsmore and her two new assistants.

All had to be registered and separated into their various standards so it took William and Martha most of the morning to record each child's name and address and other details in the new record books. After that, lessons were begun much the same as elsewhere, with some reading from books which had been provided by benefactors, others doing arithmetic and the infants learning to write the letters of the alphabet, learn their numbers and recite their times tables.

By the end of the second week, the numbers attending had risen to more than a hundred and seventy, which precipitated a hasty meeting of the parochial school's managers: every day more and more scholars were leaving and turning up at the gates of the new school. They did so to escape the harshness of Miss Dunsmore's methods of teaching – the twist of the ear, the smack of the hand across the back of the head, the rap of a ruler across the knuckles and almost once a day by then a caning as she became more and more agitated at her own failings and the vicar and the management board began to ask questions about the falling pupil numbers, since it would affect the annual grant.

As was to be expected, the sudden exodus from their school was the subject of a heated debate at the parochial school's management meeting. Having lost upwards of two hundred of their scholars, with more defecting weekly, the newly constituted board decided it must somehow discredit the new British School.

Overnight, posters, proclaiming that the architect who had designed the new chapel thought it entirely unsuitable to be used as a school, particularly if their number were to reach two hundred and more pupils, were pasted up around the town. The same posters alleged that, consequently, the Department of Education had refused to accept the building as a school or make any conditional promise of giving it an annual grant. Therefore, any children who left the parochial school to go there would not be examined by the school inspector and, thus, if of leaving age, would not be able to obtain their 'labour certificate.' 'The parochial school,' it boasted, 'is the only acknowledged Government school in the town!'

The managers of William's school responded with posters of their own, where possible pasting them over the parochial school posters in the dead of night for everyone to read in the morning: all claims made by the vicar were denied absolutely. It was further stated: *'The fees at the British School will be less than those of the parochial school. The parents of all children attending the British School can rely absolutely on the full support of the British School Committee, who will protect them in all things connected with the education of their children. The British School has been placed under the Government for inspection so that parents need not be afraid of summonses for non-attendance, as has been reported by the vicar and his board. All parents are invited to the British School on Saturday for an afternoon tea with entertainment...'*

Not to be beaten, the Reverend Scrope next persuaded the chairman of the council's health committee, who was a churchgoer and owed him an obligation, to visit the new school, so it was no surprise when he reported back: 'There are only two filthy closets, one of which stands very close to the schoolroom, and neither is suitably adapted for use by smaller children. The school is also overcrowded and the nuisance arising from the closets ought to be rectified or, with such a large number of children on the premises and the heat of the summer soon upon us, an epidemic could well be produced...'

It was perhaps just as well that the managers had already taken the precaution of getting the carpenter, Thomas Chiddup, to begin building two extra bucket lavatories: they, too, had been caught out by the influx and the two extra lavatories were hastily installed the day after the chairman's visit, so that the chapel school's managers could smile happily back at any member of the parochial school's management board whom they passed on the High Street.

The vicar's next attack came in the parish notices he gave out at the end of his services. With tongue firmly in cheek, the Reverend Scrope declared that he was heartily glad that they now had more school accommodation in the parish than was actually needed as it would put off a School Board forever. 'Competition is good for all,' he told his dwindling congregation, without batting an eyelid, 'and we are quite content with our number and with our pupils' progress.'

Some days William and Martha had no idea how many children would turn up at the chapel: a girl or boy walking towards the parochial school, perhaps going under duress from their parents, who still went to church on Sundays, might join a group of former friends going to 'Warburton's School,' as it had come to be known, and would suddenly decide to follow them into their 'classroom.'

Five boys from the church school caught playing truant even used the chapel school to escape a caning from Miss Dunsmore: they joined the classes at the British School for three days and then, when they hoped the threat of the caning had been forgotten at the parochial school, they went back to their pals there – though one stayed.

However, seeing their elders and betters in the town resorting to open hostility, it was not at all surprising that, with children from the two schools walking together up the same High Street and a short way up Head Street together before they diverged, the more unruly older scholars of each should begin a rivalry of their own.

It began with girls from the parochial school having their pigtails pulled by boys from the rival school: then girls from the chapel school had their hats seized off their heads and shied into puddles and up on to nearby rooftops by boys from the parochial school. The next morning, a boy on one pavement, egged on by his friends, suddenly launched himself across the road to punch one of his 'enemies' on the opposite pavement. Thereafter, fist fights and stone fights between the two groups were commonplace: and it was only after a shop window was shattered by one errant stone-thrower that the town's two constables took to standing on the corner at the junction of Head Street and the Wivencaster road as the scholars went by, just to keep them apart and ensure the peace.

Conflict and stone-throwing were not confined to the street: on the fourth week after the British School had opened, as William's third and fourth standards were practising a song late in the afternoon before going home, the front door of the chapel was flung open and several of the older parochial scholars ran in with handfuls of pebbles, which they shied everywhere, injuring five chapel children who were not quick enough to duck under the benches, one who suffered a severely cut eye and another a cut on the head.

Honour was avenged the next day when eight boys from William's school burst into the parochial school, seized the hand bell and rang it loudly, disrupting everything, toppled the assistant-teacher Miss Sawyer's blackboard before she could stop them and scattered copybooks and writing slates everywhere before running out, shouting obscenities.

That was enough: the matter had to be dealt with – the war had to be ended. Though the latter culprits sprinted back to their own school, they were rooted out when the assistant-mistress complained and one of the constables visited the chapel. Reluctant as he was to cane anyone for it, William lined up all eight boys and, in the presence of the three pastors and the constable, he gave each of them three hard strokes across their backsides.

The following week, giving the lie to the vicar's posters, the assistant schools inspector called at the new school, making a surprise visit to examine the same eight, who had all applied for a labour certificate, hence the wildness of their earlier conduct: all passed in reading, writing and arithmetic and there was a smile upon the face of each of them as they left that day.

Soon after, the Reverend Scrope learned to his dismay that the Non-conformist school management board had purchased the field next to the chapel and plans had already been drawn up for a new brick school, with the hope that the foundations might be dug sometime in the next year – if the present school could continue as successfully as it had begun.

Worse, the vicar was told, the hundred pounds for it had been donated by none other than the aged mill-owner, Sir Thomas Oldcourt, who, while he was prepared to give to the Non-conformists, would not give to the parochial church because he had heard too much that was dislikeable about the vicar...

SIXTY-THREE

THE GARDENER'S BOY, William Upson, saw them together: he had left his coat in the potting shed and had gone back to the vicarage to fetch it late one evening. The vicar's study curtains were drawn, but, seeing some movement inside and, just out of curiosity, he went up to the window, shaded his eyes and peeked through the tiny gap that had been left.

What he saw amazed him and soon became the subject of ribald gossip among the youths of the town – Hannah Hodgson, the former pupil-teacher now working as the nursemaid at the vicarage, was lifting her dress for the vicar, then sitting on his lap and allowing him to kiss her and to fumble between her legs. And when she stood up to get off him, he saw her exposed bum, which meant she had no drawers on! He had run off then in case he was seen, in case a difference in the sliver of twilight showing through the windows had been noticed.

If the youths of the town are gossiping about a subject as salacious as the vicar consorting with a girl they know, how long before their older brothers and fathers and uncles want to share in the laughter and make crude jokes of their own in the inns and ale houses? And how long after that before one of the landladies hears and passes the same astonishing gossip on to her friends? And how long after that before the rumour is spread all over town?

In Steadshall, not long was the answer. From the time the gardener's boy peeped in and saw them to the time it came to the attention of one of the town's two constables took exactly nine days. Late the following Saturday night on the High Street, an inebriate labourer from the lower end of the town was pulled out of a shop doorway, where he had hoped to sleep away his intoxication.

He objected most strenuously. 'Why don't you go and arrest that dirty old vicar up yonder for what he's doing to that young nursemaid o' his, instead of bothering decent folks who just want to sleep?' the angry inebriate had demanded.

In his short time in the county constabulary, Constable Trott had heard many a drunken rant, but this was the first time he had ever heard one about a vicar and a young girl: it intrigued him. He had no liking for the Reverend Hugo Scrope and thought him a pompous fool: so what was this gossip about him?

'Oh, yes,' he sneered, taking hold of the drunk's coat-front and jamming him up against a lamppost, 'and why should I want to arrest the vicar of Steadshall?'

The man was not afraid: he was far older than the young constable holding him and, besides, he had been arrested several times before: if he were taken in that night, it would not be the first time he had slept off a drunken stupor in a police cell. The downside, of course, was the fine he had to pay at the magistrates' court later for being drunk and disorderly in a public place.

'Pah!' snorted the man. 'You bobbies don't know anything! The parson's been seen, for Gawd's sake! Seen doing it! She was seen sitting on his lap with no drawers on and he had his trousers round his ankles. It's him you should be arresting, not me!'

'Seen by who?' the constable demanded: for, if that were true...

He was quickly apprised of who and the details of what half the men in the town had been laughing about for the past week.

'Right, mate, bed is where you sleep tonight,' the constable said, giving the man a hard shove down the hill towards his home and getting some satisfaction when he rebounded off a shop wall: then he went straight back to the station to report to his sergeant.

The following day, the sergeant hauled the gardener's boy out of his mother's house to ask him some questions and, having been told what he was told, he went straight back to the station, wheeled the police cart out of the stables, harnessed the pony into the shafts and drove over to the superintendent's station house at Shallford.

In the early afternoon, the superintendent from Shallford and the inspector from Hamwyte, with the sergeant seated beside them, all looking grim-faced, called at Widow Hodgson's cottage at the lower end of the town: they had been told her daughter visited her there on her Sunday afternoon's off. Could they speak to her, please?

Hannah was called in to the parlour from the scullery, where she was sitting with her three younger siblings, clipping the ends of gooseberries. How old was she, they asked her first, and nodded when she told them. Certain rumours were being spread about the town concerning her and the Reverend Scrope, she was told next: what could she tell them about that? For instance, were they true? The girl began to cry, her mother began to rail, her three sisters, trying hard to listen through the door of the scullery, shushed each other, though they did not understand what was being asked. Had their sister stolen something that three policemen should visit their mother?

It took half-an-hour of patient coaxing, but a statement was eventually written out, which Hannah signed in the presence of her mother, the superintendent, the inspector and the sergeant: then a neighbour's child was dispatched with a note, to be handed directly to Miss Agnes Scrope at the vicarage, informing her that Hannah had been taken ill and would not be returning to the vicarage that evening, but would be spending the night in bed at home. It was a lie, of course, but, in the opinion of the superintendent, a necessary one: she could not be allowed to return to the house, not even to act as nursemaid to little Elizabeth. She was not only the principal witness, but the victim also: her employer was the perpetrator: it would put her in an intolerable position were she allowed to return, for, if the vicar got wind of the fact that three policemen had called at her mother's cottage, he might seek to influence her evidence...

Instead, she was taken round to Dr. Iveson's house and ushered into his surgery, where, in the presence of her mother, she was examined: the poor woman almost fainted with relief when the doctor reported: 'She is practically *virgo intacta* still.'

Privately, to the superintendent, he stated that the small deviation he had discovered from the norm could possibly be put down to minor sexual activity of 'an invasive kind,' but short of actual sexual intercourse. Other than that, he could not say any more.

Thus it was, early on the Monday morning, that the Shallford superintendent, accompanied again by the inspector from Hamwyte, arrived a second time at the police station in the constabulary's cart, collected the sergeant again and drove together up to the vicarage.

Agnes, who in Hannah's absence, had risen early to prepare breakfast for Elizabeth, opened the door to them and looked quite shocked when the two senior officers asked if they might speak to his reverence on a matter of urgency and, no, they were not prepared to wait till he rose: they had come early for a reason and required to see him at once, if she pleased.

She showed the three into the parlour and went to wake her brother, who was not best pleased to be woken so early – it was just after six-thirty and nine o'clock was his normal hour for rising, except on

Sundays when he rose at eight. After taking a quarter-hour to dress himself, he went down to them, complaining not only of the earliness of the hour to find three policemen standing in his front parlour, but the fact that their cart, which everyone knew belonged to the Shallford superintendent, was standing outside for all to see. For what possible reason had they come?

They could do nothing about the cart, he was told: it had to be parked somewhere and outside was as a good a place as any: they had come early because they wanted to conduct their business without the prying eyes of neighbours observing them. They were there to question him about certain rumours which were rife in the town and to serve a warrant on him. He was given the facts of the rumours: what did he know of them?

'I really am not going to answer such questions,' the vicar retorted. 'Anything which has happened in this house is a private matter. It concerns no one but myself and Miss Hodgson. Everything which has happened between us has at all times been by mutual consent. There has been no coercion. You have no right to pry into my private affairs. It is utterly disgraceful. I shall have words with your superiors about this...'

Undaunted, the superintendent exchanged glances with his inspector: with one statement, the vicar had unwittingly confirmed that the rumours were true. Calmly, he told the vicar he might do as he wished, but that first he would have to accompany them to Shallford, where he would have to answer before an occasional magistrates' court, which was to be convened specially for him that very morning.

'Magistrates!' the vicar blustered. 'Why should I be taken before magistrates?' He began to smile. 'I think you should know, Superintendent, that I myself am a Justice of the Peace. I know almost every Justice of the Peace throughout the county. They will make quick work of this nonsense, I have no doubt.'

After that, he stood on his dignity and would answer nothing further, saying only: 'I reserve my defence. Do as you will. I shall say nothing more, but you may rest assured, if I am put before my fellow magistrates, I shall take my complaint to your superiors – to the very highest authority, to Parliament itself, if necessary...'

The superintendent, who, in his time, had arrested men more pompous even than the vicar of Steadshall, replied to it all matter-of-factly: 'As you wish, sir. However, in view of what has been stated here this morning, I am arresting you, Hugo Scrope, for having had carnal knowledge of a girl aged thirteen.'

The Reverend Scrope could not help himself, the policemen's information was wrong: he threw up both hands in the gesture of one who cannot fathom why others do not seem able to understand what he understands. 'She is fourteen, sir,' he said glibly. 'She had her fourteenth birthday three weeks ago.'

He would say no more, he told them, till he was standing before his brother magistrates so that the whole sorry saga could be resolved.

Obediently, he gathered up his hat and his cape from the hallstand and followed the superintendent and the inspector out, with the sergeant following behind. There was not one word of remorse for what he had done, not one blush of shame. Only at the front door did he think to turn to his distraught sister and inform her: 'I expect I shall be back later when this matter has been cleared up. I do not think it necessary to inform Mr. Wyndham or anyone else just yet where I have gone.' Then he climbed into the cart alongside the superintendent and the inspector.

In the house, a horrified Agnes, who had heard the whole of the proceedings through the open fanlight, was slumped upon the hallway floor, her back against one wall, staring blankly into space, her mind numbed by the shock of it all. Many dazed minutes were to pass before she climbed to her feet and, almost like an automaton, went slowly up the stairs to the nursery and young Elizabeth...

SIXTY-FOUR

WHEN THE POLICE CART carrying the vicar and the two senior policemen arrived at Shallford courthouse a little after nine o'clock, the superintendent indicated for one of the policemen outside to open the gate to the rear yard so that his prisoner might be taken in through the back door. The Reverend Scrope was indignant: in his experience, only the guilty went in and out that way: people who had committed no crime went in through the front door and came out the same way.

'Stop this vehicle, I shall go in through the front,' he cried: and, flanked by the two policemen, he stepped down and walked boldly up the steps and through the front door.

Inside, he was taken into the clerk's office, where he was advised to send for a solicitor: the names of several in the town were given to him and an offer made to fetch the one he chose, but he waved the list away. There was no need for him to employ a solicitor: it would be an unnecessary expense, he told them, a waste of time and money for a man who could prove that he had committed no crime under the law: and he knew the law even if the police superintendent did not. He would surprise them all with his knowledge: he knew for example, that the age of consent applying to girls had been twelve years for the past six hundred years ever since the reign of King Edward the First: he knew, too, that twelve years previously, it had been raised to thirteen. Carnal knowledge of a thirteen-year-old girl was not a crime – not in England. Besides, Hannah was now fourteen.

He would have told the superintendent and the inspector that, if the two of them had not been so pompous, so officious, so sure of themselves and so ready to accuse him of being a criminal when all he had done was to show love towards a young girl who one day he might well marry – if she attended the ladies' college at Wivencaster, if she turned out for the better, better than she was at the present, anyway. He would see the superintendent damned first! Once this business was over, he would make sure that not only the chief constable at Melchborough heard of it but the lord-lieutenant of the county as well: he had met the lord-lieutenant twice and so would be able to approach him as an acquaintance if not an actual friend. They could keep their solicitors, he would defend himself: after all, he was a Justice of the Peace and knew the law.

The proceedings against him were scheduled to start at eleven-thirty. Outside, a crowd was gathering: when he had arrived, there had been only a few people standing by the steps: but somehow, they had got wind of the fact that a clergyman had been brought to the court and was to be charged with some serious offences committed against a young girl. A constable had 'tipped someone the wink' and within the hour a hundred or more Shallford townsfolk, mostly women, had hurried to the courthouse so that, when at last the Reverend Scrope was ushered into the courtroom and shown to the table at which the prisoners always sat, he found that the court was filled with people. Surely, they were not there because of him: there must be another reason, a later trial perhaps? Even so, he would have preferred it to be empty: but what did it matter? He would soon tell them and clear his good name. What a farce it all was!

The only upsetting thing was that all three magistrates were unknown to him – a colonel and a captain, both retired, whose names he had never heard before, and the deputy chief constable of the county, who, while he had met his superior, he had not met him. He had hoped that they would be men with whom he had served on the Bench at some time, the better to converse with them as an equal and disprove the wording of the indictment or whatever charges it was the superintendent had got up against him.

The magistrate's clerk rose to read the warrant, brushing at his gown as he did so: 'If it pleases your worships, we are asking for a remand in this case in that the prisoner – '

The Reverend Scrope did not like his use of the word 'prisoner': it was common: he was not a 'prisoner,' he was a defendant wrongly indicted...

' – in that the prisoner, Hugo Scrope, a clerk in Holy Orders at Steadshall, is charged in that, on divers dates this year, he did commit unlawful offences against a child, a girl of thirteen years...'

A gasp went around the court, followed immediately by loud shouts of derision which drowned the clerk's final words, not that the Reverend Scrope was listening very hard, anyway: he was too busy turning to those hissing at him to see if he knew any of them, quite prepared to call for them to be evicted from the courtroom if needs be.

Neither did he like the way the clerk was reading the indictment: there was a clear measure of distaste in his tone: it was as if he were trying to make the whole thing out to be a sordid affair of an older man and a young girl, which it decidedly was not – well, not entirely. It was more than that: he had asked her to marry him, had he not? He had been honest with her. If they asked, he would say that he intended to keep his promise. Goodness knows what Hannah had told them – what the superintendent had made her reveal, what he had made her say that was untrue.

'May I say something?' he asked, rising to his feet.

The colonel, the chairman of the bench, looked down at him over his spectacles, a frown upon his face. 'No, sir, you may not,' he said bluntly, as if addressing a junior on the parade ground. 'This is a hearing for a remand, not a trial. It would better if you waited and had your say later when you appear in a higher court.'

'That is what I am trying to avoid,' the Reverend Scrope protested with a wearied sigh. 'I am not guilty of these charges. If you would only hear me out, sir – '

'The prisoner will be silent!' the colonel rapped, banging his gavel down hard upon the bench top. 'I say again, this is a remand hearing. You are not being asked to plead, only to listen. If I have to tell you again, I shall have you removed from the court.'

At that, the vicar slumped back on his chair, feigning injured pride and giving a dismissive wave of the hand, as if he had no further interest in the proceedings. He had tried: it was not his fault that the charade had to continue: he had asked them to let him speak and end the farce and they would not let him: he had done his best.

'I understand you were offered the services of a solicitor, but have declined to have one here and intend to conduct your own defence,' the colonel went on. 'I would strongly advise you to reconsider.'

Solicitors, barristers and judges, with years of experience in the twists and turns and the pedantry of the law, seldom have any sympathy for the unlearned layman who wishes to conduct his own defence: so it was not surprising that there was an obvious sneer in the voice of the prosecuting solicitor when he rose to lay the facts of the case before the court: that between the dates named in the indictment, the 'child' referred to as 'Miss A' had said in a signed deposition, taken down at her dictation by the superintendent of Shallford – and witnessed by others – that she had been living in the accused's house, working as a nursemaid to his young daughter for several months. She had known the prisoner since she was a small girl and, while living at his house, she had gone several times into the prisoner's study, at which point he had locked the door and drawn the curtains across and had put her on his knee and kissed her and taken 'certain liberties with her.'

The superintendent of Shallford then gave evidence of the 'prisoner's' arrest, declaring that it had been made with the inspector of Hamwyte and another police officer, who had returned to his duties, but who would be called in due course. He would also vouch for the statement from the girl as having been taken down in his presence and that of his inspector.

In the view of the Reverend Scrope, the whole matter was becoming absurd: denied the chance to speak, he had listened with growing restlessness to what was being recited for the depositions: finally, exasperation got the better of him again and he decided he must make one last effort to put an end to the nonsense.

'I keep telling you, the girl is fourteen years of age,' he cried, jumping to his feet again. 'I can show you the church's baptismal record at Steadshall, if you wish, which will confirm this. If the police superintendent had bothered to listen to me, all of this could have been avoided. She is fourteen now, I say, and she was already thirteen when she came to the vicarage.'

'Then all the more reason that you should be remanded,' snapped the prosecuting solicitor and, turning back to the Bench he said matter-of-factly: 'That is all the evidence I offer on this charge at this juncture, your worships. I think it sufficient to justify a remand and, therefore, I ask for a remand for eight days.'

'I do not understand. Why am I to be remanded if I am innocent of any offence?' the Reverend Scrope cried.

The prosecuting solicitor turned to him with a look of utter contempt upon his face. 'Because it is our belief that you are not innocent of the offences for which you have been indicted, sir,' he retorted. 'You keep repeating that the girl is fourteen years of age. She may well be. So be it. You also keep saying that you have done nothing wrong. That will be for another court to decide. All that matters to us here is that the girl, "Miss A," is not of the age of sixteen and that is quite sufficient for me to proceed.'

The Reverend Scrope thought he had misheard. 'Do you not mean thirteen?' he asked.

'No, sir, I mean sixteen,' the solicitor informed him, with the irritation of one who did not like being corrected by a layman, even if he were a Justice of the Peace.

'The age of consent is thirteen years,' the vicar corrected him again in a firm voice and, by extension, the Bench and the whole court. 'It was raised from twelve years to thirteen several years ago, was it not?'

'Yes, it was,' the prosecuting solicitor replied, nodding, 'by Act of Parliament eleven years ago.'

The Reverend Scrope looked triumphant: he was having to inform a prosecuting solicitor of a law which he should have known. On the Bench, the colonel, the captain and the deputy chief constable exchanged uneasy glances and the two policemen seated beside the vicar smiled to themselves: at the back of the court, the spectators leaned forward and waited.

'Are you not aware, sir,' the prosecuting solicitor said quietly, looking straight at the Reverend Scrope, 'are you not aware that the age of consent for carnal knowledge of a young girl was raised again to sixteen two years ago? Have you not heard of The Criminal Law Amendment Act, which repealed sections forty-nine and fifty-two of the Offences Against the Person Acts of 1861 and the whole of the Act of 1875? Where were you, sir, out of the country? Everyone else knows it. There was a great brouhaha over it at the time. Did you not know that, sir? You ought to have known, you being a Justice of the Peace – '

The vicar did not answer: he was slumped upon the floor in a dead faint...

SIXTY-FIVE

AS A MATTER OF COURTESY, the Reverend Scrope, being a clerk in Holy Orders still and most likely from then on 'a former' Justice of the Peace, was taken in a private carriage all the way to Melchborough Gaol, whereas other prisoners were handcuffed to a uniformed policeman and taken first to Hamwyte and from there to the county gaol by the public train for all to see and to snigger at. The Shallford superintendent accompanied him, but deigned to change out of uniform into private clothes, as the vicar requested, not even for an acquaintance of the chief constable and the lord-lieutenant: he did, however, allow the carriage hood to be pulled over.

One month later, on the opening day of the Quarter Sessions at Melchborough, the Reverend Scrope was driven the short distance from the gaol to the town's Shire Hall in a hansom, this time accompanied by a more humble police sergeant, who was dressed in private clothes. The vicar had complained to the chief constable by letter, as he had threatened he would, and, more to placate the Bishops of Wivencaster and Melchborough, the chief constable had thought it better to acquiesce.

Not that it made any difference: each remand he had had to undergo had attracted a larger and larger crowd, everyone eager to see the pompous vicar of Steadshall standing in the dock: thus, on the day of his trial, an even larger crowd, forewarned that he would be put up first, had gathered outside the Shire Hall. Jeers and catcalls greeted the hansom when it came up: and, as the carriage passed through the throng, several of the women, who predominated again, rushed forward and attempted to rock it violently and it took a half-dozen constables pushing and pulling and punching to force a way through for it.

At ten o'clock precisely, the Reverend Scrope was escorted to the bar: immediately before him, lying on the prosecuting barrister's table, were two dozen labelled items, among them a pencil case with a flowered top, a curl of red ribbon, a pair of pink gloves, a silver bracelet, a garnet ring, a silver necklace in the shape of a heart and the illustrated Bible, the very 'gifts' he had given Hannah each time.

Immediately, the doors were opened, more than a hundred members of the public pushed their way into the courtroom, again most of them females, eager to hear the full details of what a man of the cloth had done to 'a poor innocent girl.' The judge, however, had other ideas and, no sooner had he sat down, than he ordered the police to clear the court of all females: only males would be allowed to remain.

Suffice it to say, the women did not go willingly: five policemen went into the gallery and a further ten into the body of the court: faces were scratched and kicks were aimed at knees and ankles and other sensitive parts. The police, however, were not to be deterred, especially as the chief constable sat watching: he was pleased to see that the heavy ends of their truncheons were prodded into rib cages and rotund stomachs to force the women out. It was to a chorus of angry shouts, screams and blasphemies that the doors were finally closed, though the police had to guard them to stop the women from breaking in again.

The ten gentlemen of the Press, crammed together on a single long bench, were then requested to refrain from printing the more salacious details which might be contained in the evidence 'to spare a young girl's feelings.' Most, in scribbling their stories for their editors, dwelled on the fact that the vicar had locked his study door and pulled the curtains across before carrying out the assaults and that he had asked the girl to 'commit certain acts upon himself,' as they phrased it. What made it better was that he was an Oxford-educated man, yet he had asked a 'poorly educated, fourteen-year-old town girl' to marry him simply as a means to enable him to carry out 'indecent assaults upon her person,' especially as he had told her he could not marry her for several years.

The trial lasted for five hours, with an hour's lunch adjournment: Hannah, Agnes, Bertha the cook and Hannah's widowed mother were all closeted away from the public's gaze in rooms in the courthouse before being called to give their evidence. Hannah told her story as she had told the superintendent, emphasising that the vicar had told her each time not to say anything to anyone. Agnes, Bertha the cook and Hannah's mother all declared they had not known anything of what had been going on.

The Reverend Scrope had given up on the idea of defending himself and, while in gaol, he had obtained a solicitor and he had briefed an expensive barrister from London. For most of the time, the man questioned nobody, but sat twiddling his glasses.

When his time came to address the court, he simply stressed as his client's defence that Hannah must have consented to everything for it to have gone on for so long and she had not submitted under his client's influence, so, therefore, no 'actual wrong' had been done. It did not convince the jury, however: at the end of five hours, they were out for only twenty minutes before they returned and the foreman rose to say: 'We find the defendant guilty and we find that the submission was under his influence. It was not consent.'

The barrister's plea for leniency in sentencing also fell on deaf ears. 'The Reverend Scrope's health is broken by his time in gaol, m'lud,' he informed the judge. 'With this verdict, he has lost everything in his life which matters to him – his calling, his service to his God and to his Church. At home, he has a motherless child, a two-and-a-half-year-old daughter. I place these reasons before you in the hope that your honour will make some mitigation of the sentence, especially so far as hard labour is concerned.'

The judge was totally unsympathetic. 'With regard to what you have said about the child's age during the trial, it makes it ten times worse that you did what you did,' he told a stunned and disbelieving Reverend Scrope. 'It seems you were waiting for some age when you thought you could do these things to the girl with impunity. As far as your health is concerned, it will no doubt be carefully watched by the prison doctor while you are in gaol. You are hereby sentenced to two years' hard labour in Melchborough Gaol. Take him down.'

According to some, especially the Dissenters in Steadshall, what happened next twenty miles away in the town was 'God's punishment – God's anger.' Over the years since, not unnaturally among the pious and the fearful, a myth has grown up that, at the exact moment the foreman of the jury was pronouncing the vicar 'guilty,' a lightning bolt came out of a clear blue sky and struck the tower of his former church.

Work on repairing the tower had finally begun during the Reverend Scrope's remand. In the highly likely event that he might not be 'able to return,' a stand-in vicar, a semi-retired clergyman from Wivencaster, had been sent to look after the parish in the week following his arrest till a full-time replacement could be appointed. With the authority of the Bishop and a substantial donation from the Diocese's coffers to bridge the subscription shortfall, the stand-in vicar had sought to take the people's minds off the disagreeable court case by having work on the tower begun immediately upon his arrival. Six men from Elijah Crowfoot's builder's yard had dug ten feet down to underpin the north-western buttress with concrete and, now that it had set, they had spent the morning removing the unsightly props which had been holding it up for the past several months and erecting the necessary scaffolding so as to turn their attentions to the tower's front elevation.

What is not in dispute is that sometime after four o'clock, just as the foreman of the jury was delivering his verdict, a loud roar rent the air around the parish church and a great cloud of dust went rolling down the broad slope of Steadshall High Street like some great pestilence, covering the poor unfortunates caught in its path in a choking brown fog.

Immediately the dust had cleared, people began running towards the scene: at first, it was thought all six labourers were beneath the ruins and the shrieks of the women were dreadful to hear. Fortunately, just five minutes before the catastrophe, Elijah Crowfoot had noted that the tower was in a more unstable condition than he had been led to believe and he immediately ordered his men off the scaffolding. They were standing by the low wall dividing the churchyard from the street, waiting for the surveyor to come and wondering what they could do to right the problem, when the higher part of the tower suddenly came crashing down in a great deluge of stone. The men got clear by leaping over the wall on to the road and running for their lives.

The vicar's former parishioners disputed any inference by the Non-conformists that it was caused by God's anger against them – divine retribution for what was happening in Melchborough that very day: it was just a coincidence, they said: there was not thundercloud to be seen anywhere in the sky that afternoon.

Some even swore blind they had felt an earth tremor just before the tower toppled, a minor earthquake, just like the one which had struck Wivencaster and the villages to the south of it just three years before and which had caused similar damage to two church towers and had even damaged a rectory. It had nothing whatever to do with God and retribution…

A few minutes after the same hansom which had brought the Reverend Scrope to court left the yard bound for Melchborough Gaol, with the vicar securely handcuffed to the same police sergeant, a second vehicle, a pony and trap, trailed them as far as the gaol, which lay on the edge of the town, a short way along the old Roman road leading first to Hamwyte and eventually to Wivencaster. But when the first vehicle turned off and crossed the gravelled concourse to pass through the great gateway into the gaol, the pony and trap, though it slowed so that its occupants might observe the disappearance of the other, eventually picked up speed again and continued on towards Hamwyte.

It was driven by the former curate, the Reverend Smallwood: and seated beside him, with her arm linked through his, was the vicar's sister, Agnes. They were on their way back to Steadshall: they had a child to pick up at the vicarage and a new life to begin...

Made in the USA
Charleston, SC
12 February 2013